Praise for Claire Douglas
and *Just Like the Other Girls*

"*Just Like the Other Girls* is a chilling novel showcasing Claire Douglas's trademark brilliantly claustrophobic settings and tightly plotted twists. Impossible to know which of the well-drawn characters to trust and very hard to put down."

—Gilly Macmillan, bestselling author of *What She Knew*

"Douglas's best yet—an ingenious concept with a corker of a twist halfway through. *Just Like the Other Girls* grips and thrills."

—Gillian McAllister, bestselling author of *The Evidence Against You*

"*Just Like the Other Girls* is just the sort of distraction I need at the moment: an immersive page-turner with numerous red herrings and a twist I didn't see coming."

—Sarah Vaughan, bestselling author of *Anatomy of a Scandal*

"A wickedly clever page-turner of a psychothriller."

—Emma Curtis, bestselling author of *One Little Mistake*

"Deliciously spooky. You simply have to discover what happens."

—Jane Corry, bestselling author of *I Made a Mistake*

"A thriller that will leave you in a spin."

—*The Sun* (London)

"If you like thrillers with plenty of killer twists and turns, then *Just Like the Other Girls* should definitely be high on your reading list."

—*My Weekly*

Just Like the Other Girls

Just Like the Other Girls

a novel

CLAIRE DOUGLAS

HARPER

An Imprint of HarperCollins*Publishers*

Originally published in Great Britain in 2020 by Penguin Random House UK.

HarperCollins books may be purchased for educational, business, or sales promotional use. For information, please email the Special Markets Department at SPsales@harpercollins.com.

FIRST U.S. EDITION

Library of Congress Cataloging-in-Publication Data has been applied for.

ISBN 978-0-06-313811-7 (pbk.)
ISBN 978-0-06-321127-8 (library edition)

22 23 24 25 26   LSC   10 9 8 7 6 5 4 3 2 1

To Juliet

The rising fog mingles with the dark night, turning everything opaque. I can barely see, yet I know someone else is on the suspension bridge with me.

I can hear them breathing.

How foolish I've been.

Nobody will come to my rescue. It's too late at night – even vehicles have stopped driving across due to the weather. I clutch the railings tightly with gloved hands to anchor myself.

Someone calls my name. I turn, but I'm disoriented and I can't tell which direction the voice is coming from. I just know I've been lured here. I need to find a way off this bridge. I let go of the railings, stumbling in panic, my breath quickening.

Don't lose it. I must stay calm. I need to get out of this situation alive.

Suicide. That's what they'll say it was. Just like the other girls.

I hear a laugh. It sounds manic. Taunting.

And then a figure steps out of the fog, clamping a hand across my mouth before I've had the chance to scream.

BRISTOL DAILY NEWS

Carer/companion wanted for elderly lady * young female preferred * must live in * Clifton location * competitive salary * room and board included * Telephone Mrs Elspeth McKenzie . . .

October 2018

It's even more stunning, more perfect than I remember. I stand and stare for a while at the place I will soon call home.

The scene before me is like a photograph in a glossy magazine, or the opening shot of a romantic film. I can almost hear the swell of background music as I take in the row of Georgian townhouses painted in different pastel shades, with their mint-humbug-striped canopies, delicate wrought-iron balconies and rooftops that reach up towards a cloudless blue sky. Trees, their leaves turning red, brown and orange, line the pavement, and a stretch of grass divides the street from the suspension bridge. A handful of people sit chatting and laughing, basking in this rare mid-October sunshine. Beside me, an older couple are huddled on a wooden bench overlooking the bridge and the Avon Gorge, sharing a drink from a Thermos flask. Beyond them, a young father helps his son with an oversized kite.

There is an electric charge in the air that makes me think anything is possible. I smile to myself as I bend over to pick up my small suitcase with its broken wheel. Ignoring the fluttering of nerves in my stomach, my fingers find the torn-off newspaper advert still in the pocket of my denim jacket. I can't bring myself to get rid of it. It's my talisman.

This is it. My new job. My new life.

I've waited a long time for this.

I twiddle the ring on my little finger, like I always do when I'm nervous or apprehensive: this is so different from anything I've ever done before. I'm going to be living with strangers for the first time in my life. I'll be out of my comfort zone.

I take a deep breath, swallowing my anxieties, as I stride towards the McKenzie house. This job is going to solve all of my problems. What could go wrong?

part one

1

Ice crunches underfoot and I have to tread carefully in my boots, made for fashion and not for Arctic conditions. Even so, I slip and save myself from falling on my arse by grabbing on to the iron railings for dear life, my legs splaying as I try to regain my footing. Two teenage lads stroll past and one lets out a bark of laughter. I resist flicking the finger at them just in case my would-be employer witnesses me and decides I'm too uncouth for the job. Instead I try to get my legs under control and gingerly continue down the pavement, stooped like an old lady, until I reach the McKenzie house. I stop, my hands still clutching the railings, ice seeping through my woollen gloves, and stare up at it in awe.

It's the colour of strawberry milkshake, curve-fronted, with four floors and Georgian sash windows that overlook the suspension bridge. There is a balcony on the first floor and a black-and-white-striped canopy that has been pulled back. For a brief moment I consider turning and running – which would actually be impossible in this snow and ice. Why did I ever think I'd get a job like this? I'll be working at the care home with Randy Roger and Surly Cynthia until my dying days.

I dust snowflakes from the front of my best – my

only – coat. It's maroon with a black velvet collar. It makes me look younger than my twenty-two years, but it was my mum's favourite. She bought it for my eighteenth birthday from a vintage shop in Camden Town. We used to love our trips to the market there. We made it an annual event, travelling back late at night in Mum's beat-up Alfa because it was cheaper than getting the train. This coat had cost her nearly a whole week's wages. I still remember how her silver eyes lit up as she watched me unwrap it.

I swallow the lump in my throat. I can't be sentimental today. Where will that get me? Mum would want this for me. I have to do my best. I've only ever had one interview before and that was just after I finished college.

The gate sticks against the snow, and I have to shove it hard to open it. Salt has been scattered on the pathway leading up to the house but I still tread carefully, scarred by my earlier slip. I notice a movement at the huge sash window and swallow again, my throat dry.

There is a slate sign on the house, partly covered by snow. I swipe it away with my gloved hand to read 'The Cuckoo's Nest'. A strange name for a house like this. It's kind of creepy. I knock loudly on the front door (which is four times the size of my own) and feel like I've wandered out of Lilliput and into Gulliver's world. It has stained-glass panels and glossy black paint. I stand back expectantly.

To my surprise, a woman in her late forties answers. I was imagining someone much older. She's what my mum would call frumpy, in an unflattering shapeless skirt, high-necked blouse and oversized cardigan. But then my mum was still pretty cool in her late forties, with her bleached-blonde crop and leather biker jacket. I'm doing it again. I shake thoughts of her from my head and try to concentrate on the woman standing in front of me.

'Hi. Mrs McKenzie? I'm here for the interview.' I take off my gloves and thrust out my hand enthusiastically. 'My name is Una Richardson.'

The woman stares at my proffered hand as though there's dog shit in the palm. 'I'm not Mrs McKenzie. I'm her daughter, Kathryn.'

I blush at my mistake and retract my hand. She must think I'm stupid as well as rude. Not a great first impression. She purses her thin lips as she surveys me, her face radiating disapproval as she takes in my not-warm-enough coat and my cheap New Look skirt. Then, without speaking, she stands aside to allow me in.

I step over the threshold, trying to prevent my mouth from falling open. I've never been in a home so . . . well, so *grand*. I feel like I've stumbled into a giant doll's house. There are ornate brown and blue Victorian tiles on the floor, an arched wall with pillars on either side, and beyond that, a sweeping staircase with a blue-and-cream-striped runner. A grandfather clock stands proudly against one wall. Everything is painted in tasteful neutrals. The hallway is bigger than my whole flat.

'I'm glad to see the recent snowfall didn't hinder your journey,' she says stiffly, almost regretfully, as though she'd hoped I wouldn't make the interview.

I have to stop myself apologizing for showing up. 'The main roads are clear. And luckily my bus was running.'

'Yes. What luck.' She turns on her sensible low-heeled shoes towards a closed door on the left. I shove my soggy gloves into my coat pocket, then follow her. My nerves crank up a notch at the thought of meeting Mrs McKenzie, especially if she's anything like her daughter.

'You can go in.' Kathryn doesn't try to hide her irritation, which shows in her voice. Up close, I can tell she's attractive. Her eyes are hazel behind her large glasses and she has the type of skin that looks as though it tans easily. Her hair is thick and a rich chestnut. But she's wearing such a pinched expression that I don't warm to her.

She tuts under her breath when I don't move, and leans across me, engulfing me in a wave of musky perfume, to open the door.

Come on, get a grip. This is my chance to start over and get away from that awful care home, although I will miss the residents.

Tentatively I move into the room. It has high ceilings, with mismatched high-backed chairs and an inky blue velvet button-backed sofa. There's a mahogany writing desk in the corner, next to the sash window. A well-dressed woman in a tweed pencil skirt and a pale blue sweater, pearls at her throat, sits on a chair by a huge marble fireplace, her legs crossed elegantly at the ankles. Her hair is completely white and gathered in some kind of fancy updo. She has a clipboard on her knee with what looks like notes attached, which she's flicking through.

She lifts her eyes as I approach. They are small and a startling bright blue, like the bubblegum-flavoured Millions sweets my best friend, Courtney, used to eat when we were younger. Even though she's sitting down I can tell she's tall – taller than me, anyway – slim, and looks robust and strong for a woman in her late seventies.

'Hello,' she says, without getting up. She doesn't take her eyes off me, even when Kathryn sits in the chair next to her. 'You must be Una. An unusual name.'

I smile and nod as she indicates for me to sit on the sofa opposite. 'My mum was a fan of the actress Una Stubbs. You know, who played Aunt Sally in *Worzel Gummidge*?' I perch on the edge of the sofa, crossing my ankles, like her, and pulling at the hem of my skirt, which, in the presence of these two women, now feels obscenely short. 'I know her best from *Sherlock*...' I'm gabbling now.

Mrs McKenzie frowns. 'I don't know about that but I do know who you mean. I've seen her in the West End,' she says, without smiling. My eyes flicker around the room. There is no television. She clears her throat and I sit up a bit straighter. 'So, tell us a little about yourself.' Her voice is plummy and I make an effort to speak correctly in what my mum used to call a telephone voice.

'Well...I...' I swallow. *Come on, Una, don't mess this up. Don't be intimidated by these people just because they're posh.* I notice Mrs McKenzie's eyes go to my legs and then back to my face. Maybe I don't seem responsible enough. I know I look young for my age. I'm forever getting asked for ID. 'I've been working in a care home for the past four and a half years, since I left higher education at eighteen. I've several qualifications from the college I went to on day release –'

'Sounds like prison,' interjects Mrs McKenzie, without smiling.

I giggle nervously, not sure if she's making a joke. 'It's what they call it when your job allows you to have a day off to attend college.'

'I see.' She glances down at the notes on her lap and I realize it's my CV.

'I've got NVQs . . . and first aid.'

She looks up again. 'So I see. Go on.'

'And . . . um . . . I'd like a new challenge.'

'You do understand that this is a live-in position?' she says. 'You'd have your own bedroom. I would need you on Saturdays but you get Wednesdays and Sundays off. We really would prefer someone without any . . . commitments.'

'Commitments?'

'Husband. Children. That kind of thing.'

'No. I've no commitments.'

'Family in the area? Boyfriend?'

I glance towards Kathryn, who is staring at her hands in her lap but something I can't read passes over her face. Are they worried I'll be bringing men back to the room?

'No. No boyfriend or family. It was just me and my mum but she . . . well, she died. Last November.' I can feel my cheeks grow hot. I didn't want to mention Mum. When I tell people about her their expressions change, their voices soften and they look at me with pity, not knowing what to say.

Although that's not the case with Mrs McKenzie. 'I'm sorry to hear it,' she says crisply, not sounding particularly sorry. 'So,' she continues, after a beat of awkward silence, 'a little bit about me.' She sits up straighter. 'I'm eighty next year . . .' she pauses, presumably for me to tell her that she looks good for her age, which of course I do '. . . but have suffered from ill health since a fall two years ago.' She looks in great health to me. 'I'm not as agile as I once was,' she continues, and Kathryn gives a little har-rumph from across the room. Elspeth ignores her. 'So, I need someone to help me dress, bathe, et cetera. To accompany me to events – I go to lots of events and I want to continue with that. Trips to the theatre, shopping. Anything, really.'

Excitement bubbles inside me. It sounds so much more interesting than my current job, where the highlight of my day is accompanying one of the residents out into the small garden, weather permitting.

'Does that sound acceptable to you?'

I nod. 'It sounds perfect. What . . . um, what about cooking? I'm a terrible cook – I even burn cheese on toast.' My cheeks flame as I realize I said that out loud.

She laughs. A proper laugh this time. 'Oh, you wouldn't have to worry about that. I have a cook. And a cleaner. No, it's just a companion I need. You're probably thinking I have a daughter for that. My one and only child.' She glances at Kathryn sitting mutely in the chair, then fixes her eyes on me again. It's an odd thing to say. 'But Kathryn has a family and two very demanding boys. She doesn't have the time.'

'You know I have the time,' mutters Kathryn, still star-ing at her hands, and I sense tension between them.

'Nonsense.' She turns her attention back to me. 'I like to be surrounded by youth. It keeps me young.'

I'm sure I hear Kathryn make a derisive sound through her nose, but either Mrs McKenzie doesn't hear or she chooses to ignore it. 'I think you'll find the salary is competitive,' she says, and tells me a figure twice my cur-rent salary – which isn't hard considering that's barely minimum wage, but still. With no rent or bills to worry about I can begin to pay back my credit card, which has reached its limit, thanks to my ex, Vince. My dream of travelling actually has a chance of being realized. She stands up. Kathryn and I follow suit.

'I'll be in touch. Kathryn will show you out.'

'Thank you, Mrs McKenzie. It was lovely to meet you.' I extend a hand and she takes it with a little jolt of surprise, as though she hadn't expected me to have any manners. I want this job so badly, despite Kathryn's brooding presence.

'Please,' she says, holding on to my hand. 'Call me Elspeth.'

It's dark by the time I get home. I had to take two buses from Clifton to Horfield, where I live. Thankfully, the main roads are mostly free of snow now, but even so the journey took over an hour.

The flat I share with Courtney is above a pharmacy and consists of a poky kitchenette/lounge/diner, two small bedrooms and a bathroom. I wasn't exaggerating when I said the whole flat could fit into Elspeth McKenzie's hallway. But it's all we can afford on our wages. Courtney likes to tell people she works in fashion, but really she's a hairdresser at a salon on Gloucester Road. I already know she won't be home yet. She works late every other Friday.

The alleyway that leads around the back of the pharmacy to our flat is dark and thick with ice and, for a fleeting moment, I think of Vince. If we were still going out he'd have cleared the snow for us. But we haven't spoken since our huge fight on New Year's Eve, eighteen days ago – not that I'm counting. Don't get me wrong, I don't want him back. Not after what he did.

I climb the concrete staircase that always smells of piss, my heart heavy. Usually, after a day like today, I'd ring my mum. I'd tell her all about Elspeth McKenzie and her posh house and her uptight daughter. Or we'd get together and laugh about it over tea and biscuits – Mum loved her tea: she drank at least ten cups a day – and then she'd advise me gently not to judge a book by its cover, that they might not be what they seem. Grief washes over me, as it often does, that she's not at the end of the phone or a few streets away, that she's gone forever. I have to swallow the lump in my throat. It's not yet been three months. I've been through a Christmas and a New Year since she died and it's still so fresh and raw, and I can't see an end to it. I know I'll always feel this way. I'll miss her for the rest of my life.

I let myself into the tiny hallway, switching on the lights, which only highlights the drabness of the place: the brown scratchy carpets, the beige melamine kitchen units, the magnolia walls. Courtney and I have tried to cheer the place up with colourful throws, which I crocheted, on the old, worn sofa, bright prints and photos of us taken on numerous nights out to cover the woodchip wallpaper, but it has made little difference. After Elspeth's magnificent house, the flat seems even more dreary, cramped and tatty.

Dumping my bag on the pine table that's shoved up against the wall to make room for the sofa, I shrug off my damp coat and hang it on the back of the chair. I have to make a concerted effort to be tidy around Courtney. In that regard we're the total opposite. Mum and I always argued about the state of my bedroom when I lived at home, and Courtney is so tidy it borders on obsessional.

The flat is freezing and I turn the storage heater up a little, blowing on my hands, which look like two slabs of raw meat. They start to itch and I place them under my armpits to warm up – a tip Mum gave me years ago. I switch the kettle on and take a Co-op meal for one out of the freezer. While it's in the microwave I sit at the table, staring at nothing. I have to change my life. A new year, a new beginning. Things can't go on as they have been. I don't even see that much of Courtney anymore as we work different hours and she's spending more time with her boyfriend, Kris with a K.

My mobile springs to life, startling me. I reach for it, expecting it to be Courtney, so I'm surprised to see a number I don't recognize flash up on the screen.

'Una?' says a clipped voice, when I answer. 'It's Elspeth McKenzie. I think you'd be perfect for the job. When can you start?'

Elspeth ends the call and I stare at my mobile in surprise. I can't believe I've got the job. A bit of luck, at last.

A clatter outside makes me jump and I pull aside the horrible office blinds that our landlord insisted on putting in every window. Our trash can has been overturned, lying on its side in the snow, like a drunk. I'll wait until Courtney gets home to tackle it. I'm about to close the blinds when I see a figure standing at the end of the alleyway. I can't make out if it's a man or a woman because their face is obscured by shadows and they're wearing dark clothing. But something about the way they're standing, facing me, unflinching in their pose, hands in pockets, shoulders squared, unnerves me. I pull the blinds closed, determined not to let it rattle me. They're probably waiting for someone, although the pharmacy is closed. I stand for a few seconds, deliberating. I've never been worried about being in the flat by myself and I'm not about to start now, just because Vince is no longer in my life.

A thought strikes me. Could it be Vince? I pull aside the blinds again and press my nose to the glass, but whoever it was has gone.

So you're the new one. The chosen one. I can see why she's decided on you. That same fresh-faced, raw beauty, the same silky blonde hair. Eyes that are slightly too wide, a rosebud mouth, petite and skinny but with a full bust. All clichés. And they say that's what men want. It seems women do too.

I followed you home. I watched you in your maroon woollen coat and your cheap boots as you tried to navigate the snow without falling. You care about what other people think of you. I saw the way you spoke to the bus driver, all demure smiles and fluttery lashes. Did you hope he'd find you attractive? I saw how you gave up your seat for the old lady with the sausage legs so that you had to stand in the aisle, reaching up to hold the bars above your head. Do you know you have a very small hole in the armpit of that coat? Are you really that nice? Or is it just for appearances? You're a people-pleaser.

You live in a hovel. Of course you do. That's why you're so impressed with her airs and graces, her ridiculously expensive house and her money. All that money. But she's as tight as arseholes. You'll soon see. Oh, yes, you'll soon regret taking that job.

2

Elspeth is perched on the edge of her favourite armchair as she chats into the receiver. Her eyes are burning with an excitement that Kathryn hasn't witnessed for weeks.

She lets out a sparkling laugh, which sets Kathryn's teeth on edge. 'Oh, you are sweet,' she coos. 'Well, I'm looking forward to seeing you too. Thank you for letting me know. See you on Saturday. Goodbye for now.'

Goodbye for now. Urgh. Kathryn feels queasy.

Elspeth replaces the handset in its cradle – she's the only person Kathryn knows who still has a landline and refuses to own a mobile – and glances up at her daughter, her cheeks flushed. 'That was Una. She's managed to organize it so she can start in three days' time.'

'Of course she has,' mutters Kathryn, under her breath, when her mother's back is turned. No doubt Una Richardson is impressed by the grand house and the Clifton location, just like the others had been.

It's five days since the interview, and every subsequent day that's passed Kathryn has tried to talk her mother out of hiring Una – hiring anyone – but Elspeth McKenzie has always been a stubborn woman who has never taken Kathryn's advice. Why would she start now?

As soon as Kathryn had opened the door to Una

Richardson last week, and seen that elfin face, those big grey eyes and her long swishy blonde hair, she'd known she'd get the job. Her mother's like a magpie the way she swoops in on beautiful things: a dress, a piece of jewellery, a painting, a pretty face.

Kathryn has often wondered how her life would have turned out if she'd given her mother two delicate blonde granddaughters instead of large-boned, boisterous grandsons. They'd have been invited around for Sunday lunch a lot more. And maybe she would have felt that she truly belonged to this family. She would have watched with a sense of pride as her mother fawned over them, doting on them, instead of the polite indifference she doles out to her grandsons.

Kathryn steps into the sitting room, pulling on her coat. She needs to get back to Ed and the boys. It's past their dinnertime and she doubts her husband would have thought about what to cook, even though she'd given him clear instructions this morning on what was in the freezer. 'How will you cope for the next three days before Una starts?'

She knows all too well that her mother will be fine. Because, the truth is, she doesn't really need someone to care for her. She has Aggie the cook, Carole the cleaner, and an ever-changing stream of gardeners and handymen on call. She's perfectly capable of caring for herself because she has more than enough money to fund every whim. No, the problem with her mother is that she can't bear to be on her own, even for a few hours. She's never been at ease in her own company, like Kathryn has. Even as a younger woman, Elspeth had to fill her days with events or errands so that every hour was accounted for. It was as though she thrived on the hustle and bustle and general business of her life, of running the galleries, or travelling across the country to buy antiques or fussing over Huw – going to London to buy specially tailored suits or his favourite aftershave, which could be found only in Harrods. She used to wish her mother would just stop sometimes and spend some quality time with her family. And now, as she's aged, she has no choice but to stop, and Kathryn can see that it drives her crazy.

Elspeth picks up a book from the side table. It's a first edition by some highbrow author whose name Kathryn can never pronounce. She wonders if her mother has ever read it. It's always seemed more of a prop. Growing up, Kathryn was never allowed a television – 'Not cultured enough, darling. Much better to go to the theatre or read a book', not that her mother ever sat still for long enough to read – and Elspeth still didn't have one in the house. Huw would escape to the garden to watch cricket on a portable TV he'd set up in the shed.

Elspeth clears her throat, turning the pages slowly without reading a word. 'Well, I have you, don't I, darling? You've been here every day to check up on me,' she says, without glancing up.

'Of course you have me. I don't know why you bother paying someone else.' Kathryn goes to the window and closes the heavy curtains, shuddering as she catches sight of the suspension bridge. It still gives her the creeps at night, even after all this time. 'I can pop in every day. Why waste your money?'

'We've discussed this,' her mother says, in a bored tone.

'I have more than enough money to spare. I'd rather have the assurance of someone being with me all day. What if I fall again? You have a family and a job. I can't rely on you.'

Kathryn suppresses a sigh. Two years ago her mother had slipped coming down the stairs. She insists she knocked herself out and was lying at the bottom of the stairs for hours until Aggie found her. Aggie had called an ambulance but, apart from a sprained wrist, she had been fine. After that Elspeth suddenly got it into her head that she needed a companion, as though she was one of those aristocratic ladies from the late 1800s, and it seemed only a young blonde girl would do. Within weeks of her fall she had employed the first of them, an attractive bubbly girl called Matilde, without even talking to Kathryn about it.

'You know I'd give up my job if you're worried about being alone and falling again. Surely it would be better for you to be looked after by family rather than some – some stranger.'

'And who would run your father's gallery?' Elspeth asked, without looking up from the book she's pretending to read. She hasn't turned one page.

'I could do it around the gallery. Daisy can cope without me . . . she's very capable and –'

'No. I need someone with me full time. And I pay you more at the gallery than you would earn as my companion.'

'You're my mother! You know I'd do it for free!'

'Don't be ridiculous. You couldn't afford to do it for free. Not on what your husband earns.' And there it is. The little dig she always makes whenever Ed is mentioned: that Kathryn married for love rather than money is a personal affront to Elspeth. Her mother snaps the book closed and places it back on the side table. She scrutinizes Kathryn, with her bright, penetrating gaze. Kathryn has to concentrate on not rolling her eyes. She knows Elspeth has never approved of Ed because he isn't some fancy lawyer or surgeon from a well-bred family. Instead he has a normal job in IT and went to a state school. But what her mother has never bothered to find out was that she fell head over heels for Ed because he made her feel safe. He made her feel that he'd never leave her, or hurt her. When they met, at university, he was the first person with whom she'd felt she could be her true self.

'But we're doing okay,' she lies. 'The mortgage is nearly paid off . . .' She doesn't reveal that they've borrowed more because she hopes she'll inherit enough from her mother in the future to pay it off.

'I don't want to discuss it.' Elspeth's tone is sharp. 'Una will be my companion and that's the end of it.'

Kathryn bites her lip in frustration. *Fine*, she thinks. *But don't expect me to fill in in the meantime.* But she knows she won't say it. Of course she won't. She never does.

'I think it's best you go home,' Elspeth says coldly. 'Aggie is here to cook my supper. I'm sure she won't mind helping me to bed tonight.'

You're perfectly capable of getting yourself to bed, thinks Kathryn, her heart thumping in fury. She can't trust herself to speak as she stalks out of the room, her low heels clattering on the tiles as she crosses the hallway to retrieve her bag from the cupboard.

'Goodnight,' Elspeth calls cheerfully, as Kathryn is half out the door. She slams it behind her.

That's what annoys Kathryn most about her mother. She always has to have the last word, leaving Kathryn choking on hers, in case she says something she might regret.

It's only a five-minute drive from her mother's place to where Kathryn lives on the other side of the Downs, but due to the rush-hour traffic, and the snow and ice still covering parts of the smaller roads, it takes a lot longer tonight. Plus she's still getting used to this huge car, which feels like a tank, even though she's had it for five months.

She pulls the SUV carefully on to the driveway. Snow is still banked around the edges, even though Ed scattered grit this morning. She sits for a few minutes, just staring at the house she shares with him and the boys: a roomy 1930s semi, with a garage, but none of the charm and a fraction of the size of her mother's elegant townhouse. Even though the curtains are closed, Kathryn knows Ed will be in the living room, slumped in front of the television, maybe even asleep, his mouth wide open, his hands resting on his belly. The boys, she expects (she hopes in Jacob's case anyway), will be glued to some electronic device and neglecting their homework. She sighs, bracing herself for the battles ahead. She would love it if she didn't have any responsibilities. No demanding, stubborn mother, no lazy husband or wayward kids. She could just come home, kick off her shoes, open a bottle of wine and relax in front of Netflix. Instantly she feels guilty. She loves her family, of course she does. She'd be lost without them.

And although her mother drives her mad, Kathryn knows how much she owes her.

The nasal voice of a football commentator and the cheers of the crowd in the background greet Kathryn as she lets herself into the hall. Is there a more annoying sound? Then she hears her kids fighting upstairs and Harry shouting, '*Muuuuuuum!*' at the top of his lungs. Indeed, it seems there is. She tries relaxing her shoulders from where they've risen around her neck and swallows her irritation.

She smiles patiently as her eleven-year-old bounds down the stairs, his face furious. 'Jacob keeps killing me on Minecraft,' he wails.

Jacob, four years older, and already looking like a man at fifteen, appears at the top of the stairs. 'I don't want to play this crap game with you anyway. It's babyish!'

'It's not babyish,' shouts Harry, stamping his foot and sticking out his lower lip. 'Is it, Mum? Just because *he* always wants to play some stupid shooting game.'

Kathryn folds her arms across her chest. 'You shouldn't be playing *anything*. Why haven't you done your homework?'

At the mention of homework, Jacob disappears while Harry blushes and tugs the back of his thick, dark hair. 'Um. Don't have any. What's for dinner?'

'I don't know yet. But it'll be ready in the next hour. Where's your . . .' But Harry has raced back upstairs before she can finish her sentence.

Just as she'd predicted, Ed is in front of the TV,

although he's ignoring the football and seems transfixed by whatever he's reading on his laptop. He looks up when she enters the room, a smile spreading across his face at the sight of her. 'Oh, hello, love. You're back early.'

'It's gone six thirty, Ed.'

He sits up straighter, clearly flustered. 'Oh, right. I didn't realize the time.'

'The boys had their tea?' She knows the answer but she wants to see what he says.

'Er, actually, no, not yet. I didn't know what to cook.'

'There's a lasagne in the freezer. I told you that this morning.' She shakes her head. 'Never mind, I'll do it.'

He follows her into the kitchen and hovers behind her uncertainly. She scans the butcher-block worktops and white Ikea units with a critical eye. There's a carton of milk left on the side, and two plates with the remains of toast that she knows the boys must have made when they got home from school. The fridge has been left ajar and is beeping, and there is a stain down one of the cabinets. She closes the fridge door and bustles about, clearing away the dirty dishes and wiping down the units. Ed stands in the doorway, looking as though he'd rather be anywhere else. 'How's your mum?' he asks eventually.

'Her usual charming self,' she replies, throwing the dishcloth into the sink and retrieving the lasagne from the freezer. She doesn't know what she would do without Aggie's meals. Her mother would disapprove if she found out that her cook makes extra for Kathryn and her family.

She switches the oven on and stands with her back to it to face her husband. He's still in his work clothes, his tie askew and his shirt hanging out. Although he's nearly fifty, something about Ed reminds Kathryn of an over-grown schoolboy. He still has all his golden brown hair, only a touch of grey at the sides, although it's thinning on top a bit now. Does she still fancy him? She supposes she does but, God, he annoys her at times. Like now.

'You do too much for her,' he says gently. 'You look done in. I'll put the kettle on.'

'She's hired a new companion. Young, impossibly pretty . . .'

He clicks the kettle on and reaches for the teabags. 'What's happened to Jemima?'

How many times? He's got the memory of a bloody goldfish. Still, his bad memory has its uses, she thinks, as she watches him slop hot water over the worktop as he pours it into the mugs. 'Ed. Wipe that off, will you? It'll rot the wood.'

He grabs a white tea-towel and Kathryn closes her eyes, pinching the bridge of her nose with her thumb and forefinger. It's best not to look. She'll sort it out when he's left the room.

'You all right, love? Headache again?'

Yes, you, she wants to say, *you're the headache,* but doesn't. She knows her irritability is down to her mother and that she would be taking it out on Ed, which is unfair. She gets the cloth and wipes up after him while he watches with a faintly bemused expression.

'Go and sit down,' he urges, after she's finished. He hands her the mug of tea. He's put too much milk into it but she takes it anyway and perches at the kitchen table, kicking her shoes off. She has a blister on her little toe.

'Jemima left. Remember? Before Christmas. She'd only been working for Mother since October. Didn't even last three months.'

Ed pulls out a chair opposite her and sits down heavily. She smiles to herself. Ed is the proverbial bull in a china shop. The smell of lasagne starts to fill the kitchen and makes Kathryn's stomach rumble. She hasn't eaten anything for hours. 'Well, your mother's not easy.'

She knows that. Why does he have to say it? He reaches across the table and squeezes her hand. He's being kind, she reminds herself. That's the lovely thing about Ed. He's always on her side. No matter what.

And then the little voice she tries to repress pipes up inside her head.

But would he be so loyal if he knew what you've done?

3

Una

My hand rests on the wrought-iron gate, suitcase at my feet, and I stare up at the house, my feelings oscillating between anticipation and fear. Now that the snow and ice have melted away, the house looks more beautiful, more regal than it did the first time I saw it, backlit by wintry sunlight and a cloudless sky. It's still cold, freezing in fact, and I'm wrapped up warm in my scarf and gloves, but right now I can almost imagine it's spring.

'Are you coming in or what?'

A male voice startles me. And that's when I notice him. He's almost hidden by the large evergreen bush in the front garden, his head just peeping over the top. He's handsome in a rugged, outdoorsy way, with olive skin and light eyes. He is wearing a grey woollen beanie, with dark curls peeking out of the sides. He's grinning at me. 'Were you talking to yourself?'

'Um . . .' Oh, my God, was I thinking out loud? Courtney's always laughing at me for doing that. My whole face is burning. 'It's my first day. I'm a little nervous.'

He climbs down from his ladder. He's really tall, with broad shoulders, and looks a few years older than me. 'Well, you'd better hurry up then, the old lady doesn't like shirkers.'

'I'm not a shirker, I'm . . .' But his eyes are twinkling. He's just teasing me. I push the gate open and he strides over to me to help with my case.

When we reach the front door he thrusts a gloved hand in my direction. 'I'm Lewis by the way.'

'Hi, Lewis By The Way. I'm Una.'

A languid grin spreads across his face. 'I hope to see you around. *Una.*'

And then the door opens and Kathryn is staring at me disapprovingly, as though she's caught us in a compromising position.

'You're late,' she says, even though it's exactly nine o'clock, the time Elspeth asked me to arrive. 'And haven't you things to be getting on with?' She fires this question at Lewis. 'The greenhouse needs emptying.' He flashes her an apologetic smile and lopes away.

I step into the house. I was hoping Kathryn wouldn't be here today. Doesn't she have a job to go to? I wonder if this is what it's going to be like working for Elspeth, her grumpy, disapproving daughter looking over my shoulder all day. It will be worse than Surly Cynthia – and I hadn't thought anyone could be *that* bad. Even Randy Roger, with his leers and suggestive remarks, didn't compare. I suddenly yearn for my old life: my flat with Courtney, the job I've had for the past four years. The familiarity of it all. I feel like I did on that rainy school trip to Wales in Year 6 when I wanted to be at home with Mum, huddled in front of the TV, dunking Digestives in our mugs of tea instead of hiking across fields and sharing a room with five other homesick girls.

Kathryn's face softens, as if she's sensed my distress.

'I'll show you to your room and give you half an hour or so to settle in. Then you can come and see Mother. I'll need to head to work for ten a.m. Is that okay?'

Mother. It sounds so formal.

'I . . . Yes, that's great.' I lug my case up two flights of stairs to the top of the house, in what I imagine was once the servants' quarters. When we get to the top there is a small landing and one door. She opens it and says, 'This is your room.'

I walk in, my mouth falling open. It's more of a suite than a room, with an en-suite bedroom, leading into another smaller room, which has been set up as a lounge.

'To give you some space if you don't want to be in the sitting room with my mother,' Kathryn says, as I gaze at my surroundings in awe. 'Believe me, there will be times when you'll be glad to get away.' She laughs then, loud and throaty, which catches me by surprise. It's the first time I've heard her laugh properly. She hands me a key. 'You can also lock your door,' she says.

Why would I want to?

Kathryn is looking around the room, a wistful expression on her face. Then she suddenly seems to remember I'm there and comes to. 'Right, well, I'll leave you to unpack.'

When she's left the room, I perch on the edge of the sleigh bed that's been pushed up against two sash windows overlooking the suspension bridge and vow to keep it tidy. The duvet cover is white with pink rosebuds dotted over it, the walls are painted a soft grey and the floorboards are sanded and varnished. It's a lot nicer than my room at the flat. I get up, smoothing the bedding where I've just sat, and wander into my lounge area. A wooden desk faces another large sash window, there's a grey linen sofa with pink scatter cushions, and a lamp next to a small TV.

This window overlooks the back garden, which is vast, with a shed and a greenhouse. I can see Lewis piling rubbish into a wheelbarrow, his back bent, his breath steaming. Right at the back of the garden, poking through the trees, is an ugly wooden structure that might once have been a tree house. I imagine Kathryn playing there as a kid. I wonder if she was lonely in this big house with its huge garden, no brothers or sisters to play with. I'm an only child and I was never lonely. But then it was always just me and Mum. We were a team, a unit. Self-contained and all the happier for it.

I go back through to the bedroom, unpack my clothes and put them away in the ivory French-style wardrobe and chest of drawers. I resist the urge to toss them all into one drawer, as I would have done at the flat. I pull out a framed photograph of me and Mum at the beach, taken a year ago. Before the cancer diagnosis. I hold it for a while, remembering our holiday in Devon and wishing I could go back to that time when everything was simpler, then place it on my bedside table.

I fill my bottom drawer with the snacks I'd bought on the way here. All my favourites: Cheddars, Oreos, a packet of Penguins and a couple of cans of Sprite. I know my meals are catered for, but I do love my snacks. And I don't feel comfortable helping myself to whatever Elspeth has in her cupboards.

I take my toiletry bag into the bathroom. It's small but well equipped, although I can't help the little thud of disappointment that there's only a walk-in shower and no bath. It's my way of relaxing, although it used to drive Mum mad when I was a teenager and my bath bombs left a coloured ring. Still, a shower is good and, more importantly, I won't have to share this bathroom with anyone else. Courtney could spend hours in the morning messing with her hair extensions and her fake eyelashes and self-tanning cream. I finger one of the plush grey towels. Everything has been thought of, right down to the White Company room spray sitting neatly on top of the cistern.

I open the cupboard under the sink and shove my cosmetics bag on the lower shelf. I'm about to close it again when something glints in the corner, catching my eye. It looks like a balled-up chain. I reach for it. It's old, tarnished, the chain in knots, but at the end is an oval locket. I try to open it, but age has made it stick together and I almost break one of my fingernails trying to prise it apart. I place it on my bedside table instead. I'll ask Kathryn about it later. It must have belonged to the girl who was here before.

I can hear footsteps outside my room and Kathryn calls through the door. 'Are you ready? Mother is asking for you.'

'The room is lovely, thank you,' I say, as I follow her along the landing.

'That's down to Mother. She likes everything to be just so. You'll learn that about her.'

'Right.'

'And you've got the floor to yourself so at least it warrants some privacy,' she says, walking down the stairs. She keeps talking about privacy as though the house is full of people, but as far as I'm aware it will be just me and Elspeth at night. We reach the next floor where I assume the other bedrooms are. It looks like there are four off the wide landing, but I don't get the chance to be nosy before I'm ushered down the next flight of stairs.

Elspeth is perched upright in a high-backed chair in what Kathryn calls the sitting room but I call a lounge. She gets up when she sees me and rushes over, embracing me like she would a long-lost daughter. She has to bend down quite a bit. She's at least four inches taller than I am. 'Una! It's so lovely to see you! I do hope you've settled into your rooms okay.'

My rooms. I want to giggle. I feel like I'm in *Downton Abbey.*

And then she turns to Kathryn, as if noticing her for the first time, and her expression darkens. 'What are you still doing here? You can go now.'

I can't help but flinch at her cutting tone. I can tell Kathryn's hurt, although she's doing her best to hide it. Her shoulders are pulled back and her chin juts as though to ward off unkind words. She stalks off, without saying goodbye to either of us, and closes the door firmly behind her.

'Thank goodness she's gone. She's such a kill-joy,' says Elspeth, straight-faced but with a twinkle in her bright blue eyes. I want to laugh at her forthrightness, while also feeling slightly appalled that she is speaking about her daughter in that way. My mum would never have talked about me like that behind my back. 'Right, come on, let me show you around.' She takes my arm and leads me through the house. She's surprisingly sprightly for an older lady who needs a companion and carer, and I wonder again why she's hired me. Is she just lonely? But how can she be, with Kathryn always hanging around?

She shows me the library at the back of the house, with built-in floor-to-ceiling shelves stacked with books, mostly classics – there's not a Danielle Steele or a John Grisham in sight – large French windows and a terrace with steep steps that lead down to the garden; the snug – a small, square room with squashy sofas where her grandsons usually spend their time when they come over; and the kitchen, which is down another flight of stairs, and takes up most of the lower ground floor, apart from a small room that Elspeth calls her 'study'. I notice none of the rooms has a TV and I'm grateful for the one in my bedroom.

'The kitchen is a recent addition,' Elspeth says, staring at the units lovingly. They are beautiful, hand-crafted, according to Elspeth, and painted in dove greys and soft beiges, with a limestone-tiled floor and doors leading on to the garden.

I wish my mum could see all this. She'd hardly have been able to believe it. The only thing that strikes me as a bit strange is the lack of photographs. The house I grew up in was full of family shots of me, Mum and Gran, of me in all my stages of growing up, Mum and her closest friends, holiday snaps. Even in the flat I shared with Courtney we had photos on the walls and in frames on the sideboard, strips of silly ones taken in booths stuck to the fridge. Here, there's artwork on the walls, painted landscapes and a few line sketches, one of which looks familiar, but nothing to show the family. Not even her grandsons.

We're just about to leave the kitchen when we hear a cheery 'Hello!' behind us and a large woman in her late sixties with tight grey curls and the biggest boobs I've ever seen is bustling over to us. 'Just had to pop out for some eggs,' she says. 'Still want quiche for lunch, Elspeth?' She doesn't wait for an answer as her gaze sweeps over me. 'You must be the new girl! I'm Agatha. Everyone calls me Aggie. I'm the cook.'

I just have time to introduce myself before she's talking again. 'Now, shoo, out of my kitchen. I've got lunch to prepare.' She turns away from us and starts washing her hands at the huge Belfast sink.

Elspeth links arms again. 'Let's get our coats and explore the garden,' she says gleefully, as though she's just announced we're off on a cruise.

'Just be back in time for midday,' Aggie calls over her shoulder, like we're two kids.

We go upstairs to fetch our coats and then I follow her through the library – marvelling again at the bookshelves: my mum, an avid reader, would have loved them – and out of the French windows. The lawn is crisp with dew and our breath steams in front of us, but Elspeth huddles against me.

'The girls used to love playing out here,' she says, as we stroll along the lawn. The wind whips at our hair and the hem of my coat. 'My late husband built that tree house, God rest his soul.'

'Do you have other children then, apart from Kathryn?' I ask.

Immediately I sense I've asked the wrong question: her arm stiffens against mine and she doesn't speak for a few seconds. Eventually, 'No. It's just Kathryn.'

I'm puzzled. Who was she talking about, then? What girls?

She's still clutching my arm as we circle the garden but she's silent now. I wait it out, not wanting to put my foot in it again. Despite myself, I can't help but scan the garden for Lewis. There's no sign of him now, although there is a wheelbarrow by the side gate filled with bracken.

Elspeth doesn't begin talking again until we're back inside the house. 'Would you mind making me a cup of tea?' she asks, as she settles herself into her favourite arm-chair in the lounge and picks up a book from the side table. The curtains are open, highlighting the views of the suspension bridge. From here I can see a young couple on the bench overlooking the Avon Gorge. They must be cold, I think. 'And please make one for your-self. You must treat this place as your home now.'

I smile and leave the room, happy to be away from her and her silent mood, even for the briefest of moments. Maybe this isn't the right job for me after all. But then I think of the money – it's the best-paid job I'll be getting any time soon. And I need it if I'm to travel. It's the one thing I promised Mum before she died, that I'd fulfil my dream to see the world. That was her dream, too, but she never got the chance to do it. We used to sit together while she was going through chemo, on those horrible plastic armchairs while the drugs pumped into her veins, and talk about the countries we'd visit, the food we'd eat, the clothes we'd wear, the playlists we'd make. We imagined the smells of the beach – coconut sun-cream and sand – trying to distract ourselves from the stench of disinfectant in the ward. We planned our route for South East Asia:

Thailand followed by Laos and Vietnam. And then, when she knew she was dying, she made me promise I'd see it all for the two of us. When I took this job I vowed to myself I'd stay just until September, not that I'll admit to Elspeth that I see this job as temporary, a way to earn enough to fund my dream.

I swallow the golf ball in my throat. It's going to take a bit of getting used to, this job, but it's only my first day. I can do this.

The smell of pastry hits me as I enter the kitchen. Aggie is sitting on one of the bar stools flicking through recipes, her large frame spilling over the seat. She looks up when I come in. 'She'll be wanting her mid-morning cuppa,' she says, shifting herself from the stool and going to the Aga.

'Shall I do it?' I ask.

'No. You're all right. Sit yourself down and talk to me. I know you've only been here a few hours but how's your first day going?' She has large red cheeks that remind me of shiny apples. There's something about her that makes me feel completely at ease straight away. She's homely. Warm. The opposite of Kathryn and Elspeth. She reminds me of Gran, my mum's mother.

'It's great,' I say, conscious that my voice is pitched too high, like it always is when I'm not being entirely truthful.

She fixes her hazel eyes on me. 'It'll take a bit of getting used to, I expect,' she says kindly. 'Having to work and live in the same place. It can be a bit . . . isolating.'

I bite my lip, wondering if I can be honest. 'It's a bit weird,' I admit, as I slide onto one of the wooden stools. They're high and my feet dangle like a little kid's. Mum and I used to laugh that we felt like children, swinging our feet on such chairs. That's the problem with being barely five foot. 'It's very quiet here after the care home.' I can't admit that I feel a little homesick. 'And usually I'd have Saturdays off,' I add instead. Then I blush, wondering if I've said too much. What if it gets back to Elspeth that I've been moaning already? I'm known for putting my foot in my mouth. Courtney's always teasing me about it.

She makes a funny clicking sound with her throat. 'Well, I hope you last longer than Jemima. She was only here three months. Shame, really, as she was a nice girl.'

'When did she leave?'

The kettle whistles. She gets up and moves it on to another part of the hob. She bustles about with mugs and teabags, talking with her back to me. 'Just before Christmas. It was all a bit odd. She left with no warning. Didn't give notice or anything. I think she was a bit of a free spirit. There were rumours that she went travelling. Some say she did a runner. That she was in some sort of trouble. Not that I'm the type to gossip, mind you.'

I smile to myself. Aggie reminds me of a younger version of one of the residents at the care home, Esme. She loved a gossip.

I hope I last longer than three months. Courtney is about to move her boyfriend into our flat, so I can't go back there if things don't work out here. No, I tell myself. They will work out here. They have to.

'Was there a girl before her?'

She turns to me and hands me a tray laid out with bone-china mugs and a teapot. 'Here we go.' I take it from her with thanks, although I'd rather stay in the kitchen talking and not have to go back up to Elspeth. 'Ah, the lovely

Matilde.' Her face falls. 'She was here for a few years. It was sad what happened to her.'

I feel a prickle of unease. 'What did happen to her?'

She hesitates, as if wondering whether she should be telling me this. She lowers her voice, her eyes flicking to the door. 'She was killed. In a hit-and-run last August. Oh, it was just dreadful. It was her night off and she was walking home in the dark, a little drunk I imagine – Matilde did like to party. She'd been to a bar in Park Street. Happened on the road out the front. It was raining heavily that night, I remember. She must have just stepped out without seeing the car.'

I'm too ashamed to admit to Aggie that I never read the news. And that last August I was rushed off my feet looking after my mum in between my job at the care home. 'Oh, Aggie, that's awful. I am sorry.'

Her eyes soften. 'I was fond of Matilde. A lovely, bonny girl. Good fun. A breath of fresh air around the place.'

'Did they ever catch the driver?'

She shakes her head, her chins wobbling. 'Unfortunately not.'

I'm just about to ask more when I hear Elspeth at the door. 'What on earth is keeping you so long? I could have made my own tea in the time it's taken you.' She turns on her heel and, carefully so I don't drop the tray, I follow her up the stairs.

At this rate I won't even last the morning. I'll be the one Aggie will be gossiping about to my replacement. The girl who didn't make it past her first day.

I've been watching you. I'm like a cat, stealthy and light on my feet. It's a fun game and you're easy to spot with your long hair that shimmers down your back. It stands out from the bland January skies. Sometimes you wear a big fluffy Russian hat and then you're even easier to spot. You have your own style. You don't run with the crowd. You like to think you're different.

I watch you come and go from the big house like you own it, and I bet you wish you did. I bet you like to imagine that you're the mistress of that house, that you're rich, don't you? Sometimes you have that old bag on your arm and sometimes you're alone. Well, you're never actually alone. Because I'm always with you. You just don't know it. And when you least expect it, I'll pounce.

4

Una

Thankfully, I last the morning. I even make it to Wednesday – my day off.

I know it's only a few days, but I can't lie. There are times when I'm bored out of my skull in this job. I was so busy at the care home – there was always some duty to perform and because there were so many residents I had variety to my routine. Then, when my shift ended, I'd rush home to visit Mum. But here, with Elspeth, a large amount of my time is spent sitting next to her on the sofa while she reads – although I never actually see her turn a page – and nods off. Yesterday I made the mistake of getting up and exploring the house while she was napping, hoping to bump into Aggie or Lewis – anyone I could have a chat with – but when Elspeth woke up and found I wasn't there she began calling for me, panic in her voice, as if I'd left her to die or something. I had to pretend I'd just gone to the bathroom.

The only time I have a small reprieve is when she asks me to go down to the kitchen and fetch her some tea. Then I can have a chat with Aggie, but not for too long or she comes to find me. I've not had a chance to ask about Jemima or Matilde again.

Luckily Elspeth is in bed by nine thirty so I can escape

to my room, watch TV, while munching junk food, and take the smile off my face, as Mum would say. I never knew how emotionally draining it would be living and working in the same place. It's like I'm never off duty.

Elspeth is an early riser so she expects me to get her up at six thirty. She likes to shower every morning, with my help. She doesn't mind standing naked in front of me, not like some of the residents at the care home, who tried to hide themselves behind a towel. No, Elspeth is happy to walk around in the buff. I imagined she was like that as a younger woman, never worrying about her nakedness. I didn't grow up in a household like that. My mum and I were much more prudish, even though it was just the two of us. And I'm expected to be by Elspeth's side at all times. It's only when she's in bed that I can truly relax. I imagine this is what it must have been like over a hundred years ago being a lady's maid.

This morning, because it's my day off, I have a lie-in until nine o'clock. But even though the sleigh bed is large and comfortable, I can't relax as I stare up at the beads of light dancing on the sloping ceiling, from the weak sun filtering through the cream curtains. I can hear traffic, the shriek of a child, a faraway police siren. What am I supposed to do all day? I can't hang around in my room watching TV, and if I go downstairs I'll feel like I'm working. I half expect Elspeth to be calling for me now, in her pinched, clipped tone.

I sit up and peer through the gap in the curtains. The sunshine glints off the suspension bridge, and the sky beyond is white, as if a screen has been pulled over the sun. In spite of my reservations about this job, I feel a rumble of excitement rippling through me that I'm living in such a stunning location. And, okay, my role might not be that exciting, yet – although Elspeth did promise me a theatre trip on Friday night, and talked about visiting an arcade she funds (I'm pretty sure she's not talking about the sort of arcades I used to go to in Weston-super-Mare as a teenager) so at least I have those things to look forward to – but I'm right here, in the heart of this gorgeous city. In what my mum called 'the posh part', living in a house that I could only imagine existing. I'm so lucky to have landed this job. It's an adjustment, that's all.

I reach for my phone and text Courtney. It would be great to see her. It's strange not living with her. She texts back straight away and we arrange to have lunch in Clifton. I shower, more energized now that I have a plan, and pull on jeans and a jumper in my en-suite bathroom – *my en-suite*. I still can't get over it! I feel awkward when I get downstairs. *It's my day off*, I remind myself. *You're not supposed to be working.* So why do I feel as if I'm skiving? Elspeth keeps telling me to treat the house like my home, that even on my days off I can help myself to food and Aggie will cook for me if I want it. But I still feel uncomfortable because I don't know if she's just being polite. Sometimes I feel I need to read between the lines with Elspeth. Yesterday, for example, I left a scarf and a dog-eared paperback of Agatha Christie's *The Moving Finger* on the coffee-table in the lounge (Elspeth always corrects me when I call it that – 'It's a sitting room, dear') and she told me, curtly, that my things must stay in my room.

On Sunday, my first morning waking up in the house, I helped Elspeth dress, as she'd instructed me to do on my first day (I was shocked to see her wardrobe was filled with identical twinsets, just in different colours, not a pair of trousers in sight) and then we went down to the kitchen for breakfast. Elspeth had to cling to my arm because she was worried about losing her footing on the stairs (although that didn't seem to be an issue on the occasions she's come looking for me). Sunday, I was informed, was sausage, bacon and eggs day. Today is salmon and avocado on toast.

The house is eerily silent as I descend the stairs. Where is Elspeth? She told me yesterday that Kathryn would come over to look after her today but there's no sign of either of them. I carry on down to the kitchen, hoping to bump into Aggie. But she's not there either. Instead there's a tray with a floral tea-towel laid over it. As I step closer I can see a note that reads: *For Una*. My heart swells. How lovely of Aggie to think of saving some breakfast for me. I remove the tea-towel, like a magician about to reveal a trick, expecting to see avocado on toast, but instead there is nothing. Just a large empty plate with a few crumbs and a chunk of tomato. I stare down at it in shock. I can't believe someone has eaten the breakfast that was meant for me. Who would do that? I shrug it off. There must be some mistake, although I'm desperate for coffee.

I stare at the Aga hob. I have no idea how to use it. The kettle is one of those heavy orange affairs that you don't have to plug into a socket. I've never used one of those, either. I suddenly feel like a Neanderthal. I place my hand against the side of the kettle and discover that it's still warm. Then I open all the wall cupboards, trying to remember where Aggie kept the mugs, until I find one as well as a jar of coffee. I sit at the kitchen table with my freshly made coffee trying not to feel as though I'm trespassing.

'Made yourself at home, I see.'

I jump. Kathryn is striding into the kitchen. She reminds me of the terrifying headmistress I had at school. She has on a navy wool coat and is wearing the frumpy skirt and sensible shoes she seems to favour. I look down at my jeans and jumper, feeling underdressed.

My cheeks grow hot and I'm annoyed at my body for betraying my feelings. 'I . . . just made a coffee.'

'Helped yourself to breakfast, too.' She glances across at the empty plate on the kitchen island and the tea-towel I'd tossed aside.

I smart. Hasn't her mother told her how the food situation works? 'Actually . . . no, I didn't eat that. It had my name on it but . . .' I don't know how to explain it. She might think I'm accusing her.

She folds her arms across her chest and juts her chin. 'There's no need to lie about it.'

I blink at her. Is she serious? Why is she being so antagonistic? 'I'm not lying,' I splutter. 'I'd never lie.'

She pushes her glasses further up her nose and assesses me silently for a few minutes. 'Okay. I just don't want to see my mother being taken advantage of, that's all.'

'I'd never take advantage of her,' I mumble, wondering where all this is coming from.

'Well.' She clamps her lips together. 'Some of the other girls weren't quite so honest.'

I wonder who she's talking about. Is that why Jemima

left so suddenly? I think of the necklace I'd found upstairs. I'd completely forgotten to give it to Kathryn. What if she sees it and thinks I'm trying to steal it? It can't be worth much. It's doubtful it's even silver, but I'd hate her to think I'm dishonest in any way.

I push my coffee mug away. I'm used to instant coffee but I have a feeling this is that cafetiere stuff. 'Um, talking of the other girls, I found a necklace in my room.'

She stands up straighter. 'A necklace?'

'Yes. It's in my bedside table. I think it must have belonged to that last girl . . . Jemima, was it?'

She looks taken aback that I know the name of my predecessor. I shouldn't have said it. Now it looks like I've been gossiping and I'm worried I'll get Aggie into trouble.

'Would you mind fetching it for me? I can post it on to her.' She's trying to be nonchalant but I can tell from the way her fingers scratch at her wrist that she's anxious about something. Bertha, one of the residents of the care home, used to do it when she was stressed. Her arms were always a mass of scratches, like she'd been attacked by a cat.

I stand up. 'Sure. I'll go and get it now.'

Kathryn's presence has sucked all the air from the room and I rush out of the kitchen, relieved to get away from the oppressive atmosphere. *Why does she care so much about a worthless old necklace anyway?* I wonder, as I climb the stairs. Aggie said something about Jemima leaving in a hurry one evening. It didn't sound like she'd left a forwarding address. Anyway, it's not my business. Kathryn is my boss's daughter, she wants the necklace, end of story.

I'd learnt at the care home not to ask too many questions when my bosses asked something of me.

It's curled in the corner of the top drawer of my bedside table and I take a while to unpick the knots. Then I turn the locket over in my hand, trying to find any distinguishing features, but it's quite plain. It looks old – maybe it's an antique. I'm conscious of Kathryn waiting for me downstairs but I'm intrigued enough to try the lock again. This time, to my surprise, I manage to prise it apart and the little door pings open.

Inside is a coloured photograph, not more than 2 cm tall. It appears to be a recent shot of a girl around my age, although it's hard to tell because you can see only her head and shoulders. Her hair is long and ash blonde, like mine, and there's something familiar about her face. It takes me a while to figure out why, but then it hits me.

The girl in the photograph looks uncannily like me.

5

Kathryn

Kathryn watches from the upstairs bedroom window as Una saunters down the street in her maroon coat with the black velvet collar turned up against the cold. She's wearing one of those furry Russian hats in black. She reminds Kathryn of a young Julie Christie.

She hates to admit it, even to herself, but Una seems decent. Not like Jemima. Certainly not like that snake Matilde. No, Una seems genuine. Quite naïve. Young for twenty-two in some ways, unworldly and innocent, despite what she's obviously been through with her mother's death. But then again, what does she know? Una could be a first-class manipulator. After all, Kathryn's been wrong before. And even if Una is a good person, she knows she can't allow her to stay. Matilde stayed for too long and look how that turned out.

Her mother has to stop all this. Kathryn hoped Elspeth would get the message after the other two, but obviously not. Typical, really. As much as she loves Elspeth she knows her mother has a tendency to be arrogant and stubborn.

Kathryn examines the necklace in her hand. As soon as Una told her she'd found it, she'd known straight away who it belonged to. How could she have overlooked it?

She slides it into the pocket of her coat and moves away from the window. Her mother will have finished at the hairdresser's soon and will expect to be picked up. Since her fall, Elspeth doesn't like going anywhere by herself. Kathryn had to drop her at the salon first thing and promised to be back within the hour to fetch her. Her mother used to be so active, so independent, running the gallery, setting up the foundation for impoverished artists, being interviewed for the Bristol press as some kind of local philanthropist. It's important to her that others think well of her, even though she hides her true self underneath her upper-class twin-set veneer. But Kathryn knows. And Kathryn's kept quiet. Because, despite how easily her mother can drive her mad, she loves her and will never forget how much she owes her. And, in a lot of ways, she feels sorry for her.

But it's more than a sense of duty. Even though Kathryn tries to convince herself otherwise, she's only too aware that she's her mother's puppet, unable to do anything without her pulling the strings. Too much depends on it. And if the strings are cut, Kathryn will fall and the life she's built for herself will be over.

She glances at her watch. If she's even a minute late Elspeth will be furious, demanding to know where she's been. It's only a short walk to Elspeth's favourite salon and Kathryn knows her mother could make that journey on her own, especially with the walking stick she refuses to use, even though she visits the salon once or twice a week and has been doing so for as long as Kathryn can remember. Her mother isn't particularly frail, despite being nearly eighty, but Kathryn understands the fall two years ago has knocked her confidence. She has tried to persuade her to use the walking stick, just so she'd feel less wobbly on her feet, but Elspeth refuses. No, Elspeth would rather have a pretty young thing to prop her up.

It's cold and fresh, the sky grey and threatening, as she lets herself out of the front door, her handbag slung over her shoulder. She made sure to pack her umbrella. She stands at the threshold for a few moments as she drops the keys into her bag and slides her fingers into her leather gloves. The necklace Una gave her is in her coat pocket, ready.

'Good morning.'

She looks up to see the gardener by the front gate. She can't remember his name. She's surprised to see him here again so soon. During the winter they only need him to come once a month at the most. 'Hi . . . er . . .' She smiles tightly, not wanting to stop and chat although he has a look on his face that suggests he has something to say.

'Lewis.' He grins at her and blows on his bare hands. He doesn't sound as if he's from Bristol, although she can't place his accent. He's handsome and tanned, and she wonders if he's been travelling. She regrets never doing so herself when she was younger. Everyone seems to be at it, these days. When she was young all she could think about was going away to university. Somewhere she could put all the bad things behind her, reinvent herself. Edinburgh had been that place, where she'd met Ed, fallen in love. But Bristol, and more specifically her mother, had pulled her back, like a magnet. 'I know we haven't met properly.'

That's true. Kathryn never bothers getting too friendly

with the gardeners. There's no point as the same one never lasts longer than a few months. Elspeth always finds some fault in them.

'I'm Kathryn, Elspeth's daughter, but I expect you know that.'

He raises his eyebrows, suggesting she's right. 'I'm from the agency,' he says. 'Not much work to be had this time of year for a gardener.' He has a kind face, with a quick-to-smile mouth and striking eyes. He reminds her of someone. 'So I was wondering if you had other work you might need doing? In your own home maybe. I'm good at all kinds of handiwork.'

Kathryn has the urge to laugh in his face, this boy who is young enough to be her son. He has made the same mistake numerous others have in the past. The mother is rich, so therefore the daughter must be too. 'Sorry to burst your bubble but I can't afford a gardener, even though I'd love one,' she says stiffly, hoisting her bag further up her shoulder. 'Now if you'll excuse me, I need to get on. My mother is expecting me.'

He looks crestfallen but tries to hide it by dipping his chin and staring at his feet. Without another word he stands aside, and she feels a pang of guilt for being so abrupt. It's hardly his fault. He's just trying to make a living. She flashes him an apologetic smile as she walks briskly past him. And then she stops, and turns to him. 'But I have friends who might need someone. I'll ask around.'

Relief floods his face and he expresses his thanks before heading towards the house. She feels better for doing a good deed even though she doesn't think any of her friends will be in need of a gardener. She wishes she could afford to employ Lewis. There's a set of shelves in the spare bedroom that Ed has been promising to put up for months now. She knows he'll never get around to doing it.

She strides towards the salon but stops when she reaches a bin. She retrieves the necklace from her coat pocket, and then, glancing around to make sure nobody is watching, she deposits it in the bin, before quickly walking on.

When Kathryn arrives at the salon her mother is finished, her hair set into her preferred chignon and sprayed with so much lacquer that even if there was a gale-force wind a hair wouldn't fly out of place. She's sitting in the waiting area wearing her favourite purple Chanel coat and chatting to another customer, an attractive woman with strawberry blonde hair, who looks to be in her thirties. 'Ah, there she is,' Elspeth says, to the woman, as Kathryn comes blustering in, a gush of cold air in her wake. 'This is Beatrice. She designs jewellery. I was just telling her about the arts foundation.' She turns her attention back to the woman. 'I have a shop if you ever want somewhere to showcase your work,' she says, rummaging in her bag and conjuring up a business card. 'We're always looking for new talent.'

Kathryn has to resist rolling her eyes. Can't her mother go anywhere without promising the world to any pretty young thing?

Beatrice takes the card with thanks. A hairdresser with a black blunt bob bustles over and whisks her away before she can say anything more.

'Isn't she a bit old for you?' Kathryn mutters, when they're out of earshot.

'What, dear?' Elspeth says, gathering up her things.

'And you're late.'

'I'm really not. You're finished early.'

Elspeth stands up, assessing Kathryn through narrow, critical eyes. 'Don't you want to make an appointment for yourself? You could do with a haircut.'

Kathryn touches her hair self-consciously. Ed prefers it longer and it's now skimming her shoulders. 'I like it this length.'

Elspeth purses her lips but doesn't agree. Instead she holds out her arm for Kathryn to take. 'Can we go home now, please? I've got lots to sort out today.'

Kathryn doesn't ask her mother exactly what she has to sort out. She has people running every aspect of her business so that she doesn't have to worry about anything. Elspeth takes her monthly dividends, gives the accounts a cursory glance once in a blue moon and leaves the running of the art gallery to Kathryn. She has gardeners, a cleaner and a cook. And now Una. Her mother is cosseted in every aspect of her life and always has been. People seem to do whatever she asks of them. Including lie.

There is a police car outside her mother's house when they return home. At first Kathryn doesn't think anything of it. This is Bristol, after all. Just last week there was a disturbance outside the local pub and the police had had to be called. Her mother might live in one of the most desirable roads in the city but it isn't crime free.

The sky has clouded over and it has just started to

drizzle. All Kathryn can think about is getting her mother into the house and putting the kettle on. She hopes Aggie has left out something warm and nourishing for lunch. Elspeth is walking painfully and unnecessarily slowly, talking all the while about Patricia, her friend who lives in the next street whose husband recently died, and how she can't bear this weather and is looking forward to spring.

As they let themselves through the front gate Elspeth is still wittering on but Kathryn isn't listening. Instead she's focused on the two plain-clothed police officers getting out of the car – a young man and an older woman. Her heart speeds up as they come towards them, the woman officer holding up a badge. Despite the cold, sweat breaks out under her armpits.

'Are you Elspeth McKenzie?' asks the woman, ignoring Kathryn and directing her question to her mother.

Elspeth, who has been completely oblivious to their presence until now, stops with her gloved hand on the gate. 'Yes. Can I help you?'

'I'm Detective Sergeant Christine Holdsworth and this is Detective Constable Joe Phillips,' says the woman, tucking her badge back inside her coat. She has red curly hair that is as short as a boy's and getting frizzy in the rain. 'May we come in and ask you a few questions?'

'What is this about?' Kathryn asks, fear making her sound more clipped than she intends.

'We just want to ask you a few questions about a girl you employed here at the end of last year.'

Elspeth frowns. 'Do you mean Jemima Freeman?'

'Yes,' says DS Holdsworth.

Elspeth stands up straighter. 'What about her?'

Two teenage girls are walking down the street, laughing and talking over each other. They look so carefree, thinks Kathryn, with nothing to worry about apart from boys and shopping. Right now, she wishes she was one of them.

'We'd rather not say standing here in the street, if you don't mind,' says the other officer, DC Phillips. He doesn't look much older than Jacob. He's tall and skinny with a mop of fair floppy hair and a large Adam's apple.

Elspeth pushes open the gate. Kathryn and the police follow. Her mother has suddenly forgotten she needs to walk slowly and is racing along the path to the front door. Nobody speaks until Elspeth has unlocked it and they troop through the hall and down the stairs into the kitchen.

Aggie is at the sink, up to her elbows in water, soaking vegetables. She opens her mouth to speak when she sees Kathryn and Elspeth, but closes it again when she notices they aren't alone. She moves away from the sink, wiping her wet hands on her apron, one eyebrow arched.

'This is Aggie,' says Elspeth. 'And these are the police.' Kathryn notices that the younger detective raises his eyebrows when her mother describes Aggie as her cook.

'The police,' says Aggie, wringing her hands. 'What are they doing here?'

'It's about Jemima,' whispers Elspeth, as if the police aren't standing there.

'Please take a seat,' offers Kathryn, and they sit side by side at the oak table. They look awkward and out of place in her mother's beautiful kitchen. 'Aggie, would you mind making some tea?'

The woman detective gets out her notebook and starts flicking through it. Kathryn is desperate for a glass of wine. She's been expecting this visit for some time. 'Mother, you'd better sit down too.' She pulls out a chair at the head of the table and her mother sinks into it.

Kathryn slumps into a seat next to her. Her legs feel weak. What do the police know?

'What's going on, Officer?' asks Elspeth, peeling off her fur gloves slowly.

'When was the last time you saw Jemima Freeman?' asks DS Holdsworth.

Elspeth frowns, placing the gloves on the table in front of her. They look like two dead animals. 'December. A week or so before Christmas. She used to work here and then she just upped and left one night, taking her stuff with her. Why?'

DS Holdsworth looks grim, her mouth pressed in a firm line. 'Didn't you ever wonder what'd happened to her?'

Elspeth shakes her head. Her hair doesn't move. 'Of course. She was a good girl. She'd only been with us a few months. She loved travelling, was a bit of a free spirit. I assumed she got bored with just an old lady like myself for company all day.'

'And you never heard from her again?' asks DS Holdsworth.

Her mother's drawn-on eyebrows knit together. 'No. Nothing.'

DS Holdsworth sits up straighter. 'I'm sorry to have to tell you this,' she says, glancing at them all in turn, even Aggie, who is hovering by the Aga waiting for the kettle to boil and pretending not to be listening, 'but Jemima Freeman has been found dead.'

There is a stunned silence until Elspeth pipes up, 'I'm very sorry to hear that. I liked her. Very much. But, what does that have to do with us? Surely she has family. She left her employment here over a month ago. I don't know what she would have been doing in the meantime.'

Kathryn cringes. Why does her mother have to sound so insensitive?

'Well, that's the thing,' says Holdsworth, glancing around at them all with the same grave expression on her face. 'Jemima died on the nineteenth of December.'

Elspeth frowns, and Kathryn can see her trying to make the connection. 'But . . . that's the day . . . that's the day she left here.'

'I know,' says Holdsworth. 'It appears that you and your family, Mrs McKenzie, were the last people to see Jemima alive.'

6

Courtney is sitting in the window of a café on Gloucester Road, near where she works. I love Gloucester Road, with its independent shops and delis and the colourful graffiti on the walls. It's always bustling, even on a drizzly grey day like today. I watch her for a moment, her head dipped as she reads something on her phone, with a serene half-smile. She's probably on Instagram, posting another carefully orchestrated shot. Anything mundane looks good through Courtney's eye: a hairstyle she's just done, a flower covered with raindrops, a spider's web, her shoes against a brick wall, the retro sweets she's addicted to. Her glossy copper hair is gathered up in a high ponytail and she's wearing the white T-shirt and black skirt combo that is her uniform at the salon where she works. I only moved out on Saturday morning, it's only been four days – we've been apart for longer when I was going out with Vince – yet it feels like I haven't seen her for years. My heart swells for her. My oldest friend, the closest thing to family I have now.

We grew up in the same 1950s cul-de-sac in Filton. Our mums got on well, so we were always in and out of each other's houses as kids. We've been best friends since starting school at the age of four.

The bell on the door tinkles as I go in and she looks up from her hot chocolate – she doesn't like caffeine, and it's a running joke that we always say we need to meet for coffee when she doesn't drink it. Her face breaks into a huge smile when she spots me. She leaps from her chair to hug me. 'I've missed you,' she says, leading me to the table. 'God, it feels weird in the flat without you.'

I shrug off my coat and place my hat on the chair next to me. It looks like a cat curled up on the seat.

'You aren't just away or at work or staying with a boyfriend. You've moved out. Actually moved out.' She throws her hands into the air to emphasize her point. She's always gesticulating, and the two of us talk so fast when we're together that nobody can understand us. 'Your stuff's all gone. The place seems empty and smelly now I'm sharing with a man, although,' she chuckles, 'he's actually tidier than you. And not to mention we've got damp.' She grimaces. 'Luckily the landlord is dealing with it. And thank you for leaving all the throws and cushions we chose. Kris thinks they're too girly, but they're staying.'

'How's it going living with him?'

She pulls an exasperated face, then catches a waitress's attention to order me a cappuccino. We're creatures of habit, me and Courtney. I surprise her by asking for a croissant to go with it. I'm starving, thanks to the stolen-breakfast incident. When the waitress has gone she says, 'I'm regretting letting him move in.'

'Really?'

'He leaves his clothes everywhere. Wet towels on the floor, pants on the carpet. It's like he thinks I'm his mum.

He's twenty-six years old and this is the first time he's lived away from home.'

I laugh. 'I thought you said he was tidier than me.' I'm not a huge fan of Kris, not that I've ever admitted as much to Courtney. I just think she can do better. She's fiercely loyal when she decides she likes you. Although, as she'll say herself, she has a resting-bitch face. Kris plays the drums in Vince's band, and when he met Courtney he told Vince he didn't like her because 'her head's stuck up her own arse'. She doesn't give her friendship easily. Unlike me. I know I'm quite laid-back in that respect. It takes a lot to annoy me but Courtney is less tolerant. In the end, Kris realized how genuine and kind Courtney is and won her around. She says he makes her laugh. I suppose he can be funny, in the immature way that boys at school could be, but there is a side to him I don't like. He takes people for granted. I used to see him do it with Vince and now I'm noticing it with Courtney. He's the one who'll never pay for a round of drinks, who always expects others to drive, who won't go out of his way to help someone. Everything has to be on his terms. I've always felt Kris was a kind of stop-gap for Courtney. Although now he's moved in, I worry she'll be stuck with him.

She smirks. 'He is! Although I'd trained you well. And you didn't expect me to pick up after you.'

'True. Is he working today?'

She shakes her head, nearly whipping herself in the face with her long ponytail. 'That's another thing. He still refuses to think about a proper career even though the band is going nowhere.'

We've discussed this at length, many a time. Kris and Vince are dedicated to their band. Everything, even a possible career, is put on hold just in case they make it big.

'They really believe they're the next Arctic Monkeys.' She laughs.

I roll my eyes. The thing is, it's not as though they're bad. They're actually quite good. The lead singer, Dexter, has a gorgeous, gravelly voice and the looks to go with it. Vince is an excellent bass player, their songs are clever and catchy, and Kris is an enthusiastic drummer. But they're just another band on the Bristol scene, gigging the local venues and hoping to be the next big thing. And everything is on hold until they 'make it'.

The waitress appears at our table with my order. Courtney is thoughtful for a few moments as she sips her hot chocolate. 'I told him he needs a back-up. Go to college part time, get some qualifications. Like me.' Courtney would like to have her own hair salon one day. 'Anyway, enough about me. How's the job going?'

'It's good . . .' I lie, buttering my croissant. But Courtney knows me too well. I can see she's not convinced.

'I thought you'd landed on your feet.'

'It's great. Don't get me wrong, it's better than the care home, it's just . . .' I take a bite of croissant, careful not to wolf it.

She leans forward expectantly. 'What?'

I swallow and tell her about the boredom, and about Kathryn. 'She's always watching me, like she suspects I'm about to steal the family silver or something.'

Courtney laughs. 'You're the most honest person I

know. Remember when we found that wallet full of money in Castle Park?'

I do. We'd been heading to the shops when we saw a wallet on the ground bulging with twenty-pound notes. There must have been at least three hundred pounds. Courtney had wanted to keep the money – we were only seventeen, after all, and broke – but I'd insisted on taking it straight to the police station.

I shrug. 'I wish Kathryn was as sure of me. She makes me feel uncomfortable.'

'But she's not there all the time?'

'No, thank goodness. She was there today.' I fill her in on the morning's events, including my missing breakfast.

She raises her thick eyebrows. She takes ages in the morning to make sure those bad boys are expertly filled in and she's always trying to get me to do mine, even though I'd look weird with thick dark brows and light blonde hair. 'Do you think she ate your breakfast?'

'That would be weird. Why would she?'

'Just so she could have a go at you?'

I shake my head. 'I can't imagine her being that petty. She's old. Nearly fifty. And sensible. A bit dowdy, you know? Like Mrs Bird across the street. She's got two kids and a husband. I can't imagine her doing something like that. But it's not all doom and gloom. There's a hot gardener.'

Her face lights up. 'Tell me more!'

I wipe my mouth with the napkin, half tempted to order another croissant. 'He's very handsome. Like stunning. He looks a bit like that *Poldark* actor but with bright blue eyes.'

She makes appreciative noises.

'He's worth coming to work for.' I laugh.

'What about Vince? That's definitely over?'

I cup my hands around my mug. 'I've not heard from him. Nothing. Since we split up.'

She reaches out and touches my wrist. 'I'm sorry.'

'Does Kris say anything?'

'Only that he thinks he still loves you.'

'Has he . . . has he met someone else?'

'Nope. Kris says he doesn't seem interested and that he's still pining after you.' My heart leaps at the thought that Vince might not be over me, even though I know it could never work between us. I need to move forward with my life. 'So, do you think you'll stay?'

'Yes. Of course.' The thought of returning to the care home is unbearable. 'It's a cushy job, really. It's just going to take a bit of getting used to, that's all. And it's great money. Especially if we're still going travelling at the end of the year . . .' I eye her warily. It's all we've talked about since Vince and I finished. 'Unless you don't want to leave Kris?'

'Are you kidding? I'm desperate to take a few months off work and see the world. You know that.' Courtney is self-employed at the salon and her boss has said she can continue there when she gets back. I doubt it'll be the same for me with Elspeth. But that's nine or ten months away. Anything can happen before then. I only have to give a month's notice, anyway.

I lower my voice. 'Something a bit weird happened earlier.'

'Oh, yes?'

I tell her about finding the necklace. 'I think it belonged to the girl before me. Her name was Jemima apparently. But the strange thing is, she looked a lot like me.'

She stirs her hot chocolate thoughtfully. 'That's a bit odd. If it was Jemima's, why would she carry a photograph of herself inside it?'

I hadn't thought of that. Courtney has always been the more analytical one of the two of us. 'So you don't think it belonged to my predecessor?'

She shrugs. 'Unless she thought a lot of herself.'

'Then why would Kathryn tell me it was Jemima's?' I think back to our conversation. Did Kathryn say it was Jemima's? Or did I just assume that?

Courtney bends down to retrieve her bag. 'I need to go. My shift starts in ten minutes. But before I do . . .' She takes her phone from her bag and snaps the two of us together.

I roll my eyes.

'Come on! You're so photogenic.'

'Just this once.' She knows I hardly use Instagram. I have about two photos on my account, both of fluffy dogs.

She winks at me as she does up her coat. It's nearly ankle-length in the softest powder blue and looks a lot more expensive than it was. Courtney has a way of making anything look stylish.

'What are your plans for the rest of the day?' she asks, as I push my chair away.

'I'm not sure. I'm at a bit of a loose end, really.' I must look a bit crestfallen at the thought of spending the rest of the day alone because she says, 'Why don't you come to the pub tonight? Kris and the guys are playing. I know you don't want to see Vince, but all the gang will be there. They're your friends too. And you'll have to face Vince sometime.'

She's right. I've been very unsociable since Christmas. And it would be fun to go out this evening. Otherwise it will be another night in with Elspeth, which will feel like work even though it's my day off.

'Okay,' I agree. 'Are they playing at the Pig and Calf?'

She rolls her eyes. 'Don't they always?' It's in White-ladies Road, which is probably only a twenty-minute walk from Elspeth's. Once again it strikes me how lucky I am to live so centrally when I used to have to take a bus from Horfield.

I've got hours to kill before tonight, though. We go to the counter to pay and then leave the café. It's started raining and we huddle in the doorway for a few minutes while Courtney applies lipstick expertly without looking in the mirror. 'Do I have it on my teeth?' She flashes them at me and I shake my head. 'Right. I'll text you later. Love you.' She hugs me, engulfing me in her favourite Marc Jacobs scent, then wafting away. I watch her walk down the street, the furry pompom on her bag swinging with each step she takes, her large umbrella nearly poking the eyes out of a passing man. I press my hat firmly on to my head and walk in the opposite direction, wondering how I'm going to fill my day.

It's boredom that makes me do it. There are only so many clothes shops you can look around when you haven't got much money to spend. And after finding the locket and hearing Aggie talking about Jemima leaving so suddenly, and the girl before her, Matilde, killed in a hit-and-run, I want to know more. One of my mum's favourite sayings was 'Curiosity killed the cat', which she usually aimed at me because I'm so nosy. So I take a long, slow walk to the central library and pay to use one of their computers. I don't have a laptop and the Wi-Fi at Elspeth's isn't great. Most of my friends are social-media queens, but I'm not a huge fan. Being off social media makes me feel protected somehow, like I'm in my own private world, although lately I have become a bit addicted to Instagram. There's something so engaging about scrolling through other people's photographs. It's perfect for the voyeur in me.

I settle myself at one of the computers and soon have Google up. It takes me a while to find anything because I don't know Matilde's surname so instead I just type in Matilde + Elspeth McKenzie + Clifton and soon an article that was published last week in the *Bristol and Somerset Herald* flashes up on screen.

13 January 2019

Police are still no closer to finding the driver of the car that killed a young woman in a hit-and-run in Clifton last summer.

Matilde Hansen, 23, was on a night out with friends on Wednesday, 21 August when she was knocked over crossing the road. She had been drinking and was returning alone to the house where she lived and worked in Sion Hill when the accident occurred.

Unfortunately, the part of the street where Matilde was struck down doesn't have CCTV and there were no witnesses.

Alexandra Stein, 23, a friend of Matilde's who was with her the night she died, said: 'We left the pub just after 11.30 p.m. It was pouring with rain and we had our umbrellas up. I walked a little of the way with her, before turning off to go to the bus stop. Matilde would only have been on her own for about five minutes before she reached her house. The roads were pretty quiet, especially as the weather was bad. It was a Wednesday night but Matilde liked going out on Wednesdays as it was her day off. I can't believe this happened. She was such a fun, bubbly girl.'

Her employer, local philanthropist Elspeth McKenzie, told the *Herald:* 'My family and I are in shock. She worked as my carer and companion for the last two years and she helped me back on my feet after a fall. She was caring, kind and considerate. She will be sorely missed and I am deeply sorry for her family's loss.'

Matilde, who was originally from Denmark, had no family in Bristol. Her mother died when she was a child and her father still lives in her home country.

Police are still appealing for witnesses to come forward.

I sit back in my chair, digesting what I've just read. Poor Matilde. How horrific, so close to where she lived and where I'm living now. How could a person knock someone down and just drive off? It must have been panic. And fear. I don't have a car but I know that if I was ever in such a situation I'd stop and help. I couldn't just leave someone dying in the road. The thought of it makes me feel sick.

There is no photograph of Matilde but I Google her name and her Facebook profile comes up as *Remembering Matilde Hansen* and then a photo of her beautiful face, her long blonde hair, her laughing pale eyes.

I feel as though all the breath has been knocked out of me.

I sink back in my chair, unable to believe what I'm seeing.

Matilde looks remarkably like Jemima.

And me.

Maybe Elspeth warms to young blonde girls. Perhaps we remind her of someone, although I can't think who. It's definitely not her daughter. Kathryn is tall and dark. There must be a reason for it, though. Even if it's unconscious. Because I don't believe in coincidences.

I scroll through the other links attached to Matilde's name until I read something that makes me gasp out loud. A line in a news article published today.

Jemima Freeman, 24, was an employee of local philanthropist Elspeth McKenzie. Her predecessor, Matilde Hansen, was killed in a hit-and-run last year. Jemima was found dead two days ago. Police suspect suicide.

No. I don't believe in coincidences.

Have you realized yet that you look just like the other girls? The two who came before you? Do you know you'll end up just like them? I've been watching you. But you wouldn't have noticed me — as I've said, I'm good at this. I've had a lot of practice. I walked past you at one point. So close I could smell the perfume you wear, and the coconut shampoo of your hair, but you didn't recognize me.

I fantasize about it. About you. When the time comes. And it will. I imagine how your breathing will change, how your big grey eyes will fill with alarm, the fear on your face. You won't be so smug then, will you? You will never be lady of the manor. Not after I've got hold of you.

7

Kathryn

Jemima had been lying dead for over a month, hidden for the most part by the snow and then, when that had melted, by the earth and the rocks of the Avon Gorge. The police suspect she jumped from the Clifton Suspension Bridge, although there were no witnesses.

Kathryn listens in a stupor as DS Holdsworth imparts this information in her flat, toneless voice. When she's finished there is a stunned silence at the table. Even Aggie can't think of anything to say, but stands at the Aga, her face pale.

Kathryn takes a few deep breaths, trying to push down her nausea. *What has she done?*

Elspeth is the first to speak. 'Well,' she says, fingering the pearls at her neck, 'I'm . . . well, I'm shocked.' Her face crumples in on itself and for the first time Kathryn thinks her mother looks older than her years. She's a good actress, Kathryn will give her that.

'What exactly happened on the last day of her employment with you?' Holdsworth asks. 'Was there an argument? Did she leave under a cloud?'

Elspeth catches Kathryn's eye, then looks down at the table, studying the fine grain of the oak. 'No,' she says. 'Like I said, she took her belongings and left. She didn't tell me she was leaving.'

Holdsworth frowns and consults her notes. 'But you said she was a live-in employee. Didn't you notice that she was leaving the house with all her stuff?'

'She didn't have much,' adds Elspeth, still avoiding eye contact. 'Just a backpack's worth. I was at a meeting – about the gallery I run – and she would usually have come with me but she said . . . she said she had a headache and wasn't feeling well so stayed behind. She ordered me a taxi. I was only gone a few hours. When I got back she wasn't here. I thought she might have nipped out, although there was no note. When she didn't return I went up to her room and saw that she had taken all her belongings.'

'And you didn't report it?'

'Why would I?' Elspeth scoffs, her head shooting up, no longer avoiding Holdsworth's gaze. 'She was old enough to make that decision. Before she came to us she'd spent two years backpacking around South East Asia. She was a free spirit, I could see that. I always knew she wouldn't stay long. But I liked her. So I was willing to take that risk.' She leans forwards on her elbows, her bright blue eyes flashing. In this moment Kathryn can see how formidable her mother really is and Holdsworth shrinks back a little in her seat. 'You have to like who you employ when they live with you, work with you, and are your constant companion. Do you see that, Detective? I wouldn't have taken her on if I didn't *like* her.'

They are interrupted by Aggie, who approaches the table with a tray. She places it in front of Elspeth.

'Please help yourselves to tea,' says Elspeth to the two detectives, as though she was the one who had gone to the effort to make it. Aggie sidles away to continue cooking, but Kathryn can tell she's still listening. She knows Aggie will be loving this. Something to tell her husband when she goes home this evening, no doubt.

Holdsworth pours tea for herself and DC Phillips. She offers a mug to Kathryn but she hasn't the stomach for it and shakes her head. Her mother takes one, although Kathryn notices she doesn't drink it.

Holdsworth sips her tea and puts the mug on the table. 'Did Jemima ever show signs of depression?'

'No,' Elspeth says vehemently. 'Not at all. She was a sunny girl. A breath of fresh air. After Matilde . . .'

'Ah, yes, Matilde Hansen. She died in a hit-and-run . . . What was it? Two months before you took on Jemima?'

Elspeth nods. 'That's right. I was very fond of Matilde. Very attached. She was my first companion and she became like family to me. Like a daughter.'

Like a daughter. The words stab at Kathryn's heart.

Elspeth continues, oblivious, 'Her family were in Denmark, you see, so she had nobody else.'

Kathryn clenches her fists at her sides. Oh, yes, her mother certainly doted on Matilde. There were times when Kathryn wondered if her mother loved Matilde more than her. Elspeth showered Matilde with gifts, like a lovesick teenager, albeit a rich one – designer shoes, beautiful dresses, the latest handbags. It had been sickening to watch Matilde blatantly taking advantage of her. Not least because the only gifts her mother has ever bestowed on Kathryn were on her birthday or at Christmas, and usually something practical, like an iron. In her mother's eyes, it seemed Kathryn wasn't deserving of beautiful things.

'I see. I understand that Jemima also had no family. Is that true?'

'She was estranged from her mother. She never mentioned her father. And, as far as I was aware, she had no siblings,' says Elspeth, still cupping her mug.

Holdsworth taps her pen against her teeth, which instantly grates on Kathryn. She feels overly sensitive to any sound, as though all her nerves are on edge. 'Unfortunately her mother passed away a few months before Jemima. She was an alcoholic.'

Elspeth puts her hand to her heart. 'That's awful. I didn't know.'

'But she has a brother. He wants an inquest into her death. He doesn't believe she would take her own life.'

Elspeth sits up straighter, surprise on her face. 'I would have said the same, but you never know what's really going on in someone's head, do you, Detective?'

Holdsworth murmurs her agreement. She takes another swig of her drink, then gathers up her belongings, much to Phillips's apparent disappointment – he won't get to finish his tea. 'Come on, then,' she says to the younger officer, standing up and taking her wet coat from the back of the chair. Phillips reluctantly does the same. 'Anyway,' she adds, 'we'll get out of your way. Sorry for disturbing you and for having to be the bearer of such bad news.'

Elspeth puts her mug down and stands up too, although she seems shaky on her feet and holds on to the edge of the table for support. 'Thank you for letting us know.'

'Sit down, Mother. I'll show the detectives out,' says Kathryn. She can't get them out of the house fast enough.

'Feel free to contact us again if you need any more

information,' she says insincerely, as she ushers them to the front door. The rain is coming down heavier now and both detectives do up their coats before braving the elements. 'But, really, we hardly knew Jemima.'

She shuts the door on them before they can say anything else.

When the police have gone and Elspeth has picked at the ham ploughman's that Aggie has prepared (Kathryn can't face any lunch herself, the visit from the police quashing any appetite she previously had), she asks if Kathryn can help her upstairs.

'I just need to lie down and rest for a bit,' she says, as she clutches her daughter's arm, climbing each step slowly, deliberately. For once she appears frangible, her bones thin beneath her cardigan. When did she start losing so much weight? She clings to Kathryn as they shuffle along the corridor to her room, and Kathryn helps her on to the four-poster bed. It's as if all her energy has been snuffed out of her, and she looks as withered as a decaying flower. 'I'm exhausted,' she says, as she stretches out and rests her head against the plump pillows, her face white.

Kathryn gently removes her slippers, making sure she's comfortable and tucked up, like a child. Just as Kathryn is about to leave, Elspeth grabs her hand. 'Will you send Una up when she gets home?'

'It's her day off, remember?'

'I know.' She squeezes Kathryn's hand, her grip surprisingly strong, her eyes closed. 'You're a good girl.'

Her words surprise Kathryn. Her mother isn't one for praise, at least, not to her. It takes her back to when she was eleven years old and would do anything to make Elspeth keep her. If she was good, if she was quiet and respectful and considerate, if she did everything Elspeth asked of her, she wouldn't send her away. Those little words, *You're a good girl, Kathryn*, were music to her ears. It meant she was on the right track to being the perfect daughter.

The perfect daughter. Would she ever stop playing that role? It's a full-time job.

She kisses her mother's crêpy forehead, then walks around the huge bed to pull the curtains across the sash windows that overlook the suspension bridge. It's still raining and the drops tap against the glass in a rhythmic thud that Kathryn's always found soothing. Afterwards she leaves the room to the sound of Elspeth's breathing.

She can't bring herself to ask her mother why she lied to the police about Jemima's last day. And if she had been trying to protect Kathryn, or herself.

8

Una

I can't stop thinking about Matilde and Jemima as I return to The Cuckoo's Nest. Both my predecessors are dead. I can't get my head around it.

It's not even five o'clock but it's already dark as I let myself in. I kick off my boots and am about to walk away but remember to put them neatly in the cupboard as is the rule. I pad across the cold tiles towards the sweeping staircase. The door to the lounge is ajar and I can see Elspeth perched in her favourite chair next to the mantelpiece. A fire is raging in the hearth and she's staring wistfully into it. I move away, wanting her not to notice me. My jeans are damp, as well as my coat, and I feel chilled to the bone. I just want to go up to my room, shower and rest ahead of my evening with Courtney.

But no such luck. Kathryn is coming up the stairs from the kitchen. She jolts when she sees me, as though I'm an apparition. She frowns and grabs hold of the banister. She looks pale. 'Oh,' she says, when she's recovered. 'You're back.'

'I got caught in the rain. I'm going upstairs to shower.' I feel slightly queasy and I'm sure it's the prospect of seeing Vince tonight. I've been putting it off for too long, but I need to speak to him.

'Okay.' She looks exhausted. I'd love to ask her about

Jemima but it's not the right time. And then a thought strikes me. Maybe she doesn't know. She took the necklace from me earlier and said she'd post it to her. Why would she do that if she knew she was dead?

I ask her if there is anything I can do to help, even though it's my day off.

She smiles and, for once, it seems genuine. 'No. Thank you. Ed is with the boys so I'm staying over tonight. Just in case Mother needs me. I do it every Wednesday and Saturday. She doesn't like to be in this huge house by herself at night.'

'But I'm here.'

'I know. But it gives you the chance to stay elsewhere, if you want to.' I frown. It seems a bit odd. Where else would I stay? They know I'm single. I'm sure it's just Kathryn wanting to make herself seem indispensable to Elspeth. She lowers her voice in case Elspeth can hear, although she's in the other room. 'She's been in bed this afternoon. She's not feeling well.'

'Oh, I'm sorry to hear that.'

She continues as though I haven't spoken. 'Mother should sell this house, really. Get something smaller.'

'How long has she been living here?'

'I was eleven,' she says, without missing a beat. Something dark passes across her face, like an eclipse. I sense she doesn't want me to ask any more questions. She stiffens and clutches the banister tighter.

'Okay, well, I'd better get into the shower,' I say, holding a tendril of my wet hair to illustrate my point, wondering why Kathryn is being weird.

She nods curtly and I carry on up the stairs to my room,

grateful to be away from her. How can what I consider to be an anodyne question provoke such a change in her? It was the same with Elspeth when I asked about the tree house. Maybe this is what posh people are like. Maybe it's not the done thing to ask questions.

I'm beginning to realize that this house and the family within it are full of secrets.

I feel uneasy as I shower. I pull on my jeans and a long-sleeved fitted top, thinking of the girls who lived in this room before me, now dead. I sit on the edge of my bed and towel-dry my hair. What would Mum make of all this? What would she say to me if I could ring her now and admit that I feel scared because two other girls who lived here before me have died? Girls who looked like me. She would tell me not to let my imagination run away with me. That I have a good job. That Kathryn and Elspeth are harmless. That Matilde had an unfortunate accident and Jemima must have been suffering from depression. The two things are unrelated. Completely different circumstances.

I get out my phone and log on to Instagram. It takes a while to load, but when it does I find myself searching for Jemima Freeman. She might not have had an account. I scroll through a few Jemimas until I pause on a photo of a familiar-looking girl. She has sea salt in her hair, a healthy tan on her face, and she stands smiling on a beach with the most brilliant blue skies I've ever seen. My stomach drops. Is this the girl from the locket? I scroll through more of her photos: more beach scenes, then market stalls and the exotic streets of foreign countries that I dream of visiting. She resembles the locket girl, just like she resembles me and Matilde, but I can't be sure if it's the same person. The girl in the locket looked younger, maybe mid-teens, with finer eyebrows.

A shout from the garden shakes me from my thoughts. I drop my phone onto the bed and rush to the window, cupping my hands around my face to block out the light in my room. It's dark outside, but the patio lights are on, illuminating two figures. A man and a woman. I blink, and crane my neck to get a better view. I'm four floors up so it's difficult to tell, but the man looks like Lewis. He has his beanie pulled down over his hair and he's gesticulating. The woman has her hands on her hips and her hair in its famous chignon. It's Elspeth. What is she doing out in the cold and rain? Kathryn will be furious.

I open my sash window a fraction so that I can hear, cringing when the hinges screech, hoping they haven't heard and can't see me.

'I don't want to discuss it anymore.' Elspeth's angry voice drifts up to me.

Lewis says something but his voice is too deep and indecipherable.

'I think you'd better leave. I have nothing more to say on the matter. I'm not interested.'

Now it sounds like Lewis is pleading with her. What's going on? Is she sacking him?

'I've said no,' she snaps, turning on her heel towards the French windows to the kitchen. I hear them slam behind her. Lewis stands there for a few seconds. I wish I could see his expression, but his features are obscured by shadows. Then he thrusts his hands into his pockets and walks around the side of the house. I dart across my sitting area and around my bed to look out of the other window, which has the view of the suspension bridge. I watch and wait and, sure enough, Lewis emerges from the side of the house, trudging through the front garden, a cigarette hanging from his mouth. At the gate he stops and looks up at the house, unsmiling. I can't read his expression – not angry as such, more resigned maybe. I don't know if he can see me so I wave but I don't think he notices as he dips his head and lets himself out of the gate. I watch as he continues down the street until he's out of sight. I find myself feeling heavy with disappointment that I may not see him again.

The pub is already packed when I get there, despite it being a Wednesday evening. The band hasn't started playing yet, and as soon as I walk in I spot Vince at the bar with Kris and Dexter. My stomach flips at the sight of him. I was hoping that the month apart would have lessened my attraction to him but, if anything, it's stronger. He is wearing a black leather jacket, his dirty-blond hair touching his collar. I can only see his face in profile, that chiselled jaw. My queasiness returns. I'm not ready to see him. It brings it all back. My mum's death, the aftermath, that hideous Christmas and then our argument on New Year's Eve. I suddenly feel too hot in my coat. Just as I'm about to turn around and leave, Courtney weaves towards me with a pint in her hand. 'You made it!' she says, coming over to hug me and sloshing beer onto the floor in the process.

I grimace. 'I nearly bolted.'

She links her arm through mine and guides me into the pub. 'Come on, you need to break the ice with him.'

'He owes me five grand,' I say, through clenched teeth.

Not to mention the other thing he did. The thing I've not been able to admit to anyone, even Courtney.

'I know. He says he's got some money to give you.'

About time. It's only taken him a month.

She leads me towards Vince. When he spots me our eyes lock and his cheeks redden. He steps forwards, his face serious. 'Hi.'

'All right,' I say, trying to sound nonchalant.

The bar is busy, and with the cacophony of voices, the dull thrum of the background music and the chink of glasses, it's hard to have a proper conversation. He leans towards me and I get a whiff of his scent mixed with tobacco. 'Do you want to go outside? We need to talk.'

'We haven't got anything to talk about,' I reply. 'Let's not drag it all up again.'

His eyes burn with disappointment. 'You're a tough nut to crack.' He smiles briefly, but it's tinged with sadness.

I have to stay firm, resolute. I can't let him sweet-talk his way out of what he did. 'You still owe me five grand.'

'I know.' He reaches inside his leather jacket and hands me a cheque. 'It's only five hundred pounds. But I will pay you back. All of it.'

I take the cheque. 'It'd better not bounce.'

'It won't.' He hesitates. 'How have you been?'

'Fine,' I lie.

'I've thought about you a lot. I keep thinking about your mum too . . .'

I stiffen. I don't want to talk about her with him. It's too soon. Otherwise I'll start crying here in the pub, surrounded by people I haven't seen for over a month.

'I should have been there for you.' When I don't say anything he adds, 'We had such a great two years, but your mum dying . . . well, that was hard on our relationship . . . and what I did . . .'

How dare he? I feel a sudden flash of anger. 'No. Not because my mum died. Because you lied. Because you cheated me out of five thousand pounds, you fucker. That's why we ended.' I push him in the chest, hard. I only come up to his shoulder but he still stumbles backwards.

He steadies himself, his face shocked. I hardly ever lose my temper. Placid Una. A walkover. But not anymore. A few people at the bar turn to stare at us. 'Jesus, Una. Calm down.'

'What are you going to do? Grab me around the throat,' I lower my voice so that it's more of a hiss, 'like before?'

His face goes grey and when he speaks it's more of a whisper. 'I'm . . . I'll never forgive myself for that.'

I take a deep breath. I will not lose control in front of him again. I won't show him how much he frightened me that day. How I really thought he was going to hurt me. I didn't think he was capable of that kind of anger. 'Look,' I say, trying to keep my voice even, 'it doesn't matter. Not anymore. I just want my money back.'

'And I've promised I'll give it back.'

I stare at him. There is so much I want to say. But what's the point? I move away from him to go and find Courtney.

'Great to see you and Vince getting along,' Courtney shouts in my ear, later, while the band are playing. We're standing to the side by the toilets, jigging along to the music and sipping our pints. I've only had one – I don't want a hangover at work tomorrow. Somehow I doubt that would go down well with Elspeth and Kathryn. Every time the door to the toilets opens I get a waft of bleach and urine. But the bar is packed so we stay where we are.

'We're not.'

'You were chatting for ages.'

'Not for ages. I can't forgive him,' I shout over the music.

Courtney sips her pint. 'For the money?' she shouts back.

Not just that, I think, but I don't say it. Courtney and Vince are friends and I don't want to ruin that by telling her the whole truth. She's already punished him by ignoring him for weeks after we split up. If she found out about his loss of control she'd never speak to him again. 'For everything. But mainly for not being there for me when I needed him the most.'

She nods understandingly. 'At least you can be on speaking terms and don't have to avoid coming out with us anymore.'

'S'pose.'

She puts her arm around my neck. 'The guys have missed you.'

I watch them onstage. They're not bad, but I don't want this to be my future. I don't know what I want. I just know I want more than this. My mum's death has created a gulf between me and my friends, except Courtney. I feel different from how I was before. More knowing, somehow. It's matured me. Made me see there's more to life than working in a dead-end job, pubbing it at the weekends and staying in the area where you were born. Life is short. As soon as I've saved, and Vince has given me back the money he owes me, I'm off. I've got nothing to keep me here now.

I notice a girl at the front, near the stage, talking to Dexter's girlfriend. 'Who's that with Hannah?' I ask Courtney. She's giggling and dancing provocatively. I can only see her profile but I can tell she's pretty and petite. She's wearing a strappy top that shows off her (I'm assuming fake) tan, and I know straight away that she's Vince's type. I get a strange feeling in the pit of my stomach. If she's here for Vince it's not my place to get territorial over him. I don't want him back. I touch my throat, remembering his hands around my neck. It was only for the briefest of moments and then he'd stood back, alarm and shock on his face at his actions. But it was enough. It was the first and only time he went for me. The money is bad enough, but that split second of violence cemented my decision.

'Oh, that's . . .' She pauses and frowns. 'I can't remember her name. Velma or something. She's a groupie, I think. I've noticed her here a few times.'

I laugh. Courtney is terrible with names. 'Velma? Has she come to find Scooby-Doo?'

She punches my arm playfully. 'Idiot.'

Despite my reservations about coming out tonight, the evening flies by and I stay until the pub closes. I try to get Courtney on her own to tell her about Matilde and Jemima, and all I've found out in the library, but I don't get the chance. Somehow it doesn't feel right to have that conversation at the pub when I have to raise my voice over the music and the chatter.

After the band has finished playing I go to leave but Courtney grabs me. 'Let me and Kris walk you home.'

I shake my head. 'It's not far.'

'It is. And it's late, too dark to be walking back by yourself.'

'I'll be fine. It's just a few streets away.'

She doesn't look convinced but Kris pulls her away, his arm around her neck, and she relents. Kris's white-blond hair is stuck to his head with sweat and his jumper has holes in it. He wears his jeans too tight so that his legs seem milk-bottle-shaped. I don't know what she sees in him. She breaks away from him to hug me, then the two of them wander off, arms around each other.

I don't say goodbye to Vince and he doesn't leave the pub with the others. I wonder if he's gone home with Velma. I smile to myself. Vince and Velma. It sounds stupid. I thrust my hands into the pockets of my coat and make my way back to Sion Hill.

I walk fast, my breath clouding in front of me. It's still raining and a few people are out and about, but as I round the corner they fall away and it becomes quieter. I feel a sense of unease as I pound the pavements. Maybe I'm being reckless walking home by myself, but it's only 11 p.m.

Suddenly I hear footsteps and a hand grasps my shoulder. I let out a scream.

'It's me,' says a familiar voice, and I spin around, my heart hammering.

'Vince, for fuck's sake! You scared the shit out of me.'

He has the grace to look contrite. 'Sorry. I was calling you.'

'Well, I didn't hear you.' I begin walking again and he falls into step beside me. It's silly, I tell myself, to be scared of Vince. This is the man I shared a bed with, a life with, for nearly two years. And in all that time he was only violent towards me once. Still, it shows what he's capable of. But are we all capable of it if we're pushed?

'Courtney told me about your new job. Fancy,' he says.

'It is. The house is amazing.' I don't want to antagonize him so I play along.

'Maybe I could come over sometime.'

I grimace. What planet is he on? 'I don't think my boss would like that very much,' I say, trying to keep my voice calm.

He shrugs and lights a cigarette. He doesn't offer me one. I gave up as soon as Mum became ill. After watching her dying of lung cancer at the age of forty-nine, I'll never smoke again.

He doesn't say anything else and we walk along in silence. The streets are slick with recent rain, and the light from the lampposts is refracted in the puddles.

'You shouldn't walk home alone late at night,' he says suddenly, breaking the silence.

'I'm not alone. You're with me.'

'You know what I mean. It's not safe.'

I roll my eyes. 'What do you want, Vince? Why are you walking with me?'

He flicks his cigarette to the kerb. 'I still love you.'

'Vince . . .'

'I know. I know. We can't go back. But . . . well, I just wanted you to know that.'

I sigh. How can I tell him that I'll never forgive him or trust him again? What if he turns on me, like he did the night we finished?

'Love isn't enough sometimes, though, is it?' I say, as

we turn onto Sion Hill. The suspension bridge is lit up in the distance and a fine rain is illuminated by the old-fashioned lampposts. 'This is me,' I say, halting outside Elspeth's house, and he gives a low, appreciative whistle.

'Wow. The old lady must be loaded.'

I shrug. 'I don't know. I think she's had the house a long time.'

'Still. This is worth a couple of mil.'

Vince is obsessed with money. I turn to look at him as he stares at the house, no doubt imagining that's the sort of place he'll buy when he's 'made it'. And then I feel a stab of guilt mixed with pity. Why not have those dreams? Who am I to judge? After all, I have dreams too. Vince has had a shit time: a dad who beat him up, a mother who turned a blind eye. Music was an escape for him. He must see me assessing him as he bends over and touches my cheek. I wince, and hurt flashes in his eyes. 'I wish I could take it all back. Be the man you needed me to be. I would never hurt you. I'm not my dad.'

'It's in the past . . .'

His eyes glisten and he looks as though he's about to cry. 'It's not, though, is it?'

I hang my head in answer.

He lights another cigarette. Then he leans towards me and his lips brush mine. 'I'm sorry,' he whispers.

I watch as he walks down the street, his collar up against the cold, his familiar lumbering gait, the tip of his cigarette glowing amber in the dark.

As I push open the gate, I glance up at the house and freeze. Someone is standing at the window of my bedroom, watching me.

9

Kathryn

Has she seen me? Kathryn darts away from the window. What was she thinking? Stupid, stupid. She needs to be more careful. The visit from the police today has unnerved her, sent her into a bit of a spin. When Una went out she couldn't resist coming up here, to what was once her bedroom, long before it was Matilde's or Jemima's or Una's. Long before those other girls came and took away her mother's attention. This room was different then, of course, not as plush as it is now, no en-suite bathroom or varnished floorboards or tastefully painted walls. Just two interconnecting rooms that had once held the things nobody wanted, which had been hurriedly thrown away when she'd moved up here. Funny how she'd ended up in this room, another thing nobody wanted. She remembers how excited she'd been when Elspeth said she could decorate it however she liked. Elspeth had taken her shopping, revelling in showing her all the lovely expensive wallpapers, vetoing anything she considered cheap and tacky, so in the end the turquoise paper dotted with pink hummingbirds that had adorned the walls – now stripped and painted a tasteful dove grey – hadn't been Kathryn's choice. But it had been a big improvement on what she'd had before so she'd been grateful.

The sound of the front door banging reverberates through the house. Una can't seem to do anything quietly. She'd better get out of here before Una catches her. How would she explain this?

Kathryn lets herself out of the bedroom, then takes the key out of the pocket of her cardigan and re-locks the room, just how Una left it. Then she slips down the stairs onto the landing that leads to the spare room where she sleeps for two nights a week. The room she wasn't allowed to have as a kid. It's a double, like the other three bedrooms on this floor, with sash windows that look out onto the garden and pretty rambling-rose wallpaper, a four-poster bed and mahogany bedside cabinets. Every room here is done in a chintzy style. Kathryn's house is the opposite, all clean lines and minimalist furniture.

She hears Una's tread on the stairs. She hopes she's taken her shoes off. Kathryn will have to go down in a minute and check whether Una locked the front door properly – she won't be able to sleep until she does. She glances at the clock on her bedside table. It's nearly midnight. Who was the man Una was with tonight? She said at her interview she didn't have a boyfriend. She can't see her mother liking that very much. Elspeth wants her girls to be at her beck and call, with no family ties or commitments. When Matilde had acquired a boyfriend, all hell had broken loose. Luckily he hadn't lasted long. Her mother had put an end to that.

She wonders how Ed and the boys are doing. Despite spending two nights every week with Elspeth (much to Ed's chagrin, mainly because he has to get off his backside and take some parental responsibility), she still misses her family when she's away. Her real, imperfect, annoying family. Being in this house stirs up memories she'd rather forget, even after all this time, although Elspeth has more or less wiped away any sign of the past. But Kathryn is still haunted by it. And by Matilde and Jemima. She can still see their mark on the walls, the carpets, still feel their energy in every room. They are like spirits that refuse to be exorcized.

Kathryn sits on the edge of the bed and gathers her thoughts. They are all over the place, like wayward toddlers running off in different directions. She tries to bring them together in her mind: her mother, Jemima, Una and the boy she was with, and Lewis. Lewis. Her mind pauses on the gardener. What was her mother arguing with him about in the garden? She'd gone down to the kitchen to talk to Aggie and seen her mother and Lewis having a heated discussion out on the patio despite the rain settling on their shoulders and hair. What has Lewis done wrong now? Another gardener about to bite the dust, no doubt.

When Kathryn's sure that Una is safely ensconced in her bedroom, she pads down the stairs to check the front door. Una forgot to double-lock it, just as Kathryn had suspected she would – she'd have to talk to her about it tomorrow. Kathryn turns the bolt clockwise, latching it into place. Then she stands with her back to it, surveying the large hallway and the doors to the rooms coming off it: the library, the snug, the sitting room, the dining room that nobody uses, the stairs that lead to the basement kitchen. The only light comes from the landing upstairs. Her mother is fast asleep – she checked on her about an hour ago. She's a heavy sleeper so Kathryn doubts she heard Una come in, or Kathryn walking about the house.

The Cuckoo's Nest. She remembers when her mother named the house. She hadn't long moved in. It was typical of Elspeth's dark, sadistic sense of humour. 'The cuckoo,' she'd said, stroking a finger down Kathryn's silky eleven-year-old cheek. 'It's perfect, my dear, because that's exactly what you are.'

Kathryn runs her hand along the gleaming teak banister as she returns to her room. This house will be hers one day. She's worked hard for it, put up with her mother's bad behaviour, her moods and her put-downs and her demands over the years. She's put Elspeth before her own family. Yes, Kathryn deserves it. And she's waited a long time for it. Nothing will get in the way of that. No, it will be hers and hers alone. The cuckoo. The cuckoo's nest.

10

Una

It must have been Kathryn in my room. I can't imagine it would have been Elspeth. She's asleep by nine thirty most nights and she finds the narrow staircase that leads up here tricky to navigate. Kathryn must have a spare key. I'm shocked that she took the effort to unlock the door and creep in, knowing I was out. Why? Why was she invading my personal space and watching me from the window? Was she spying on me? I shudder at the thought.

I glance around my room. Has she touched anything? Maybe she'd been looking for something. I pick up the clothes I left on the bed and, remembering my vow of tidiness, I fold them and put them away in a drawer. Nothing seems out of place.

Kathryn must have seen me with Vince. She'll have got the wrong idea about us. I'll have to find a way of setting the record straight tomorrow – although I have to be tactful because I don't want her to think I'm accusing her of being in my room. Even though I know it was her, I can't actually prove it. And it is her mother's house, after all.

I find it hard to sleep. I keep tossing and turning, thinking of Vince and the pub, of Kathryn and Elspeth. When I do drift off, I dream that I'm morphing into Matilde, then Jemima and that someone is chasing me but

I can't see who. I wake up sweating, my heart racing. I'm exhausted when the alarm on my mobile goes off at six the next morning, ready for another day.

Elspeth's eyes light up when I come into her bedroom. I help her to the bathroom and turn on the shower for her. Her en-suite has been converted to accommodate a walk-in shower with a seat so that she doesn't fall. I turn away and pretend to organize the towels on the rail as she gets undressed. I wait for her in her bedroom as she showers, busying myself straightening her bed and throwing open the curtains. Usually she'll come out wrapped in a towel. But today she calls me. 'Una! I need help getting up.' I rush into the bathroom, assuming she's fallen, but she's perched on the edge of her shower seat, gripping the handrail but not moving, her arms rigid as though she's seized up.

'Are you okay?' I say, pushing the panic from my voice as I reach into the cubicle and turn off the shower. The water sprays up my arm and shoulder, drenching my top.

She shakes her head. She's shivering. Goosebumps have popped up along her body, her flesh wrinkled and sagging, like the skin on an uncooked chicken breast. I grab a towel and try to wrap it around her, but she pushes it off angrily. 'Just help me up,' she snaps.

I do as she says, not sure where to grab her, her skin wet and slippery. She clings to me as we clumsily make our way into the bedroom. She sits on the edge of the bed, still naked and not at all self-conscious about it, while I hover with a towel, trying not to look as though I'm uncomfortable with her nudity. She snatches it out of my hand. Still she doesn't cover up with it, but pats herself dry. She must be freezing but she takes ages over it. I retrieve the outfit she's chosen to wear – another twinset. Usually she's happy to dress herself and I only need to assist with doing up buttons, but this time she sits there like a child while I help her step into her underwear. She doesn't speak while I do all this, and I wonder if I've managed to offend her somehow.

Once she's brushed her teeth and tidied her chignon – it's stayed in place since her trip to the hairdresser yesterday – she turns to me. 'You'd better change your top. You're soaking.' She stares pointedly at my now see-through T-shirt. 'In fact, take it off now. Carole can dry it. She'll be in later.' I hesitate. 'Oh, Una,' she sighs, 'for someone so young, you're awfully priggish. We're all girls together.'

She's right. I'm being ridiculous. I take off my T-shirt and hand it to her. It's my favourite. I've had it forever but I love the rose colour and the shiny metallic star that decorates the front.

'Thanks,' I say stiffly, as she takes it.

'Go on, then,' she says, when I just stand there as though rooted to the plush carpet. 'I'll wait here for you while you change.'

'Right. Okay.' I run from the room, confused. What was all that about? Elspeth was perfectly fine to get out of the shower herself. I grab a jumper and return to her. She is waiting patiently on her bed. There is no sign of my T-shirt.

Aggie is already in the kitchen, although it's only seven. She's doing a 'healthy' fried breakfast with chicken sausages and grilled bacon today. I notice that Kathryn is already sitting at the table, tucking into her food. She's dressed in her usual shapeless skirt and floral blouse. She looks up when I enter and surveys me without smiling, her eyes running over my short skater skirt and thick tights. Elspeth's already told me she leaves early when she stays over so that she can pop home and take the boys to school before heading to her job at the art gallery.

'So, how was your day off?' Kathryn asks, when we've all sat down. Aggie is hovering with the tea. I could get used to this. All my meals cooked, and being waited on. Although, if I'm honest, I don't feel comfortable with Aggie doing all this for me when I'm just 'the help' too, like her. She doesn't seem to mind waiting on us, though – in fact, she seems to enjoy it and buzzes around us like a wasp that's ingested too much sugar.

'It was good, thanks,' I say, after swallowing a mouthful of bacon. 'I met up with Courtney –'

'Who's Courtney?' interjects Elspeth, looking at me sternly over her bone-china mug.

'My best friend. We used to live together but now her boyfriend has moved in with her instead.' I don't know why I tell her this extra snippet of information. Maybe because I want her to know I can't move back in with Courtney, that I'm not about to do a moonlight flit, like Jemima did.

Elspeth frowns, her bright blue eyes boring into me. It unnerves me so I concentrate on the plate of food in front of me. I wonder if Kathryn's told her she saw me with Vince. I don't know why I feel guilty about it, like I'm breaking some rule. It's not like I sneaked him into my room and spent the night with him.

There's an uncomfortable silence and I eat, not knowing how best to break it. Aggie is busy wiping the worktops, humming quietly to herself, seemingly oblivious to any tension.

'I think there's something you should know,' says Elspeth, after a few moments.

'Mother!'

'Kathryn, she has a right to know. I'd rather Una hear it from us rather than through idle gossip . . .' Her head inclines towards Aggie, who appears not to notice, although her shoulders tense slightly and she stops humming as her cloth slides along the marble worktops.

Kathryn's brows form a V and she puts her knife and fork down with a clatter, sighing theatrically. But she doesn't say anything – she doesn't need to: her body language is speaking volumes. She obviously doesn't want Elspeth to tell me whatever it is she's about to say.

Elspeth clears her throat, as though she's an actor or a politician about to give an important speech. 'Jemima, the girl who worked for me before you, has been found dead.'

I sit up straighter and widen my eyes in surprise, hoping my expression doesn't betray that I've already found this out.

'The police were here yesterday to tell us. Until then we didn't know a thing about it, did we, Kathryn?'

Kathryn shakes her head vigorously but doesn't speak. In fact, she's turned slightly green.

'The police think she took her own life. We didn't realize she was depressed. It was only that last day . . .' She shoots a glance at Kathryn, who gives her a warning look.

'Anyway, it doesn't matter about all of that. She was evidently depressed and, well, she jumped from the suspension bridge, the same day she left here.'

'The same day?' I say, surprise in my voice. I hadn't read that in the newspaper.

'It would appear so, yes. She took all her stuff and left. I thought she'd had enough. This job isn't to everyone's taste. But . . .' she puts her mug down '. . . I thought she was happy here.'

There are so many questions I want to ask. What time did she leave? What did she do with all her belongings before she jumped? Did they have no clue she was so unhappy? But I've already learnt that Elspeth and her daughter don't like to be asked too many questions. So I just say how sorry I am to hear this and that it must have been a shock for them.

Kathryn gets up, straightening her skirt and carrying her plate to the sink. Aggie eagerly swoops in, taking the plate away from her and stacking it in the dishwasher.

'I've got to get to work,' she says. 'Please excuse me.' She smiles at me stiffly and plants an obligatory kiss on her mother's cheek before disappearing out of the room. Nobody speaks until her footsteps have receded and we hear the front door close behind her. Then the three of us take a collective breath as the tension in the kitchen eases. Aggie joins us for breakfast and we spend the next half-hour talking about neutral subjects, mainly Aggie's pregnant daughter, who's married to a vicar and lives in a village outside Bristol. She's got a two-year-old boy whom Aggie dotes on. Elspeth sits back in her chair, relaxed for once, an indulgent smile on her face as Aggie describes her grandson's visit to the zoo at the weekend.

Just as I begin to feel at ease for the first time that morning, Aggie has to go and ruin it. 'Who was that handsome young man I saw you with last night, then?' she says, helping herself to some toast and plastering it with butter.

Elspeth turns to face me, her eyes cool. 'Who's this?'

It was gone eleven thirty when I arrived home with Vince. What was Aggie doing here this late? She doesn't live in. 'Oh, an old boyfriend. He just walked me home.'

'An old boyfriend, eh?' laughs Aggie, winking at me. I can feel the blood rushing to my face. 'He's a bit of a dish. Is a reconciliation on the cards?'

'We're never getting back together,' I insist, even though Elspeth is dabbing the corners of her mouth with her napkin, no longer looking in my direction, as though she couldn't care less what I do. 'He . . . well, he stole from me.'

Elspeth's eyes soften as she turns to me. 'Stole from you?'

'He used my credit card to buy some expensive amp equipment without telling me. I only found out when the credit-card company wrote to me to tell me I'd exceeded my limit.' I don't mention the row or how he'd pinned me against the wall by my throat.

Aggie tuts. 'That's awful. I'm sorry, pet.'

'He's paying me back. But I can never trust him.'

Elspeth reaches over and places her hand on mine. 'No, you'd never be able to trust him again. It was a wicked thing for him to do. You deserve better.'

To my shame my eyes fill with tears. It's the sort of thing I'd longed to hear from my mum, but she'd already died when I found out what Vince had done. I'd felt so alone, with nobody to turn to, apart from Courtney. And now Elspeth and Aggie are comforting me, showing me that I'm worth more, that they're on my side.

Elspeth has a lot of appointments today. First I have to accompany her to the doctor's, which is only a five-minute walk away. 'Just for a check-up,' she says, squeezing my hand as though to assure me that she's not about to croak it at any minute, and then to a tailor to get a ripped lining mended. She walks slowly, clutching my arm, so by the time we've performed these errands and taken a detour to the florist to pick up some flowers – 'It's so important to have fresh flowers about the place, don't you think, dear?' – it's nearly midday when we get home.

Elspeth says she'd like to rest before lunch so I help her into bed, close the curtains and retreat to the kitchen where I know I'll find Aggie. I've been hoping to bump into Lewis but I haven't seen him all day, although I did notice his abandoned wheelbarrow overturned in the garden. I wonder if he'll be back after his row with Elspeth yesterday.

'Would you like a cup of tea, pet?' asks Aggie, as I offer to help cut up carrots for the stew she's making for dinner.

'Yes, please.' This is my favourite time of day, when Elspeth is having a nap and I can sit in the cosy kitchen with Aggie and have a chat. I've been desperate to ask her about Matilde and Jemima.

'What do you think about Jemima?' I ask, as I slice a carrot. Aggie is chopping an onion and has to keep wiping her eyes.

'Shocked. She didn't seem the kind of girl to take her own life.'

'Did you think she was depressed?'

'Not at all. She was a chirpy little thing. Always going about the place singing. You know . . .' She swipes at her eyes again. They're streaming. 'Sorry. Bloody onions. They get me every time.'

My mum used to be the same. 'Here,' I say, taking the knife out of her hand. 'Let me do it. They don't make me cry. Maybe because I wear contacts.'

She sniffs, 'Oh, you are a lamb,' and we swap jobs.

'What were you about to say?' I probe, as I cut into the onion.

'What? Oh, yes. I was just going to say that you remind me of Jemima.'

'Really? In what way?' I think of the photograph in the locket. 'Do you mean in looks?'

'Yes, but also personality. You're both bubbly, easy-going. Happy. You brighten up the place. I can see why Elspeth likes having a young companion. Especially as Kathryn can be so –' She stops herself as if suddenly remembering where her loyalties lie. 'Kathryn is a good person, just more reserved, that's all.'

I don't say anything but concentrate on chopping the onions into small cubes as instructed.

'And she worries about Elspeth. It'd been just the two of them for years before she decided to employ Matilde.'

'How long have you been with the family, Aggie?'

She pauses mid-chop to consider this. 'A long time.' She chuckles. 'I started after Elspeth's husband died back in 1987. Kathryn was fifteen then and Viola nearly seventeen.'

I pause, knife in the air. 'Viola?'

Aggie looks up at me guiltily as though she's said too much. 'Viola is Elspeth's elder daughter.'

I'm taken aback. Nobody's ever mentioned her. 'Where is Viola living now?'

She shrugs, her round face colouring. 'I shouldn't be telling you this, really. Elspeth is still funny about it all these years later. Viola ran away from home when she was eighteen. A year after I joined.'

'Ran away? Do you mean she doesn't keep in contact with her family?'

She shakes her short grey curls. 'Nobody's heard from her since. It broke Elspeth's heart.'

I'm stumped. I don't know what to say. 'How awful. Poor Elspeth. At least she's got Kathryn.'

Aggie purses her lips as though she's afraid more revelations will spill out of her mouth involuntarily. She doesn't say anything for a while, then blurts, 'I don't think Viola would've run away like that if Kathryn hadn't come.'

I frown. 'What do you mean?'

She puts her knife down and carries the bowl of chopped carrots to a pan sitting on the hob of the Aga. 'Kathryn was eleven years old when Elspeth adopted her.'

'Adopted? Kathryn's adopted?' I wasn't expecting that. I think back to their interactions – Elspeth is very dismissive, almost cold towards Kathryn at times. Is that why? Or would she be the same even if Kathryn was her biological child?

'Oh, yes,' says Aggie. 'Elspeth couldn't have any more

children after Viola. So when Viola was thirteen she and Huw adopted Kathryn. I'm not saying it was Kathryn's fault that Viola left. I'm fond of that girl. Woman now, of course. And, my goodness, she had a lot to contend with growing up. But it was only natural that Viola would feel pushed out.'

I hand Aggie the plate of onions for her to add to the pan. 'Imagine not knowing where your own child is. She'd be – what? Late forties now?'

'Nearly fifty. Elspeth has heard nothing from her in all these years. She doesn't even know if she's alive or dead.' She shakes her head. 'A sorry state of affairs.'

'Did Elspeth ever look for her?'

'I think so. At the beginning. But it was like Viola disappeared off the face of the earth. She didn't want to be found.'

The faces of Matilde and Jemima swirl in my mind. Did Viola really run away or is she dead too?

11

The Cuckoo, July 1983

As the big orange car she was travelling in hurtled down the M4, Katy felt she might be sick with nerves. Her social worker, Fiona, sat rigid and upright next to her in a hot-pink short-sleeved blouse, her hands firmly in the ten-to-two position on the steering wheel, every now and again turning to flash her a reassuring smile as they sped towards Bristol. It was stifling in the car, despite the windows being wound down and the fan on full. Katy had been allowed to sit in the front because of her travel sickness. She preferred it at the front: it was easier to see out. The sky was a clear blue with a few streaky clouds in the distance, and the sun beat down, glinting off the hood. Fiona had the radio on, low so as not to distract her too much while driving apparently, and 'Club Tropicana' was playing. Katy liked the song. It made her feel happy. She took it as a good sign.

The lush green countryside sped past her window until they turned onto another road, smaller this time, and the fields of sheep and cows fell away to be replaced with glassy buildings, ugly concrete car parks and shops. Her new family lived in a place called Clifton. She liked the way it sounded on her tongue, sharp and precise. She hadn't been to see her house yet. Her new mum and dad,

Elspeth and Huw McKenzie, had visited the children's home in Gloucester and taken her out for tea a few times at the local hotel. She liked them, although they seemed a bit posh. When she was with them she felt as though she needed to be extra polite. But, still, she was excited even when Tommy Evans, an irritating eight-year-old that the grown-ups seemed to find cute, returned after living with the McKenzies for a week saying they were stuck up and he couldn't do anything right. She'd heard rumours that he'd been kicked out because he was naughty and the McKenzies couldn't cope with him. She'd never found out exactly what he'd done, but Fiona told her they felt a girl would suit their family better. And it seemed that the girl they wanted to adopt was her. She would no longer be plain old Katy Collins, but Katy McKenzie. She'd have a new sister too. A girl with a name that sounded a little like 'violin'. Katy always wished she'd learnt to play the violin but the home didn't allow it because lessons were too expensive. Fiona was very excited about this 'match', as she called it. After the initial interview she'd said something about how 'affluent' they were. Katy didn't know what the word meant, but from the way Fiona's freckled face broke into a huge grin when she said it, she knew it must mean something good.

They drove a bit further through what Fiona called the city centre, past a theatre with 'Hippodrome' written across it in big bright letters, up a hill and then a long road where everything started to look prettier with more trees and bigger houses.

'Look over there,' said Fiona, pointing at a long bridge that crossed what looked like two cliffs. 'That's the suspension bridge. It's famous, and at night it's all lit up. You'll be able to see it every night from your new house.' And then she pulled up in front of one of the grandest houses Katy had ever seen. It was the colour of cotton candy and had a balcony on the third floor with a black-and-white-striped awning stretched over it that reminded her of humbug sweets.

She had just stepped out of the car and onto the pavement when the front door of the cotton-candy house was flung open to reveal a beaming Elspeth. Her blonde hair was held back in a banana clip so that when she turned her head the curls fell past her shoulders. She was wearing a smart jacket with padded shoulders and a matching knee-length fitted skirt. Katy couldn't believe this elegant lady was going to be her new mum. She looked like the mum out of the film *E.T.*

Elspeth came rushing towards them, her husband, Huw, close behind. He was older than Elspeth by nearly fifteen years. Katy knew this because Elspeth had told her over a cream tea when she last visited. Huw certainly looked older, with his receding hairline and his bushy grey beard. He was something to do with hedge funds, so Elspeth had said, sitting up straighter and looking proud when she revealed this nugget of information. Katy didn't know what hedge funds were but she thought it had something to do with gardens. And judging by the box hedging in the McKenzies' front garden she could imagine Huw out there trimming them into the perfect right-angles.

Elspeth darted out of the front gate to greet her. 'Darling girl,' she said, holding her shoulders. 'Let me look at you. Just as pretty as I remembered.' Katy blushed. She didn't feel pretty. She wasn't like Isla at the home with her silky black hair, pert nose and skinny limbs. Elspeth placed an arm around Katy's shoulders, guiding her down the pathway and into the house. Huw was hovering, grinning manically but not saying anything, as though he didn't really know what to do. Katy understood how he felt. Fiona followed with Katy's battered old suitcase. 'This is our new home,' trilled Elspeth. 'We only moved in here recently. Oh, I do hope you like it.'

Katy stared at the hallway in awe. The staircase was like something out of *Dynasty*, and a huge crystal chandelier hung above their heads, the droplets catching the sunlight that streamed through the stained-glass window above the door, casting rainbow colours onto the pale walls. Even Fiona couldn't help but gawp at the interiors, exclaiming over a portrait of a man in old-fashioned dress on the wall, which Katy thought was ugly.

'Where's Viola? She's desperate to meet you,' said Elspeth, looking around with a frown on her face. Viola, that was it! Such an unusual name. 'Oh, the naughty girl, I bet she's out in the garden again. She'll get her dress mucky.'

Katy stared down at her own velvet knickerbocker jumpsuit. It was her very best outfit, reserved for special church services and Christmas Day, but now she felt underdressed and not quite right for this posh house and the posh people within it.

'I'll go and find her,' said Huw, treating Katy to a reassuring wink and then setting off through a room with floor-to-ceiling bookcases. Katy wondered how she'd ever be able to find her way around this house. The children's home was quite big, but she'd been living there for three years now and she was used to every nook and cranny. It still wasn't as big as this house, though, and definitely not as grand. There, she'd had to share a room with two other girls, the carpets were worn and the place needed decorating. She'd had posters of Spandau Ballet on her walls just to cover the cracks and the dirty handprints.

Elspeth ushered Katy into another room, with a view of the famous bridge, and she and Fiona perched on the velvet sofa that was the colour of ink, Katy's old brown suitcase at their feet. Elspeth stood by the fireplace. She seemed on edge, jiggling about as though she needed the bathroom. On the coffee-table there was a tray of little cakes and a jug of lemonade. Katy still had the annoying butterflies flapping around in her stomach but she could really eat one of those French Fancies. The yellow ones were her favourite. She didn't dare ask, though, and Elspeth didn't offer. Instead she stood there wringing her hands and fidgeting, her beautiful face crumpled with concern. 'I don't know where they've got to,' she said, to nobody in particular. 'I wanted Viola to come here to greet you.'

Katy heard Viola before she saw her. A screech and a high posh voice shouted, 'Get off me! I said I'm coming!' And then there she was, standing in the doorway, resplendent in a pink gingham dress with long white socks that wrinkled around her ankles. There were grass stains on her knees. She was pretty, like Isla at the home, with long white-blonde hair and a perfect oval face. Katy had already been told that Viola was eighteen months older than her, although two school years above, which would make her nearly thirteen. She didn't look it, though. She looked young and innocent in that dress. It was more like something an eight-year-old would wear. She had a matching Alice band atop her long fine hair that she'd pushed forward too much so it made her ears stick out. She scowled at Katy and Katy's heart plummeted. She'd really hoped they would become best friends as well as sisters. Elspeth moved so that she was standing behind Katy, her arms around her. She liked being in Elspeth's arms. It made her feel wanted and she smelt sweet, like Love Hearts. 'This is your new sister,' she said, to Viola. 'I hope you'll make her welcome.' Then Elspeth turned to Fiona, not bothering to lower her voice: 'It will do Viola good to share. She's becoming a little spoilt. I couldn't have any more children, sadly.'

'I. Am. Not. Spoilt,' cried Viola, stamping her foot.

'Now then, Viola, that's not polite, is it?' said Huw, who was standing beside Viola in the doorway. She stuck out her tongue at him and ran off. They all stood in silence as her shiny patent sandals clomped across the tiles in the hallway.

Elspeth sighed theatrically. 'I don't know what we're going to do with that girl.' She turned to Katy. 'But it's not something you need to worry about. I've been told you're a good girl.'

Fiona stood up, looking concerned. 'Is Viola going to come around to having Katy here? I don't really want to leave Katy in a hostile environment.' She glanced at Katy worriedly. As far as social workers went, Katy knew she was lucky. Fiona genuinely seemed to care about her welfare, which wasn't the case with her last one, Derek, who had told her to put up and shut up when she was placed with a foster family who used her as an unpaid skivvy. Luckily he was sacked and Fiona replaced him, with her freckled face and warm smile. She could see how unhappy Katy had been at the Morgans and had whisked her out of there and back into the children's home within the day.

'Why don't you go and find her in the garden? I'll show you. Come on.' Elspeth held out her hand to Katy and led her through the library, then outside and down a few steps onto a terrace. 'She'll be in that tree house, I expect.' Elspeth made an encouraging face and Katy tentatively walked across the huge garden, wanting to please her new mother. When she got to the back of the garden where the tree house was a hand pulled her to the ground. It was Viola's.

'You're not wanted here,' she hissed at her, surprisingly strong for such a slight girl. 'I'm going to make your life hell and then you'll be begging to go back to that puky home like hideous Tommy.'

Katy stared into the girl's perfect face in shock. How could something so pretty be so . . . so *mean*? She felt her eyes fill with tears.

'Oh, great. Another weakling,' said Viola, getting to her feet and dusting off her dress. 'No wonder your real parents didn't want you. I'll break you within a week.'

Katy watched Viola stomp off, anger rising in her throat.

Katy had spent years wishing for a new family. And now here was her chance and she wasn't going to let that brat Viola spoil things for her.

12

Una

I laugh at something Elspeth is saying as we walk through the arcade on Friday morning. She's on good form today, as though getting out of the house has lifted her spirits. We've just come from the wool shop because Elspeth said she'd like to take up crocheting again. She was surprised when I told her I also liked to crochet and that my mum had taught me. We used to sit and make blankets for the NSPCC while she was recovering from chemo, chatting about travelling to an exotic destination. When I relayed this to Elspeth in front of a triangular display of blue-hued wools she went quiet and gripped my arm, her fingers surprisingly strong. 'What a wonderful thing to do,' she'd said. 'I'd love to make a blanket for charity. Will you help me?' I'd agreed eagerly and we spent a pleasant half-hour picking out the colours we would use. She refused to let me pay for any of the bundles and as we left the shop I felt relief that we'd found something we have in common – tinged with sadness that I can no longer do it with my mum.

Afterwards, she shows me her antiques shop, Viola's, and the jewellery store, Kat's. I like that she's named them both after her daughters. I want to ask about Viola but Mum's voice pops into my head: *Curiosity killed the cat, Una.* And I know she's right. Particularly about this.

Elspeth's arm is linked through mine and she's telling me how she used to drive to the markets in northern France to pick up bargains for the antiques shop back in the early 1990s, when I notice Kathryn ducking into a card shop. I'm sure she saw us. I don't mention it to Elspeth but let her talk as she steers me down the corridor and towards the art gallery. It's called simply McKenzie's.

'Kathryn runs this one for me,' she says, as I push open the door. The bell tinkles. Inside, the space is quite big, with some beautiful paintings on the wall – not that I know anything about art – but there are no customers milling about. 'Oh,' says Elspeth, looking around her. 'I thought Kathryn would be here now.' She checks her watch. 'It's ten o'clock.'

A girl younger than me emerges from the back, clearly surprised to see us – it's as though she was expecting someone else. Elspeth introduces her to me as Daisy, Kathryn's assistant. 'Do you know where my daughter is?'

Daisy is wearing bright red lipstick and her caramel-streaked hair is gathered on top of her head in a mass of curls, held back by a floral headband. She's attractive with a wide, smiling face and a 1940s vintage look about her. 'She went out to check the other shops.'

Elspeth looks puzzled. 'We've just come from the other shops. We didn't see her.'

'Oh.' Daisy shrugs. 'She might have gone to get a coffee. She doesn't really like the instant stuff,' she says, pointing vaguely towards the back of the shop, presumably where the 'instant stuff' is kept.

Elspeth stiffens. 'Very well. Can you please tell her I

popped in.' It's not a question. Elspeth offers her arm to me and I take it. She doesn't bother telling Daisy my name and this rankles a little. Am I that disposable? As we leave, I throw Daisy a warm, conspiratorial smile, which she returns.

Something is clearly bothering Elspeth after we leave the gallery. As we walk through the arcade in silence I notice how her eyes dart about and I know she's looking out for Kathryn. She only saw her yesterday morning. I've known them just a week but I can't get to grips with their relationship. When Elspeth is with Kathryn she acts as though she finds her presence an annoyance, but now it's clear she's disappointed to have missed her.

'I know!' Elspeth exclaims, when we've exited the arcade. The rain has stopped, the pavements are all shiny, and there's that fresh-washed smell in the air. The sun is struggling to come out from behind a cloud. 'Let's go for a cup of tea. There's a quaint tea room around the corner that does the most delicious cakes. Would you like that?'

I'm surprised by her sudden change in mood. Elspeth's dark expression has cleared and she's beaming again.

'That sounds lovely,' I say. Anything to fill the hours. The day stretches ahead of me, long and dull.

'Here we are, then,' says Elspeth, as we head into a little tea room with rose-printed bone-china cups and rustic furniture. I order a carrot cake and Elspeth has some banana bread. I shove the bag of wool under my chair.

'Have you ever thought about using your walking stick more?' I suggest, when the waitress has brought our drinks and cakes. We have a table by the window and sit opposite each other. The place is surprisingly full. 'One of the residents of the care home had one and it gave her that little bit of confidence on her feet . . .'

Elspeth's scowl stops me in my tracks. I've said the wrong thing *again*.

'I don't need that stick. I'm not an invalid.'

'Well, no . . .' I'm flustered. 'But I've seen yours at home and . . . it's just . . . you know, after your fall . . .'

'Why would I need a stick when I have you?' she says, cutting her banana bread into squares. 'And it's only pavements I have a particular concern for. And stairs.'

I want to say that she's wasting her money having me live in. That I could just as easily come over for a few hours a day to sit with her or help her dress, not that she really needs that. She's perfectly capable of dressing herself and is steadier on her feet than she gives herself credit for. I wonder if she'll ever go into a home. With her money she could afford a really plush one, not like the one I was working in. But it's clear it's companionship she's after, and not just the type you get from a few hours' meeting up with friends. She wants a constant companion. I wonder why she never married again.

I smile in response and scrape the cream off the top of my carrot cake with my spoon and eat it, enjoying the sugar rush. 'I haven't seen Lewis around much,' I say, in an attempt to change the subject.

'You want to stay away from that young man,' says Elspeth, harshly, glaring at me over the rim of her bone-china cup. 'He's no good.'

I blush. 'Oh, I'm not interested in him like that,' I lie. I can't deny that I find Lewis attractive, and he seemed like a nice guy.

'Yes, well, he's left now anyway. It didn't work out.'

'Oh.' I feel a thud of disappointment, even though I suspected as much after overhearing them arguing the other night. I'd looked forward to spotting Lewis's handsome face every day.

'I'm fed up with having men about the house. Next time I'm going to ask for a woman gardener,' says Elspeth, taking a cube of her banana bread and popping it into her mouth. I wonder what happened in her life to make her dislike men so much. Did her late husband abuse her? Belittle her? Aggie told me he sounded like a kind, self-effacing person.

'He seemed nice,' I say meekly, not wanting to disagree with my boss but at the same time feeling she's judged Lewis unfairly. 'What did he do?'

She shakes her head, the lines around her mouth puckering. The frosted lipstick she applied this morning has almost vanished, leaving behind a rim on her top lip. 'Nothing that concerns you. He's lazy and didn't do as I asked of him.' I find that hard to believe. Lewis seemed very hardworking. But what do I know? I've probably been blinded by his good looks, like I was with Vince.

I take a sip of my cappuccino. It's too milky and it sloshes uncomfortably in my stomach. We sit in silence for a few more moments. I don't know what to say. Perhaps it's best for her to lead the conversation. Every time I try, I seem to put my foot in my mouth.

'So,' she says, taking an elegant sip of her tea, little finger crooked, like a comma, 'what did you think of the shops?'

'They're great,' I say. A slice of sunlight falls onto the table and onto Elspeth's hand, causing her wedding ring to glint. 'Do you miss running them?'

'Of course,' she says, putting her cup down and playing with a chunk of her banana bread. I've noticed she's eaten hardly anything. 'But I still like to keep an eye on everything. It keeps me young.' She grins, showing off a set of unnaturally white and even teeth for her age.

'I like the way you've named them after your daughters,' I say. When I notice her expression change I realize what I've said. I inwardly groan. *Nice one, Una.*

'I haven't named them after my daughters.'

'Oh . . . sorry. I thought, with Kat . . . Kathryn . . .'

'It was already called Kat. We just decided to keep it.'

'And Viola?'

'I don't have a daughter called Viola.' Her eyes lock with mine, daring me to contradict her. And I can't say anything because if I did it would mean she'd know Aggie has been talking about her. 'Can we get something straight?' She doesn't wait for me to answer. 'As far as I'm concerned I have one daughter.'

'I . . . Okay.' Why won't she admit she has another? Did Viola hurt her that badly?

The sun goes in and a shadow falls onto Elspeth's face making it appear harder and more angular than usual, the foundation settling into the deep grooves of her skin. She picks up her knife and cuts into a cube of banana bread. 'Jemima asked a lot of questions.' Her sapphire blue eyes flash. 'And look what happened to her.'

My pulse races and I stare at her in shock. I don't know if she's referring to Jemima leaving, or her death. Either way it sounds like a threat.

13

Kathryn

The gallery is shrouded in darkness when Kathryn arrives on Friday morning. Daisy hasn't turned up yet, even though it's nine thirty. Kathryn will have to reprimand her about her time-keeping. She'd asked her to open at nine on the dot, even though they haven't been very busy lately. Sales have taken a downward turn in the last year, not that Kathryn's admitted as much to Elspeth. She doesn't want to worry her unnecessarily.

McKenzie's is in a small shop in the faded Victorian grandeur that is the Clifton Arcade. Apart from the gallery, her mother also owns two other units in the arcade: a jewellery store and an antiques shop. Kathryn's job is to oversee them all, even though she spends most of her time in the art gallery, mainly because the other two businesses have competent managers. The shops had been Huw's passion, really, something for him to do when he retired. By then Elspeth had set up her foundation for impoverished artists, and Huw had wanted a project of his own. It had started with the antiques and then he had decided to branch out into art. He had died prematurely, at the age of sixty-one, when Kathryn was fifteen, from a stroke, leaving the business in the very capable hands of his younger wife. When Elspeth felt too old to continue with it, she handed it over to Kathryn. By then Viola was long out of the picture.

Kathryn switches on the lights — it's darker down this end of the arcade — and aligns one of the paintings, which seems to be on a slant: a stunning Paris watercolour by local artist Benjamin Percy. She stands in front of the painting, tipping the gold-edged frame until it's straight. Funny, she was sure it wasn't like that when she left yesterday. She notices two half-empty wine glasses on Daisy's desk. The only other person apart from herself and Elspeth who has a key is Daisy. But Daisy had left before her last night.

She hangs up her coat and bag in the room at the back and turns on the heater. It's freezing here. She can't wait until the spring. The constant grey clouds and drizzle make her feel down. She prefers the cold winter days when the skies are blue and there is frost on the ground to this incessant rain.

The doorbell tinkles and she hears Daisy's voice echoing through the empty shop. 'So sorry I'm late. Overslept and missed the bus.' She strides in, slipping off her coat and bag simultaneously, chatting all the while about a date she had last night that went much better than she'd thought it would, and how he'd ended up staying over and she'd had to sneak him into her room so that her mother wouldn't see. Kathryn wonders if Daisy brought him back here last night, which would explain the wine glasses. She'd have a word with her about it. She can't bring all and sundry to the gallery after hours.

As she watches the twenty-one-year-old making coffee while keeping up her monologue, not caring in the least that Kathryn hasn't spoken a word, she envies the younger girl's youth and confidence. It's really true what they say – youth is wasted on the young. Daisy is a curvy girl with big boobs and a tummy to match but that doesn't stop her wearing tight plunging tops or jeans so skinny you can see every ripple and roll of fat. At forty-eight Kathryn could do with some of Daisy's confidence. Daisy is pretty with that cherub face and full mouth, chocolate-brown eyes and caramel hair, and is popular with the customers. But Kathryn often leaves the gallery at the end of the day with a niggling headache from having to listen to Daisy's constant stream of chat for hours on end.

Still, the girl is harmless enough and it's marginally better than being stuck here by herself all day.

Kathryn walks into the main gallery carrying the too-strong coffee that Daisy has made and settles herself behind the register. Daisy is still talking but Kathryn has zoned her out. She takes a long sip. That's better. She needs the caffeine today. She feels utterly exhausted. She spent half the night awake worrying about Jacob. He'll be sixteen next month, and will be sitting his GCSEs in the spring yet he refuses to do any work. All he's interested in is that blasted PlayStation, but that's preferable to how he was acting last year, so she doesn't feel she can complain too much. It would help if Ed wasn't so bloody ineffectual. Jacob refuses to listen when his father tries to lay down the law. It's too little too late. Still, she reminds herself, it's better than Jacob roaming the streets with his old mates from the estate. He's promised not to get involved with them again and she hopes he's keeping his word, but every time she gets home she has the same nagging worry that he might not be there. That he might have relapsed.

Kathryn's shoulders sag under the weight of her anxiety. She wishes she had someone to talk to. Really talk to. Elspeth had insisted on sending both her grandsons to a private school and paying for it, much to Ed's disapproval. Kathryn had got to know a few of the other mums, but since the boys went up to the seniors they've caught the bus home so even those friendships have fizzled out. And she can't talk to her mother about any of it. Elspeth already thinks her grandsons are wayward and undisciplined. She'll only judge and make Kathryn feel like a bad mother.

Daisy, oblivious to Kathryn's mounting irritation, hovers by the register, still droning on about this new boyfriend.

'Daisy,' Kathryn snaps, when she can't bear it any longer. 'It's great that you've met someone but can you please remember to open up at nine if I ask you to?'

Hurt flickers on the girl's heavily made-up face. 'Sure. Of course. I'm really sorry. It was a one-off.'

'Good. And please can I remind you not to use the premises after hours to entertain your boyfriends. This isn't a knocking shop.'

An uncomfortable silence falls between them, and after a few minutes of Daisy slurping her coffee, she moves away to the other side of the shop. Kathryn sits where she is for a while, feeling mildly guilty for snapping at the girl, and remembers the paperwork that needs sorting. Daisy turns on the radio and jigs about to some pop song that Kathryn doesn't recognize as she bubble-wraps a painting that the buyers are due to collect today.

Kathryn stands up. She needs to get out of here. 'I'm going to check in with the other stores,' she calls. Daisy nods but doesn't say anything. Kathryn doesn't bother with her coat or bag, mainly because she doesn't want to have to walk past Daisy to get them. She's not in the mood for small-talk. The arcade is covered anyway.

Kathryn closes the door to the gallery behind her and is just about to head towards the antiques shop, which is only a few doors down, when she notices her mother and Una ambling towards her, deep in conversation. Her mother is dressed in her smart Burberry coat and Una is wearing her Julie Christie fur hat. They haven't seen her and she watches them, heads bent together, arms linked. Elspeth is laughing at something Una is saying and a hard ball of jealousy lodges in Kathryn's chest. Will she be cast off too? The inheritance that she desperately hopes will transform her life one day and get her and Ed out of debt recedes in front of her eyes. Those girls, she thinks, as she darts into a card shop before they see her, are like bind-weed: they look pretty but they're deadly, entangling themselves around the other flowers, eventually strangling them. And it doesn't matter how many times they are cut down, another always grows in its place.

I'm not going to let anybody stand in my way. Certainly not you. You with your youth and your beauty. You, who beguiles that old witch. I've been planning this for a long time. And you are my prey. I've watched you hanging out with your tarty friend, her short skirts and her fake hair. I've watched you sitting together in your favourite café, or your local bar. I even know where she lives. Courtney. Common Courtney, with the loud laugh and the big brows. Although she's not a patch on you. But I expect you know that. Oh, yes. I know everything about you. And when the time is right I'll step from the shadows and show you exactly who and what I am.

14

Una

'Wait! So you're saying she threatened you?'

Courtney sounds incredulous on the phone and I lower my voice even though it's just me and Elspeth in the house and Elspeth went to bed over an hour ago. After the awkward experience in the café we went home and fell back into our usual routine, as though nothing had happened. I made sure not to ask any more questions, just listened when Elspeth wanted to talk, my heart lifting when she suggested we begin our crocheting. As we worked she opened up to me, about her husband, Huw, and how adrift she'd felt after he died, although she didn't mention Viola. 'You know, you spend so long with someone that you're not even sure if you love them in the end or if it's just companionship,' she'd said cryptically. 'It was the done thing back then. Marry and have children. If I had my time again, my choices might have been different.' She didn't elaborate and I felt I couldn't ask. And then she changed the subject, telling me she had theatre tickets for a play at the Hippodrome that evening. It was a bit stuffy, but Elspeth enjoyed it and it was good to have an opportunity to dress up. I tried to look as conservative as possible in black trousers and a satin shirt. She ordered a taxi to drop us off at the entrance and I was surprised when we were shown to our seats in one of the boxes, with a great view of the stage.

'I don't know,' I reply, moving a pile of clothes I'd discarded earlier to the end of the bed. 'It did sound a bit threatening but she's been lovely to me since.' I tell her about the crocheting and the play. I lie back against the headboard. The curtains are closed, the only light coming from my bedside lamp. 'Why would you deny your daughter's existence?'

'I don't like the sound of that woman. Maybe you should move back in here. Get your old job back.'

I sigh. 'I need the money. And you have Kris living with you now. Anyway, she's harmless enough. I mean, she's old. She's not exactly a threat, is she? I'm not saying she murdered Jemima or anything. When she wants to be, she can be really kind.' Although she still hasn't given me my T-shirt back. When Carole – a short, dark-haired woman in her forties – came in to clean yesterday I asked her if she'd washed it and she didn't seem to know what I was talking about.

'Still, you have to admit it's odd that both of the girls who worked there before you are now dead. The McKenzies could be like some Mafia family and the girls had found things out about them.' She puts on a rubbish Marlon Brando voice: 'Don't go asking questions.'

I laugh. 'Maybe they've got dodgy business dealings or are doing some money laundering. Whatever it is, I couldn't care less. I was just being nosy about her daughter.'

'You couldn't care less if they're involved in something criminal? Christ, Una.'

I cross, then uncross my ankles, noticing a hole in

the knee of my pyjamas. 'I'm only joking. Of course they aren't criminals.'

'Maybe they're psychopaths, luring girls into their lair and killing them. You have heard of the Craigslist murders, right?'

I sit up. 'What? No.'

'This psychopath guy put an advert on Craigslist, advertising for lonely single men to come and work on his ranch. When they arrived he hunted them. Actually shot them like they were deer.'

'Where was this?'

'In America somewhere.'

'So what are you saying? Elspeth is putting adverts in a newspaper for a companion only so she can kill her?' I laugh. 'Do you know how ludicrous that sounds? Matilde was here for two years before the accident. And, okay, Jemima was only here for a few months but . . .' I shake my freshly washed hair and a wet tendril hits me in the eye. 'No. It's crazy.'

'The Craigslist murders are true. These things happen. There are some right weirdos out there. You'd be surprised. I see many of them in the hair salon.' She chuckles at her own joke but then she sobers up again. 'Just be careful, that's all I'm saying.'

'Kathryn and Elspeth aren't secret psychos. I think Elspeth has trust issues and she's obviously got a chip on her shoulder about her elder daughter for some reason. She's just very private. And I shouldn't have been asking questions anyway.'

'Jeez, you're entitled to ask questions. Who told you about Viola?'

'The cook, Aggie.'

'Hmm ... Kris, get off me, I'm on the phone ...' There's a rustling sound and then Courtney says, 'Sorry about that. Kris is being a twat. He's gone out now. Band practice.'

'How is living together working out?'

She groans. 'Okay. I suppose. Are you coming out tomorrow night? The usual place. Vince will be there but that's okay, isn't it? He said you two are friends now. He's really sorry for the way he acted, you know.'

'Courtney ...'

'I know you can never go back there. He fucked you over. I know.'

I swallow the lump that's formed in my throat, wishing I could go back. To before Mum got ill, to before Vince 'fucked me over', as Courtney so eloquently put it. I blink back tears. But, of course, I can't. This is my life now and I have to get on with it.

We hang up, promising to see each other tomorrow night, and I lie on the bed for a few minutes. I get up and, to be on the safe side, I lock my bedroom door.

A noise wakes me. I blink in the darkness, feeling disoriented for a few seconds. I hear it again. The creak of floorboards. I rub my eyes, propping myself on my elbows and notice that my door is ajar, letting in a sliver of silvery light from the landing. I remember locking it before I went to sleep. I know I did. Is someone in my room?

I'm wide awake now and sit up straighter. I start when I see a figure by my wardrobe and then realize it's just my dress on a hanger that I never got around to putting away.

My throat is dry as I swing my legs out of bed. I go to the door, peering out onto the small landing. Nobody's there. I hear a cough from Elspeth's room. There's only the two of us in the house. Does she need me? I pad downstairs to her bedroom, cold in my thin cotton pyjamas, and poke my head around her bedroom door. But she looks as though she's asleep, her eyes closed, her chest rising and falling gently. Why do I have the feeling she's pretending?

I leave, but as I do so I have the strange sensation that someone is behind me, their breath hot on the back of my neck. I run to my room and shut the door, my heart pounding. Oh, God, what if there's an intruder and they're now in my room? I feel like a kid as I frantically check under the bed and in the wardrobe, relief coursing through me when there's nobody. I know I locked the door before I went to sleep and the only people with keys are Kathryn and Elspeth. I poke my head into the en-suite, just to be sure, but it's empty. I take the key from my bedside table and lock the bedroom door again. And then I drag the chair from my desk over to it and jam it under the handle. Only then do I feel safe enough to return to my bed.

The next morning I hear Kathryn arrive early, but as it's my day off I peer over the duvet to make sure my door is still locked and the chair in place. When I see that it is, I pull the duvet over my head and go back to sleep. By the time I wake up later the house is blissfully quiet. I dress quickly in a jumper and jeans, making sure to choose the ones without holes in the knees after Elspeth made a remark about my needing to darn my trousers, then go down to the kitchen. Aggie is clearing away the breakfast things. She looks up when she sees me, her big friendly face breaking into a smile. 'Hello, ducky. Do you want something to eat?'

I feel exhausted. After returning to bed last night I spent the remaining few hours tossing and turning until I saw the reassuring early-morning sunlight filtering through my curtains. 'Toast and a cup of tea will be more than enough,' I say. 'But I'll get it.'

'Don't be silly. Sit yourself down. I'll do it for you.'

'Thank you.' But I don't take a seat, instead I help her clear away the breakfast things that must have been Elspeth and Kathryn's and stack them in the dishwasher.

'Go and sit yourself down. Are you sure you don't want an egg with your toast?'

I shake my head. 'No, thanks.' I pat my stomach. 'I still feel full from your amazing meal last night.'

She beams. 'How was the theatre?'

I hesitate. 'Yeah. The play was . . . good.'

I obviously don't sound convincing because she laughs. 'Elspeth has some strange tastes,' she says. 'What was it about?'

'It was too highbrow for me. I didn't get most of it.' I remember how Elspeth had taken my hand between both of hers afterwards and asked, her tone a little patronizing, how I'd enjoyed my first theatre experience. It had niggled me that she'd assumed – rightly – that it was my first time, unless you count the pantomime I went to with Mum when I was seven.

Aggie hands me my toast and pats me on the shoulder.

'You're lovely as you are,' she says. 'It's nice to have a bit of unpretentiousness about the place. I miss that.'

I don't tell Aggie how Elspeth had said yesterday as we were crocheting, 'Oh, you do have a delightful West Country accent. I know a very good elocutionist if you ever fancied making it more . . .' she'd paused, her eyes assessing me as though she was trying to find the right word '. . . euphonious.' I didn't want to admit I didn't know what the word meant.

Aggie sits opposite me with a cup of tea between her large hands. I need to be honest with her. 'Aggie – I'm so sorry. I think I put my foot in it with Elspeth. I asked her about Viola. One of the shops was named after her. But she was very defensive about it and basically denied having a daughter called Viola.'

Aggie's usually good-natured face clouds. 'I don't know what went on there,' she says, shaking her head and making her chins wobble. 'Viola could be a little madam, don't get me wrong, and the mind games the two girls played, well . . .' She purses her lips, then takes a sip of her tea. 'There was often fireworks. But it wasn't Kathryn. Kathryn was as good as gold. She was the perfect daughter. I suppose, really, she made Viola look bad without meaning to.'

'And she was in a children's home before then?'

'That's right.'

'It must have been hard.'

'She never seemed troubled, though. She had her head screwed on, that one. It was like she came here determined to make it work. She said to me once that she'd do everything she could to be the perfect daughter so as not to get sent back to the home.'

I feel a stab of pity for Kathryn. 'Do you know what happened to her parents?'

'Her dad wasn't around. I'm not sure what happened there. And her mum,' she lowers her voice, even though it's just us in the room, 'drugs. She took an overdose. Kathryn was the one who found her and called the police. She was only eight, bless her.'

'How awful.'

She shakes her chins. 'But Elspeth has been a brilliant mother to Kathryn. And Kathryn is a dutiful daughter.'

Yet I sense that something is off about their relationship. It's obvious Kathryn avoided us yesterday. And it's clear she doesn't agree with Elspeth employing a companion. Although it could be that I'm comparing their relationship to the one I had with my own mother, which, in my eyes, was perfect.

We sit in silence for a few minutes. My eyes stray to the French windows and the garden beyond. I'm disappointed that Lewis has gone. It would be better if there were other young people about the place, someone to talk to. I had Cherry at the care home. She was a few years younger than me, but the two of us used to have a right laugh. I live for my days off when I can see Courtney. The rest of my spare time – not that there seems to be that much of it – is spent scrolling through social media in the sitting room, where the Wi-Fi works better, looking up Matilde and Jemima, trying to glean as much as I can about what they had been like. Sometimes I feel as if I knew them.

Aggie gets up from her chair and takes her empty mug to the dishwasher. 'Right,' she says, gathering her coat from the peg by the back door. 'I'm off. Kathryn's taken

Elspeth to Frome to look at a painting, so they won't be back until teatime. The cleaner will be here at four and I'll be back around five.'

'I'll be going out soon,' I say, necking the remains of my tea.

She winks at me. 'Don't get up to any mischief.'

I laugh and pull a 'What – me?' expression.

'See you later, ducky,' she calls, as she bustles past me and up the stairs. I hear the front door bang shut and everything falls silent. I've got the whole house to myself for several hours before I'm due to meet Courtney at the salon. I know I shouldn't do it. My mum and Courtney would never approve. But I can't resist having a snoop around.

I don't know what I'm looking for, really – evidence of a break-in last night maybe, even though, deep down, I know that can't have been the case. In reality, the only person who could have unlocked my door is Elspeth. Unless Kathryn came over in the dead of night, but why would she?

I've been in the sitting room and the library, but they are all meticulously tidy. There are no papers that belong to Elspeth. My mum always had a stash of bills, documents, insurance papers and birth certificates in a suitcase under her bed. But there is nothing like that in Elspeth's room. Kathryn's is also very tidy, but that's because she's only using it now and again when she stays over. Considering Elspeth has lived here for nearly forty years, the house is surprisingly clutter-free. Sometimes it feels as though I'm in a National Trust property, not in someone's home at all. The most lived-in part of the house is the kitchen, but that might be because Aggie occupies it. Then I remember the study, the small room that Elspeth never goes into on the lower ground floor at the front of the house, next to the kitchen. I run back down the stairs and stand in the square lobby, poking my head around the kitchen door just to double-check that I really am alone and Aggie hasn't come back. But when I can see it's empty I go to the only other door off the lobby, dismayed when I discover it's locked. I stand staring at the door in disappointment. And then I mentally shake myself. What am I doing? Am I really expecting to find evidence of foul play or criminal activity, or am I just looking for excitement in a job I'm finding a bit dull? Matilde's death was an accident and Jemima killed herself. *But they both looked like you,* a little voice in my head says. *Isn't that a bit odd?*

Urgh. I'm driving myself mad with these thoughts. I'm going to kill Courtney when I see her. This is all her fault with her talk of the Craigslist murders.

But why did Elspeth come into your room last night?

I put my hands over my ears to stop my relentless thoughts. Elspeth wouldn't hurt me. She's not capable of it. And it's not like the other girls were found stabbed in their beds. I'm letting my imagination run away with me.

I move away from the door and return upstairs. I need to get out of this house and clear my head. I'm just about to run up to my room when the front doorbell rings. The sound reverberates through the hallway. I stand still for a few seconds, wondering if I should answer it, until I pull myself together. It's probably the postman, for goodness' sake.

I open the heavy door and a gust of cold air hits me in

the face. Standing on the threshold is a man in his twenties, with bright blond hair and eyes the colour of icicles. He's wearing a puffy yellow jacket.

'Oh, hi. Can I help you?' I have to peer up at him because he's so much taller than me.

'I'm looking for Elspeth McKenzie,' he says, with a London accent. He has a checked scarf pulled up around his throat, and a large beauty spot on his left cheek.

'I'm sorry, I'm afraid she's not in.'

His whole body deflates with disappointment. 'Do you know when she'll be back? I've come a long way.'

'Not until around teatime. Can I help at all? Or pass on a message?'

'And you are?' He doesn't smile. He has a very square jaw and a muscle twitches just under his ear.

'I work for Mrs McKenzie.'

Why does he look so annoyed? 'I'm Peter Freeman. Jemima was my sister. She worked here before you.'

'Oh . . . of course. I'm so sorry to hear about –'

'She would never have taken her own life.' His voice cuts through my words like a guillotine through paper.

'I – I'm afraid I didn't know her.'

His face collapses and, for one moment, he looks on the edge of tears. Instinctively I reach out to him and touch his shoulder lightly. He's weighed down by grief. I recognize it. I live with it too. His pain touches me and, to my horror, my eyes fill in sympathy. He steps away from me. 'Okay. Well, sorry to bother you,' he says.

He's going to leave. I can't let that happen. This is the perfect opportunity to find out more about the girl whose life I'm living.

'You want to go for a coffee? There's a café around the corner. I could meet you there in five minutes,' I say, my words tumbling out in a rush. I sound desperate and I am. I've been stuck in the house on my own all morning.

Surprise flickers on his face, but he nods. 'Thank you. I'll see you in five minutes.'

I watch him walk out of the front garden and down the street, his shoulders hunched, his grief almost palpable. And then I go back inside the house to fetch my coat and bag.

15

Peter is standing at the counter behind a line of people
and he looks up when I walk into the café. I'm relieved
when I see him. This is the closest café to Elspeth's house,
but I was worried he'd walk straight past it as it's tucked
away between a row of imposing Georgian buildings in
what looks like a residential street.

The café is only small and the tables are all taken. 'Shall
we get a takeaway and go for a walk?' he says, when I
reach him. 'It's so pretty around here.'

I say okay and we stand awkwardly in the queue, not
speaking until we're served. We both order cappuccinos,
then head out into the cold clasping our cups with gloved
hands. We wander across the green, our feet sinking into
the wet grass, and towards the suspension bridge. It's
shrouded in a faint drizzly mist.

'I just need to understand how she died,' Peter says,
after a while. He stops and stares at the bridge, horror in
his eyes. 'It's so high.'

'Do you want to walk across it?'

He looks surprised. 'You can do that?'

'Yes. It doesn't take long.'

He nods and we stride towards the entrance of the bridge.
He looks faintly sick as we walk along the pavement, past

the barriers where the cars have to pay. 'I don't understand how she could have jumped from here,' he says. 'Look at the fences. They're high.'

It wouldn't be impossible to climb over them, I think, but don't say. Instead I sip my coffee, enjoying the warmth. It's so cold up here. I wish I'd brought my hat. 'At the other end there's a wall which would be easy to climb over.'

He winces as though imagining his sister tumbling over it and onto the hard ground below.

'Did you come down from London today?' I ask, after we've been silent for a few minutes.

He nods. His nose has gone red from the cold. 'I came on the train. I just wanted to come here to . . . well, to understand. It was just the two of us, you know? Since Mum died.'

'I'm so sorry.'

'I can't get my head around it. I don't believe she'd kill herself. Just before Christmas. She loved Christmas. I dunno . . . I just . . . Don't believe it.'

An uneasy feeling travels through my body. 'Then what do you think happened?'

'I don't know. I spoke to her only a few days before she died.'

I wait, biting my tongue to prevent myself asking any questions. Sometimes it's better to let the other person tell you things in their own time. I'm learning that, thanks to Elspeth.

'She sounded happy. She'd met someone, she said.'

'Really?'

'Yes. He worked for Mrs McKenzie apparently. She seemed smitten.'

Could it have been Lewis? Was he working for Elspeth last month? Aggie said that the gardeners never lasted long as Elspeth always found fault with them, but I'm sure Lewis had implied he'd been employed by the McKenzies for several months.

'She was excited about Christmas. She wanted me to meet this guy.'

'Did she say what his name was?'

He shakes his head, a lock of white-blond hair falling into his eyes. He brushes it away with one hand. The gesture is endearing and my heart goes out to him. I want to help him, this man who wears his grief like a shroud.

'I called her once a week. I was her older brother. I felt responsible for her. I spoke to her on the fifteenth of December. I wasn't able to see her on Christmas Day as I was working – I'm a firefighter,' he explains, his voice dipping, and I regard him over my coffee with renewed interest. 'But she was okay with it. She said she was spending it with him. When I rang her on Christmas Eve her mobile went straight to voicemail.'

So it was a serious relationship, I think, as I sip my coffee. Vince and I had spent only last Christmas together, because I would have been on my own otherwise. My heart contracts and I try to concentrate on what Peter is saying.

'Jemima could be like that. Sometimes she went off the radar for weeks. She liked to do her own thing. So I wasn't too worried at first. But when she didn't call on Christmas Day, or the week after, I started to stress about it. I tried the McKenzies. I spoke to a woman called Kathryn.'

'Elspeth McKenzie's daughter.'

'She said that Jemima had left out of the blue. That

there had been a bit of a disagreement and she'd taken all her things and cleared out. But she wouldn't have done that without ringing me. She had nowhere else to go.'

The coffee curdles in my stomach. *A bit of a disagreement.* I didn't know that.

By now we've reached the end of the bridge where the railings give way to a walled terrace. Peter steps forward and looks down onto the water and the thicket of bushes. 'This must have been where she jumped. Apparently she was found down there.' He points to the wild undergrowth. It's exactly where I thought it must have happened. 'Nobody noticed her body for nearly a month.' His voice breaks.

I don't know what to say. 'What do you think really happened?' I ask eventually.

He sniffs, and I can tell he's concentrating hard on not crying in front of me. He stares straight ahead at the view of the gorge. 'I think someone pushed her. She was scared of heights. She wasn't depressed. The McKenzies . . .' He swallows his emotion. 'They know more than they're letting on. I'm certain of it.'

'You don't think they hurt her?'

'I don't know.'

'What about this boyfriend? Maybe it was him. Or maybe he knows more about it.'

He turns his head to look at me. 'I've told the police about him. But I didn't even know his name. Do you think you could find out? Ask the family? They might know something. I came here today to ask Mrs McKenzie. But Kathryn was so cold on the phone. It was like she didn't care about Jemima at all.'

I promise him that I'll try, and we swap numbers.

'Where does this lead?' he asks, pointing towards the area where the bridge ends.

'Leigh Woods.'

'Woods?' He chews his lips. 'That's interesting.'

I don't really know what to say so I remain silent and we walk back across the bridge.

When we've reached Sion Hill he pauses at the trash can on the green and drops his coffee cup into it.

'I've just remembered something,' I say. 'I found a necklace when I first moved in. A locket. I gave it to Kathryn. She said it was Jemima's and that she would post it on. She made it sound like she had a forwarding address.'

I sense Peter freeze beside me. 'What? When I spoke to her she told me she didn't know where Jemima had gone.'

By the look on his face I can tell we've had the same thought. Why would Kathryn lie?

16

Kathryn

'She keeps asking questions,' says Elspeth, as they leave the gallery. They'd spent a good couple of hours with Fleur Honeywell, a willowy whimsical woman about Kathryn's age. Kathryn had liked her a lot, but her mother had been less keen, her eyes glazing over when Fleur talked. She could tell Fleur's paintings weren't to Elspeth's taste either – too bold and colourful. Her mother preferred pictures as delicate as everything else she admired. Still, Kathryn knew she had a better eye for what sold than her mother did. Kathryn disliked her job most of the time, mainly because there was a lot of waiting around, but she knew she was good at it.

'Who? Fleur?'

Her mother tsks. 'No. Una.'

She has to suppress a shiver and pulls the scarf further up her throat. It's getting dark now, and the streetlamps have come on, giving the cobbled street a ghostly, almost Victorian glow. 'What about?' she asks, trying to sound nonchalant as she helps her mother over the cobbles, Elspeth gripping her arm too tightly. Maybe her mother won't be enraptured by Una, after all. The right looks but the wrong personality. Too nosy by the sound of it.

'About Viola. Aggie told her.'

'Has Aggie been gossiping again? For crying out loud, Mother, why don't you say something to her?'

Elspeth looks appalled. 'Aggie has been part of this family for over thirty years.'

'She shouldn't be gossiping to the staff.' Kathryn would never admit it to her mother but she loves Aggie. She's like the mother Kathryn wished she'd had. She looked after her when nobody else would, kept her fed and warm, was a shoulder to cry on, even more so after Viola. But, still, she can't have her gossiping. Who knows what she could reveal about their family?

'I don't like to be reminded of Viola.' Elspeth's voice sounds frail in the gloaming. 'Can you talk to Una for me? Tell her that? I don't want to have to fend off her questions all the time. It's utterly exhausting.'

Kathryn inwardly sighs. *This is what you get*, she wants to scream, *if you invite people into your home. If you employ silly young girls as your companions.* 'Why don't you get someone else to run the gallery? I could stay and help you instead.'

Elspeth stops walking and turns to Kathryn. 'The gallery will be yours one day. Don't you want to run it?' Her face is a white halo in the light.

'It's not that. It's just . . . I don't know. Maybe you should get rid of Una. Get someone to pop in a few times a day instead. Like a nurse.'

'What is it about them that you dislike so much? First Matilde, then Jemima, and now Una. I need more than a carer, you know that. I get lonely. They're harmless, Kathryn. They aren't a threat to you.'

Aren't they? Like Kathryn wasn't a threat to Viola? Her mother is lying. Should she tell her? But then she'd have to confess that she'd read her will. That she knew what her mother had done.

She'll never forget the shock she'd had when she first stumbled upon her mother's will. She'd been looking for the buildings-insurance papers for the gallery after the boiler broke last July. Her mother had gone out somewhere with Matilde, and Kathryn had let herself into The Cuckoo's Nest and found the key to Elspeth's study – her mother always hid it in the same place, behind *The Great Escape* in the library. She'd found the will in the desk drawer, already signed and updated. She'd read it, of course. How could she not? And there it was in black and white. Half her mother's money went to her, but the other half went to Matilde. A girl her mother had known for five minutes. In that moment she'd thought her mother must be losing her marbles. Why would she do that? Why not leave the remainder of her estate to Harry and Jacob? Everything, the shops, the foundation, the house – oh, God, the house – it would all be divided between her and Matilde.

Matilde, the manipulative little cow, had hoodwinked her stupid, gullible mother.

Elspeth starts walking again, pulling on Kathryn's arm so she has no choice but to do the same. 'Do you miss her? Viola?' Kathryn asks, her voice thick. She feels like a little girl again. Small, vulnerable and in dire need of love and reassurance.

'You know I don't like to talk about her. She hurt me.'

'I know.'

'I'll never forgive her.'

'I know that too.'

How unyielding and conditional her love is, Kathryn thinks. She'd forgive her own two sons anything.

Elspeth sighs, her breath fogging in front of her. 'But yes . . . yes, I miss her.'

Kathryn pats her mother's hand, wishing she'd never asked the question.

Kathryn is surprised to see the lights on in the sitting-room window when they arrive back at The Cuckoo's Nest. She was expecting Una to be out with the man she pretends isn't her boyfriend.

'I think you should be careful about ordering too many of Fleur's paintings,' Elspeth is saying, while Kathryn shrugs off her coat. 'They're an acquired taste.'

'I think they'll sell.'

'Let's hope so, because we need to see the gallery making a profit. Sales have certainly dipped in recent months.'

Elspeth hangs up her coat and Kathryn follows her into the sitting room. They both halt in surprise to see Una sitting on the velvet chesterfield sofa with a man. He's handsome, Nordic-looking and, for a sudden, heart-stopping moment, she wonders if he's related to Matilde.

Una stands up when she sees them. She looks awkward and keeps playing with the ends of her long hair. 'Hi. This is Peter.' She indicates the man on the sofa, who also gets to his feet. He's very tall, towering over Kathryn's five-foot-ten-inch frame. 'This is Jemima's brother.'

Jemima's brother. Of course. Now Kathryn can see the resemblance. The same platinum hair and ice-blue eyes. She'd always thought Jemima's hair was dyed that colour.

Her mother finds her voice first. 'I'm so sorry to hear

about Jemima,' she says, her tone imbued with a warmth Kathryn rarely hears.

It seems to throw Peter, who mumbles, 'Thanks.'

'Can I offer you some tea? Coffee?'

Peter asks for tea and Una starts to leave the room but Elspeth stops her, her voice crisp. 'You stay here, Una. Kathryn can fetch the tea.'

Damn it. Kathryn wanted to hear what Peter had to say. Goodness knows what her mother will reveal in her absence. She hopes Aggie is in the kitchen.

But the kitchen is empty. Kathryn boils the kettle and gets the tray ready with her mother's tea things. Within five minutes she's back upstairs.

'I'm just trying to understand what happened,' Peter is saying, when Kathryn re-enters the room. She places the tea tray on the coffee table but only Una thanks her.

Her mother is sitting upright in her favourite armchair, looking like a formidable headmistress, her glasses on a chain around her neck.

Kathryn perches on the chair next to Elspeth. When there is a pause in the conversation, she asks Peter to help himself to the tea. When he doesn't move she pours him a cup and he takes it, almost absent-mindedly, his gaze focused on Elspeth. 'She would never have killed herself. Please. Can you talk me through that last day?'

Elspeth sits up a little straighter. 'Well. I had to go to a meeting. Jemima would normally have accompanied me but she said she had a headache. She was acting a little oddly –'

He jumps in. 'In what way?'

'I didn't really think much of it at the time, but in hindsight she seemed jittery. Almost a bit nervous. I sensed she was lying about the headache. And when I got back she had gone. I thought – I assumed she'd been unhappy here and didn't have the nerve to tell me she wanted to leave.'

'That would have been out of character for her,' insists Peter. 'Did you owe her any wages?'

'I paid her the day before. I pay my staff weekly.'

Kathryn is proud of her mother. She's giving nothing away.

'What about the disagreement?' he asks.

Kathryn's heart speeds up.

'What disagreement?' Elspeth looks genuinely baffled.

'When I spoke to your daughter, a few days later, she told me that Jemima had left after a disagreement.'

All heads swivel towards Kathryn. She clears her throat to give herself time to respond. 'I didn't say there was a disagreement. I wasn't here. I just said there *may* have been a disagreement. My mother isn't known to hang on to her staff.'

He frowns and inches forwards in his seat. 'Wasn't the last girl with you for two years? I remember my sister saying as much because she felt she had big shoes to fill.'

Kathryn wants to tell him to fuck off. Him and his probing questions. 'Well, yes, she was . . .'

He frowns. 'Do you know who Jemima was dating? She said she was going out with a guy who worked here too.'

Kathryn shrugs. This was news to her. 'I have no idea.'

Peter stares at Kathryn for such a long time that sweat breaks out on her top lip. Eventually he asks, 'And what about the necklace?'

Kathryn's eyes dart towards Una and back to Peter. 'Necklace?'

'Una told me she found Jemima's necklace in her room and gave it to you. You said you'd forward it to her. Why would you say that when she'd left in such a hurry? Did she leave you a forwarding address? I thought you weren't here that day.'

Una has the good grace to look guilty and averts her eyes from Kathryn, studying her hands in her lap.

Kathryn breathes in deeply through her nose. 'Because it wasn't Jemima's necklace.'

Una lifts her eyes towards Kathryn in surprise.

'Initially I thought it was hers, but then I realized it must have belonged to someone else.'

Una opens her mouth to say something but Kathryn gives her such a withering look that she shuts it again, doubt creeping over her face.

'I'm so sorry for your loss.' Elspeth's voice cuts into the silence. 'But, as you can see, we know nothing about what was going through Jemima's head that day.'

Kathryn watches Una place her hand on Peter's arm. Either in sympathy or reassurance. She's not the only one who's noticed this small act of togetherness.

Her mother looks furious.

Earlier, Kathryn had found the part-crocheted blanket and her heart had sunk because her mother had something in common with Una. Elspeth had tried, and failed, to teach Kathryn to knit in the past. Kathryn had found it too fiddly and kept dropping the hook.

This thing between her and Una is like a game of tennis – a point to her, then to Una. But the ball is back in her court now. She knows Una is losing. Her mother will see her cosying up to Peter and believe – in her warped, misguided way – that it is some kind of betrayal.

Una is on borrowed time.

17

Una

'It's all just a bit odd,' I say to Courtney, later that evening. She's come to Clifton so we can go to a bar, just the two of us. We've chosen a new place that opened recently, all chandeliers, glass tables and velvet button-backed sofas. 'Peter seems convinced that Jemima didn't kill herself. And I remember Aggie saying she was a bubbly, bright thing. She thought we were quite similar, in looks and personality.'

Courtney sits back against the soft cushions. Her thick copper hair is piled high on her head in a jaunty ponytail, which cascades over one shoulder. She's wearing a long-sleeved dress with lace panels and looks stunning. 'Do you think Peter is just in denial, though? Remember when we found out Charlie from school had depression and he tried to kill himself? We were shocked. He was one of the most popular boys, had everything going for him, looks, brains. You know as well as I do that people can hide depression.'

I run my finger along the rim of my mojito glass. 'I know. But what if he's right? He wants me to try to find out who Jemima was dating. Apparently it was one of Elspeth's staff. The only men she employs are the gardeners.'

Her green eyes light up. 'Ooh! Do you think it could have been Lewis?'

'Maybe.'

'Then you need to find him.'

'But how?'

She leans forwards conspiratorially. 'Find his mobile number. Elspeth is bound to have it.'

'I can't just ask her for it, though, can I?'

'Why not? Say you know someone who needs a gardener.'

I shake my head. 'It won't wash with Elspeth. She's wily. She knows I thought he was good-looking and she'll think I'm after a date. She also told me she sacked him because he was lazy. So she knows I wouldn't pass on his number.'

'Oh, Una. I can tell you're not going to be great at this. You need my help.'

I laugh. Ever since I can remember, Courtney has loved solving 'mysteries'. When we were twelve she convinced herself, and me, that Mr Hadley from number twenty-four had done away with his wife because she hadn't been seen for a week. Cue days of following him around, watching him from our bedroom windows. We even got Courtney's brother, Theo, involved. We'd been mortified when we found that Mr Hadley's wife had been laid up in bed with flu and he hadn't murdered her after all.

I sip my cocktail. 'And how are you going to help?'

She raises one of her thick eyebrows. 'I have my ways. People tell hairdressers everything.'

'Yes, well, unless he's about to go to the salon for a haircut I can't imagine Lewis spilling the beans to you.'

'Find his phone number. That's all you need to do. Look through Elspeth's things if you have to.'

I blush when I remember I've already tried to do that.

Courtney notices. 'You've had a snoop, haven't you? I know you. You're so bloody nosy.'

I hold my hands up. 'Okay. Yes. But her study was locked.'

'Then find the key.'

'Easier said than done.'

We fall silent for a few moments, both sipping our cocktails. I can't bring myself to admit to Courtney how I've been scrolling through Matilde's Facebook page and Jemima's old Instagram posts, searching for clues, similarities. Anything, really. By the look of things Matilde had been bookish, posting about novels she'd enjoyed – she'd particularly liked romcoms – and Jemima's photographs were mostly of her travels to exotic locations. I've examined them all, my heart breaking that these vibrant, seemingly carefree girls' lives had been cut so short.

'There's something else, too. Something weird happened last night.' I explain about finding my locked door ajar. 'And when I went to check on Elspeth I was sure she was pretending to be asleep.'

'That's creepy.' Courtney exhales, her face aghast. 'Do you think she was watching you sleeping?'

I almost choke on my drink. 'Stop it! You're not helping!'

She laughs. 'Sorry. Maybe she's infatuated with you.'

'Of course she isn't!'

'You said yourself you look like the other girls. She's obviously got a thing for young blonde things. Maybe she's in the closet.'

I push her gently so that her drink nearly slops onto her

lap. 'Stop it.' I laugh. I tell her about the necklace and Kathryn's insistence it had belonged to someone else.

'Who did she say it belonged to?'

I shrug. 'I have no idea. But I don't believe her. I think it was Jemima's.'

Later, I walk with her to the bus stop and she leans over to hug me. She smells familiar, of alcohol and Marc Jacobs perfume. I wait with her until her bus arrives, then walk the few streets back to The Cuckoo's Nest. It doesn't feel right to call it home. Home is still the flat in Horfield with Courtney. This is just temporary, I remind myself.

The street is empty by the time I turn onto Sion Hill. Clifton Suspension Bridge looks eerie in the distance, the mist haloing around the lampposts and the lights blurring against the inky dark night. I can't help but think about Matilde, walking home alone on a night out. How did she not see the car coming? It must have been driving fast.

A twig snaps behind me. I spin around but nobody's there. I pull my hat down further over my head and walk faster towards Elspeth's house. I can hear footsteps getting closer. I break into a jog, my imagination running wild. That's all this is, I remind myself, just like the monsters I imagined under my bed, or the witch trying to get in through my window, or the person breathing down my neck last night outside Elspeth's bedroom. I can almost hear my mum's soothing voice, telling me there's nothing to worry about.

I stop running when I reach The Cuckoo's Nest, and wrench open the metal gate, darting down the front path. I almost drop my key in my haste to open the door. I can't get into the house fast enough. I'm only brave enough to peek through the crack in the glass panel of the door when I'm safely inside. And that's when I see a figure in a dark coat, the hood pulled up, crossing the road towards the suspension bridge.

I blink, trying to focus on the person scurrying away, but my contact lenses are irritating me, causing my vision to blur. As I turn away, though, I can't shake the disconcerting feeling that it was Vince.

I was stupid. You saw me, didn't you? I could have given myself away. I tried to get too close, too quickly. The time wasn't right. I could have ruined everything. Patience isn't my strong point. If I hadn't stood on that fucking twig you'd never have known I was there. I was with you long before that. I was with you when you left the bar with your tarty little friend. I was with you when you both wove your way to the bus stop, giggling and acting younger than your twenty-two years. I was with you when your friend got on the bus and you waved her off. And I was with you when you walked home alone. I could so easily have reached for you, placing my hands around your long, slender neck.

You need to be more careful.

18

Una

I don't get a chance to do any amateur sleuthing for the next week or so because Elspeth is constantly by my side. When we're not in the house I'm accompanying her on excursions, or sitting patiently in one of her shops while she discusses business with the manager. I also have to walk her to her twice-weekly hair appointments. Unfortunately she doesn't use the salon where Courtney works (it would have been great to catch up with her for a chat) but a more upmarket affair in the village. When I saw the price of a cut and colour I nearly passed out.

I'm sure Kathryn is deliberately avoiding me. When she comes over she's polite but distant – even colder than usual. I think she's angry with me for telling Peter about the necklace. Perhaps she thinks we're ganging up on her, accusing her of knowing more about Jemima's death than she lets on. But that's not what this is about. Yes, I believe she lied about the necklace, but I can't believe she harmed Jemima. Why would she?

Peter keeps in touch by text. He's much more communicative by phone than he is in person. He had to go back to London for work. But he's promised to visit in a few weeks, saying he'll stay nearby in a bed-and-breakfast. I told him I'll try to find out who Jemima's mystery man was before he returns.

Sometimes, when I'm alone in bed at night (door locked with the chair jammed under the handle), I miss Mum so much it physically hurts. The weight of her death sits heavily on my chest so that I feel suffocated by it. I understand Peter's pain. If I thought someone had harmed my mum I would go to the ends of the earth to find out the truth. I'm not stupid – I know that my interest in Jemima's death is also a distraction from my own grief, from my failed relationship and my boredom in a job where I mostly have an old lady for company, even though these days – since I stopped asking probing questions – we get on well. I know all this. The only thing that gets me through these depressing cold winter days is the thought of the hot climes I'll visit in September.

One evening after I've put Elspeth to bed I retreat to my room and scroll through Jemima's Instagram page. I can't stop looking at it: the beaches she visited and the towns. Talking to Peter has made her feel even more real to me. I feel as if I know her. I wonder if we would have been friends.

I google Peter's name and wait while it loads. There are lots of Peter Freemans but none of them is Jemima's brother. I try Peter Freeman + firefighter but still nothing. Even though his sister had a presence on social media it seems Peter is a ghost. He has no digital footprint at all.

It's February and I've been in the job for over a month when Kathryn finally corners me. It's Wednesday, my day off, and she's arrived bright and early for her daughterly duties. That makes me sound scathing. Don't get me wrong, I admire how kind and diligent Kathryn is to her mum. I'm being selfish because having her around instantly changes the atmosphere and I find that I'm on edge, as if I'm tiptoeing over a floor of broken toys not wanting to make a sound to alert her to my presence. It's obvious she doesn't like me and disapproves of me being here. It emanates from her every pore.

When I come downstairs I expect the house to be empty. Kathryn usually takes her mum out first thing because Elspeth is such an early riser. But she is standing in the library doorway with a book in her hand and a startled expression, as if I've caught her doing something she shouldn't. She's got what looks like a key in her hand. She slips it onto the shelf and replaces the book in front of it. She does all of this in a flash, like a magician performing a sleight-of-hand trick, obviously hoping I won't see, and I pretend not to have noticed as I go to the cupboard to get my boots. Courtney's got today off so we're going shopping at Cabot Circus.

'Una, can I have a word?' she calls, as I'm pulling on my coat, her voice echoing around the hallway. I wonder where Elspeth is. My heart sinks but I fake a smile and go over to her. She beckons me into the library and shuts the door behind me.

I rarely come into this room, even though it's beautiful with the floor-to-ceiling bookshelves and the two high-backed armchairs in a plush mustard velvet positioned on either side of the French windows. It's peaceful and relaxing, yet apart from the books there is no personality to this room. Nothing to say who the McKenzies really are:

no ornaments from a memorable holiday or a paperweight on the little round table. Not even a candle or a diffuser, which Courtney and I had in abundance in our flat, mainly to hide the smell of mould.

'Take a seat,' she says, indicating one of the chairs. I do as she says, puzzled and a little anxious as to what she'll want to talk about. She doesn't look particularly angry. Her face is set in its normal neutral repose so it's impossible to read what she's thinking. She sits opposite me and leans forwards, elbows resting on her lap, like we're the best of friends about to have a cosy gossip.

'I hope you don't mind me bringing this up . . .' she takes a deep breath '. . . but Mother asked me to have a word with you about Viola.'

The mysterious Viola. My senses are on alert. 'Okay.'

'Mother doesn't like to talk about her. She hurt us all badly when she ran off. As far as Mother is concerned, Viola no longer exists.'

Of course I want to ask questions. They're inching up my throat, but I know it's not the done thing in this house so I stay quiet and nod. I can feel heat making its way from my neck to my face.

She sits back in the chair, looking satisfied. 'And also, while we're here, I didn't appreciate you bringing Peter Freeman back to the house. What was all that about?'

I explain about how he'd called around while they were out, and I took pity on him and walked him to the suspension bridge.

'I know he doesn't want to believe that his sister killed herself but, Una, you shouldn't get involved. If there's any doubt over her death then it's a matter for the police.'

I nod again, feeling like a five-year-old being told off.

She gets up and I realize it's now or never. 'Um, weird question, I know, but do you happen to have Lewis the gardener's number?' I blush as I say it and she raises one of her finely arched brows.

'No, but I can find it for you.' She gives me a friendly wink and it's like the Kathryn I know has morphed into a different person in front of my eyes. I've only seen her like this once before and it was the day I moved in. 'If I were you, I wouldn't tell my mother you're planning on dating Lewis. She's not a fan.'

Later, when I return to the house after a day of shopping with Courtney, I run into Kathryn as I'm going to my room. I don't know what she's doing on my floor, perhaps she'd been waiting for me to come home, but when she sees me she presses a folded piece of paper into my palm without saying anything, then turns and walks away. I unfold the paper. It's a mobile number that I assume belongs to Lewis. My heart beats faster and I remind myself I'm doing this for Peter. For Jemima. And not because I want to see Lewis again.

It's a bitter evening. February is even colder than January was. Too cold for snow, my mum used to say. Ice coats the pavements, like sparkly fairy dust, glinting under the amber glow of the streetlights and crunching beneath the soles of my boots. Windscreens of parked cars are already frosting, and I pity their owners tomorrow when they'll have to scrape the ice away. The cold weather doesn't stop the university students, though, and the streets of Clifton are busy as I head to the pub around the corner. I'm pleased it doesn't feel lonely out tonight, and vow to get Lewis to walk me home. A few times over the last couple of weeks I've had the creepy feeling that I'm being followed. When I turn there's never anybody behind me but, on occasion, I've felt breath on the nape of my neck, or eyes boring into my back. I'm sure it's my imagination, and I've put it down to the unease I can't help but feel at walking in dead women's shoes. It's usually only when I'm alone, although the other day when I accompanied Elspeth to the hairdresser I'm sure I felt someone behind me, walking too close for it to be natural.

I push open the pub's door. Lewis is sitting on a stool at the bar, his feet resting on the base. He's wearing black jeans and a thick woollen jacket, his shaggy dark hair touching the collar. He's even better-looking than I remember.

He'd been surprised to hear from me when I called. I didn't reveal what I wanted to see him about but when I asked if he was free this evening, and apologized for the short notice, he'd agreed.

He doesn't look round until I'm by his shoulder. Then he must sense my presence because he glances up from his pint. 'Great to see you,' he says, as though we're old friends, not people who have met just once. 'What can I get you to drink?'

I order a small white wine. It's still early, not yet seven thirty, so the place is still relatively quiet and we find a table in the corner. I sit opposite him, a candle flickering between us, and I feel a flush of embarrassment. It looks like we're on a date and I wonder if I've given Lewis that impression.

'Thanks for agreeing to meet me,' I begin tentatively. Now that I'm here, I'm not sure how to broach the subject of Jemima. 'What have you been up to since leaving Elspeth's?'

'Oh, you know, a bit of this and that. Not many people want gardeners this time of year.' He cups his pint and I notice his hands are calloused and strong. For a fleeting moment I imagine them on me and blush.

'How is it, working for the old battleaxe?' He smiles to take the sting out of his words.

'I . . . She's . . .' I hesitate, not wanting to be disloyal. 'She's okay. I'm sorry she sacked you, though.'

He shrugs. 'It is what it is. She never liked me.'

'I think she prefers the company of women,' I say, thinking of what Kathryn said earlier.

He surprises me by laughing. 'You don't say.'

'How long did you work for her?'

He raises one of his eyebrows, his gaze not leaving mine. 'A few months.'

My tummy flips. I try to get my thoughts in order. 'Did you know Jemima? The girl before me.'

His face clouds and he pushes a lock of hair away from his eyes. 'Yes, I knew Jemima.' The flirtiness has gone from his voice. He picks up a coaster and begins picking at the edges of it with his long fingers. 'Is that why you wanted to see me?' He's not looking at me now, just at his hands as he tears the cardboard. 'I did wonder why you contacted me out of the blue like this when we don't know each other. I thought maybe . . .' He trails off.

I feel heat rising to my face. He did think I wanted a date. 'I met up with her brother.' And then I explain about

Peter, and his visit. 'He said he thought she was seeing someone and I wondered if it was you.'

He shakes his head. 'We went on a few dates back in October. We were both new at the same time and hit it off. She was a great girl. But it didn't last long. A couple of weeks at the most. I don't think her brother could have meant me.'

I'm disappointed but I try not to let it show. 'Peter said she was seeing someone when he spoke to her, just before she died. Do you know who?'

He swigs his pint and replaces it on the table before answering. 'Jemima was a lovely girl but very private. She didn't open up easily. After we'd gone out a few times and it was clear it wasn't going to work, she avoided me. I thought we could be friends but . . . I don't know. I really liked her, but she could be very up and down.'

'Do you think she might have been depressed?'

'It wouldn't surprise me. There was the fun Jemima, you know, the girl who was sweet and funny and liked to have a laugh, and then there was this other side to her. This darker side. She could be quite sulky. Uncommunicative. I never knew which Jemima would show up for our date.'

'Is that why it didn't work out?'

He sits back in his chair. 'God, Una, you do like to ask questions.'

'Sorry. I'm sorry. I just want to try to understand . . .'

He sits forward. 'Why? You didn't even know the girl.'

'For Peter. Mainly.'

'So you and this Peter. Are you together?'

'What?' I laugh. 'No. No, of course not.'

'So what, then? You're just helping him out of the goodness of your own heart?' His tone takes on a teasing quality, but it rankles.

'No. Selfishly, I'd like to know if there was anything suspicious about her death when I'm literally, you know, living her life. Employed by the same people, living in her room . . . and then before her, Matilde, also dead . . .' The fear is evident in my voice.

He surprises me by reaching across the table and taking my hand. 'I'm sorry. Of course it must be horrible. But honestly, Una, I don't think you need to worry. I heard about Matilde. It was a hit-and-run. Terrible, but it happens. And Jemima, well . . . Like I said, I think she had some problems. I know you said her brother can't accept she took her own life, and I know I only dated her for a few weeks, but let's just say I'm not surprised.'

Lewis's hand feels warm and reassuring in mine and relief washes over me. It's only just hit me how scared I've felt. But being here with Lewis, listening to him rationalizing it all, makes me see how paranoid I've been.

19

Kathryn

Kathryn pulls the duvet over her head and groans. She's been tossing and turning for hours and she knows why. She's been waiting for Una to get home. She pulls back the covers and gets out of bed. It's no use. She won't sleep until Una's in the house and she's gone down to check the front door. It doesn't matter how many times she tells her mother's latest companion to double-lock the fucking front door, she never does it. She stands in the middle of the room and takes a deep breath. In and out. Just like the therapist told her. It's not Una's fault. How can Una know that Kathryn lives with the crippling fear – especially when she's ensconced in her 1930s house with Ed and the kids – that one day there will be *that* knock at the door?

She's coming back from the bathroom when she hears the creak of the front gate and low voices. She checks her Fitbit, which she wears at night because she likes to track her sleep. It's nearly 1 a.m. Where has Una been all this time? She watched her go out earlier. She'd left the house at seven twenty-five dressed in tight black jeans with so many rips that Kathryn wondered what was the point in wearing them at all. She must have been freezing.

Before she has time to think about it, Kathryn finds herself in the spare room – Viola's old room – that looks out onto the front garden. The curtains are already open: nobody comes in here to close them. Every trace of Viola was wiped from the room many years ago. Now there's just a double bed with a new, crisp duvet that is never used and different furniture, heavy mahogany instead of white. It's like Kathryn and her mother have this unspoken rule. Despite the stripping of Viola's personality, it will always be her room, and even though it's been thirty years since her older 'sister' left, Kathryn can still sense Viola's presence here. She can almost smell her White Musk perfume from the Body Shop.

The sound of Una giggling brings Kathryn back to the present and she rushes to the window. Una and Lewis are standing by the gate. He has his arms around her tiny waist and hers are slung around his neck. She's looking up at him, and as he bends to kiss her, Kathryn feels a bolt of jealousy rip right through her that's so intense it makes her feel sick. She can't remember the last time she kissed Ed. Not properly. Not like the abandon she's witnessing before her. It feels so long ago that she was Una's age, when someone as handsome and sexy as Lewis was interested in her. She can't bear it. She turns away. And in that moment she feels pure hatred for Una, for how easily she swans through life with her doe eyes and her long blonde hair and her pert tits, getting whatever she wants, *whoever* she wants. How unfair that life was never like that for Kathryn. She had to work so hard and put so much effort into achieving the life she's got now. Years of being the perfect daughter, the perfect wife, the perfect mother. And for what? For girls like Una to snatch it all from her by charming their way into someone's affections?

She goes back to bed and lies there, her whole body tense, feeling frumpy and unattractive in her flannel pyjamas. She wonders what Una wears to bed. Something sexy, no doubt. She strains her ears, listening for the front door, and eventually she hears the tell-tale creaks, bangs and muffled swearing of Una letting herself in.

Kathryn gets out of bed and drags her dressing-gown around herself as she pads out onto the landing. A slice of moonlight from the side window casts shadows on the walls and she clutches the banister to steady herself. As she descends the stairs, she sees Una sitting in the middle of the huge hallway trying to take off her boots. She's giggling to herself.

'Have you double-locked the front door?'

Una looks up in surprise to see Kathryn standing there. She puts her hand to her heart. 'Oh – you scared me.'

Kathryn doesn't say anything. She continues down the stairs and, ignoring Una, waltzes past her. She tries the door. Just as she thought, it hasn't been bolted. 'What is wrong with you?' Kathryn hisses, all the resentment and fear building up and spilling out of her. 'How many times have I told you to double-lock the door, for fuck's sake?'

Una stands up, her boots in one hand. Even in the dark Kathryn can see that the younger girl looks mortified. 'I'm sorry, I didn't think . . .'

'You have to be responsible,' continues Kathryn, in the same angry whisper. 'My mother doesn't want a bloody burglar alarm but surely even you can see this house is a target.'

'I . . . yes . . . I suppose –'

'If you forget to do it again I'll have no choice but to

give you a disciplinary warning.' The words are out before Kathryn has thought about them. What is she even saying? Her mother has the last word on her staff – but there can't be any harm in scaring the girl a little.

Una hangs her head, her long hair falling in front of her face. She's so small and she looks so vulnerable standing there in her socks, with a hole in the big toe of one, and her coat that is a little large for her. Kathryn knows she's being a bitch but she can't help it.

'I don't want to have to keep waiting up for you just to make sure you've done it,' she says, aware that she sounds like a nag.

'It won't happen again, I promise.' Una tucks her hair behind her ears.

Kathryn strides past her. 'Good. See you in the morning.' She stops at the bottom of the stairs and turns to Una. 'And, really, one o'clock on a work night is a little late to be coming home.'

Una juts out her chin. 'It won't have any impact on my ability to do my job,' she says levelly.

'I hope not. Good night.' And then Kathryn climbs the stairs and goes into her bedroom, making sure to close the door behind her.

The next morning Una is quiet at breakfast, and looks pale beneath her barely there makeup. Kathryn watches her across the table as she pushes a sausage around her plate and can't help but feel a little smug that Una is obviously suffering. Maybe now she'll think twice about staying out so late on a work night cavorting with handsome ex-employees.

She should have known when she gave Una Lewis's number that they'd end up on a date.

Her mother is chattering away. She's in a good mood this morning. Yesterday she wasn't. Yesterday she listed all the things that Kathryn does to annoy her, including holding her arm too tightly when they walk down the street and making her tea too 'builders'. There were numerous times yesterday when Kathryn wished she was back in the gallery with the effervescent Daisy rather than listening to her mother's never-ending criticisms, all of which seemed to scream, 'You're not Viola!'

She watches as her mother laughs at something Una says, throwing her head back so that Kathryn can see down her pink throat. She can't bear to witness her mother's obvious devotion.

Kathryn puts her knife and fork down with a clatter, and clears her throat. 'How are you feeling this morning, Una?' she asks, her voice ringing out clearly in the large kitchen. Aggie has stopped bustling around and has now joined them with a cup of tea.

'Ooh, did you go out last night, ducky?' Aggie's button eyes assess Una fondly. It makes Kathryn's blood boil. Even the lovable Aggie is smitten by her.

'She did,' interjects Kathryn, before Una has a chance to speak. 'She was on a date. With Lewis.'

It has the desired effect. The others fall silent. Even the normally tactless Aggie seems surprised.

Her mother's demeanour changes in a flash, just as Kathryn had known it would.

Her cold blue eyes glint dangerously and Kathryn can

hardly contain her glee. 'You went out with Lewis? As in our ex-gardener, Lewis?'

Una looks even paler than she did earlier, if that's possible. 'Um . . . not a date, exactly. I was . . . it was just to . . .' She appears to have run out of words.

'We're all ears,' says Kathryn, leaning forward on her elbows.

Una shifts in her chair. 'There's nothing to say, really.'

Kathryn smiles. 'I did wonder why you wanted his number. I don't blame you, he's a good-looking guy.'

Una reddens and her mother looks sickened. 'That's enough, Kathryn,' she snaps. 'You're old enough to be his mother. And, Una, I'm surprised at you. I thought you had more taste.' She pushes her chair back with such force that the legs screech across the limestone tiles. She stands up. 'Now, if you'll excuse me, I've got a headache. I'm going to rest in the sitting room. If you could bring me up a cup of tea, Una, I'd be grateful.'

'Of course,' mumbles Una, from behind her hair. Her cheeks are still pink.

They don't speak until Elspeth has left the room. Kathryn watches her mother's stiff back, and how steady she is on her feet today. 'Well,' she says, finishing her coffee, 'I'd better be off. Have a good day.'

She smiles to herself as she leaves the house, knowing Una's day is ruined.

Jacob is waiting on the stairs when she returns, dressed in his school uniform. The black blazer looks smart on the other kids but for some reason never does on her son, probably because he walks like an ape. His navy blue regulation rucksack is by his feet. It looks empty. She knows better than to ask him about it if she doesn't want to get her head bitten off.

'You're late,' he says, as soon as she steps inside the hallway. She isn't. She's never late.

'Where's your father and Harry?'

'Harry's on a sleepover and Dad's gone to work.'

'Harry's on a sleepover? On a school night? Who decided that?'

Jacob stands up. He's so tall, he towers over her now. 'Dad did. You're never here.'

'I was with Grandma.'

'You're always with Grandma.'

'She's old. She needs looking after.'

'Isn't that why she's got Una?'

'Well, yes, but Una needs a day off.' She bites back her irritation. 'We've been through this.'

He mutters something under his breath but she doesn't catch it. 'We need to go.' He hurls his rucksack onto his back. 'I'm gonna be late for school.'

'What about the bus?' He always takes the bus. He says he likes it because it gives him the chance to catch up with his mates, not that they look like they're catching up when Kathryn sees them. They're usually glued to their phones or their ears are plugged into them.

'I missed it.'

Again. Last week he didn't turn up at school. He'd taken the bus that day and she'd assumed he'd arrived okay – she has Find My Friends on her phone to keep track of him after his behaviour last year – but his phone was turned off. And he usually got the bus with Harry.

Then she'd received a call from the headmaster to say he hadn't turned up for registration. She'd rushed out of the gallery and driven around until she'd found him, walking on the Downs, in the cold, his breath clouding in front of him. When she'd asked him where he'd been, he told her he'd missed the bus and decided to walk and had then got lost in the fog. She hadn't believed a word of it, of course. He'd been living in Bristol all his life and his school was a forty-minute walk at the most. Yes, it would have made him late but there's no way he would have got lost going from Stokes Bishop to his posh school near the centre of town.

'Well, lucky I'm here, then,' she says, trying to keep her tone light so as not to antagonize her once placid son.

It was when he turned fourteen that he changed, practically overnight, from a chilled-out kid to an angsty, defensive bag of hormones. She'd heard it could happen from friends with older kids but she'd never thought it would apply to her boys. She'd brought them up well – being a good mother was just as important to her as being a good wife and daughter. Her own disastrous childhood, before she'd come to live with Elspeth, had made her determined to be the best mum she could be to her kids. And she'd thought she'd succeeded. Until last year.

Not that she could admit any of it to Elspeth. Elspeth wouldn't understand. She knows her mother prefers girls. She remembers only too well how her mother had sent back little Tommy, a boy she was going to adopt before Kathryn because he'd been 'too naughty'.

'Did Grandma ask after us?' Jacob asks from the front passenger seat.

'Of course. Always,' she lies. The sad truth is, Elspeth doesn't give a shit about her grandsons. Kathryn worked that out years ago. She remembers visiting her mother with a newborn Jacob, a beautiful chubby baby with big brown eyes and apple cheeks. Elspeth had looked faintly disgusted when Kathryn handed him to her, as though he was some mangy animal that smelt. She'd swiftly returned him to her with a rictus smile, and Kathryn had been so hurt she'd gone home and cried. Throughout Kathryn's second pregnancy she could see how hopeful her mother was that she'd have a little girl. Every time Kathryn saw her Elspeth had announced that she was carrying this baby differently. Comments like 'Your bump is all around the side and you're looking swollen. I think it's a girl,' or 'You've not been nearly as sick this time. Have you noticed?' And when she gave birth to Harry her feelings had oscillated wildly. On one hand she knew that if she'd given her mother that much-wanted granddaughter she'd lose all control and Elspeth would take over, but on the other a granddaughter might have made her mother love Kathryn more.

'I haven't seen her in months.' Jacob's voice brings her back to the present.

Kathryn tries to hide her surprise. 'Do you want to see her?'

He grunts. 'Not particularly. She never asks me questions. Not like Nanny Mols.' Nanny Mols – Molly – is Ed's mum, a lovely, plump-cheeked, smiley lady who dotes on Ed, as well as her only grandchildren.

'I think Grandma has a lot on her mind. And she's older than Nanny Mols, remember. I wouldn't take it personally. Grandma is like that with everyone.'

'I'm not taking it personally,' he snaps, and Kathryn wants to kick herself for saying the wrong thing. Again.

She wants to scream at him. To tell him to be thankful for the home he has, for the life he's got. *You could have had a childhood like mine,* she's tempted to say. *A mother overdosing in front of you. Being pushed from pillar to post. And then finally finding a family only to discover they have their own demons and dark secrets.* But she doesn't say any of this, of course. She bites her lip and they drive the rest of the way in silence.

20

It was 31 October. Viola's thirteenth birthday.

Katy thought it was apt that Viola should have her birthday on Halloween. In the three months she'd been living under the same roof as her sister, she had come to realize that something very dark lurked behind Viola's beautiful veneer.

She had done everything in her power to make friends with Viola, not least because she knew that was what Elspeth expected, and she had vowed to do whatever her new mother wanted to avoid being sent back to the home, like Tommy. She'd hated it there. Nothing in the home had belonged to her – everything was shared: the TV, the tatty second-hand toys in the playroom. Worse than that, there was no love. She even let Elspeth call her by her full name, Kathryn, when nobody else did. 'I don't like to shorten names, darling girl,' she'd said, wrinkling her nose.

Once when passing the sitting room she overheard Elspeth talking in a low voice to Huw about how she'd assumed adopting a girl would help Viola become a 'nicer person and less spoilt'. Her voice had been filled with disappointment, which terrified Katy. Would they send her back if Viola didn't like her?

Her new bedroom was supposed to be across the landing

from Viola's but her sister had made such a fuss that, in the end, to appease her, Elspeth had said Katy could live in the attic.

'I'll decorate it for you however you like,' promised Elspeth, her blue eyes silently pleading with her not to make a fuss. Which Katy would never do. She was there to make Elspeth happy. And it was clear Viola made her mother very unhappy. Viola seemed to make it her mission to behave as appallingly to her parents as possible. 'You can have your own bathroom and everything.'

'As long as she's not sleeping anywhere near me, I don't care,' snapped Viola, her eyes blazing. 'I don't want to catch her fleas.'

Elspeth had screamed at her, told her she was spoilt and selfish, while Huw looked on with a worried expression on his usually benign face. 'Now hang on a minute, Elspeth, that's a bit harsh,' he said, as Viola pushed past them on the landing and ran crying to her bedroom. Katy was pleased that Elspeth had stood up for her while Huw did nothing. He was like a big bear that always seemed to get in the way and Elspeth was always snapping at him, as if she found his presence particularly irritating. He was too laid back. He should be telling Viola off for being rude instead of accusing Elspeth of being harsh. She could see why Viola was so spoilt with a father like him.

Elspeth had come over faint then, stating that she was exhausted and had to lie down, leaving Katy and Huw standing awkwardly in the doorway of the bedroom that was no longer going to be Katy's, not knowing what to say to each other. Eventually Huw had patted Katy's shoulder and said he'd make the attic look nice for her. In the meantime she had to bed down with the boxes and cobwebs, spiders and dust, until the builders came in to make the bathroom and knock the two rooms into one. Katy didn't mind. She had a good view of the garden from up there, and she could hear the conversations that filtered through the windows from below. She had her own private space – her own floor – in a beautiful house and that was all that mattered to her.

For weeks, Viola had been talking about a Halloween party to celebrate her birthday. She was going to invite her friends from school, she'd say loudly, whenever Katy was in earshot. Already Katy hated the snooty girls' school she had to attend, with the stuffy pinafore and starched-shirt combo she was forced to wear. Everyone made fun of her accent when she opened her mouth, so she decided the best thing was to keep quiet. Even though Viola was two school years above her, her popularity and hatred of Katy filtered down through the pupils, which resulted in everyone giving her a wide berth as though she was infectious and riddled with lice – which was probably what Viola had been telling everyone. Katy tried not to care. She was used to keeping herself to herself. It had served her well at the children's home and it would protect her here.

Elspeth had gone to town on the house, decorating every inch of it with fake cobwebs, furry spiders, pumpkins with sinister faces carved into them (Katy was made to help with this and hated it because the orange flesh stuck to her fingers), ugly gargoyles, witches' broomsticks, hanging bats. It was grotesque and changed the feeling of the house from pretty and dreamlike to ugly and nightmarish.

Viola's friends were to arrive at five o'clock for some food, then go trick or treating. It wasn't clear to Katy if she was invited, although Elspeth had given her an unflattering witch's costume with stripy tights that kept falling down and a pointed hat that itched her head. Viola looked beautiful in a white dress, even with the scary face paint. She wasn't quite sure who Viola was supposed to be but she admired the long Victorian-style dress, all chiffon, lace and petticoats, and glanced down at her own costume feeling like Cinderella in rags.

Viola's friends were dressed in similar outfits to hers, Gothic and glamorous-looking, with red-painted lips, white faces and too much perfume. And they pranced about the kitchen, giggling and dancing, whispering behind their hands while Katy sat at the end of the table alone. Nobody spoke to her, except Elspeth and a kind-faced older woman called Franny, who was a cook-housekeeper, which Katy soon found meant she did all the jobs that Elspeth didn't want to do.

And then eventually Viola and her sycophantic cronies gathered as a crowd in the hallway, moving en masse as though they were one living organism, and Katy hung back, by the staircase. 'Viola, make sure you look after your sister,' called Elspeth, as she handed out plastic bags for them to collect their sweets. 'And don't be back too late.'

Katy noticed how Viola shuddered at the word 'sister' and her obvious loathing made Katy's eyes smart. Viola was determined to hate her – and, as a result, to cast herself in the role of tortured, misunderstood princess in her own little film, while Katy was the ogre.

Viola carried on out of the door, surrounded by her six friends, like maids-in-waiting, while Katy trailed pathetically behind. But they didn't head to the nearby houses, as she'd expected them to: they continued towards the suspension bridge.

'Um . . .' called Katy, running to keep up. 'Aren't we going trick or treating?'

'That's for babies,' one of Viola's friends scoffed, a pretty girl with long red hair and freckles.

'And the old farts around here won't give us anything interesting,' added another girl, with black hair and a green-painted face. Casey or Cassie. 'Half of them won't answer the door.'

'Then where are we going?' Katy could hear the panic in her voice.

But nobody answered. Instead they linked arms and giggled, running on ahead. She thought about going home but she was so desperate to join in, to show Viola she wasn't a baby, that she followed as they trudged across the bridge, the pavements shiny with rain, the lights refracting in puddles, trying to ignore her sweaty palms and feeling of dread. She had been in Bristol just a few months, miles away from the children's home in Gloucester, and still hadn't got her sense of direction but it seemed they were walking a long way. Too far. After they had crossed the bridge Viola and her friends continued, splashing through puddles and giggling, and Katy felt she had no choice but to follow, more despondent with every step. The road was dark on the other side of the bridge, with fewer streetlights, and dense trees that seemed to leer at Katy as she passed, their twigs like bony fingers pointing and jeering at her. And then they turned off the main road and skipped down a narrower street and then . . . And then they were climbing over a fence into a wooded area. Viola was atop the fence, laughing as her skirts caught and her friends were trying to release her, and all Katy kept thinking about was why they were going to the woods in the dark on Halloween.

Still she followed. She wasn't sure how to get home, and even if she could figure out the way she didn't fancy the walk in the dark by herself. She felt spooked. She'd have nightmares tonight, she just knew it, up in that attic room by herself. She trailed behind the other girls as they led her through the maze of trees, tried not to trip over the roots sticking out of the ground, like bones. The cold was biting at her ankles, like an angry monster. She could feel the wind through her thin witch's costume. Eventually they came to a clearing with a dip where there was a rope swing and a few logs. Viola and her friends stopped and gathered in a little circle around Katy. Their faces seemed sinister with the paint and the moonlight, and she had a feeling she knew what was about to happen.

'Fancy a game of hide and seek?' asked Viola. Katy could see something mean glinting in her eyes. It was dark, despite the full moon, with shadows elongating the trees so they looked threatening against the inky sky. She definitely didn't want to play hide and seek in the woods.

'I thought we were going trick or treating,' she said feebly. The other girls looked at each other and laughed.

'No. Trick or treating is for babies, like we've already said. Hide and seek is for big brave girls,' said Viola, standing in front of Katy. 'And you're going to be the one to count. Okay?'

No. It definitely wasn't okay. Katy didn't want to be left alone in the clearing to count while the others hid. She didn't want to be left alone at all. But she could hardly say that for fear of looking like a baby. She wanted – she needed – Viola to like her. To respect her. If Viola hated her Elspeth might send her away. She couldn't bear to go back to that children's home. Or the one before. That place had been even worse, with bars at the windows and a teenage boy who tried to get her into trouble and hid a penknife under his pillow, threatening to cut her if she told. She'd never had a proper family. She hadn't known her dad, and her mum had preferred going out and partying to staying at home and looking after her. Until that dark day three years ago when she had fallen asleep on the sofa and never woken up. She had sat with her mother for a full night and a day before she realized that something was very wrong and had gone to get Gladys, the sweet older lady from next door. That day she'd lost the little family she'd had and she couldn't lose this one. So, she found herself agreeing meekly and stood by the tree, her eyes shut while she counted loudly into the night. There was the smell of damp and bonfires in the air. She heard the scurry of footsteps, the bark of laughter, then nothing. Just the haunting shriek of a fox and the rustling of branches.

After she'd finished counting, Katy called their names, then wandered around the clearing, desperate to catch sight of Viola's white dress or Cassie's green cloak, hoping they were hiding behind the thick tree trunks. But eventually, when it was obvious they'd dumped her in the woods and weren't coming back, she screamed for them, her throat hoarse from crying.

She tried to find her way out, but all the paths looked the same and she was sure there was something up ahead, its yellow eyes watching her, slinking through the undergrowth. An owl hooted from one of the trees and there was another sound, something animalistic and frightening. In desperation she ran back to the clearing, tearing her costume on brambles and branches in her panic, slumping at the foot of the large oak tree where they'd left her, rocking and crying, her arms folded around herself as though to ward off the horrors. She was going to die. She knew that with a certainty she'd never felt before. She was going to be killed in these woods. And if she did die, would anyone care?

She wasn't sure how long she was out in the cold and the dark, for sheer terror numbed all her senses, but eventually she heard voices. Adult voices and then, like a miracle, Huw and Elspeth were standing before her, Viola hovering behind them, crying. Huw scooped her up in his big bear arms and carried her through the woods, through the night.

21

Elspeth is sitting in her favourite chair in the lounge, pretending to read a book. I've come to realize it's her way of sending me to Coventry, as my mum used to say. When she's in this mood I have no choice but to sit there with her. I have nothing to read as I left my book upstairs, and the one time I brought it down with me Elspeth had stared at me disapprovingly, as though I was slacking. As if I couldn't do my job properly unless I sat, watchful and quiet, like a guard at Buckingham Palace. She even made a disparaging comment about how I should be 'expanding' my reading material to 'open' my mind. So I stare into space and try not to feel uncomfortable while, every now and again, puncturing the torturous silence with 'Would you like a cup of tea?' which she always refuses, probably because she doesn't want to give me the luxury of going down to the kitchen to talk to Aggie. I've come to understand that this is what Elspeth likes to do best: play mind games.

I've not heard from Lewis since our kiss the other night. And I have a feeling I won't. There was something final, almost aggressive, about that kiss. I felt it was his way of saying goodbye to me. It would be hard to make it work, what with Elspeth detesting him. I called Peter a few times to tell him about my meeting with Lewis, but he didn't answer his phone and I never left a message.

I make an excuse that I need the bathroom, anything to get away from Elspeth and her moods for a few minutes. I sit in the bathroom just off the huge hallway for longer than I need to, staring at the china-blue patterned wall tiles and the ornate bone-white basin. I feel lonely and isolated. When I was working at the home and was having a bad day I had Cherry to gossip to. Here, there's no one I can chat to who understands how I feel, who's in the same position. The only other people who have been here before me are dead.

When I return to the lounge, she's no longer there. I feel a flutter of panic. What if she's wandered off somewhere and fallen down the stairs? Kathryn will accuse me of being negligent. I rush down to the kitchen, but it's empty. Aggie is out shopping for ingredients for dinner tonight. Maybe Elspeth's gone upstairs to lie down. I dart out of the kitchen and I'm just about to mount the stairs when I hear music coming from the direction of Elspeth's study. It sounds old-fashioned, something classical I vaguely recognize. I'm as silent as I can be on the flagstone tiles in my socked feet. I've never been in Elspeth's study before. It's usually locked. Now the door is open an inch or so and I stand outside, watching through the crack. At first I can see a mahogany desk and floor-to-ceiling bookshelves that span the whole wall to my left. But then I glimpse Elspeth.

She's dancing.

I take a step forward, unable to believe my eyes, but I'm not mistaken. Elspeth is dancing around the room, her arms framed as though in a waltz with an invisible partner. I'm so shocked that I can only stand there for a few minutes, frozen to the spot, watching her waltz around the room. Then the song comes to an end. She stops and I take a step back in case she sees me.

'Una!' she calls, her voice breaking the silence and I jump. I run to the stairs, trying to make out I've only just come down. 'Is that you? I'm in the study. I need your help.'

I return to the study where she's slumped into a chair, her hand on her heart. There is a film of sweat above her top lip. 'Can you help me up? While you were off doing God knows what, I got so fed up waiting for you I had no choice but to come down here alone. Now I'm out of breath and can't get out of this chair.'

I stare at her, puzzled. I long to tell her I saw her dancing around the room just a few minutes ago but I can't. She shoots me a look as though daring me to challenge her. Does she know I saw her?

'Well, don't just stand there,' she snaps. 'Help me up!'

I go to her and she grabs my arm as I lever her out of the chair. She clutches me as though she can barely walk and we return to the lounge in silence, my mind whirling. I've always suspected Elspeth wasn't as frail as she tried to make out, but still. The sight of her prancing around the room like a woman half her age and then her pretence at being unable to stand up has shocked me. She's even more manipulative than I thought.

The day is unbearably long. We don't go anywhere, and the only person I see is a postman delivering a canvas swathed in bubble-wrap that is nearly my height, which

I have to lug across the hall and into the library, while Elspeth says, 'Be careful, that's an expensive painting,' every five seconds. By the time we head to the kitchen for what Elspeth calls supper but I call tea I'm desperate for someone, anyone, to talk to. Aggie is bustling around us but we can't have a proper conversation with Elspeth's brooding presence sullying the atmosphere. She's perfectly pleasant to Aggie, which just highlights exactly what she thinks of me at the moment.

When Aggie goes out of the room, grimacing at me in solidarity over her shoulder as she leaves, I can bear it no longer. If I want to keep this job, I have to play the game too.

'You know,' I say, as I pick at my meat pie and potatoes, the atmosphere between us diminishing my appetite, 'I won't be seeing Lewis again. It was a mistake.'

She's sitting opposite me but she doesn't glance up from her food. And at first I wonder if she's even heard me as she pops a forkful of potato into her mouth elegantly and swallows. Then she looks up. 'That's good to know.'

'Can I ask . . .' I clear my throat, my palms sweating, hating myself for stooping to her level, but I need the money. I have to think of the future. '. . . why you dislike Lewis so much?'

She doesn't answer straight away and the silence that ensues makes my scalp prickle.

Eventually: 'He's got no prospects. He's a roamer, a loser. And I could smell . . .' she wrinkles her nose as though the memory troubles her '. . . marijuana on him.'

I want to laugh, but I don't. So that's why she sacked him. She thinks he's a pot head.

'I don't want a boyfriend,' I say truthfully. 'I've had it with men.'

I must have said the right thing, for once, because she looks at me, properly, for the first time today, her eyes lighting. 'Good for you,' she says. 'Now be a dear and go and fetch some wine from the cellar. I think this is cause for a celebration.'

I despise myself for matching her manipulation but I know I have to suck up to Elspeth if I want to survive this job for the next seven months. I diligently oblige her, even though I don't want a glass of wine, and go to the cellar, if you can call it that. It's a small room built underneath the house below the garden. You get to it by going out of the French windows and descending a few stone steps. It has a latched wooden door, with a padlock that, according to Elspeth, doesn't have a key but is more of a deterrent.

I push open the door and the smell of damp and rot hits me straight away. The ceilings are low, and even though I'm small, I still have to crouch as I enter. It's dark and a bit creepy with the cobwebs and rat droppings, and I have to hold my phone in front of me to light the way. I've never been in here before, and this is the first time Elspeth has suggested wine. Her moods swing faster than the pendulum of my gran's old grandfather clock. In the corner I notice a huge wine rack, the bottles covered with dust. They must have been down here for years. I wouldn't know an expensive vintage from a cheap bottle at Asda. I select one that looks like a white, although it's hard to tell in this light, but the label is pretty and it has Château

Something-or-other on the front. I hope it isn't too prestigious – it will be wasted on me. I don't even really like wine. I prefer shots that taste of peaches or strawberries.

I grip the bottle and make my way to the entrance when my leg knocks against something. I turn sharply, my heart pounding, worried I've brushed against a rat or some other animal, my phone casting an arc of light where I've swung my arm, eventually landing on the shape at my feet. I bend down. It's not an animal but a bag. On closer inspection I see that it's a canvas duffle bag, the handles fraying. Courtney's suspicions come back to haunt me and, for a mad moment, I wonder if the bag contains money. I said it in jest, but maybe I'm right. Maybe they are involved in something dodgy. I've obviously watched too many heist movies with Vince because, when I open the bag, there are only women's clothes shoved inside, as if someone has packed in a hurry. I'm about to dismiss it as old things ready to take to the charity shop but I notice a pair of jeans from a shop called Chelsea Girl. I can't imagine Elspeth or Kathryn ever owning such an item. Curiosity gets the better of me and before I know what I'm doing I'm rummaging through the bag, the bottle of wine forgotten at my feet. There's more clothes, a crop top, a floaty summer dress, a tatty pair of white tennis shoes, a few cardigans, two pairs of pyjamas with Snoopy on the front, as well as some Body Shop toiletries and a comb. There's no phone, or purse, and I'm just about to stuff everything back into the bag when I notice a passport tucked into one of the inside pockets. I take it out and open it, shining the light from my phone onto the photo.

A girl of around my age with blonde hair and a familiar face stares back at me. It's Jemima.

I hear a movement in the garden and I quickly return everything to the bag, zip it up, my heart pounding while my mind is still trying to process why Jemima's clothes are in Elspeth's cellar.

The door banging against the wall makes me jump. I turn. Someone is standing there.

22

Kathryn

She's found the bag. Of course she bloody well has. What did Kathryn expect? She should have hidden it better, buried it even. But she hadn't expected someone to be snooping in the cellar. It's usually only her that goes in there.

Una's trying to look nonchalant, which is hard when she's stooped, with a pained expression on her face. She witters on about Elspeth sending her here for some wine but Kathryn can tell by her panicked air and the way her eyes dart, almost unconsciously, towards the bag, that she knows.

What is she going to do now? *Think, Kathryn, think.*

She contemplates blocking Una's way, but what would that achieve? It would cause a scene, not to mention alert her mother. No, she wants to keep Elspeth out of this. And she can't very well trap Una in the cellar forever, tempting though that is.

Una walks towards her, the bottle of wine held in front of her, as if she's brandishing a weapon. Kathryn has no choice but to stand aside without speaking, and Una almost runs past her, while trying to appear as if everything is normal. It's almost comical.

Kathryn breathes in the dank smell of the cellar, her

mind working overtime. Then she kicks the bag further into the corner of the room. She'll have to come back and retrieve it. Burn it, if necessary. Maybe she could convince Ed to light a bonfire, until it dawns on her that Ed has never started a fire in his life and probably wouldn't know where to begin, and if she did go home requesting such a thing, how suspicious would it look?

Damn it. This wasn't supposed to happen. Nobody uses the cellar. Why has her mother decided to ask Una to come down here? And why can't anybody find the fucking key for the lock? It went missing years ago and nobody's ever bothered to replace it. Kathryn slams the door and stomps up the stairs towards the French windows. She'd only popped over to collect a painting her mother had bought from a local artist. Bloody ugly piece of a woman in a rocking chair holding a dog: the background is too dark, while the figures are cumbersome, as though the artist has used paint that was too thick. Kathryn worries that her mother's eye for art isn't as good as it once was. And when Elspeth had told her Una was in the cellar, Kathryn remembered with a sudden panic that that was where she'd dumped the bag.

When she returns to the kitchen, Una and her mother are sipping wine from Elspeth's best crystal. Not that Una seems to be enjoying it. Every swallow looks to be an effort. She doesn't meet Kathryn's gaze.

Elspeth's eyes are bright. Too bright. Playful. Cruel. Kathryn braces herself for some acidic comment that's obviously brewing in her mother. And, sure enough, 'Checking up on Una, are we?' she says to Kathryn, a smirk on her lips. 'Satisfied she hasn't made off with the Pétrus?'

Kathryn bristles. Why can't her mother make her feel, just once, that she's the most important – the most loved – person in the room? Instead she's always the butt of her nasty comments. She doesn't bother to respond. Instead she throws her mother a withering look and turns to Una. 'Well, I'd better be off. Una, would you mind helping me carry the painting to the car? I'm parked right outside.'

Una looks as if she'd rather do anything else but she pushes her seat back obligingly and follows Kathryn to the library, like an obedient pet. She doesn't speak and neither does Kathryn as they heave the painting from the house and into the trunk of Kathryn's SUV. Kathryn can just make out the ugly hues and clumsy paint strokes from beneath the bubble-wrap. A Picasso it isn't.

'You'd better get back inside,' says Kathryn, closing the boot on the painting. There is ice on the ground, sparkling under the streetlamps, like tiny crystals. Una is shivering in her thin jumper, with the cut-out shapes in the arms, and her ripped jeans. Una pauses, as if wondering whether to say something, but must decide against it as she turns away and walks back into the house.

Kathryn has no choice but to drive to the end of the road and then wait. From here she still has a view of the house and, more importantly, of her mother's bedroom window. She must be mad, she thinks, as she chews her nails, a habit that hasn't disappeared since she was that anxious eight-year-old. She wonders what Ed is doing. She hopes he's putting the boys to bed. It might be only 9 p.m. but Harry needs his sleep and Jacob is probably still on the PlayStation. Ed is much more lenient about that kind of thing than she is. She hopes Jacob's been studying. His GCSEs are in a few months.

Does she worry about them more than is natural, her two boys? She wouldn't know. Elspeth never seemed to worry about her or Viola. Kathryn wants to give them the childhood she never had, with parents who love them unconditionally, but Jacob is so prickly, so troublesome. Although she's hopeful he's settled down now. Last year . . . well, last year was the worst of her adult life with Jacob truly rebelling, first running away from home so that he could stay over with whoever. And then there was the time she found him drunk on the Downs with a group of older boys. She'd done everything right, yet she was terrified that Jacob would end up like her birth-mother. Maybe it was in the genes and had skipped a generation.

She rings Ed to tell him she's been held up at work and to remind him to make sure Jacob's off the PlayStation. He sounds sleepy, distracted, but agrees, telling her not to worry, that she can rely on him. She ends the call wondering if she can.

It's over an hour before she notices Elspeth's bedroom light is on. She's freezing and her body aches from being in the same position for too long. She watches Una's silhouette in the sash window as she closes the curtains.

When Kathryn's certain she won't be seen, or heard, she creeps out of the car, down the street, into the front garden, slipping through the side gate until she's standing in front of the cellar again. She pulls the padlock from the bolt and pushes open the door. The creak reverberates into the dark night. Her plan is to take the bag and put it into the car until she can decide where to dispose of it.

The passport will be the main problem. Using her phone as a torch, she's almost on her hands and knees as she feels her way to the corner, where she'd kicked the bag earlier. She reaches out her hand, hoping to feel it, to see the familiar canvas bag. But it's an empty space, just cobwebs and dust. The bag has gone.

23

'I've got the bag here,' I tell Courtney. I'm sitting cross-legged on the bed with the duffle bag open in front of me. 'It's got to be Jemima's. Her passport's here.'

Courtney takes a sharp intake of breath. 'Shit. I can't believe you took it.'

'I had to. I knew Kathryn would go back for it.'

'But what are you going to do with it?'

This is the part I've not really thought through. I just knew I had to get it before Kathryn moved it. Because it's evidence – I know that much. Kathryn said Jemima had left without a word, taking all her stuff with her while Elspeth was out. But her stuff is here. So somebody is lying.

I pull out a floral summer dress, my heart contracting for a girl I didn't even know. The girl who used to sleep in the bed I'm sitting on now, used to live in this house, this room. The girl whose job I'm doing, whose life I'm living. The girl who had been around the world, who liked to take selfies on exotic beaches, who looked like me. She'd even been out with Lewis too, kissed him, like me. I suddenly feel sick. 'Do you think I should go to the police?'

'Definitely,' says Courtney, firmly.

I groan. My first thought is that I could lose my job. My

dream of travelling disappears in front of me. Mum would be so disappointed. I think of my promise to her: to see the places she'd never get the chance to see. That dream will take a lot longer to come true without this job.

I fold the dress up carefully, respectfully, in the same way I handled my mother's clothes after she died, and place it back in the bag, my mobile clamped between my shoulder and my ear. The dress smells old and damp and there are black mould spores dotted in the fabric. 'I need to tell Peter.'

'Peter?'

'Jemima's brother. Remember? He was here last month because he wanted to find out who the guy was that Jemima was seeing. I tried calling him after meeting up with Lewis but haven't heard anything back.' I'm surprised I haven't heard from Peter. He was so adamant that we keep in touch, wanting me to find out who Jemima's mystery man had been. It's strange that he hasn't got back to me.

Courtney's voice is serious when she next speaks. 'I think you should stay here tonight. I don't think it's safe.'

Despite myself I laugh. Which is a normal reaction for me when I'm nervous or scared. When my mum broke it to me that she had cancer my first reaction was to laugh. 'It's only Elspeth here with me tonight. She's an old lady. She wouldn't have harmed Jemima.'

'What about the daughter? That Kathryn? She sounds like a heartless cow from what you've told me. And you said yourself she's never liked you.'

Even though everything I've told Courtney is true, I can't believe that Kathryn is a murderer. I say as much to my friend. 'But she might not have set out to kill her,' says Courtney, impatiently. 'Something's obviously happened, though. Kathryn told you Jemima left with her stuff and that they'd all assumed she'd gone off travelling. Yet now we've learnt she died that same day. And Kathryn was obviously lying. Otherwise why would she have her stuff in the bloody cellar? Christ, Una, what other conclusion is there? And,' she continues, barely drawing breath, 'when she goes back to the cellar and sees the bag's missing she's going to know you took it.' She exhales, as though exhausted by her outburst.

I haven't really thought any of this through. It was instinct that made me take the bag. And now I'm regretting it. 'Maybe I should just put it back,' I mumble. My phone feels hot against my face so I move it to the other ear. My hands are sweating. 'Pretend I never saw it.'

'What? No. You can't do that! You've got a responsibility to give it to the police.'

'But it will open up a massive can of worms. There might be a simple explanation . . .'

'There might be. Although I can't think what. Do you want me to come with you to the station tomorrow?'

'No, it's fine,' I say, when the truth is I don't know how I'm going to give Elspeth the slip. I'm with her all day. I'm going to have to act normally around her and Kathryn, even though, now I know they lied, the thought of being alone with either of them fills me with dread. My heart starts to race. What am I going to do? Kathryn will know I've taken the bag. Courtney is right to be worried. 'We've got a few days,' I say, trying to sound more positive than I feel. 'Kathryn won't be over until Saturday now, anyway, so even if she does look for it then . . .' I pause as I notice a shadow moving under my bedroom door. I lower my voice. 'I think she's here.'

'What? Are you sure?'

'I don't know,' I whisper. 'There was a movement under my door like someone walked past. Elspeth is in bed.' I let the implication hang in the air.

Courtney sounds horrified. 'Have you locked your door?'

'Yes.'

'Then she can't do anything.'

'I think she has a spare key. I've caught her in my room before and I told you about the other night '

'Oh, for goodness' sake, Una.' She sounds like my mum. 'I told you, didn't I? I said you should leave after you found out that both Matilde and Jemima are dead. But you thought I was overreacting. And now look.'

'Courtney, stop it. It'll be fine, she's not about to murder me in my bed. I'd better go. I'll ring you in the morning.'

She starts to protest but I end the call and throw my phone to the end of the bed. Even though we're the same age Courtney has always been the mature one, the leader of us both. Like a big sister. Maybe she's right. Maybe I should leave. But I need this job. I don't know what to do. I have to think it through before I make any rash decisions.

I can't admit to her that I am actually scared. I wish I'd never found the bag. But then I think of Jemima. The same age as me and dead. Her brother doesn't believe she took her own life, so what does that mean? That she had an accident? Was murdered? Either way, Peter deserves to know the truth. And if Kathryn is responsible, or knows more than she's letting on, she should be punished. Courtney's right. It's my responsibility now. I have to take Jemima's bag to the police and I have to tell them where I found it.

I get up and look wildly about the room. Where can I hide it? Then I remember the cupboard under the sink where I found Jemima's necklace. The panel is loose. I go to the en-suite, getting on my hands and knees with the bag next to me. I inspect the panel. Yes, there's just enough room to shove the bag behind it. Once I've done so, I stand up and tiptoe to my bedroom door, feeling slightly foolish, but if Kathryn is standing there, listening, I need to know. Quietly I turn the key and throw open the door. But the corridor is empty.

Your hair is hanging loose, the roots are too dark and a little greasy. You have bruises under your eyes and there is a spot on your chin. You try to look nonchalant as you take that old hag on her frivolous trips to the hair salon. But it's getting to you. I'm getting to you.

Your fear is so visible. It's in the way you hold yourself, too stiffly, as you walk. It's in the way your features pinch as you try to laugh. It's in your greasy hair and your pallid skin.

You're more problematic than the one before, more inquisitive. Nosy. You won't leave things alone. But your nosiness has cost you, dear Una.

I've enjoyed watching you. Playing with you. I'd have happily done so for a little bit longer. But you've left me no choice.

This has to end.

24

Una

I wake early the next morning, the darkness inching its way around the edges of my curtains and filling the room so that I feel oppressed by it. Why does everything seem so much worse in the dark? I barely slept last night – every little noise had me on edge – and now I'm exhausted and emotional.

I reach for my phone. Still no word from Peter. It's only five thirty and, if he's working nights, or is asleep, he might not pick up. But I dial his number anyway. When it goes straight to voicemail I decide to leave a message for once, and whisper into my phone. 'Peter. It's Una. Sorry for the early hour. I really need to speak to you. I've . . .' I hesitate, not wanting to say too much in a message '. . . I've found something. I think it's important. Please call me back as soon as you can.'

Half an hour later, as I'm helping Elspeth dress, my phone buzzes. I can tell she's not pleased at the intrusion as her eyes flicker disapprovingly to where it's wedged in the back pocket of my jeans. I ignore the call and continue assisting her into her favourite pale green tweed skirt and silk blouse. I'm hoping it's Peter, but even if it is I can't speak to him with Elspeth in such close proximity.

My phone rings again. 'Aren't you going to answer

that?' snaps Elspeth. She's perched on the edge of the bed and I'm bending over to help her with her 'indoor shoes'. She refuses to call them slippers.

I stand up and reach for my phone. Courtney's name flashes up on the screen. I press decline and turn it off. 'No, it's not important,' I say.

While Elspeth has a midday nap, I tap out a quick text to Courtney: *I'll ring you later. I can't go to the police today. I'm working. I'll go tomorrow as it's my day off. Xx*

A reply pings back straight away: *I think you're mad. You should take it today! It could be important.*

I'm beginning to wish I'd never told Courtney. As much as I love her, and we complement each other as friends, we are different. Courtney is bossy, opinionated and always thinks she's right. Usually I respect her opinion. She's always been wise beyond her years, but I have to handle this in my own way. It's my job on the line. And my home. I can't go around ruffling feathers. I wish I could ring Mum for advice. Although I know she'd agree with Courtney. Damn it. I hate it when Courtney's right. But logistically I can't just say, 'Oh, by the way, Elspeth, I'm off to the police station to turn your daughter in because I've found Jemima's stuff that she's hidden and she's obviously lying about what happened the day she died. But please can I keep my job?'

Then I think of the bag hidden in the en-suite upstairs, like an unexploded bomb that could go off any second, destroying us all. I owe it to Jemima to take it to the police. If she didn't take her own life, if something else happened that day, then her family – Peter – deserves to know. And if Kathryn did hurt her, she deserves to be punished.

'Penny for them, ducky.'

I'm so deep in thought I don't hear Aggie come into the kitchen until she's right beside me. I look up at her round, friendly face. She's known the McKenzies forever. Can I trust her? Then I think of how much she's gossiped to me and know I can't. I like Aggie, she makes this job bearable, but she's been here since Kathryn was a teenager. Surely her loyalty will lie with her. And I can't risk her telling Kathryn. But then Kathryn will know I took the bag. Who else could it have been? Urgh, I'm doing my own head in.

'I'm fine,' I lie. 'Just tired.' I try to smile but she doesn't look convinced.

She takes a seat next to me and lowers her voice. 'I know working here can be . . .' she glances around to make sure Elspeth isn't creeping into the kitchen '. . . problematic, but stick with it. It's good money, the house is lovely, the location convenient.' She pats my hand. 'I know it can be boring for a young girl like yourself to be stuck with old folk like us, but do it for a year and think of the money.'

I laugh in spite of the turmoil I feel. 'Thanks, Aggie. I intend to.' And then I find myself telling her a little about Mum and her illness, the promise I made to her.

Her face is full of sympathy and I flush when she gives me a quick hug. 'I'm so sorry to hear about your mam. Hopefully one day you'll go off and see the world for the both of you.'

I don't tell her I'm hoping to do it by the end of the year in case she lets slip to Elspeth. Although I can't think that far ahead at the moment. All I can think about is that bloody bag upstairs.

'Aggie . . .' I pause. She's been so kind to me, so warm and understanding about my mum that I suddenly feel closer to her. 'I found Jemima's stuff. In the cellar.'

She looks puzzled. 'What do you mean?'

And I explain about getting the wine last night and finding the bag, how Kathryn had come into the cellar and how I was worried she'd come back for it so I hid it in my room.

'How do you know Kathryn put it there?' she asks, after I've finished.

'I . . .' Why *do* I think it's Kathryn? She's right. 'I don't know. She was acting weird. And her eyes went to the bag at my feet and I could tell she knew exactly what it was. And it's hardly going to be Elspeth, is it? She'd find it hard getting down those steep steps by herself.' And then I remember her dancing, her surprising agility, although she did seem out of breath afterwards. Maybe those steps wouldn't be a challenge.

Aggie shakes her head, her face troubled. 'Maybe you should just put the bag back. Forget you found it.'

'Aggie!' I gasp. 'I can't do that! Don't you think it's suspicious?'

She gets up and wanders over to the Aga. I feel a thud of disappointment. I should never have told her. My initial instincts were right. She's been with the family too long. Of course she'll try to protect them.

I get up and go over to her. She's busying herself making tea but I can tell her mind is working overtime.

'What if Kathryn is responsible for Jemima's death?' I say.

She rounds on me, her apple cheeks pink. 'Of course

she's not. She wouldn't hurt a fly, that one. The poor girl. All these years playing second fiddle first to Viola, then to whatever waif or stray her mother took under her wing, or whichever new cause Elspeth had – those impoverished artists or fundraising for the local church. And then to Matilde and Jemima. Of course she's going to be resentful. But murder Jemima? Of course not.'

'Aggie . . .' I hesitate. 'Jemima's brother is adamant she'd never take her own life. Something happened.'

Aggie waves her hand dismissively. 'Of course her brother doesn't want to think his sister killed herself. Who would want to think that?'

'Then why would Jemima's stuff be hidden in Elspeth's cellar?' My tone is harder than I intend but I'm starting to feel frustrated.

Aggie opens her mouth to speak and closes it again. She leans against the bars of the Aga, clearly deflated, and I wish I hadn't told her. I've burdened her with this secret now. I can see she's already weighed down by it.

I place a hand on her shoulder. 'I'm sorry. I should never have told you.'

She shakes her head and I notice tears in her eyes. I can tell she's struggling to speak but then she straightens up and my hand falls away.

'I love Kathryn. I worry about her.'

I hang my head. 'I know.'

'She was a teenager when I first started this job and she was so . . . beaten.'

'Beaten?' I ask, horrified.

'By life,' she clarifies. 'She'd had such a sad childhood and then she comes here and Viola is the golden girl. But

Viola was always a free spirit, wilful. She didn't want to conform to Elspeth's old-fashioned rules. Kathryn, on the other hand, was so eager to please. She was like a loyal puppy, the way she followed Elspeth everywhere. And then Viola fell in love with a boy Elspeth said was unsuitable and ran away with him as soon as she turned eighteen. And it was good for Kathryn, in a way, because it gave her the chance to shine. Elspeth was so angry with Viola that she told her never to darken her door again. I think she regrets that now, of course, because Viola's stayed away. Nobody knows where she is. And I think, on some level, Elspeth always blamed Kathryn for Viola's disappearance.'

A chill runs down my back as I let Aggie's words sink in. 'What do you mean?'

'Well, she felt it was Kathryn's fault Viola left. And she began to resent her. And the more she resented her, the more Kathryn tried to please. It broke my heart to see it.'

Aggie pauses, a wariness in her eyes as she assesses me. 'You know, when Matilde started here it was obvious as soon as I saw her.'

I frown. 'What was?'

'How much she looked like Viola.'

The breath has been knocked out of me.

'And Jemima. And you. You all look like her.'

The realization hits me. 'So you're saying Elspeth chose us because we look like the daughter who ran away?'

She nods. 'I think so. Yes.'

'But that's – that's messed up.'

We fall silent, but I can tell Aggie hasn't finished. She pours hot water into a cup and dunks a teabag. 'There's something I've never told anyone,' she says ominously.

I'm still reeling from the Viola revelation. 'Okay,' I say, as she hands me a mug. We're talking in hushed voices even though nobody else is around.

'The day Jemima left. I came back into the kitchen because I'd forgotten the potatoes. Elspeth said I could take them home for my tea. My Stanley dropped me off so I could pick them up. And I heard them.'

'Who?'

'Kathryn and Jemima. They were in the hallway and I could hear them screaming at each other.'

'What time was it?'

'Well, it was already dark, so I'd say about five. Five thirty.'

'And what were they arguing about?'

She picks up her mug and clasps her meaty hands around it, but doesn't take a sip. 'That's the thing. It was hard to tell, exactly. I'd come in halfway through but I heard the words "will" and "gallery". Then I heard the front door slam and silence.'

My heart picks up speed. 'Silence? Do you think they both went out?'

'I can't be certain, but I think so.' She sips her tea thoughtfully. 'And that was the last time I saw Jemima. I turned up for work the next day and Elspeth said Jemima had gone, taking her belongings with her.'

'When really her belongings were in the cellar,' I say.

Aggie nods gravely, then puts a warm hand on my arm. 'Take the bag to the police, ducky. I can't see what else you could do.'

25

Una

I'm alone in my room, eating a packet of Cheddars from my snack drawer. Elspeth is in bed and Aggie has left for the night. I keep mulling over what she said about Kathryn arguing with Jemima on the day she died. I wonder what happened. Did Kathryn follow Jemima that day? Did they continue their argument? How did Jemima fall off the bridge? Did Kathryn push her? Was it an accident and Kathryn was too scared to tell anyone, so she hid Jemima's stuff and pretended she'd moved away?

I get out my phone to ring Courtney when a text comes up from an unknown number.

This is Peter. My phone broke so I had to get another, hence the new number. I'm in Clifton. Would you meet me at the bridge? We need to talk.

I look at the clock. It's nine thirty. Does he mean now? *When?* I text back.

His reply is instant. *ASAP.*

Adrenalin surges through me. Could I do this? Leave Elspeth in bed and sneak out? It's one of Elspeth's rules. She doesn't like being in the house on her own at night. But I'd be gone half an hour at most, I reason. She's asleep. She'll never know. But it's unprofessional. I begin pacing my 'rooms'. I don't know what to do. I glance out of the front window. It's so dark and fog rolls over the hills in the distance, obscuring the top of the suspension bridge. It's only a stone's throw away. Maybe I could go and meet him, then sneak him into the house. We could go into the kitchen and if Elspeth does wake I can answer her, but she won't see Peter. It's not something I would normally contemplate doing, but this is important. It's not like I'm sneaking out to meet a boyfriend. I have to tell him about his sister's bag. And then – my heart beats faster when I think of it – he could take it to the police. Which means I don't have to hand in my employer's daughter. Kathryn need never know I had anything to do with it. She might suspect, yes, but she can't prove it. I'll be off the hook.

I've lost my appetite so return the Cheddars to my drawer. Then I pull a brush through my hair and grab my maroon coat from the wardrobe, slipping it on and pressing my furry hat onto my head. I hesitate. What am I doing? Is this safe? Do I really want to be walking to the bridge alone in the dark? Jemima died there. I stand in the middle of the room, deliberating. It's Peter, I reason. He can hardly come to the house to meet me. I grab my phone and decide to text Courtney. It's something we've always done since we were teenagers if we were about to go somewhere alone. It was drummed into us by our parents: Tell Someone Where You're Going. *I've heard from Peter. He wants to meet. I'm going to tell him about the bag (which I've hidden) and he can go to the police. I'm about to meet him now. Xx*

And then I leave the house, mobile in hand like a weapon.

It's cold outside, the sky moonless. The fog gets thicker and more dense as I head to the bridge. The road outside

Elspeth's house is empty on this cold Friday evening in February, and as I walk across the green, the grass snapping underfoot, I almost turn back. Am I crazy? I'm meeting a near-stranger at night on my own. But it's only nine thirty, I reassure myself. It's not late. People are still about: a man's letting his dog sniff the bench over there, and a couple are strolling towards the pub at the end of the road. There aren't many cars but that's because it's so foggy. It's fine. It's fine. I repeat this to myself, like a mantra, as I step onto the bridge.

There's no sign of Peter. Not that I can really see: the fog seems thicker up here. I look over the bridge and it's almost as if I'm floating on a cloud. I can't see the gorge beneath me. I can hardly make out Elspeth's house from here, either. The comforting lights at the windows and the figures of other people have been blocked out by the weather.

I text Peter's new number. *I'm at the edge of the bridge where the cars come in. Where are you?*

I wait with the phone in my hand for his reply but there's nothing.

Then I see a text from Courtney. *Are you mental? Don't meet Peter in the dark. Get him to go to the house. Xx*

She's right, this is a stupid idea. I was lulled into thinking it was okay because it's not that late and the bridge isn't too far away. But with the fog and the silence, well, it's eerie up here. I feel like I'm a million miles from civilization. The fog is all-consuming, wrapping around me, like cotton wool. I can only see a few inches in front of me. Maybe Peter didn't mean the bridge, maybe he meant somewhere else like – I trip and my phone shoots out of my hand. I hear it land with a crack on the pavement. Shit. Shit. I crouch on my hands and knees. Where's it gone? I can't see it. Has it gone over the side?

'Peter!' I shout. My voice is tinged with panic and disappears into the ether. 'Where are you?' There's no answer and I freeze, my heart in my throat, as I realize that Peter isn't coming. Was it even Peter who texted me? It could have been anyone. It could have been Kathryn. I stand up, blindly trying to reach for something to cling to. 'Who's there?' My heart beats faster and I walk through the fog, towards where I know the entrance is.

I think of my mum. Is she watching over me? She'd be furious that I've put myself in this position. *Oh, Mum, I'm sorry.*

The rising fog mingles with the dark night, turning everything opaque. I can barely see yet I know someone else is on the suspension bridge with me.

I can hear them breathing.

How foolish I've been.

Nobody will come to my rescue. It's too late at night – even vehicles have stopped driving across the bridge due to the weather.

Someone calls my name. I turn, but I'm disoriented and I can't tell which direction the voice is coming from. I just know I've been lured here. I need to find a way off this bridge as quickly as I can. I let go of the railings, stumbling in panic, my breath quickening.

Don't lose it. I must stay calm. I need to get out of this situation alive.

Suicide. That's what they'll say it was. Just like the other girls.

I hear a laugh. It sounds manic. Taunting.

And then a figure steps out of the fog, clamping a hand across my mouth before I've had the chance to scream.

part two

26

Willow, March 2019

There's something going on in this house. They try to hide it from me, but it's evident in the whispered discussions I hear them all having with each other. The old woman, the cold fish of a daughter and that cook from the kitchen. They do it when they think I'm not listening. Not that I *am* listening. I couldn't give two hoots what they're wittering on about to each other. This is a short-term thing for me. Just to get some cash before I decide what I really want to do with my life.

It was Arlo who told me about the job. It was advertised in the local newspaper at the end of February. I think it was mainly because he was fed up with me staying with him in his manky studio apartment in Weston-super-Mare while I did the odd shift at the local café. 'Willow,' he'd say, putting on that serious big-brother expression whenever he was about to give me a lecture, 'You need to have direction,' as though he had some high-flying career when really he was driftwood, the same as me. He must have been moaning about me to one of his mates down the pub because they told him that a friend of a friend had seen this job advertised. Something like that, anyway. Arlo tends to waffle on a bit and I was only half listening because I was in the middle of watching reruns of *Line of*

Duty on Netflix. Anyway, I decided to go for it. A live-in position, in a grand house with my own bedroom away from my brother's stinky feet and foetid flat, is a plus point. And the money was really good for a carer role.

I'm apparently younger than their previous employees. This was told to me rather sniffily by the daughter, Kathryn, at the interview, as though youth is something to be embarrassed by. I'm twenty, love, I wanted to say. I'm hardly a child. And I have experience of caring for people. I was training to be a nurse at one point. I did the first year at university and everything. And I'm telling you, training to be a nurse is hardcore. They should be getting big salaries for what they have to put up with, honestly – all those long night shifts and bedpans and cleaning old men's private parts. Yes, I did it all and I'm not embarrassed to say I couldn't hack it – although, of course, I omitted to say that at the interview. I didn't want them to think I couldn't stick at things. I just went on about a bereavement and lack of money forcing me to leave, which was a bit of a white lie, but it got me the job.

So here I am. Two weeks in and already counting down the days until I can hand my notice in. Still, the job's a doddle, really. It didn't take me long to work out there was nothing wrong with the old woman. She just wants a bit of pampering and companionship. She can get to the toilet by herself, thankfully. And I make her laugh. I like that. I like to see her throw her head back so that her throat goes all crêpy and she properly belly-laughs. It's like, in that moment, she forgets she's some posh, stuck-up pensioner. It's the most honest I've seen her. And when I came she didn't look like she'd laughed for a long time.

There's a sadness about her blue eyes, too, as though she's lost many people in her life, and I can relate to that. Not that I've lost many people. Just a few important ones. Just enough to make me feel as though I'm adrift in the huge rough ocean that is my life.

I don't think I'm the cleverest person in the world – probably one of the reasons why I didn't pass my first year of nursing. But I believe I can read people, that I'm tuned in to them and can sense what they're feeling. And, in a weird way, I feel like that about Elspeth.

The daughter, on the other hand, I don't feel attuned to her. She's got a barrier around her so strong it's like a forcefield.

I'm allowed Wednesdays and Saturdays off, and apart from those days – when her daughter stays to cover me – I'm expected to be on hand 24/7. Not that I've got any friends in Bristol anyway. I'm not really familiar with the place, although I enjoy exploring on my days off. I quickly realize that Clifton is the posh part, with its Georgian houses, boutique-style shops and upmarket cafés, which are very different from the one where I worked in Weston-super-Mare. It's fun at first, accompanying Elspeth on her excursions to the hairdresser, or to the shops she owns. The other day I had to take her to a council meeting – something to do with the funding she raises for impoverished artists. Sometimes she just likes me to take her for a walk, and Clifton is beautiful in the spring, with the cherry blossom lining the pavements, like confetti, and the smell of flowers in the air. I love spring – it's like a fresh start. A renewal. Everything wakes up, like Sleeping Beauty, after a long sleep, blinking and marvelling at the sunshine with the birds singing and the smell of cut grass.

Elspeth likes to hear my stories of growing up in a hippie commune in Norfolk, or my experiences of moon-bathing. She's even fascinated by the strands of pink I have running through my dirty-blonde hair. I'd contemplated changing them after the interview, especially when the daughter, Kathryn, made some sarky comment about how could I expect to be taken seriously with 'coloured bits that look like dental floss' in my hair.

While I wouldn't say I actually enjoy the job, I've fallen into a routine. Kathryn tries to psych me out sometimes but I ignore her. I've met worse than her. Aggie, the cook, is a little cold towards me. She's perfectly polite and makes small-talk over lunch or if I'm in the kitchen preparing one of Elspeth's many cups of tea, but I feel she's holding something back. I'm sure I'm one in a long line of companions who have come and gone over the years. Perhaps she thinks I won't last long so there's little point in getting too attached to me. Or maybe she thinks I'm a weirdo with my pink-streaked hair, the ring in my nose and my tie-dye harem trousers. I don't look like I fit in with this posh house and all its finery, I know that. Frankly, I'm surprised they gave me the job. Maybe there weren't many applicants.

It's Saturday, my day off, and I decide to head to Gloucester Road for a change. It's a sunny day, fresh, hopeful. Hot-air balloons float in the distance, children are running about on the green fields adjacent to the suspension bridge, and couples walk arm in arm, their dogs beside them. There are people sitting outside cafés, families, lovers and friends.

There's still a nip in the air but next week it will be April. I'm wearing my favourite floral bomber jacket with loose-fitting silk trousers and cherry-coloured DM boots. I've got an appointment at a hair salon. I found a card in my room – it must have been left by my predecessor. The card was funky with bright colours and snazzy fonts. I knew I'd never be able to afford the place Elspeth goes to, so I thought I'd give A Cut Above a try.

The place is just as I'd imagined, all bright lights and loud music and hip stylists with radical haircuts. Radical is good. I'm waiting in Reception as instructed and flicking through *Cosmopolitan* when a girl with bright copper hair approaches me. It's so long it has to be extensions, I think, as I follow her through to a chair right at the end of the room next to the sinks.

'How can I help you today?' says the girl, as she assists me into a gown and I take a seat. She has very white teeth and thick, well-groomed eyebrows. She doesn't offer her name but she looks about my age. I wonder how much experience she has. Her skin is a flawless beige and I'm sure she's wearing fake eyelashes. They look as though they're weighing her eyes down, which, on closer inspection, look puffy as though she's not slept. Her heavy foundation isn't concealing the dark circles I detect either. She doesn't appear particularly friendly, not like the hairdressers I've had in the past, who natter away about their boyfriends and holidays and *Love Island*. She looks like the type who wouldn't be out of place as one of the popular mean girls in a US high-school drama.

I take a strand of pink between my fingers. 'I'm getting bored of the colour. Can I change it to blue?'

She smiles, but it doesn't reach her eyes. 'Sure, but I'm going to have to bleach it first.' She scoops up a handful of my hair. 'It's not great for the condition. Can I suggest you go back to your natural colour, then come in a few months to put in the blue?'

I wanted the blue to piss off stuck-up Kathryn. But maybe it's not a bad idea. Especially as I'm new to the job. Perhaps I'll impress the old lady, make her think I'm serious about the role. So I agree.

She runs her hands through my hair. 'Your last hairdresser overdid it a little on the pink,' she says, frowning.

I laugh. There's something straight to the point about this girl that's refreshing. 'Yep. It was one of my friends. She didn't really know what she was doing.'

A smile tugs at the edges of her lips. 'I can see that. Do you want any cut?'

Cut? I haven't had my hair cut in seven years. 'No, thanks. I like it this length.'

She looks doubtful and meets my eyes in the large rectangular mirror in front of me. 'I could take the ends off? Make it healthier?'

Not on your life. After the last hairdresser promised to 'take the ends off' I finished up with it on my shoulders. I'm not making that mistake again.

I decline politely and she shrugs. 'Okay, I'll just go and mix the colour.' She wanders away without offering me a drink. Another girl, who looks about fifteen with a very severe bleached buzz cut, wafts over to me in a cloud of Impulse and dumps a couple of glossy magazines in my lap without a word. Charming.

Five minutes later the stylist is back, wheeling a tray

containing bowls of bleach and colour and a pile of foils. She starts sectioning my hair, then catches my eye in the mirror. 'I'm so sorry. I didn't offer you a drink.'

I smile. 'That's okay.'

'Do you want one?'

I contemplate saying no as I don't want her to go to any trouble, plus she looks a bit stressed, but I'm actually really thirsty so I admit I'd love a cup of tea.

She calls to the fifteen-year-old, who scurries off to make it.

'So why did you want the blue?' she asks, as she brushes bleach onto my pink strands. The girl is back with my tea.

'I've just started a new job,' I say, reaching for my cup.

She laughs. It's throaty and I'm relieved she's thawed a little. 'And your employer wants you to have blue hair?'

I sip my tea and place it on the table in front of me, all without moving my body. 'No, the old woman I work for is okay. She's cool about it. It's her daughter who's all judgy. She hates the pink.' I tell her about the dental-floss jibe. 'So I thought I'd make it blue instead! Even more vibrant. Anything to piss her off. But now it will have to wait. Still,' I chuckle to show I'm joking, 'I'll have to find other ways to piss her off!'

I'm expecting her to laugh. At least to raise a smile. But she just nods and asks me where I'm from, as though she's following a script and isn't allowed to deviate from it. I tell her a bit about Norfolk and my restlessness, leaving uni and how I'm still trying to find the right career for me.

'What about travelling? Would you like to do that?'

'I did it for a bit but I need stability, really. A proper career. I have to start making money.'

She nods. She doesn't say much about herself, just fires questions at me in her endearing West Country accent, that tilts up at the end so it's like she's asking questions even when she's not. All the while she concertinas the foils and presses them to my head. I get the sense she isn't really listening. I'd rather read my magazine, to be honest, but I don't want to be rude.

After she's finished she leaves me, saying she'll be back in twenty minutes to take the foils off. I watch her in the mirror as she wheels the trolley away. There is something sorrowful about her under the haughty exterior, like she's putting on a front. It's like she's being weighed down by invisible armour. She stares into the distance as she blow-dries a woman's hair at the other end of the salon. She's just going through the motions. She's tall and very striking, with her long copper hair and porcelain skin. I watch her for a bit longer, trying to fathom her out. I do this a lot. Arlo says I'm nosy, but I sometimes wonder if I should go into psychology. I love to know what makes people tick.

I return to my magazine, glad of the peace. My jaw hurts from yabbering away. My tea has gone cold but nobody asks me if I'd like another cup.

After a while the copper-haired stylist is back. She checks one of the foils and seems satisfied, then sends me off with the fifteen-year-old to have my hair washed.

When I'm back in the chair the stylist combs out my hair. The colour is lovely, a soft ash blonde. I look more normal and I'm not sure how I feel about that. Maybe I'll be taken more seriously but, even so, I refuse to lose the nose ring.

She's drying my hair with a large brush, and it's not until she's finished that she looks at me properly. I'm busy assessing myself in the mirror and don't really notice the horror on her face until she speaks. I glance up and our eyes meet in the mirror. She's deathly white and I know it's a cliché but there's no other way to describe it. She's staring at me like she's seen a ghost.

27

Courtney

Courtney stares at this woman, *this imposter,* in shock. She's wholly aware she's being unprofessional but she can't seem to find her voice. She can't stop looking at her. She should have seen it straight away. She looks like Una: same hair and bone structure. She doesn't dress like Una, or sound like her, but she certainly resembles her physically. What was it Una had told her before? That the other companions had looked like her too. Bile rises in her throat when she remembers the conversations with her best friend and she has to swallow it. It burns in her chest.

'Are you okay?' the girl, Willow, asks, touching her newly coloured hair self-consciously. 'Is there something wrong with my hair?'

Courtney swallows the golf-ball-sized lump in her throat. 'No, sorry, it's all . . . It looks good. W-where did you say you worked again?' She had been half listening when Willow first sat down and started talking about her job. But now . . . now that she's been transformed in front of her very eyes, she remembers snatches of the conversation. *Elderly lady. Uptight daughter. Companion.* She can't be . . . can she?

Willow frowns and stands up, her black gown billowing around her like a cape. Courtney knows she should take it from her but instead she places her hands on

Willow's shoulders and forces her back into the seat. She leans forwards so that Tamsin, on her right, can't hear her. 'Is your employer Elspeth McKenzie by any chance?'

'Yes, that's right.' She looks annoyed, unsurprisingly, thinks Courtney, considering she's just manhandled her client and is keeping her prisoner in the chair.

Courtney's heart is racing. She hadn't noticed it when the girl first came in. But now . . . the resemblance to Una is breathtaking.

'Have you ever heard of a Una Richardson?'

She can tell Willow is swallowing her impatience. 'No. No, I haven't. Should I have?'

'She worked for Elspeth before you. She was . . .' She gulps. 'She was my best friend.'

Now she's got Willow's attention. She sits up straighter in the chair, her eyes locking with Courtney's in the mirror. 'Was?'

'She died.' It still feels wrong to say it. She'll never get used to it.

'Died?'

She takes a deep breath, aware she's going to sound crazy. But Willow deserves to know what she's letting herself in for. 'She died last month while she was still employed by the McKenzies.'

Willow fidgets in her chair. 'But . . . nobody's mentioned this at all.'

'And she's not the first. The first companion was a girl called Matilde. She lasted two years. She died in an apparent hit-and-run last summer. The second girl, Jemima, arrived in October. By Christmas she was dead. Suicide. And now Una . . .' Her best friend's name catches in

Courtney's throat on the end of a sob. She composes herself. She can't cry. She needs to take action. 'She texted me, just before it happened, to tell me she was meeting Peter – Jemima's brother – on the bridge. Peter, apparently, didn't believe his sister would have taken her own life. It wasn't until the next morning that Una was found. The police think she'd bashed her head on the ground after falling because it was foggy . . . It was foggy that night, you see. And cold. She died of hypothermia while unconscious.'

And she can't prove it, but Courtney knows. She knows with all her heart that Una hadn't just fallen on the bridge in the fog and banged her head. She'd gone out to meet someone – to meet Peter. Courtney had told the police all this. She'd ranted at them about Kathryn and Elspeth, and about Jemima and the bag, when she'd got to the hospital that day, but the police had looked at her as though she'd gone insane. And, of course, Kathryn denied the existence of a bag and this Peter Freeman denied the existence of any text messages to Una. And now Una was dead. Her best friend, the girl she'd grown up with, gone to school with, laughed with, lived with, was dead, her life, the essence of her, snuffed out in an instant. The girl who was kind, funny, who hated social media, who was private, who loved spreading butter on Rich Tea biscuits, who was a bit ditzy, who had never learnt to ride a bike, who wanted to see the world – gone. And everyone expected life to go back to normal when she, Courtney, knew her death was no accident.

'I'm so sorry,' says Willow, her eyes large in her petite face – blue, whereas Una's had been grey. 'That's awful. So she never met this Peter on the bridge?'

Courtney shakes her long ponytail. 'Nope. He denied ever sending a text. The police took his phone, analysed the history. All the usual stuff. But there was no evidence to suggest he had texted her that night. Just a panicked message on his voicemail from Una saying that she needed to speak to him because she'd found something. But he'd been busy with work. He's a firefighter. He'd never had the chance to return her calls or messages. Or so he said.'

'And what had she found?'

'A bag full of Jemima's clothes. In the cellar at Elspeth's house. She was convinced Kathryn took them.'

'Why would she do that?' Willow looks confused, so Courtney fills her in on what Una had told her, about the argument Jemima had apparently had with Kathryn before she left, how Kathryn had made out she'd done a runner and taken her stuff with her.

'So Kathryn knows more than she's letting on? She's a cold fish, that one, that's for sure.'

Courtney remembers. She remembers getting to the hospital after Una was found – she had been Una's emergency contact. A fruitless exercise, as it turned out, because Una was already dead and it had done nothing but give her false hope. Una had died on the bridge, enveloped in fog, like the embrace of the Grim Reaper, hidden from the world until the sun came up and chased the fog away. Kathryn had remained stony-faced while the doctor informed them of Una's passing. She hadn't reacted at all, while it was all Courtney could do to stop herself collapsing in a sobbing heap on the white-speckled hospital floor.

The next day Courtney had gone to the police station, propped up by a reluctant Kris, to tell them everything.

About the bag, Una's suspicions, Peter's apparent text message asking to meet. The police had been interested yet noncommittal in their response. They took the details she gave them, diligently without rushing her, and then they thanked her and said they'd let her know of any developments. Except they didn't. A week passed, and in the end, in desperation, she'd had to call them. That was when they'd told her about Peter and how there had been no messages on his phone arranging to meet Una. Una's own mobile, apparently, hadn't been found on her when she died. They think it must have slipped over the edge of the bridge and into the Avon Gorge, maybe when she fell. It all seemed rather too convenient for Courtney to swallow.

Kathryn had rung her shortly after Una had died, asking if she wanted Una's stuff. Not that there was much of it. Una lived lightly. But Courtney had said yes and had gone to Clifton to pick it up. It was the first time she'd seen the house where her best friend had worked. It was grander than she'd ever imagined. She hadn't met Elspeth. Kathryn told her that she was 'very upset' and was 'upstairs resting'. Then Kathryn had handed her a large backpack with a stony expression. Not even a 'sorry for your loss'. Courtney had almost snatched the bag from her before stalking off.

And now here she is. A new companion. A new victim.

Courtney had failed her best friend but she could help this girl, this stranger. She couldn't allow Kathryn or Elspeth to harm someone else. The police might not want to do anything but she'll avenge Una's death if it's the last thing she ever does. Una had a life, and someone took it. She won't give up until she finds out who – and why.

28

Willow

The house has taken on a new perspective now that I know the truth. It no longer looks like some elegant, benign building but a place linked with death. Where skeletons are locked in closets and nobody is as they seem. All very dramatic of me, I know. Arlo always said I should be an actress. Arlo says a lot of things, and usually he's being disparaging. Still, I can't stop thinking about what that hairdresser told me, and underneath the horror a little excitement bubbles, the kind of feeling you get when a neighbour has been arrested. You're not part of the action but you're near enough to it. And I don't feel in any danger from Elspeth or her daughter. Una sounded a bit naïve, foolish even, to put herself in that position. Maybe she really did fall and bang her head. Maybe Courtney's just looking for a link because two other girls who worked for Elspeth died.

Anyway, weirdly, Courtney invited me for a drink tonight. Some pub in Whiteladies Road where her boyfriend's band is playing. As I don't know anybody in Bristol, apart from the McKenzies, I agreed. And something about Courtney fascinates me, with her glamour and her grief, like a 1920s silent film star.

When I get back from the hairdresser's Elspeth is in the sitting room with her daughter. I can't resist popping my head around the door to say hello. Kathryn's eyes look as though they're about to pop out of her head. 'You've had your hair done,' she bleats faintly.

I smile. 'Yes. Back to blonde. For now.'

She grimaces in reply, but Elspeth pipes up from the corner of the room, 'I like it, it's very sleek,' which makes Kathryn's expression even grumpier.

I stifle a giggle. I'm just about to leave when Elspeth adds, 'Aggie's in the kitchen if you'd like her to rustle you up a late lunch. She's made a vegetarian casserole especially for you.'

I say thanks and head into the kitchen. Sure enough, Aggie's still here, her chubby arms elbow deep in the Belfast sink. She turns with the wary expression she usually adopts whenever she sees me.

'Elspeth said there might be leftovers,' I say, as I walk into the room.

'There's some casserole in the Aga.' She retracts her arms and dries them on the nearby tea-towel. 'I'll fetch you some. Why don't you sit down?'

She makes me feel uncomfortable with her over-helpful attitude. When we lived in the commune we all looked after ourselves, we were all equal, so I don't like people doing things for me unless I'm paying them or helping them in return. 'It's okay, I can get it, you carry on with what you were doing,' I say.

But she's already opening the Aga and extracting a large orange dish, which she places on the hob. She scoops out a generous portion, then waddles – I know it sounds rude but there's no other more appropriate word to describe her walk – to the larder and takes out a chopped up baguette. She doesn't ask me if I want any but loads some onto the plate before she hands it to me. 'Go and sit down and I'll make you a cuppa.'

There's no point in arguing with her. She's one of those people who is happiest when she's being useful to someone. I deduce she's probably a kind, considerate person. Can I trust her in this house of – as I'm learning now – devious types?

I eat my lunch while observing her bustling around the kitchen. Aggie's worked here since the late 1980s, according to Elspeth, so she must have a wealth of knowledge about the family, I think, as I chew carefully, like my mother taught me to do. *Appreciate each mouthful, Willow,* she'd say.

I swallow some casserole with difficulty, a lump in my throat when I think about my mother. 'Um, Aggie, I was in the hairdresser's this morning . . .'

'So I see. Nice colour.'

'Thanks. Turns out the hairdresser who did my hair knew Una. She told me . . . Well . . .' I throw my hands into the air. 'Everything.'

Aggie's face drains of colour. 'W-what did she tell you?'

'About the other girls and how they died. About Una finding Jemima's bag in the cellar . . .'

Aggie's beady eyes dart towards the door. 'It's best to keep this out,' she says, tapping the side of her nose with genuine fear in her voice. 'And if you want to keep your job, just forget you heard anything about it.'

'But . . . do you think Una died in suspicious circumstances?'

She shakes her head so vigorously that her many chins

wobble. 'I'm not paid to think anything,' she says curtly. 'Now, if you'll excuse me, I've got work to do.'

I'm not offended by Aggie and her rudeness. I expect she's been briefed well by Elspeth and Kathryn not to gossip to the likes of me. But I hate being told 'No'. It makes me want to rebel. I wasn't told 'No' that much as a child. I had a lot of freedom living in the commune. Arlo and I were brought up by various females, including our own mother. I sometimes wonder if that's why university didn't suit me. I couldn't cope with the amount of rules. And the more this family close ranks, the more desperate I am to find out what happened to the girls who worked here before me. I have a right to know, surely, haven't I? Especially if their deaths occurred as a result of them being employed here. Although I do find it hard to believe – Kathryn with her frumpy skirts and sensible shoes, and fragile Elspeth, who clings to me for dear life as we walk down the street, even if I do suspect it's a bit of an act, can't possibly pose a threat.

Regardless, it gives me the excuse to meet Courtney again and maybe make some friends. I get changed in the vast area that is my living accommodation. I'm used to bunking down with as many people as can fit into a room so I'm not accustomed to all this space. Even at uni I shared with another girl because it saved money. Money was something that was always in short supply when I was growing up. I sit on the edge of the beautiful hand-carved sleigh bed that Una slept in, Jemima and Matilde before her. I wonder if they had this duvet cover with the rose-buds. Did they sit at the desk by the window? Shower in the en-suite?

Shit, I think, as I get up and begin to pace the room, my Dr Martens pounding on the floorboards. This is real. People have actually died. What am I going to do?

'So you don't think I've got anything to worry about?' I ask Arlo, over the phone, as I walk to the pub that evening to meet Courtney. I'm slightly out of breath as the walk is further than I thought. At least it's a nice evening. People are converging on pavements and outside pubs. The nights are starting to draw out and the clocks go forward tonight. A group of kids are riding their bikes up and down the pavement. I swerve to avoid one, a little boy with a pudding-bowl haircut whose call 'Sorry!' floats towards me on the breeze.

Arlo scoffs. 'No, of course not. Like what? The octogenarian murderer.' He laughs at his own joke.

'She's in her seventies, not eighties.'

'Look, they all died in different ways. I don't think it's the work of a serial killer. I think you're safe. Maybe jinxed, but not about to get murdered any time soon.'

Despite myself I smile. He's right. It's a ridiculous notion. We chat a little longer about how my job is going, and how he's just started shift work at the local factory because it's good money, and I hang up feeling lighter.

Courtney is sitting alone at a round table in the half-empty pub. Onstage, the band is tuning up – or whatever it is they do with their instruments before a gig. She smiles and waves me over.

'What do you want to drink?' she asks, half out of her seat. She's wearing very tight jeans that have been slashed down the front and a low-cut top that shows off her ample cleavage.

I look down at my baggy granddad shirt and stripy leggings, feeling underdressed. 'No, I'll get mine. Do you want anything?'

She shakes her long red ponytail so I trot to the bar and order a half of cider. I notice the bass player out of the corner of my eye. He's cute. Tall with dirty-blond hair that licks at the collar of his battered leather jacket. Just my type. The barman hands me my drink and I go back to join Courtney. 'Who's the bass player with the hair?' I ask, as I sit down, mainly to break the ice. I'm used to meeting people, but this is still a weird situation.

'That's Vince,' she says, without even turning to look at the band. 'He was Una's boyfriend. Well, ex-boyfriend.'

'Oh. Right.' *Shit.*

She takes a sip of her wine, leaving a red lipstick mark on the glass. She doesn't smile easily or seem to care about whether the person she's with is comfortable in her presence. When I'm with someone new I overcompensate by laughing too much, or chatting inanely, then go home and worry about the stupid thing I said. I wonder what Una was like and how well she and Courtney gelled. Courtney said they were best friends. Does that mean Una was also rather aloof?

'Thanks for meeting me,' she says, putting her glass down. 'I know this is all a bit mad. But I really believe someone deliberately hurt Una. I want to tell you everything.'

'I thought you'd already told me everything in the salon.'

'Not quite. Not all the conversations that Una and I had about it and, believe me, there were many. I've been thinking about it a lot since I saw you this morning. I need to tell you everything as I remember it.'

So I listen as she recounts her conversations with Una. I picture my predecessor on the bed where I now sleep, chatting to her best friend on the phone, and feel overcome with sadness for Una, for this girl who was quite alone in the world, really, apart from her friends. When she's finished I've learnt more about Kathryn, about a sister of hers called Viola, who hasn't been seen in thirty years, and an argument Kathryn had with Jemima on the day Jemima walked out and apparently threw herself into the Avon Gorge.

'So Una had a theory that Elspeth is still hung up on the daughter who ran away and that's why she chooses young blonde women as companions?' I ask, thinking it sounds like something from a Gothic novel.

She nods and sips her wine.

I find it fascinating that Elspeth is trying to replace her daughter. 'Although,' I wrinkle my nose, 'wouldn't Viola be nearly fifty by now?'

'Yep. But I think Elspeth McKenzie is very fucked up and so is her adoptive daughter.' Courtney raises her strong eyebrows. They're actually a work of art. 'Please be careful, that's all I'm saying. I think they were involved in Una's death but I don't want to put you in danger.'

'So, you think Kathryn lured Una onto the bridge that night by pretending to be Peter?'

Courtney nods. I notice she blinks back tears.

'Okay. But would Kathryn have known about Jemima's brother, this Peter guy?'

Courtney shuffles in her seat. A flash of irritation

crosses her face that she doesn't try to hide. 'Yes, of course she would. Peter came to the house. Una went for coffee with him, then took him back to see Kathryn. So she knew exactly who he was and that he was in contact with Una. And it's a bit too much of a coincidence, don't you think? That Una died just after finding the bag of Jemima's clothes? It proves that Kathryn was lying and that she knew Jemima hadn't just done a runner. Una told me she took the bag up to her room to stop Kathryn coming back for it, but nothing has been seen of it since she died. I asked the police. They couldn't find any bag. I think Kathryn lured her to the bridge, hit her over the head and left her there to die. I think she went back to Una's room, took the bag and . . . disposed of it.'

'But you can't say any of this to the police because there's no evidence?'

'Exactly.'

'And you want me to see if I can find any?' I might as well ask her outright. I can't see the point of skirting the issue. She's exactly the type of person who appreciates straight talking.

She nods. 'Would you keep your ear to the ground? Try to listen in on conversations, particularly any that involve Kathryn. Elspeth too. She's not as frail as she tries to make out. Una caught her dancing once . . .'

I knew it. I knew she wasn't as infirm as she pretended to be.

'And, please, stay safe. Don't take any chances. Don't be lured onto that bridge too.'

I swallow my irritation and nod noncommittally. I want to tell her I wouldn't be that stupid but I don't. It wouldn't be fair, and maybe I would have done the same in Una's position.

I sit back in my chair. I watch the boys in the band getting ready to play and I catch the eye of the bass player, Vince, and smile. He turns away. 'Okay,' I say to Courtney, who's watching me expectantly. 'I'll do it. If Kathryn or Elspeth know anything about Una's death, I'll find out. I promise.'

I stay for a while, listen to the band, and have a couple more drinks. Courtney introduces me to her boyfriend, Kris, a cute guy with scruffy shoulder-length hair and an eyebrow piercing, then walk home alone. Maybe that's foolish after what Courtney told me, but I refuse to let some arsehole scare me into submission. And it's only ten o'clock – the streets are still fairly busy. People are queuing to get into nightclubs, and Saturday-night revellers are spilling out of pubs. It's quieter when I leave Whiteladies Road but I still feel safe as I pound the wide pavements. That's until I hear footsteps behind me. And they seem to be getting closer. I refuse to turn, instead quickening my pace until I'm walking so fast I break out in a sweat. The footsteps behind get faster, and just as I'm about to make a run for it, I feel a hand on my shoulder. I spin around, ready to poke my fingers into my assailant's eyes or kick them in the privates, when I see that it's one of the guys from the band.

I breathe out in relief. 'Vince?'

He's breathing heavily too. 'Sorry. I was trying to catch up with you. Shit, you walk fast.'

I eye him warily. 'What do you want?'

It's the boyfriend, a little voice pipes up inside my head.

Isn't it always the boyfriend? Did he kill Una because she didn't want him back?

I continue at a brisk walk and he falls in beside me. Why has he followed me?

'I just wanted to say I'm sorry for being unfriendly to you at the pub tonight.'

I shrug. 'I didn't notice,' I lie. 'And you followed me home just to tell me that?'

He laughs. It sounds abrasive in the dark night. By now the streets are narrower and quieter. 'I haven't followed you home. I'm going to the bus stop.'

'Aren't there bus stops on Whiteladies Road?'

'Not for the bus I need to take.'

I don't believe him. I continue walking with purpose.

'Courtney told me you've taken over Una's job,' he says, matching me stride for stride. He's tall, a good head and shoulders taller than me.

'That's right.' I wonder if I could bang on the door of one of these pretty townhouses if he tries to attack me. There are still lights on in some of the windows, the occupants going about their Saturday-night business, unaware that I'm out here with a potential murderer.

'Just be careful,' he says, his voice gruff, as though he's fighting his emotions. I glance at him from the corner of my eye, and even though it's dark and the streetlights cast shadows across half of his face, I can see that he's in pain. Is he warning me or threatening me?

'What do you mean?'

He sighs. 'I loved Una. There are so many things I did wrong in our relationship, things I won't bore you with, and it kills me I wasn't able to protect her at the end.'

'What do you think happened?' We're still walking at a steady pace. We pass a number of bus stops but he keeps going.

'Una was angry with me, which was to be expected after what I did.' He doesn't elaborate and I don't ask. I actually don't care. I just want to get home in one piece. 'I wanted her back but she refused. Una didn't tell me much about what went on up at the grand house, as I call it. I only saw her once or twice after we split up. But Courtney and Kris filled me in. By the sound of it something's going on behind those doors. And you look similar to Una, you know. The same height and build. The same colouring. Apart from the threads. She'd never wear the kind of clothes you've got on.'

It doesn't sound like a compliment.

'And she would never have pierced her nose.'

For fuck's sake. Why is he telling me all this? Why do I feel like I'm being compared unfavourably to a woman I've never even met?

'And you're younger . . .'

I stop and round on him, no longer scared, just irritated. 'And your point is?'

He hangs his head. 'I'm sorry . . . I didn't mean anything by it. I . . .' his voice catches '. . . I miss her.'

My anger dissipates. 'I'm sorry. It's awful what happened to Una. And I've said I'll help Courtney, okay? I don't want to be next, do I?' I force a laugh. 'It's in my best interests to find out what happened to Una.'

He nods, his face brightening a little. 'Can I walk you the rest of the way home?'

It's against my better judgement but we're only a few streets away so I agree.

Another gone. And another arrives.

You're different from Una. Your hair is a dirtier blonde, but at least you got rid of those ugly pink streaks. You've got piercings, a tattoo of a butterfly on your right ankle that you try to hide and you probably regret, although you'd never admit it. You're younger too, not as sweet or as pretty. And you're feisty, but that doesn't bother the old bag. She likes you. I've seen the way she laughs at your jokes. Or maybe it's because she appreciates you more, knowing you might be taken away in an instant, like the others.

This time, though, Elspeth McKenzie has made the right choice. You're the best girl for the job.

29

Kathryn

Kathryn isn't so sure about this new one, Willow Green. What kind of name is that anyway? It sounds like it's been pulled from a Farrow & Ball chart. She wonders if it's made up.

This one is cocky, loud and brash, with her tattoos, wacky clothes and nose piercings. She's lacking the manners Una had. She reminds Kathryn of the first one, Matilde. Is that why her mother hired her? Kathryn had hoped that Una's death would be the end of it all. But, no, the funeral was barely over when Elspeth had put the advert in the newspaper before Kathryn had a chance to try to talk her out of it. Elspeth didn't even consult her for the interviews, although she saw one girl tripping down the pavement afterwards: curvy, dark-haired, tall. In her hot-pink fluffy jacket, she looked like she'd mugged a Muppet. Kathryn knew she wouldn't be getting the job. She almost called after her, 'Don't hold your breath, you stupid cow. You don't look like my long-lost sister!' And then, just a few weeks after Una was in the ground, out popped another Viola carbon copy.

When Kathryn first clapped eyes on Willow, she'd been shocked. Yes, she was her mother's type, there was no disputing that, but she was so . . . new agey, if they were still calling it that nowadays. She looked like she should be hanging out at Glastonbury, not here in Clifton among the antiques and the upholstered furniture. But, true to form, no family to speak of, no commitments or ties. Pliable.

How many more of *these girls* would have to die before her mother got the message that she, Kathryn, is the only one she needs?

Kathryn gets up early on Sunday morning. She can hear her mother chatting to Viola in her bedroom, her laugh echoing through the house. No ... not Viola. *Willow.* What's wrong with her? Kathryn puts a hand to her head. Her forehead is hot. Perhaps she's sick. She feels like she's going mad. She dreamt of Viola last night, of the years of bullying and abuse. Elspeth and Huw could only protect her from some of it. They didn't see the rest, the tricks and the manipulation, when their backs were turned: the time Viola and her friends left her on the suspension bridge the year after the Halloween incident, or when they pushed her out of the tree house and she broke her wrist. It's still weak now and hurts when the cold sets in. Each time she lied for Viola, terrified that if she told the truth she'd be sent back to the home. After all, Elspeth and Huw were hardly going to send their real daughter away, were they? Viola knew this and used it to her advantage. But the bullying didn't let up until that last time. When Kathryn got her revenge.

Her head throbs. No, she can't think of that now. She can't think of the hatred and the bitterness that twists around her intestines, threatening to crush her whenever she remembers. She needs to keep that in a little box inside her mind, separate from the boys and from Ed, lest it spills out and tarnishes what she has, what she's built.

She sneaks out of the house without saying goodbye to her mother or having breakfast with Aggie. All she wants to do is get back to Ed and the boys, to normality. Nothing at The Cuckoo's Nest feels normal, with these replica Violas everywhere she turns, laughing at her, taunting her, proving she'll never be good enough. Since Una died, even Aggie isn't as friendly as she once was. She's not rude but she lacks her usual warmth, never stopping to chat, briskly saying she must get on whenever Kathryn tries to corner her for a bit of light gossip. She's even stopped leaving extras for Kathryn to take to her family.

She drives home too fast. Luckily the roads are quiet at eight o'clock on a Sunday. Her house is equally silent when she lets herself in. She suspects they're all still in bed, Ed snoring unattractively, one arm slung over his face, the boys buried beneath their duvets, like little moles. She wonders if she could persuade the three of them to leave Bristol, to make a fresh start somewhere else. She's always fancied going somewhere up north. Yorkshire, maybe, or the Lake District. Somewhere rural, tranquil, far away, but even as she thinks it she knows she can never do it, despite the bad things she's done. She can't leave Elspeth: the Viola-clones will only let her down in the end.

She creeps upstairs and pokes her nose around her bedroom door. Sure enough, Ed is fast asleep, in exactly the pose she'd imagined. And then she tiptoes along to her children's rooms. Harry is asleep, the duvet pulled over his head. And Jacob is . . . She walks further into his room. Jacob's bed is empty, his covers thrown back as though he left in a hurry. Perhaps he's in the bathroom. Panic swells in her chest. He'll be in another part of the house, she thinks, as she searches each room. But he's nowhere to be seen.

She shakes her husband awake. 'Ed. Jacob's missing!'

Ed's eyes bolt open and he sits up so suddenly he nearly head-butts her. 'W-what?'

'He's gone, Ed.' She tries to keep her voice low so as not to alarm Harry. It isn't the first time Jacob's done this. Oh, God, it's her fault, all her fault . . .

Ed jumps out of bed, pulling on yesterday's clothes from where he'd flung them last night on the armchair. She follows him into Jacob's room. It's how she'd left it yesterday: his desk with his study books piled high, his headphones in the corner, his guitar that he stopped play-ing years ago propped up against the far wall gathering dust.

'Did you check on him last night before you went to bed?' She rounds on Ed, trying to keep the accusation out of her voice.

'Yes, of course,' he says, looking about him frantically as though he's expecting Jacob to pop up from behind the door with a 'Boo!' like he did when he was little. Ed looks flummoxed. Even more so than usual, with his jumper on back to front.

'Do . . .' She tries to quell the panic. 'Do you think he left in the middle of the night? What if he's run away?' She pulls open his wardrobe but his clothes are still there, hanging tidily, neatly ironed as she'd left them.

Ed puts his big red hands to his face. 'He can't keep doing this.'

'I know.'

'He's just a kid.'

Ed sounds like he's on the point of hysteria. She can't have that. He needs to be his usual dependable, slightly dull, but reliable self. That was why she'd married him. He provided the stability, the calm she's always needed but never had. He can't fall apart.

'He's got his GCSEs coming up. He's going to ruin his life.' He straightens, as if remembering the role he needs to play in their relationship. 'You stay here with Harry. I'll go and search the estates, like before . . .'

Her heart falls. In the last six months, apart from the odd blip, he'd seemed to settle down. No running away to join those – those *yobs* to get drunk and, later, stoned. He'd been shocked into sobering up, to getting himself sorted. To knuckling down and studying. She and Ed no longer had to drive the streets looking for their fifteen-year-old son. He'll be sixteen next month. She'd hoped it would be the new beginning he needed.

It had started a year ago. First he'd pilfered from the drinks cabinet, topping up the booze with water. They'd only noticed it when they'd had Ed's work colleagues around one evening and Ed had nearly spat out the gin when he'd realized it was mostly water. When it kept happening they were forced to lock the cabinet and hide the key. And then the wandering began. Coming home past his curfew, sneaking out in the middle of the night. Making friends with older boys from an estate in Shirehampton. Once, they didn't find him for two nights while he slept on a 'friend's' floor. When Kathryn found him he'd been drinking, and was surrounded by empty cider bottles. Then she began to suspect drugs. He'd come home smelling of pot, or with enlarged pupils and a manic smile. She'd threatened him with the police, but as quickly as it had started, it stopped. He'd promised her he'd learnt his lesson and would never do it again. That was seven months ago and, apart from the odd time when she was sure she could smell booze on him, she believed he'd kept his promise.

But now they're back to where they started. She can feel it in her bones.

How did her son, her beautiful boy, end up this way? She'd given him all the things she'd never had until she went to live with Elspeth, and more besides: he had love. Pure, unconditional love. Not the kind of love with rules attached, like Kathryn felt Elspeth gave – still gives – her. She'd never told Elspeth of her troubles with Jacob. She knows what she'd say. She'd point the finger, accuse Kathryn's biological mother, and say, in her posh, judgemental voice, that the apple never fell far from the tree.

She kneels on the floor next to Harry's bed, smoothing his dark hair away from his sleeping face. Her, as yet, untarnished son. Why can't she keep him like this forever? Away from the disappointments and the heartaches, from finding out your parents aren't as perfect as you'd always thought. And then she hears the front door slam and she rushes downstairs to see Ed, Jacob trailing behind him, a newspaper tucked under his arm.

Ed is smiling and ruffling Jacob's hair. 'I found this one walking back from the newsagent's. He'd just gone to get a paper.'

Kathryn smiles tightly. She wants to believe it, she really does. She glances over the top of Ed's head and meets her elder son's eye. He doesn't appear to be on anything: his pupils are normal-sized. She narrows her eyes at him anyway, a warning glare. He's the first to look away, dipping his head as though trying to hide his guilt.

Later, she goes to him while he's in his room.

'You gave me a scare there,' she admits, perching on the edge of his bed where he's sprawled out, pretending to read a textbook. The soles of his socks are dirty.

'I told you I'm not into that stuff anymore. Why won't you believe me?' He tilts his chin. 'I'm not lying to you, Mum. Okay? I woke up early and was bored. I went to get a newspaper. That's all.'

She doesn't want to point out that he never reads newspapers. Or wakes up early at the weekend. But she wraps these thoughts into neat little packages and places them in a box in her mind with all the other things she's trying to avoid thinking about.

She lowers her voice. 'I know it must be eating you up. It's messing with my head and I'm a grown-up. I'm worried for you, Jake.'

His eyes flash. 'You promised me,' he hisses.

'I know. And I'll keep my promise. I'm your mother. But you have to keep yours too.'

30

Willow

I don't know where to start. I'm not a detective and I've certainly never done any amateur sleuthing before. And I do feel a bit of an idiot lurking by door jambs, hoping to hear snippets of conversation between Kathryn and Elspeth. When Kathryn is here she's always watching me, too, with those serious hazel eyes of hers. It's obvious she doesn't trust me. And since I've known the truth, I've been jittery around her. I've tried to be normal but the other day she came into the kitchen, surprising me, and I dropped one of Elspeth's bone-china teacups. She unnerves me with her looming presence, her height and her frosty demeanour.

Courtney texts me most days asking if I have any information. I feel bad when I have to reply that I don't.

And then, on Thursday, something unexpected happens.

Elspeth is feeling unwell and is laid up in bed, saying she'd like to rest. It's unlike Elspeth. She's usually up and about, shuffling around in a pair of elegant slippers, even if we don't always go out. But today she says she's got a migraine. She's lying on top of her duvet, fully clothed, when I go to check on her. I offer to help her into her nightdress but she refuses, saying she'll feel better and will be up later.

'Shall I call a doctor?' I ask, as I fuss around her, plumping up her pillows and setting a glass of water on her bedside table.

She brushes away my concern, saying the only thing for it is to rest in a dark room for a few hours. 'Would you mind walking over to the gallery in the arcade and asking Kathryn for the books?' she says.

'The books?' I frown at her, imagining lugging home a bagful of paperbacks.

'The accounts,' she clarifies. 'I haven't looked at them for such a long time. I worry that Kathryn isn't being honest with me.'

My ears prick up and I mentally file away this titbit of information to give to Courtney later. 'In what way?'

She waves a wrinkled hand in my direction. Nearly all her fingers are encircled with jewels. 'I think the gallery isn't performing as well as she tries to make me believe. It was her father's baby. And I've been busy with the arts foundation so haven't kept on top of it.'

I know from Courtney that Kathryn is adopted, although Elspeth has never told me so. I wonder if she was close to her father. I was never particularly close to mine: when I was nine and Arlo was fourteen he ran off with another woman from the commune and started a new family somewhere else, never bothering to keep in touch.

I assure her I'll go to the gallery, even though I don't relish the thought of having to interact with Kathryn, and fetch what she needs. 'You rest now,' I say, patting her liver-spotted hands, which are clutched together in her lap. I leave her alone in the dark room and head downstairs, grabbing my jacket and making my way out of the front door.

It's a beautiful early-April morning and the sun is shining, which heightens the green of the trees and the pink of the blossom scattered on the pavements. I amble towards the gallery, deliberately taking my time, enjoying the freedom of being without Elspeth, even stopping to buy a takeaway latte from one of the cafés I pass. The mood on the streets is jovial, as though everyone appreciates the beauty of the weather after the cold winter we've just emerged from. Strangers smile at each other or nod a hello. I bend over to stroke a brown shaggy-haired poodle cross – I'm informed by the proud owner that it's a Schnoodle. I want to skip. I feel happy despite everything. It's amazing how a little sunshine can brighten your mood.

And then I realize I'm being followed.

A man with bright blond hair, wearing a mustard ski jacket, has been shadowing me from Elspeth's house. At first I didn't take much notice of him, but when I saw that he stopped when I stroked the dog, and hovered around a bin pretending to be on his phone while I was getting my coffee, it hit me that he was trailing me. I actually want to laugh at him. Stealthy he isn't.

I stop at the edge of the kerb to cross the street, wondering what he'll do next, but he forces his way through the throng of people behind me so that he's standing by my side. He's tall and very angular.

'I need to speak to you,' he says, staring straight ahead, like a spy in an old film.

I turn to him. 'Are you talking to me?'

He meets my gaze. He has intense eyes and a crease between his brows that seems permanent, as though he's constantly annoyed. I don't like the look of him. 'Yes.'

'Who the fuck are you? And why are you following me?'

He physically reels backwards. I continue across the road and down the street, and hear the thud of his boots as he runs to catch up.

'I'm sorry,' he calls after me. 'I didn't mean to come across as creepy. I just wanted to get your attention. You see, I couldn't come to the house and . . . please . . .' he sounds breathless '. . . can you stop a minute?'

I stop so abruptly that a woman with a pram almost crashes into me. She moves around me, tutting loudly. I fold my arms. He stands facing me, his face red and sweaty. He doesn't look well. 'Are you okay?'

He shakes his head. 'I've had the flu. Look . . .' he stands up straighter and extends a hand '. . . I'm Peter.'

Peter? The name rings a bell and then it clicks. 'The brother of Matilde?'

'No. Jemima. She died. She worked for Elspeth too.'

I hold up a hand. 'I know who she is.'

'I was in touch with Una and then I heard she died, too, in an accident. So when I got some time off work I knew I had to come down. Because it's weird, don't you think? And then I hovered around the McKenzies' house and saw you coming out. At first I thought you were Una and there'd been some mistake but . . .' he points to my face with a sad smile '. . . the nose ring.'

I remember what Courtney had told me about Una arranging to meet Peter on the bridge the night she died. 'Una's friend said Una thought she was meeting you that night.'

The groove between his eyebrows deepens. 'The police said something about that. But it wasn't me. I was working and the police took my phone and analysed it.'

I stare at him sceptically. I wonder if he has an alibi. And he could have used a burner phone. Isn't that what they're called on those TV crime dramas?

He hangs his head. 'I feel awful about it. Una rang me a few times and left messages, but work was crazy and I was on long shifts and never got the chance to call her back.'

I'm conscious of the time ticking by and Elspeth waking to find I've not returned with the books. 'I'm sorry, I have to go. I'm working.'

'Can you meet me tonight after work?'

I pull an apologetic face. 'I'm sort of on call twenty-four/seven.'

'What?' He looks shocked. 'I don't remember Jemima having that arrangement.'

I shrug. 'She pays amazingly well for what I do. And I need the money. But I get two days off a week. I could meet you on Saturday.'

'I'm not sure . . . I've driven all this way.'

'Then contact Courtney. She was Una's best friend. She knows more about it all than I do.' I take my mobile out of my bag and reel off Courtney's number. Peter taps it into his phone. 'I'd better go. And . . . I'm really sorry. About Jemima. And Una.'

I leave him standing in the middle of the street and head towards the art gallery.

*

Kathryn isn't there when I arrive and I'm greeted by a voluptuous girl with long hair piled on top of her head and bright red lipstick. She introduces herself as Daisy.

'Do you know when she'll be in?'

She looks at her watch. 'Should be here any minute. She's late this morning. Some family emergency.'

Family emergency? I wonder what that could be. Elspeth was fine when I left her. But what if something's happened while I've been out? It's taken longer than I anticipated to get here because I ran into Peter.

I explain why I'm here and Daisy's pretty face falls. 'I really don't think I should be giving you that sort of thing without Kathryn's permission,' she says, her full lips turning down at the sides.

'But they're for Kathryn's mum, who owns this place.'

She shrugs in a what-can-I-do? kind of way.

'I'll wait,' I say stubbornly.

Daisy nods. 'Do you want a cup of tea, then?'

I've still got my lukewarm takeaway coffee so I refuse but I follow her to the end of the gallery while she makes one for herself.

The place is spacious. Everything is white – the desks, the walls – I'm assuming to highlight the artwork. The collection is varied – some paintings are bold and modernistic, others more traditional. While Daisy is boiling the kettle I take a closer look, blanching at the price tags. 'Not busy today?' I say, noting how empty the shop is.

'It comes in fits and starts.' She walks out of the back room nursing a mug. 'Come and sit down if you want.'

She leads me to a large desk by the door. She takes the chair behind it and I sit in one opposite that is meant for customers. She chats away, asking how I'm enjoying working for Elspeth, and saying how awful it was that Una died. 'She seemed really sweet, too,' she says, sipping her tea thoughtfully. 'And I liked Jemima. I never met the first one, though. I've only been working here six months.' She leans across the desk. 'Do you know if the police are investigating? I mean, it's weird, don't you think? All three girls dying like that.'

I try to look unconcerned. 'It's a coincidence, that's all.'

Daisy isn't convinced. 'It's like the house is cursed. You should be careful.'

'Lucky, then, that I don't believe in curses!'

She looks affronted and sits back in her chair. She doesn't say anything for a few seconds, and then, 'My boyfriend used to work there. Says there was always a funny atmosphere about the place. Sinister, you know?'

I put my coffee cup on the desk. 'You should be careful what you're saying. That's your boss you're talking about. And, for the record, I don't know what your boyfriend means. It's a lovely house. Elspeth has been nothing but kind to me.' I don't know why I'm sticking up for Elspeth, but Daisy is getting on my nerves.

Her large eyes widen even further. 'Oh, I didn't mean anything by it.'

Just then the door opens and Kathryn walks in. She has an air of harassment about her and is fumbling in her handbag. Her usually neat hair is a fuzzy halo around her head and her mascara has smudged. If I didn't know better I'd think she'd been crying.

Surprise registers on her face when she sees me. 'Oh, hi, Willow. What are you doing here?'

I stand up and explain about the books.

'The books?' She looks flustered. 'I . . . To be honest, I'm not sure where they are.'

'Oh.'

'Tell Mother I'll pop over with them later.'

'Okay.'

She bestows a thin-lipped smile on me. 'Sorry you had a wasted journey.'

It's my cue to leave. I say thank you and exit the shop, feeling even more confused. It's obvious she's lying. But why?

31

Courtney

Courtney's feet ache. It's been a long day in the salon with some very tricky customers, particularly Felicity Alpine, with her thick mane of hair that wouldn't be tamed no matter how hard Courtney tried. Felicity was never happy with it, yet she always came back and always requested Courtney. Usually, after a visit from Felicity, Courtney would ring Una and they would laugh about her and her wild hair, her plummy accent and condescending manner. The chasm that Una has left in Courtney's life gapes even wider when it dawns on her, as it does every time she has the urge to call her best friend, that she'll never talk to Una again.

She stops at the newsstand on the way to the bus stop to get some sweets. Una used to laugh at her love of anything chewy. Sometimes Courtney ordered the old-school sweets from the internet so she could feast on a Wham bar or a packet of Refreshers. She buys some wine gums, not her favourite but they'll have to do, and pops one into her mouth as she boards the bus.

It's packed tonight and she's lucky to get a seat. If she had to stand up, after being on her feet all day, she'd scream. There is a waft of BO coming from the man crammed in next to her as he plays Angry Birds on his mobile. The journey tonight is never-ending, the only positive being that the days are slowly drawing out and it's still light when the bus reaches her stop.

As she's walking back to her flat her mobile buzzes in the pocket of her biker jacket. The number is unknown but she answers it anyway, expecting it to be a call centre, so she's surprised when the man on the other end introduces himself to her as Peter Freeman. He begins to explain who he is but she cuts him off: 'I know who you are.'

He asks her if she'd meet him tonight for a drink as he's driving back to London later. Her heart sinks at the prospect of having to make the journey back into the centre of town, but she can't let this opportunity pass.

He must sense her hesitation because he adds, 'Or I can see you somewhere near where you live? I'm happy to meet anywhere.'

She suggests her local pub, which is just down the road from her flat and very old-fashioned, usually only frequented by the over-sixties who have been going there for the past thirty years, but it will save her feet. He says he'll see her in an hour.

Courtney lets herself into the flat. Kris has been living with her since January and already the flat smells like him. Una's once rose-scented bedroom is now filled with his drum kit, old vinyl records, an amp, stereos and other paraphernalia. Her bathroom cabinet is crammed with his aftershaves, razors, toothpicks, hair gels and mouthwash. It was only supposed to be a temporary thing because she knew, by September, she'd be off with Una, travelling the globe. And now she feels trapped. She doesn't want to see the world by herself, but she certainly doesn't want to go with Kris. She sighs. The problem is her parents. They have such a great marriage – the love they have for each other is still as solid today as it was when she was a kid. They make each other laugh all the time. When she goes home to visit them it's not unusual to see her mum doubled up with laughter in the kitchen and her dad with a smile on his face, happy that he can still amuse his wife. He often embraces her mum when she least expects it and plants a kiss on her neck. After growing up around such love, Courtney knows she'll never settle for anything less.

Kris is sprawled on the ugly brown sofa, his legs hanging over the arm, watching TV, his head resting on the bulldog cushion she and Una had picked out at Ikea when they first moved in. She wants to yank it from under his greasy hair. He has a large rip in the knee of his jeans, exposing his hairy legs. Kris doesn't have a job. He spends his time either gigging or 'working on new material'. It's a constant cause of irritation to her, especially after a day like today. He pays half the rent with the money he makes from his gigs so she can't complain. She feels like his mother sometimes, especially when she hears herself nagging him to be tidier, or when she's picking up his dirty pants from the bedroom floor and throwing them into the laundry bin, which he always ignores.

'All right, babe?' he says, without looking up from the game show he's watching. 'What shall we do for tea tonight?' Which means, 'What are *you* going to cook?'

'I thought you had a gig.'

'Nah. That's tomorrow.'

Her heart falls. 'Oh, right. Well, I'm out tonight. I was going to grab some chips at the pub.'

He looks up at her then, disappointment written all over his face. He's pretty, she'll give him that, his large blue eyes fringed with dark lashes, which are, quite frankly, wasted on a man. And he makes her laugh, when he's in the right mood. At first they'd been all over each other but now, even though they've been together less than a year, they seem to have fallen into a comfortable, slightly boring routine. She knows it isn't love. It's laziness. Neither of them can be bothered to go out and meet someone else. She only let him move in because she'd needed a flatmate when Una got the live-in carer job.

'Oh. Who with?'

'Peter.'

He swings his legs around and sits up straighter. 'Peter? Peter who?'

She explains who he is as she shrugs off her jacket and kicks off the uncomfortable pumps that pinch her toes. They're part of the salon uniform and she hates them.

'Can't I come too? He could be a weirdo. How do you know he didn't meet Una that night and cave her head in?'

She blanches at Kris's insensitivity. 'For fuck's sake.'

His eyes widen. 'What? I'm just saying. He could be a murderer.'

'You said you thought Una fell and banged her head.'

He stands up and goes to where she's hovering by the kitchen sink. He takes her hand. 'We don't know anything for certain.' She knows he doesn't believe a word of it and just wants to accompany her to the pub to check out Peter for himself, to see if he's a threat. She can't be bothered to argue. She's done in.

'Fine. Come too. I'm meeting him at seven.'

He grins in response. 'Great. I'll change my top. I've been wearing it for three days.'

'That's gross.'

'What? I've had a shower every day. The T-shirt wasn't dirty. I'm saving you the washing.' He winks at her to show he's joking.

While Kris is in the bathroom she changes out of her work clothes and into her ripped jeans and long-sleeved T-shirt. She shakes out her long ponytail so that her red hair spills down her back, way past her shoulders. Then she adds a touch more lipstick and she's ready.

They take a slow walk to the pub, her arm linked through Kris's. It's been a warm day but now that the sun is going down she can feel the chill in the air and she's suddenly grateful for the warmth of Kris's body next to hers.

The pub is quiet for a Thursday evening, a few regulars sitting at the bar with their malodorous, ageing dogs at their feet. A group of pensioners are playing darts at the other end. Courtney hasn't been in for ages, preferring the bars in town, but she used to come a lot as a kid, usually with her dad when her mum was out shopping. He'd usually settle her and her brother in the corner with a cola while he chatted to his mates over a pint. Nothing has changed. Even the heavy, dark wooden furniture and photos of horses or farmland on the tobacco-stained walls are the same.

'How do you know what he looks like?' asks Kris, in a loud whisper, as they head for the bar.

'Um. Maybe because he'll be the only other young person in here.'

Kris laughs and pulls an oh-yes-silly-me face.

A quick scan of the pub reveals that Peter is yet to arrive so they order their drinks – a glass of house white that tastes like vinegar for Courtney and a beer for Kris – and settle themselves at a table by the door.

Every time the door opens Courtney looks up expectantly, her heart in her mouth. Why does she feel so nervous? She's not sure if it's making her feel better or worse having Kris in tow. He's wittering away about a new song the band is writing, completely oblivious to her discomfort. Eventually when the door opens again, she sees a young guy walk in, wearing a yellow coat. Her first thought is that he's tall, the second that he's handsome. And as this crosses her mind her stomach flips. At five foot seven herself she's always found tall men particularly attractive. Kris is only two inches taller than her. He strides towards them. 'Hi. Courtney?' He holds out a hand uncertainly.

She stands up and shakes it. 'Peter? Hi. This is Kris.' She leaves out that he's her boyfriend, indicating vaguely in his direction instead. Kris is slouched over his pint and barely looks up. Courtney offers Peter a drink but he insists on getting his own, and when he returns, he perches on the chair between them, his knees almost to his chest.

'Thanks for meeting me at such short notice,' he says, with a ghost of a smile. He glances at Kris, then back to Courtney. 'And I'm so sorry about your friend. She was kind to me and tried to help me when she didn't have to.'

'I'm sorry about your sister,' Courtney says.

He shuffles in his seat. 'I don't know how much Una told you . . .'

'Everything,' Courtney says bluntly.

'Did she tell you about me turning up?'

Courtney nods. 'She told me you didn't believe Jemima would kill herself. And now I understand how you feel because I don't believe Una's death was an accident.'

He dips his head solemnly. 'I've talked to the police and they don't think Jemima and Una's deaths are related.'

Courtney tuts loudly. 'I don't get it. She had a text from someone pretending to be you asking her to meet them on the bridge. Why don't the police believe that?'

He shrugs, looking apologetic. 'I know I didn't send that message but I feel responsible. If I hadn't got her involved . . .'

Kris grunts and they turn to look at him.

'What?' says Courtney.

He shakes his head. 'Nothing.'

Courtney narrows her eyes at him. He looks like he'd rather be anywhere else. She doesn't understand why he bothered to come. She turns back to Peter. 'Una told me about Jemima's necklace. And about how you said she was seeing someone before she died. She tried to find out who but never had the chance . . .' A lump forms in Courtney's throat and she takes a large swig of wine to wash it away, then has to resist the urge to cough.

'Una left a voicemail on my phone that night. Said she had something to tell me.'

'It must have been about the bag.'

'The bag?'

'Jemima's holdall. It was in the cellar. Una found it and

was convinced Kathryn had put it there. She also said that the cook, Aggie, heard Kathryn and Jemima arguing on the night Jemima left. Una said Aggie had been freaked out by the bag, too, and urged Una to report it to the police. I've since reported it but the bag is now missing, so it's my word against theirs.'

'The daughter, Kathryn, is hiding something, I'm sure of it,' says Peter, his eyes flashing. 'The necklace . . . Why did she pretend she was going to post it to Jemima when she never had a forwarding address? Why did she have all her stuff in their cellar?'

Courtney opens her mouth to say something and Kris emits a bark of laughter.

'I'm sorry,' he says when they both swivel around to glare at him. 'But this is just one big conspiracy theory. If the police think their deaths are not suspicious why are you two acting like bloody . . .' he pauses, and Courtney can almost see his brain ticking overtime, trying to think of someone to compare them to '. . . Shakespeare and Hathaway?'

Courtney swallows a giggle at Peter's perplexed expression. Kris watches too much daytime TV. She's simultaneously irritated and amused by him in equal measure.

'I think their deaths are suspicious,' says Peter, seriously. She's noticed he still hasn't taken off his jacket, which puffs out around him, making him seem bigger than he is. He looks uncomfortable on the hard chair. 'The police didn't know Jemima.' He gestures to Courtney. 'And they didn't know Una. We did. It was obvious by what she told Courtney that she was lured to the bridge because she thought she was meeting me. Why have the police never found the person who sent the text?'

'So you think you know more than the police?' Kris says, and Courtney cringes, no longer amused. He's being too confrontational.

Peter sighs and pushes back his fringe. 'The police are working with facts. Because Una's phone is missing, they haven't seen a text from someone pretending to be me. So, to them, it doesn't exist. It's all hearsay from us.'

Kris throws his hands into the air. 'Don't get me wrong, man, I'm really sorry about your sister. And Una. She was a friend and her death has shaken me too. But I can't believe she was murdered. It's just an unfortunate coincidence.'

'There's something else,' says Peter, glancing at Courtney, as though Kris hasn't spoken. 'Something the police told me yesterday.'

Courtney sits up straighter in her seat and leans towards him.

'A witness has come forward to say they saw a girl matching Jemima's description that night.'

'Where?'

'Getting out of a van on the Leigh Woods side of the bridge apparently.'

'A van?'

He nods. 'It might not mean anything. She might have been getting a lift with a friend, but they need to talk to the owner of this van to eliminate – that's the word they used – them from their enquiries.'

Courtney takes a sip of her lukewarm wine.

Kris reclines in his seat, hands behind his head. 'I just can't see why someone would deliberately target these girls. I mean . . . why?'

'That,' says Peter, 'is what I intend to find out.'

32

Willow

I've put Elspeth to bed and I'm up in my room going through my washing (Elspeth said I can give it to the cleaner, Carole, to do for me) when Courtney calls to tell me about her meeting with Peter.

'He's really lovely,' she says, her voice softening.

I want to tell her not to trust him. Not to trust anybody. But I feel bad about bursting her bubble. She fills me in on all of it, making me laugh when she describes how annoyingly Kris was acting. 'That's interesting about the van,' I say. 'Was there any identifying feature on it?'

'No. I don't think so. I think it was a generic white van, from what Peter was saying. But listen, Willow, we've decided – that is, me and Peter – that the priority is to try to work out where Kathryn has hidden Jemima's bag. If we can find that . . .'

'I know. I know. Evidence.'

I end the call after promising I'll help. I search everywhere: in the back of the wardrobe, under the bed, in the chest of drawers, even though I know it's not there – it was empty when I arrived. I go into the en-suite. There's not much room in here. Not even a bath panel to conceal a bag. I open the vanity unit under the sink. The cupboard is quite small and I get on my hands and knees and almost crawl into it. The back of the cupboard is broken, the back panel doesn't quite align. I push my hand against it and peer closer, coughing as I dislodge dust motes. Yes, it would be big enough to hide a bag. I slide my hand behind the panel and feel about, but there's nothing. I retreat, banging my head on the sink as I stand up. Damn it. If Una hid the bag anywhere in this room I bet it was there. I tap out a text to Courtney telling her this.

She replies straight away: *If K found it and took it, where else could she have hidden it?*

I sit on the edge of the bed, my mobile in my hand. Think. Think. And then it comes to me. *The art gallery*, I reply.

The house is quiet as I pad down the stairs to the first floor. Elspeth's bedroom door is ajar, just as she likes it. I peer through the crack. She's lying on her back with her eyes closed, her chest rising and falling, her duvet pulled up to her chin. She sleeps with her hair still in its updo. It must be uncomfortable.

I creep past her door and continue down the winding staircase to the hallway. I know this house is fancy, but it leaves me cold. There's nothing about it that's warm and inviting. No photographs on the walls, just a bunch of ugly paintings that probably cost the earth. There are no little trinkets or ornaments. I've come to understand that the house is the perfect depiction of the people who inhabit it, myself not included, of course.

Elspeth never mentions Una or Jemima. Not even **Matilde**. Considering Una died less than two months ago it's like – from Elspeth and Kathryn's point of view anyway – she didn't exist. They've wiped her from their memories just like they did with the daughter, Viola, who supposedly ran away all those years ago. If Courtney hadn't told me, I'd never have known Una, Jemima, Matilde and Viola had ever existed, let alone lived in this very house. It gives me the creeps when I think about it.

Kathryn's cold, sneering face appears in my mind's eye and disappears again, like a fading photograph. It sounds like Courtney and Peter are sure she had something to do with Una and Jemima's deaths. And the bag Una found in the cellar is definitely suspicious – I can't get away from that. Yet something doesn't add up. Why would Elspeth employ a companion just for Kathryn to dispose of them? Is that what they do? Like the Moors murderers? One to lure and the other to kill? Kathryn doesn't like us being here, that much is obvious, but . . . *murder*? Then I think of some of the true-life crime documentaries I've seen. Ordinary people kill for all sorts of reasons and sometimes no reason at all. Maybe Kathryn is a psychopath who is compelled to do it. And, if so, when did she start? With Matilde . . . or before that? With Viola? I shudder at the thought that maybe Viola didn't run away after all.

The creak of a floorboard makes me jump. I spin around but nobody's there. *Oh, for goodness' sake, Willow,* I tell myself. *Stop scaring yourself with these ridiculous thoughts.*

I continue down the stairs. It's dark, the only light coming from the moon filtering through the pane of glass in the front door, bouncing off the Victorian tiles. They are cold beneath my bare feet as I tiptoe across them. The cupboard on the left nearest the front door has a row of keys inside, dangling enticingly on a rack, like jewellery in a shop. They glint in the moonlight. There are about eight keys, plus a small bunch containing two and a diamanté key-ring in the shape of a dog, which I know are Elspeth's because I've had to get them for her often enough. They open the front and back doors. The other keys are singles, each with their own little plastic-labelled fob. How very organized. The gallery keys must be here somewhere. I know Elspeth has a set. I cast my eye along them, but it's too dark to make out the writing and I've left my phone upstairs. I unhook one and take it to the front door to catch the light. *Study* is written on it in Elspeth's slanted hand. I return it and try another. *Attic.* I frown. I'm in the attic. I was given a key when I arrived, not that I ever use it. So this is a spare? What's the point of giving me a key if they can gain access to my room any time they want? I replace it and go through the other keys until I reach the last one. This has to be it. I'm just about to hold it up to the light to read the tag to make sure, when I hear someone clear their throat.

I jump, almost dropping the key, and spin around, my heart thumping.

Elspeth is standing in the middle of the hallway, her chignon all awry and dressed in her favourite ankle-length thermal nightdress. 'What on earth are you doing?'

I fold the key into my palm and close the cupboard. 'I . . . I was checking the front door. I hadn't double-bolted it.'

Even in the half-light I can see the doubt in her expression. 'I thought I'd double-bolted it.'

'Yes. Yes, you had.'

'Right.' She comes towards me. She looks like she's

floating in her long nightdress and I kick the cupboard closed with my foot before she asks why I'm looking in it. 'So why did you check?'

'Because I couldn't remember you doing it. And I know how you like the house to be properly locked at night. So I thought I'd check. I couldn't sleep for thinking about it.'

She smiles, reaches out and touches my hair almost maternally in a way I've never seen her do with Kathryn. Her little finger catches my cheek. 'You're a good girl,' she says, her eyes softening. 'I'm glad you're here, watching over me.'

I feel a little awkward. So I stand there smiling inanely, wondering what the correct response should be. She's so close to me I can smell her breath: mint mixed with something sour. The end of the key presses painfully into my palm.

'Will you help me back up to bed? You know how difficult it is for me to climb stairs.'

I'd noted that she had no trouble getting down them but I agree – anything to stop her breathing in my face – and she takes my elbow, leaning on me heavily, even though she's a head taller. Good job I'm stronger than I look, I think, as I help her back to her room.

She pats the edge of the bed. 'Sit with me awhile,' she says. 'Now I'm awake I'll have trouble getting back to sleep.'

She's never asked me to sit with her before. Usually I put her to bed and she falls asleep straight away. Like clockwork. Every night at nine thirty on the dot. I wonder if she asked the other girls to sit with her like this, in her pristine bedroom, with the heavy walnut furniture and the Tiffany lamps. I sit awkwardly on the edge of the bed, while she lies back against the pillows, smiling indulgently.

'I can make you some cocoa,' I say, because that's what they do in films – it gives me nausea and makes me want to pee.

'No, I don't like hot drinks before bed. Just sit. Please. Keep me company. I had an awful dream. I think that's what woke me.'

Perhaps Elspeth will open up to me at last. Maybe I can try to find out what happened to Una.

'What did you dream about?' I ask, curling my legs up underneath me, as though she's about to tell me a story.

She casts her eyes to her skinny, mottled hands resting on her lap. Her eyes, I'm shocked to note, are wet. 'My daughter.'

'Kathryn?' Why would she be dreaming about her? And then I realize she means the other daughter.

'No. I've got . . . had . . . another daughter. Viola. She . . .' she gulps '. . . she left home at eighteen.'

I pretend to look surprised.

'I don't know.' She sighs heavily. 'Maybe it's because I'm getting on. But I've been thinking a lot about her recently.'

'Does she keep in touch?' I ask, knowing the answer.

'I've not heard from her in thirty years.' Her voice breaks. I've spent a lot of time with Elspeth over the three weeks she's employed me, and I've never heard her talk with such emotion in her voice. 'I was so angry. So angry for such a long time. But now I think what's the use? What was it all for?'

'What happened?' I ask gently.

She shakes her head and swallows. Just as I'm beginning to think she isn't going to tell me, and wonder if I should excuse myself and go back to bed, she says, 'I don't know. That's the sad thing. We argued. Of course. She was a teenager and not an easy one at that. She resented me, I think, because I adopted Kathryn. Viola was very mean to Kathryn. She bullied her. And Kathryn was like an eager puppy trying to please Viola at every turn. Viola took advantage of that. Huw, my husband, and I, we . . .' she wrings her hands '. . . we had to rescue Kathryn on more than one occasion. Once Viola left her in the woods. Another time she lured her onto the suspension bridge when it was foggy and tied her to the railings as a prank. Kathryn was shaking with shock when we found her. It was . . . I was appalled that a daughter of mine could do such a thing. And I took Kathryn's side. That's how it must have looked to Viola. Then she met a boy . . . a brute, he was most unsuitable. We argued constantly. Huw had died by this time so it was just me and her, butting heads the whole time. And then, one day, she simply . . . left.'

'Without a word?'

'Nothing . . .' She shrugs and wipes at her eyes with a silk handkerchief she always seems to have about her person. 'I never heard from her again.'

'Have you ever tried to find her?' I ask.

'Once. A few years after she left, when I realized she wasn't coming back. By this time Kathryn was at university and I thought . . . I thought the conflict between them would have run out of steam, that it might be a good time for her to come back. I tried a private detective agency but . . .' she shakes her head '. . . nothing. No leads. No clues. It's like she disappeared into thin air.' She smiles at me sadly. 'You remind me of her. You've all reminded me of her.'

I know she's thinking of the others. Of Matilde and Jemima and Una.

'And they've all gone too. All gone. Like her. Like my Viola.' She touches my cheek again. 'You won't go, will you? You won't leave me too? Promise.'

How can I promise such a thing when I never stick at a job for long? I'll get bored. I've already had a stab at many different careers – nursing, dog-walking, secretary, now a carer. I know my flaws. But Elspeth looks so sad, so desperate, that I find myself promising to stay. For as long as she needs me.

I sit with her until she falls asleep and then I get up slowly, so as not to wake her. That's when I notice something on the floor: a piece of crumpled fabric. In the shadows it looks like the blanket Arlo used to take to bed with him when he was a kid. I bend over and pick it up and that's when I see it's a woman's T-shirt in rose pink with a glittery star on the front. Much too small and trendy to be either Kathryn's or Elspeth's. I hide it under my pyjama top and creep out of the room.

33

It was March when Katy found the kitten.

She was walking home from school, alone as always. Viola had gone off with her horrible mates. Elspeth had given up asking Viola to accompany Katy. It worried Katy, who lived with the gut-wrenching fear that she'd be sent back to the home.

She tried not to think about it as she ambled along the Downs, kicking through the long grass, dew soaking her knee-high white socks with the pale blue turnovers. She still couldn't get used to the smart uniform. She even had to wear a blazer and a kilt. It made her feel like she was in Malory Towers, although she hated most of the girls at the all-girls school. Only one had bothered to befriend her. Mandy was as much of an outcast as she was, with her limp hair and thick NHS glasses. She was a scholarship kid, which meant her school fees were paid for her because she was clever but her family was poor. Katy had been to Mandy's house. It was like the one she'd lived in with her mum, but Mandy's mum and sister were lovely and welcoming, and the house was cosy and warm. Katy loved going around there, although she knew Elspeth didn't really approve. Elspeth would rather she was friends with one of the more 'prosperous' families, like that brat

Cass's – she was in Viola's year. Katy was thankful for Mandy. She felt she could cope as long as her friend was by her side.

As she approached the road she heard mewing. She stopped, straining her ears over the sound of traffic. She could definitely hear something. She parted the grass, surprised and delighted when she saw a tiny kitten nestled among the long blades. He was black with white paws and a pink nose. At first she thought he was hurt but then she decided he was just lost. She scooped him up, and as he looked at her, from his little fluffy face, her heart melted.

Katy carried him the rest of the way home, hoping she'd be allowed to keep him. He nestled his head against the crook of her arm and it was so natural she already felt they had a special bond.

'What have you got there?' exclaimed Elspeth, as Katy bounded into the kitchen with the kitten in her arms.

Viola was sitting at the large pine table, her maths books sprawled out in front of her. She looked up with a disgusted expression. 'Urgh! It's some manky flea-ridden animal,' she cried.

'It's a kitten,' said Katy, stroking his head protectively. 'He's not flea-ridden.'

'Please take him out of the house,' said Elspeth, her mouth set in a disapproving line. Her adopted mother never shouted, not like Katy's real mum had.

'Can't I keep him?' pleaded Katy.

Just then Huw strolled into the room, a newspaper tucked under his arm. 'What have we got here?' he said, beaming at Katy and extending a hand to stroke the kitten's soft little head.

'I found him,' she said, reluctantly allowing Huw to take him from her. He held the kitten up, like a vicar about to baptize a baby. The kitten looked tiny in his large hands.

He chuckled. 'I think you'll find he's a she.' He tickled her chin. 'Cute little thing.'

'Can I keep her? Oh, please, please,' she begged. She was on the verge of tears. She hadn't asked for anything since arriving from the children's home eight months ago.

Viola began to protest straight away but Huw held up a hand to silence her. 'I don't see why not.'

'Now, Huw,' began Elspeth, her fine eyebrows drawn together, 'I don't think that's a good idea. I haven't time to look after a pet . . .' She moved away from Viola and pushed Katy's hair off her face. 'Really, Kathryn, you should be wearing an Alice band.'

Usually Katy liked Elspeth touching her hair, but now she felt impatient and moved away from her mother's grasp. She wanted the kitten desperately. 'I'll look after her,' she promised. Huw was still holding the kitten and his big jolly face lit up as she began purring.

'I think it will be good for Katy,' said Huw. 'A lesson in responsibility.' He winked at Katy and she threw her arms around his large middle. In that moment she'd never loved anybody more.

Elspeth rolled her eyes, but Katy could see she was relenting. 'Okay, then, as long as you promise to feed it and –'

They were interrupted by a huffing from the table. Viola pushed back her chair, threw her pen across the room and stormed out. For once, Katy didn't care.

*

Katy decided to call the cat Mittens because of her little white paws. For the first time, she experienced real happiness. The cat slept upstairs with her in the attic and every evening, after another horrible day at school where she was ignored or jeered at for being a geek, or laughed at for her strong accent by everyone except Mandy, she'd come home, cuddle Mittens and feel everything would be okay.

And every day Mittens got bigger. Katy read books on how to look after a kitten, took her out into the garden so that she could get used to her surroundings and would know her way home when she was eventually allowed outside. And as March turned to April, Katy spent hours in the garden, playing with her new pet. Viola would scowl in their direction, but she didn't seem bothered by the cat. Katy couldn't understand it. How could anyone fail to find Mittens the most adorable ball of fluff imaginable? Maybe Viola wasn't an animal person, she thought one day, while she was grooming Mittens. Katy was suspicious of anyone who didn't like animals.

One Sunday evening, as she was coming down to feed Mittens, she heard Viola and Elspeth in the kitchen. The Top Forty was on the radio and she could hear Nik Kershaw's 'Wouldn't It Be Good', which she loved. She had a poster of him on her wall.

'She's always with that stupid cat,' she heard Viola say, her arrogant voice grating on Katy's nerves instantly. 'Why did you say yes?'

'We've talked about this. The poor girl has been through a lot. More than you could ever imagine.' Katy felt a rush of love towards Elspeth, who always stuck up for her.

'Oh, Mother. I find it tiring, I really do,' said Viola, sounding much more grown-up than her thirteen years. 'Why do you always have to have some kind of project?'

She could hear Elspeth sigh. 'She's not a project. She's my daughter.'

'*I*'m your daughter.'

'I know that.' She sounded cross.

'But you're supposed to love *me* more,' Viola said petulantly.

'I have enough love for each of you.'

'You always take her side . . .'

'Because you can be mean, Viola. It hurts me to think a child of mine can be nasty.'

'So can you, Mother. I've seen the mind games you play with Daddy. How you always have to get your own way.'

'Oh, don't be so immature. You know nothing about it.'

Katy hovered by the door, Mittens in her arms struggling to get down.

'Unlike little Goody Two Shoes St Kathryn, I suppose.'

'Now that's enough.'

'What is it going to be next? Opening our house to all those tramps on the street? Or letting the impoverished artists you're always funding come and live with us?'

'I said that's enough. Why can't you be more altruistic, Viola?'

'Like *you*, I suppose.' Viola laughed sarcastically.

'I refuse to argue with you. I know that's what you want. But it's not going to happen,' she said, her voice cold. 'And turn this rubbish off. Honestly, the amount of money I spend on your education and you listen to drivel like this.'

Kathryn shrank back into the shadows as Viola charged out of the room and thundered up the stairs.

Katy had Mittens for a year. A glorious, happy year. Until one day Mittens never came home.

Katy spent every hour she wasn't at school or asleep traipsing the pavements looking for her. Huw helped her make posters, which she stuck on lampposts, and every night she cried herself to sleep.

'I'm so sorry,' said Elspeth, one evening a few weeks later, as Katy sat hunched over her orange juice. She put her hands on Katy's shoulders and gently squeezed them.

'I just wish I knew what happened to her,' sobbed Katy. 'I did everything to make a good home for her.'

'I know you did, sweetheart,' said Huw, pulling out a chair to sit next to her.

Katy could see Viola out of the corner of her eye, smirking at the kitchen sink. And in that moment she knew. She just knew her cat's disappearance had something to do with her sister.

Katy stood up so quickly that she almost knocked over her drink. She heard Huw cry out in surprise. 'It was you, wasn't it?' Katy cried. 'You've done something to her! You never want me to be happy.'

Viola looked like she'd been slapped. Katy couldn't decide if it was because she was actually standing up for herself, or that she'd accused her of doing something unspeakable. 'Of course not,' snapped Viola. 'My God, I'm not a monster. She probably just found another family. Cats aren't loyal creatures, Katy.'

Viola glanced at Elspeth but Katy couldn't read her mother's expression.

Later, as Katy was passing the sitting room, she heard Elspeth's clear voice ring out across the hallway. 'I do hope you're not responsible for Mittens going missing,' she said. Katy hovered by the door, holding her breath. She could just make out Viola sitting in the armchair by the window, her legs curled underneath her, a copy of *To Kill A Mockingbird* in her lap, with its vibrant orange cover.

'Why do you always have to assume I'm nasty, Mother?'

Elspeth pressed her lips together in answer.

Then Viola glanced up at where Katy was hovering, a nasty smile on her face. *It was me*, her expression seemed to taunt and Katy felt a surge of rage so fierce that she had to clench her fists by her sides, her nails pressing into her palms until they drew blood.

Either Viola was pretending because she wanted to upset Katy or she had had something to do with Mittens's disappearance. Either way, Katy knew she'd have her revenge.

And she was willing to wait.

34

Kathryn

'Do you have to go today?' asks Ed, sitting up in bed. He's wearing his Mr Lazy pyjamas and the T-shirt stretches over his belly. 'It's our weekend. Family time. We never see you on a Saturday anymore.'

Kathryn sits on the edge of the bed to pull on her opaque tights. 'She's my mother.'

'Adoptive mother.'

'And she has no one else.'

'Maybe she should employ two people. It's a lot for you to take on.' His hands move to her shoulders: they feel warm through her blouse. 'You've got two sons and a husband. We need you too.'

'Please. Don't make me feel guilty.' She moves away from him and steps into her skirt.

'I'm sorry. I didn't mean it to come out like that. But with Jacob and everything he's been through . . .'

'It's one day a week.'

'Two, actually.'

She tuts. 'You're at work on Wednesday and the boys are at school. You don't even notice I'm not here. I even leave you meals to cook for the boys – if you remember to defrost them.'

'Actually,' he says, and she can hear the hurt in his

voice, 'I miss you. When you're not at your mother's, you're at the gallery. You pull away from me when I try to kiss you or hug you. I'm –'

'You're what?' she snaps. 'Because suddenly this is all about you. Don't worry about the fact I've got so much on my plate I feel like I might explode. That I'm constantly worrying about Jacob or my mother or those bloody gold-diggers she employs. Or that the gallery isn't making enough money. Or that I never get a minute, not a minute, to myself. And on top of that I'm supposed to be this perfect wife to you? But do you know what?' Her voice has risen so much she's worried she'll wake the boys. 'You're just another thing demanding my time at the moment.'

He looks as though she's punched him.

'And instead of sitting there bitching to me about it, why don't you get off your backside and actually help me? Why don't you – Oh, I don't know!' She flings her arms out. 'Cook a meal so that I don't have to worry about it when I get home. Or put the washing on. Or even – here's an idea – stack the dishwasher now and again.'

He opens his mouth to speak but no words come out and his lips hang there, like a wet fish.

'That's what I thought,' she says, zipping up her skirt. 'Can you at least make sure the boys eat properly today? And, no, that doesn't mean taking them out to fucking McDonald's.' She's so angry her heart is booming in her chest. She grabs her hairbrush from the dressing-table and slams out of the room.

She stands outside the bedroom door while her heart slows, hairbrush in hand. She shouldn't have erupted at

Ed like that. He tries his best and he's put up with her leaving him with the kids every Saturday for the last two and a half years. She contemplates going back in to apologize but then she remembers the mess the kitchen was in when she got home from work last night and decides against it.

She wonders when her marriage started to become so . . . *stale*. Was it when Matilde arrived or before that? It wasn't the boys. No, funnily enough when the boys were born it brought them closer together, cemented them as a family. She'd never felt so loved as she did when she held baby Jacob in her arms and he'd look up at her with his big brown trusting eyes or grab hold of her hair with his little fist. It was hard, especially when she discovered Elspeth would be no help, but she'd felt Jacob, Ed and her were a team, a little family unit. For the first time in her life she felt like she belonged. Properly belonged. Not a cuckoo but a mother, the most important role she'll ever have in life. And later, when Harry was born, he slotted perfectly into their lives, the cherry on top of her lovely big cake. Was there a tiny little part of her that had wanted a girl? Perhaps, but she was happy with her boys even if it was obvious her mother wasn't.

Kathryn pulls up outside Elspeth's house and tries to swallow the guilt and hurt she feels at leaving her boys again at the weekend just so she can play her role as dutiful daughter. Would she be doing all this if she didn't desperately need the inheritance? Ed is on a decent wage, yet they still find it hard to make ends meet, with a large mortgage and credit-card debts. And even though her mother pays the school fees the extras all fall to Kathryn: the ridiculously expensive uniform and the foreign trips. And she hasn't taken a wage from the gallery in months because it's making a loss, which she's going to have to admit to her mother now she wants to see the books. Another thing that will be Kathryn's fault, no doubt.

It's a crisp spring morning, and despite the blue sky, there's a cold breeze in the air. It's only seven. She's running late, thanks to her argument with Ed. On the days she doesn't stay over, her mother likes her to arrive at six thirty as that's when she gets up. She stands in front of the house with her overnight bag and her heart sinks. She'd rather be in bed next to Ed's warm, reassuring body. She hasn't had a lie-in for as long as she can remember.

The neighbour's black cat brushes against her legs and she bends down to stroke it. His name is Barney and he reminds her of Mittens. She feels a pang in her heart at the thought of the little cat she had loved so much, even after all this time. For years afterwards Kathryn searched for that cat whenever she was outside, or a passenger in the car, hoping to catch sight of her bushy tail or her white paws, but she never found her.

The house is silent when she lets herself in. She suspects Willow is still asleep. She takes off her shoes and runs upstairs to her mother's room. She's still in bed although her eyes are open and she's staring at the ceiling. She turns to Kathryn standing in the doorway. 'About time. I've been awake for ages.'

'You could get yourself out of bed, Mother. You're not an invalid,' Kathryn says, trying to keep the irritation out of her voice.

'I've been plagued with migraines this week.' She places a palm to her forehead to illustrate the point. 'I feel very woozy.'

'Maybe I should call a doctor.'

'You know I hate doctors.'

Kathryn bites back a retort as she helps Elspeth wash and dress. When they go down to breakfast Aggie is already there, bustling around the kitchen, mashing avocado and spooning it onto toast. It's too early for Kathryn to eat, but she nibbles at the toast while Elspeth and Aggie chat away inanely to each other.

'This was Una's favourite breakfast,' says Elspeth, out of the blue. It's the first time Kathryn has heard her mother mention Una for weeks. 'She was such a lovely girl, wasn't she, Aggie? So pretty, so sweet. And so talented. She was helping me crochet that blanket. My hands aren't as agile as they once were.'

That fucking blanket. Kathryn hadn't heard the end of it: 'Una has such a delicate touch, she's so talented and kind,' her mother had cooed at the time. When Una died, Kathryn had taken the half-finished blanket and stuffed it into the back of her wardrobe. Her mother hasn't mentioned it until now.

'It's so sad what happened to her.' As Elspeth says it she darts a look at Kathryn. *She knows exactly what she's doing*, thinks Kathryn. *She's trying to wind me up, make me jealous, and I'm not going to bite.* It was what she had done with Viola when they were young. Not at first. But when her mother realized they were never going to get along she'd enjoyed playing them off against each other, wanting each girl to fight for her approval, especially after Huw died. Most of the time it just made Viola rebel. But not always.

'There's been some gossip,' says Aggie, her face grim. 'You know, locally. Sandra at church the other day was asking me about it.'

'Well, I'd expect nothing less,' says Elspeth. 'I've had the police here asking questions.'

This is news to Kathryn. 'When? When have the police been here?'

Elspeth waves her bejewelled hand in Kathryn's direction. 'Oh, nothing to get your knickers in a twist about. But it doesn't look good, does it?' This is directed at Aggie. 'Three of my staff have died while living here.'

'Yes,' agrees Aggie. 'But all in completely different circumstances. And, technically, Jemima had already left.'

'I know. And the police don't think there's anything suspicious. They asked about a bag. Someone – it must have been Una before she died – reported to the police that Jemima's bag was found in our cellar.'

Kathryn puts down her knife and fork. Any appetite she might have had suddenly leaves her. She notices that Aggie is avoiding eye contact with her.

'I told them they had to be mistaken. Jemima took all her stuff with her when she walked out,' continues Elspeth. She stops talking to swallow a mouthful of food. Aggie waits patiently for her to continue. She's standing at the sink holding a mug of coffee, a grey apron tied around her large middle. 'And they seemed satisfied with that.'

'Does Willow know about the others?' asks Aggie.

Did Una tell Aggie about the bag? Kathryn wonders.

That would explain why Aggie has been behaving oddly around her lately.

'Absolutely not,' says Elspeth, firmly. 'And I want it to stay that way. I don't want her to worry or to feel unsafe here.'

Aggie shakes her chins. 'I've not said a thing. And it's not like anything bad happened in the house. It's all out of your control.' She takes a noisy slurp of her drink.

'Exactly,' agrees Elspeth. 'They were grown girls. Women, really. How they lived their lives when they weren't at work was nothing to do with me. If they wanted to take unnecessary risks, or walk back home drunk late at night, or throw themselves off the bridge, then what could I do about it? I didn't own them. They just worked for me, that's all.'

Kathryn wonders if her mother can hear how insensitive she sounds. She notices Aggie flinch, then try to cover it up by sipping her coffee.

They fall silent. 'It's sad, though,' says Aggie, eventually. 'I was fond of them all. I suppose I got attached to each of them. Particularly Matilde, as she was here the longest. Even Una who was only here six weeks – I used to enjoy our chats. I feel like I don't want to get too attached to Willow.'

Elspeth, who had been cutting her toast into tiny pieces, stops what she's doing and her head snaps up. 'What do you mean?' Her tone is cold. 'What do you think's going to happen to Willow?'

'Nothing. I didn't mean anything by it. I just meant . . .'

'That she's going to die too?'

Aggie looks flustered. 'No!'

'That there's some curse on my young staff? Or do you

mean that Kathryn or I might –' She drops her knife in her anger and it clatters onto the table '– be responsible somehow?'

Poor Aggie. Kathryn almost feels sorry for her. She can see Aggie doesn't know what to do with herself. She starts flapping, gathering up the breakfast things even though they haven't finished, whisking the plate from under Elspeth's nose and taking it to the sink.

'Come on, Mother, let's go up to the sitting room,' says Kathryn, in an effort to dispel the uncomfortable atmosphere.

But Elspeth is in no mood to be pacified today. She refuses to take Kathryn's proffered arm, instead, forgetting how infirm she's supposed to be, she strides over to where Aggie stands, thrusting her cup into Aggie's face. 'I'd like some more coffee, please,' she says.

Aggie nods and takes the cup, filling it from the cafetière. Elspeth's expression is scornful, mean. Kathryn recognizes it and remembers how quickly Elspeth's moods turn. She looks as though she's about to say more to Aggie when her attention is diverted by someone standing at the kitchen door. It's Willow, still in her nightwear, her long hair hanging down her back. She looks childlike in her oversized pyjamas. Elspeth's face instantly loses its sour expression and brightens at the sight of her. 'Good morning, Willow,' she says cheerily. 'You're up early.' Kathryn and Aggie exchange knowing looks, their previous awkwardness dissipating. 'Aggie, please can you prepare some breakfast for Willow?' She walks over to her companion, places an arm around her slim shoulders and ushers her to the table, like she's a princess on a royal visit.

Una used to look embarrassed by the attention Elspeth would occasionally lavish on her but Willow is positively glowing in it. She turns to Kathryn and gives her such a self-satisfied look that it knocks the breath from her. She's another Matilde – she can feel it in her bones. If she's not careful her mother will have bequeathed half of her estate to Willow before the year is out.

When Willow first arrived, Kathryn had tried to find out more about her, just like she'd done with the other girls. But there was nothing, not even a former address. She'd found a copy of her measly CV in Elspeth's study and contacted the referees she'd listed, but both numbers rang out and Kathryn knew they were fake.

Kathryn watches as Elspeth's mood changes and she laughs and jokes with Willow. She could be at home with her family now, she thinks, walks in the park with Ed and the boys. Cycling – Harry's always on at her to go for a family bike ride – or they could be watching a movie, snuggled up beneath the blankets, eating junk food.

Her mother's sudden bark of laughter grates just as much as Willow's smug face. She'd made a huge effort to get here early to help Elspeth when she could have been at home. Kathryn stalks out of the kitchen, even though she doubts anyone notices. She'll wait in the sitting room until Willow's gone out. She can't bear to witness her mother's sycophantic behaviour a moment longer.

Kathryn is frowning over the books in the sitting room. It's been ages since she last looked at them, but something doesn't add up. She knows the gallery isn't making any money but, according to the ledger, they are further into the red than she had calculated.

When Elspeth finally joins her she's clinging to Willow's arm, suddenly infirm again.

'Are you okay now?' Willow asks Elspeth, as she helps her into a chair, flashing a pointed look in Kathryn's direction.

Elspeth pats Willow's hand. 'Thank you. You are good.'

It takes all of Kathryn's willpower not to roll her eyes.

Willow leaves the room saying she's off to get dressed.

'I thought it was her day off,' murmurs Kathryn.

Elspeth scowls at her. 'It is. But you'd just left me downstairs on my own.'

'Oh, for goodness' sake,' Kathryn snaps. 'You're perfectly capable of getting yourself up the stairs. This has got to stop, Mother.'

'What does?'

'This reliance on other people. If it's that hard then maybe you should go into assisted living and sell the house.' She's amazed that she's telling the truth for once, rather than pussy-footing around her mother like she usually does.

'Sell the house? You of all people want me to sell the house?'

'Of course I don't. I love this house, you know that. But . . .' Kathryn softens her voice deliberately '. . . I'm worried about you. It's a big place. The stairs . . .'

'I've had a thought about that and I've decided I'm going to install a stairlift.'

This is a surprise to Kathryn. 'Really?' She can't bear

the thought of the beautiful oak staircase being blighted by an ugly lift. 'You've always said you hated those things.'

She purses her lips. 'Hmm, well, needs must.'

Kathryn knows she's gone too far. Her mother is doing this to punish her.

'Also . . .' she says, smiling at Kathryn in the chilling way she's come to recognize over the years. It's the smile she bestows on her unsuspecting victims whenever she's about to impart some news that she knows won't go down too well. '. . . I've been thinking a lot lately. About Viola.'

A wave of alarm washes over Kathryn. 'What?'

'Don't look so surprised.'

'But you've never wanted to talk about her. You removed all photos of her, pretended for years she doesn't even exist.'

'That doesn't mean I've not thought about her. After all, she is my daughter.'

She says this coldly, as though to make clear that Kathryn is not.

35

Willow

When I leave the house around ten o'clock, Elspeth is in the sitting room with her cold fish of a daughter. Kathryn has brought the accounts from the gallery. When I poke my head around the door to say goodbye, they're having what looks like a serious discussion. I knew Kathryn would be here today. And I know why she plays the dutiful daughter. It's all about money, I can see that now. Money and control. Thank God my parents never had any. I'm not naïve: I can tell that Elspeth's affection for me isn't that of a normal boss/employee relationship. Obviously, I have no idea how she treated the other girls but Courtney said Una had told her Elspeth blew hot and cold. But with me Elspeth is always lovely: maternal, giving, generous. Last week I took her shopping and she bought me this boho bag with tassels I've had my eye on for ages at a boutique in Clifton. She never lets me pay for anything, even though she gives me a generous wage. I've hardly spent a thing since I moved in. I've seen her cold side, of course. The way she is with Kathryn sometimes is frosty. But, so far, she's been nothing but kind and welcoming to me. Still, it's early days.

It's another warm spring day. I only need a jacket on top of my T-shirt and trousers. I can already see a hint of summer on the horizon, tantalizingly close. Where will I be then? I've been thinking more and more about going back to studying, maybe reflexology. I'm not really a make-a-plan kind of person, but maybe that's where I've always gone wrong in the past. If I stay in this job for a couple of years I'll have enough money to return to college, get a place of my own.

Courtney has set up a WhatsApp group to include me and Peter. I told them both last night about finding the keys for the gallery. We agreed I'd go over there today to suss out if there are any CCTV cameras. If we're going after dark we'll need to make sure nobody knows we were there. Peter has today off and is driving down so we can break in tonight.

I stop for a takeaway coffee on the way to the gallery, pausing to chat to the cute barista with the dreadlocks and sparkly eyes who now knows me by name. I enjoy taking my time on the walk, savouring the fact it's my day off and I don't have to rush anywhere. I think of the texts I've been exchanging with Courtney and Peter. It's strange, really, considering I've known them just a few weeks, but they're already starting to feel like friends. Yet it's a warped friendship that the three of us have formed. They're acting out of grief, but why am I doing it? They're looking for answers on behalf of those they loved and lost.

At first I agreed to help because it was almost like a game, something to relieve the boredom of the job.

But then I found the T-shirt. When I described it to Courtney she'd been adamant it was Una's. 'I was with her when she bought it,' she said, over the phone. 'Why would

Elspeth have Una's T-shirt? When Una died I went to the house to collect her clothes.'

'Maybe Elspeth had wanted to keep a memento,' I'd suggested, which horrified Courtney, especially when I admitted I'd found it in Elspeth's bedroom, and that I believed she'd been sleeping with it.

Whether Elspeth is involved in the deaths of the other girls or not, it's obvious she has a slight obsession with all of us, is capricious and faking her frailty for attention. I sometimes wonder if maybe she's losing her marbles, confusing us so that in her mind we merge to become Viola. I don't understand it but, even so, does that make her a killer?

When I arrive, the shop is predictably empty. Daisy is sitting at Kathryn's desk, her mobile cradled between ear and shoulder, picking at her pink acrylic nails. 'Yes, that's what I'm worried about,' she's saying into the phone. When she hears the ping of the door she looks up and irritation flashes across her features when she sees it's me. 'Gotta go. Speak later.' She ends the call. 'Back again so soon?'

'Sorry to bother you. I know you're really busy.'

She rolls her eyes at my sarcasm.

'The last time I came here I think I left something behind,' I lie.

She narrows her eyes at me. 'Oh, really? What was that, then?'

'My . . .' I cast my eyes around the shop, hoping for inspiration '. . . brother's door key,' I say desperately.

'Your brother's door key?'

'For his flat. It's a spare and he'll kill me if I don't find it.'

She continues to stare at me without speaking, one of her perfectly plucked eyebrows raised.

'You know what big brothers are like,' I say, conscious that I'm rambling now. 'Do you mind if I scoot about?'

She breaks eye contact and shrugs. 'I was just about to make myself a coffee anyway,' she says, getting up. Her skirt is so short I can see the tops of her tights. 'So scoot away.' She wanders off to the back of the shop and I get down on my hands and knees on the cold white tiles, pretending to look for my brother's key and feeling foolish. What am I doing? This is harder than I'd thought.

She comes back, coffee cup in hand, and surveys me with an amused expression. 'Found it?'

I stand up and dust down my trousers. 'No. Sadly not. Never mind. If you do, though, would you let me know?'

She shrugs in answer.

'So,' I say, in my best breezy voice. 'Doing anything fun tonight?'

'Seeing my boyfriend.'

'Do you have to work late on a Saturday?'

She shakes her head. 'Only till five.'

'That's good.' I make a mental note to tell the others.

I turn to leave when I say, as if suddenly remembering, 'Elspeth told me there was a break-in down here a few nights ago.'

Daisy frowns. 'A break-in? Really?'

'Apparently. Not one of Elspeth's shops, luckily. I wonder if they have CCTV.'

'I think they do in the corridor. Not in this shop, though.'

I pull a relieved face. 'Great. Well, have a nice time with your boyfriend tonight.'

'Lewis,' she says, as I go to leave the shop. 'His name is Lewis.'

Courtney is already in the White Hart when I get there at seven as planned. I'd suggested we wear dark clothing so we wouldn't stand out. She's in black jeans and a leather jacket that looks like it belongs to her boyfriend. Her red hair is plaited and she's not wearing as much makeup as usual. Understated. I'm pleased she listened to the brief.

It was hard for me to find dark clothes, considering all my things are so bright. The best I could do was an old black anorak that I threw over a pair of ink-blue satin trousers. I'm wearing a beanie I pinched from Arlo when I moved out to hide my blonde hair.

Courtney has a glass of wine in front of her so I go straight to the bar and order a Coke. I want to keep my wits about me tonight.

She looks up in surprise when I join her at the table. 'I didn't recognize you,' she says, laughing.

I laugh, too, aware of how ridiculous I must look. 'Is this mad?' I say, as I slide into my seat.

She sobers up. 'I have to do this for Una.' Her eyes fill. 'I worry about involving you, though.'

I shake my head to silence her. 'No. I *am* involved. You know why.'

'I don't want to put you in danger.'

'I could be in danger anyway.'

'Do you feel safe at the house?'

I admit that I do. 'Kathryn doesn't like me, that much

is clear. And there've been a few occasions when I felt like I was being followed.' I tell her about the night Vince followed me from the pub. 'You don't think he'd hurt Una, do you?'

She splutters on her drink. 'Vince? No. He loved her.'

'Didn't you say he stole from her? If he killed her, he'd never have to pay her back.'

'But why would he kill Jemima? And Matilde?'

I sit back in my chair. 'True.'

'And I've known Vince for years. I can't imagine him hurting anyone. Not physically anyway.'

We look up as Peter walks in. He's wearing the same mustard jacket he had on the last time. I notice how Courtney's face brightens when she sees him. He looks as though he's bursting to tell us something. He fetches himself a pint, then joins us.

I don't know whether to mention the coat and that I'd said dark clothing. But before I have the chance to speak he blurts out, 'I had a visit from the police. I know what they said to you, Courtney, and that we didn't think they were doing anything, but they are. They're working hard behind the scenes. They told me they have CCTV images of the bridge.'

'The bridge?' Courtney asks. 'The suspension bridge?'

He nods like an eager puppy. I've never seen him so animated. 'Yep. The bridge has CCTV. I never knew that. It's been hard for them to detect anything because of the fog on the night Una died, but they've seen Jemima was with someone on the bridge that night. And it looks as though they were having an argument. Whoever it was, she knew them.'

'What about the van?' says Courtney.

'What van?' I ask.

Peter fills me in. 'But the number-plate was obscured, which makes the police think whoever harmed Jemima planned it.'

I'm speechless. And so is Courtney. We both stare at him with our mouths hanging open and I feel a stab of panic. Maybe I am in danger at the McKenzie house, after all.

'I knew it,' he adds. 'I knew she'd never kill herself.'

'But,' I say, when I find my voice, 'she died at the end of December. It's taken them three months to work this out?'

He shuffles out of his coat. 'They said something about the glare of the LED lights on the bridge and the weather conditions. She was too far away from the cameras for them to make out exactly what happened, but the fact that there was someone on the bridge with her has made them look more closely into what happened to her and Una.'

'And the other girl. Matilde?'

He looks doubtful. 'I'm not sure about that. That might just have been an unfortunate accident. Very different circumstances. But both Jemima and Una died while they were on the suspension bridge.'

'And did they say anything about Una?' Courtney asks, hope in her voice.

'No. They told me about Jemima only because I'm her next of kin.' He grabs Courtney's hand and squeezes it. 'But they'll find a connection. After this, they can't think that what happened to Una was an accident.'

Courtney flushes. 'That's true. It was foggy the night Una died, though. Will they be able to see anything?'

'I'm not sure,' says Peter. I notice his hand is still on Courtney's. Then, as if he senses me looking, he takes his hand away and sips his pint.

'Could they tell if it was a man or a woman?' I ask.

He shakes his head. 'Someone tall. Taller than Jemima anyway. Wearing a long black coat and trousers. The hood was pulled up on the coat. They suspect a man but they're not ruling out a woman.'

36

Courtney

Courtney follows the others, heart pounding. Willow is striding out in front. She's loving this, being the leader, the drama of it all. Courtney can't help but worry that Willow isn't taking it as seriously as she should be. After what Peter said tonight, it sounds as though their suspicions are correct, that Jemima and Una were murdered, and Willow could be in danger.

A lump had formed in her throat when Peter imparted his news and it hasn't left. She has to concentrate on not crying, on not thinking about Una alone on the bridge. Alone and vulnerable in that fog, believing she was meeting Peter but instead being lured to her death. The other day it hit her, like it often does, as though for the first time, and she'd raged and thrown things in the flat, scaring Kris, eventually collapsing in a heap of angry tears on the sofa. Una was so kind, so good. And she'd had such a shit time of it, first losing her mum, then Vince, and she'd handled it all so bravely.

'She's with her mum now,' Kris had said, sitting beside her and awkwardly patting her shoulder, which had just made Courtney cry even more. What did Kris know about any of it? He's never lost anyone. How can he begin to

understand the heavy pressure of grief that sits perma-
nently on her chest.

Peter is next to her, his yellow coat making him stand
out, like a beacon of light, in the darkness. She knows he
must understand exactly how she's feeling, having lost a
loved one too.

It's a Saturday night so the streets are busy but it feels
to Courtney, in this moment, as though it's just the three
of them, united in this quest.

Willow leads them through the arcade's empty corri-
dors. It's spooky at night. They have to light the way with
the torches on their phones: three beams bouncing around
the ornate ceilings and pillars. 'It's a bit scary,' Courtney
admits, her voice small in the large Gothic space as a gar-
goyle leers at them, its face twisted and ugly.

Peter takes her hand. 'It's okay,' he says. His hand feels
warm in hers, safe. He turns to her then, and she can just
about make out his smile in the darkness. Her tummy
does a weird little back-flip.

Willow stops outside the art gallery. It's painted white
with 'McKenzie's' in black letters. The grilles are down at
the windows.

'Right,' says Willow, who looks ridiculous in a beanie
and an oversized anorak. 'The camera's over there. No,
don't turn around and look,' she growls, when Courtney
and Peter are about to do just that.

'We're not committing a crime, technically,' says
Peter. 'We've got a key. So why would anyone check the
CCTV?'

Willow tuts. 'Just in case. Although you'll stand out a
mile in that coat.'

'I could have picked the lock,' says Peter. 'Just saying. I'm a firefighter, remember.'

'You could have mentioned that before,' hisses Willow.

'Better to do it legitimately. Then we won't raise suspicions.

Willow folds her arms across her chest. 'I got caught by Elspeth stealing this key.'

'You did?' Courtney asks in horror.

'Well, she saw me in the key cupboard but she didn't notice I had it in my hand. Right, come on.'

They follow her into the shop. Courtney freezes, expecting an alarm to go off, but there's nothing and she looks around in surprise. The hair salon is always alarmed when it's closed.

Willow switches on an overhead light and they blink like woodland creatures waking up after hibernation. 'We'd better not be too long, in case we're seen,' says Willow, hands on her hips. 'We need to search any areas where Kathryn would try to hide a bag.'

They split up. Courtney drifts towards the back of the shop where there is a little storage area. She has some Parma Violets in her pocket, which she keeps nervously eating. It feels eerie being here after dark, and forbidden, like a classroom after school has finished for the day. She walks past a fridge with a kettle on top and goes through a curtained area to where a number of paintings are stacked against the wall. She supposes they're waiting to be picked up or have just arrived. They're all bubble-wrapped and mostly large, some in frames, others just canvases, although she can't make out more than that. She can't see any nooks and crannies, though, where a bag might be hidden. She gets down on her hands and knees. The flooring in the storage room is linoleum and it's dusty, tickling the back of her throat. The strip-light overhead buzzes and she notices a dead fly beneath the plastic casing. She crawls along on her hands and knees until she spots a door in the wall. It's small but she opens it anyway. It's full of old cans of white paint. She pushes some aside but there's no room behind to fit a large duffle bag.

'Have you found anything?'

She turns at the sound of Peter's voice. He's standing behind her, his eyes scanning the room and the ceiling, where they land on a hatch. 'There's a loft,' he says in surprise. He raises his voice to call Willow and they hear her heavy boots pounding on the tiles as she runs towards them.

'What? Have you found it?'

'No, but look,' he says, pointing to the ceiling. 'I'm going to try to get up there.'

Peter's tall but it's still out of reach unless he stands on something. Courtney darts from the storage room to the main body of the shop. What can he use? She grabs a chair with wheels and pushes it towards Peter. 'Use this,' she says. 'We'll hold it still.'

They position it under the hatch and hold it while Peter climbs onto it. With his arms outstretched he can just about reach. He pushes against the hatch and slides it to the side. The three of them stare up into the gaping black hole above their heads.

'How are we going to get up there?' asks Courtney.

'Give me a leg up,' says Willow. 'I'm the smallest. I can climb through.'

'We can't both balance on this chair,' says Peter, doubt-fully. He climbs down and goes back into the office. Courtney and Willow follow to see him grappling with Daisy's desk. It's no more than a table with files on it and a laptop, which they move to the floor. Then the three of them half carry, half drag it into the storage room. It takes them a while to manoeuvre it through the small curtained doorway, and they have to turn it on its side, but after ten minutes of grunting and swearing – mostly from Willow – they finally have it positioned under the hatch. Peter and Willow climb onto it. Then he lifts her up, no trouble, and Willow disappears into the black hole.

'There's no lights up here,' her disembodied voice calls through the silence. 'I'm using my phone . . . Ow . . .'

'What is it?' cries Courtney.

Peter, who is still standing on the desk, glances down at her and grins, then holds up crossed fingers. A lock of his blond hair falls over his forehead and her stomach contracts. Why is he having this effect on her? She's never reacted this way to Kris, not even when they first met.

'I've found something – a bag,' Willow's voice calls.

Courtney's heart quickens in anticipation.

'I'm going to chuck it down. Ready . . .'

Before they've had a chance to reply, a bag hurtles towards Peter. He catches it in his arms, and frowns as he runs his long fingers over the logo. Then he unzips the bag, staring at the contents for a while before lifting out a short floral dress. He turns to Courtney, his face pinched. 'I don't think this is her stuff,' he says, shoving the dress back into the bag. 'My sister lived in jeans. I'm not an expert but . . .' He throws the bag to Courtney and it lands at her feet.

She kneels on the floor to riffle through it. The clothes look dated – why didn't Una pick up on that before? She reads the labels – Chelsea Girl, C&A. These shops don't exist anymore.

Peter and Willow climb down from the desk and join her. 'Whose do you think it is?' asks Willow.

Courtney's fingers close around a passport. She hands it to Peter.

'It's Jemima's,' he says, his face grim.

'But these clothes belonged to someone else,' says Courtney, shoving a long tie-dyed skirt in Willow's face. It smells musty. 'Look, this says Chelsea Girl. My mum used to talk about that shop. It was popular in the 1980s.'

They all stare at each other, until finally Willow speaks. 'I think these clothes must be Viola's.'

37

Kathryn

Kathryn is woken at six the next morning by banging on the front door. At first she ignores it, thinking it must be a mistake. After all, it is Sunday morning. The postman doesn't come on a Sunday. She pulls the duvet over her head but the knocking becomes more insistent and she's forced to get up. She pulls her grey velour dressing-gown around herself and makes her way down the stairs.

'Who is it?' calls Elspeth, as Kathryn passes her bedroom. Her door is ajar.

'Go back to sleep, Mother. I'll sort it.'

Kathryn's furious now, her heart thumping with rage. How dare someone wake them up this early? And then panic sets in. What if it's the police coming to inform her that something has happened to one of the boys or Ed? She clutches her throat as she almost runs across the hallway, the tiles cold underfoot, and unlocks the front door. She curses Willow under her breath that she didn't double-bolt it last night. She's usually so good at remembering.

The police flash their badges at her as soon as she's opened the door. The sight of them makes her breath catch. They are plain-clothed and the older of the two women steps forward. She recognizes her as DS Christine Holdsworth, who came over before to tell them about

Jemima. She's accompanied by someone different this time, a younger woman with mousy hair tied back at the neck and thick, black-framed glasses.

'Kathryn Winters?' asks DS Holdsworth, holding up her badge. 'May we come in?'

'Is everything okay?'

'We'd just like to ask you a few questions about Jemima Freeman.'

Kathryn's feelings oscillate between relief that Ed and the boys are safe to dread that they're back asking questions about Jemima.

'It's a bit early,' she says, her voice cold. It's only just getting light and there is a fine rain in the air. It settles, like dandruff, on the shoulders of the officers' black overcoats. She sighs, knowing she has to face the inevitable, and stands aside to let them in.

DS Holdsworth introduces the younger officer as DC Felicity Reid. She looks almost as young as Willow, with a round baby face and dimples. The three are hovering in the hallway when Elspeth makes her way downstairs, gripping the banister tightly, her shoulders hunched against the cold. She hasn't put on her dressing-gown and Kathryn can make out her bony frame through her thin nightdress. She looks like a ghoul, thinks Kathryn, unkindly. 'Mother, you should be in bed.'

'Una's not back.'

'It's Willow, Mother, remember? Una's dead.' She realizes as she says it how uncaring and blunt she sounds, and notices that DC Reid recoils slightly at her words. Kathryn concentrates on rearranging her face into a passive expression. 'My mother confuses names sometimes,' she explains to them. They don't say anything. DS Holdsworth stares back at Kathryn, her face hard.

'Has something happened to Willow?' Elspeth calls from halfway down the stairs.

Holdsworth shakes her auburn frizz. 'No. This is about Jemima Freeman, Mrs McKenzie. We just need to have a few words with your daughter.'

'Why?'

Holdsworth ignores her and instead speaks directly to Kathryn. 'Is there somewhere we can sit?'

Kathryn leads them into the sitting room and offers to take their wet coats. She can just imagine her mother's wrath if any rain gets onto her expensive velvet chairs. She leaves the room to hang their overcoats in the cupboard as Elspeth continues down the stairs slowly, as if every step is painful, gripping so tightly to the banister that her knuckles turn white. 'Where is Willow? She's usually getting me up by now.'

'I don't know. I've got more important things on my mind,' she snaps. 'Like why two cops have come to speak to me at this time in the morning.' When Elspeth has reached the last step, Kathryn escorts her across the hallway and into the sitting room where she settles her in her favourite chair. Kathryn takes the one next to her. The two officers are on the sofa, sitting at either end. The younger one has a notebook in her hand and is chewing the top of her pen.

'So what is this about?' Kathryn asks, crossing her legs. She remembers she's only got a T-shirt on underneath her dressing-gown. She pulls it around herself.

'I just wanted to ask you a bit more about the day of the

nineteenth of December when you last saw Jemima Freeman,' begins Holdsworth.

'I've told you all this before.'

'We'd like to hear it again, please.'

Kathryn suppresses a sigh. 'I wasn't even here. She was supposed to go to the gallery with my mother, wasn't she?' She turns to Elspeth, who nods. 'But she stayed behind because she had a migraine. My mother told you all this last time.'

Holdsworth sits up straighter and pushes her shoulders back. 'So, let's get this straight. On the afternoon she left here, you were both out? The last person to see her was you, Mrs McKenzie, and that was just after lunch? When you returned home around five she was gone, taking all her stuff with her?'

'Yes. That's right,' agrees Elspeth.

Holdsworth smiles tightly. 'So why did you have Jemima's passport, Kathryn?'

Kathryn's heart feels like it's about to stop. 'What?'

'A bag of clothes containing Jemima's passport was handed into the station. It was found at the gallery. The gallery you run.'

Elspeth flashes Kathryn a questioning gaze.

'Care to explain?' adds Holdsworth. 'Or would you rather do it down at the station?'

Kathryn sags against the cushions. What's the use? She might as well tell the truth. Or, at least, her version of the truth. 'Okay . . . The bag . . . it belonged to Viola. She was my sister.'

Holdsworth sits up straighter. Kathryn notices she has a crease down each trouser leg and imagines her getting up at the crack of dawn to iron them. 'Your sister?'

'She left home when she was eighteen. Back in 1988. It was just some old clothes she left behind. We never got around to getting rid of them.'

Holdsworth glances at Elspeth but she doesn't say anything. Elspeth turns to Kathryn. 'You had Viola's bag?'

'Yes, Mother.' She tuts. 'Just clothes we had packed away together years ago. Don't you remember?'

'No,' says Elspeth. 'I thought she'd taken everything.'

Kathryn waves her hand impatiently. 'I'm sure the police aren't here to discuss Viola.'

Holdsworth frowns, then reaches inside her suit jacket to retrieve her notebook. She flips it open with one hand. 'Why did you have Jemima's passport?'

'She left it behind after we argued,' says Kathryn, not missing a beat.

Elspeth hangs her head but says nothing. Kathryn notices strands of white hair have come out of her chignon. She's never seen her anything but composed and immaculate – except just once.

Holdsworth's face is grim. 'So what really happened?'

'Do I need a lawyer?'

'We're not arresting you, Kathryn. This is just an informal chat.'

'Okay. Well, I met my mother at the gallery as she wanted to talk to one of the artists who was going to sell their work through us. Anyway, she'd forgotten to bring the paperwork so I said I'd pick it up. I drove over here to collect it and that's when I found Jemima. She was rummaging in my mother's desk, going through her things.

We argued. I told her I'd have her fired . . . Yes, I know, not my finest moment, but you have to understand that these — *these girls* are usually only after my mother's money.' She ignores Elspeth's protests. 'I don't trust them. Anyway, Jemima was crying, begging me not to tell Elspeth and making some, quite frankly, ludicrous excuse as to why she was in the study. I'm not going to lie, I did shout at her and accuse her of all sorts, and she ran upstairs crying. The next thing I knew she was leaving the house with a backpack.'

'And you never saw her again?'

'No. I was worried I'd gone too far with my accusations. So I was relieved when she didn't come back. I went into her room and found her passport in the drawer. In her hurry to leave she must have forgotten it.'

'But why hide it?' asks DC Reid.

'Because I didn't want my mother to know we'd argued. I wanted her to think Jemima had just left because she'd had enough.'

'And you didn't wonder why she didn't come back for it?'

Kathryn nods. 'Of course. But I figured she knew I was on to her, that she'd found another victim to try to fleece and that she didn't need it. It was only the passport. She had her handbag on her with her money and things.'

Holdsworth writes something in her notebook, then looks up at Kathryn. 'You say she had a backpack on her?'

'Yes.'

'She didn't have it on her when she died.'

Kathryn shrugs. 'I don't know what she did with it.' She hesitates. 'I don't have it if that's what you're getting at. The clothes are Viola's. I just shoved the passport into that bag because I thought, at some point, Jemima would come back for it.'

She wonders who found it. Daisy probably. Kathryn had been dubious about storing it at the gallery, but she hadn't known where else to put it after Una had found it in the cellar. She'd thought it would be safe in the loft.

'Where were you at around eleven p.m. on the nineteenth of December?'

Kathryn frowns. 'I was here, wasn't I, Mother? When Jemima didn't come back I stayed to help.'

Holdsworth turns to Elspeth, who looks skinny in her chair, her face pale. 'Is this true?'

Elspeth wrinkles her brow but doesn't say anything, and Kathryn feels sweat break out under her armpits. 'I can't remember,' she says, not looking in Kathryn's direction. 'I think so. I'm sure that's true, but it's months ago now and my memory isn't as good as it was once.'

A white-hot flame of anger ignites inside Kathryn. 'You know I was here,' she snaps, turning to Elspeth. 'You hate being on your own in the house.'

Elspeth replies calmly, her face poised, 'I'm sure you're right, my dear.'

Holdsworth doesn't look convinced and she surveys Kathryn, her eyes scanning her as though she has X-ray vision and can see her every thought. It makes Kathryn feel uncomfortable. 'How tall are you?' she finally asks. 'Five ten?'

'Nearly.'

'And Jemima was what?'

Kathryn feels a prickle of irritation. 'I don't know. Five one?'

Holdsworth makes a noise through her teeth. 'We have CCTV footage of Jemima on the bridge that night. She wasn't alone.'

Elspeth leans forward. 'What do you mean? You think someone hurt her?'

'I'm afraid so, Mrs McKenzie. Someone else was with her on the bridge that night.'

Kathryn falls back against the chair. When she speaks her voice is thin, strained. 'Am I a suspect?'

'We're looking into all avenues. A witness has come forward to say they saw her getting out of a white van. Do you know anybody with a van?'

Kathryn exchanges looks with her mother. 'Handymen who have come to the house in the past, I suppose,' says Elspeth. 'A joiner came to put up shelves a few months ago. He had a white van.'

'Would he have met Jemima?'

Her mother considers this question. 'No. No, it was before she started here.'

'If you can think of anything else, please get in touch,' says Holdsworth. She stands up and the younger officer follows suit. 'Thank you for your time. We'll see ourselves out.'

After the police have left, Kathryn can't move for a few minutes. She can't even speak. Her mother must feel the same as she shrinks into her seat, looking frailer than ever.

Elspeth breaks the silence. 'I knew you'd argued with Jemima.'

'What?'

'I saw her running out of the house, crying. My taxi

had just pulled in. I didn't tell the police the first time they visited because –'

'Because you thought I might have hurt her.'

Elspeth dips her head. She has the good grace to look ashamed. Then she glances up at Kathryn, with her usual, challenging gaze. 'Why do you hate the girls so much?'

Kathryn fidgets in her seat. 'I don't trust them.'

'So that's why you wanted to put a lock on my study after Jemima left? Do you really think I'm that naïve? That I'll let some pretty young thing fleece me out of my money? Is this what it's all about for you? Your inheritance?'

Kathryn feels a flush of guilt. 'No. Of course not.' Now would be a good time to admit she knows about the will and that Matilde was down to get a big chunk of her mother's cash. But she can't bring herself to say it. It will make Elspeth believe she's only worried about money.

Elspeth stands up. She trembles in her thin nightgown. 'Can you help me upstairs?' she barks, her voice betraying her size. 'It's nearly seven o'clock. I don't understand where Willow is.'

Kathryn does as she's asked. She helps her mother into the shower, then assists her with getting dressed. Once Elspeth is resplendent in a smart tweed skirt and silk blouse she looks like her formidable mother once again. Elspeth reaches up and touches her hair, her fingers finding the loose strands from the chignon. 'Thank goodness I have a hairdresser's appointment tomorrow,' she says, pushing the tendrils of white hair behind her ears. 'My hair is a mess.'

'It looks fine.'

And still Willow hasn't emerged from her room. 'I

need to get home,' says Kathryn, thinking of the argument she had with Ed yesterday. 'Maybe Willow's overslept. I'll go and check.'

She leaves her mother sitting on the edge of her bed, applying her lipstick with a shaky hand, and climbs the stairs to the attic. It always brings her back, coming up here. The years fall away. She can almost imagine Viola on the landing below, shouting obscenities or threats. She knocks on Willow's door, but when there is no answer, she tries the handle. It's not locked so she opens the door and steps into the room.

Willow's bed is empty and looks unslept-in. She goes to the wardrobe, her heart pounding, but the girl's odd boho clothes are still there, some hanging up, others bundled in a heap at the bottom. She closes the wardrobe and scans the room, looking for more clues. Willow's perfumes are scattered on the top of the dressing-table and her makeup spills out of a soft felt bag. There's a tie-dye blouse on the bed and a pair of chunky boots by the desk. But Willow is nowhere to be seen.

'Mother!' she calls, running from the room and down the stairs. She's breathless by the time she reaches Elspeth. 'Willow's not there. I don't think she came home last night.'

You stupid girl. You stupid, stupid girl. I was relying on you. I'd hoped, believed, you would be The One. The True One. Not like the others. Different. Special. But no. You had to play detective. You had to ruin it all. You and your pathetic friends.

You're going to regret it.

38

Willow

The flat is in darkness when Peter drops us off. It's late and the area where Courtney lives is quiet, just a few youths in hoodies smoking beside a bus stop.

I get out of the car and wait on the pavement for Courtney to say goodbye to Peter. She's in the passenger seat and they're having a chat about the bag. It's cold and I pull the beanie further over my head. I'm beginning to feel completely out of my depth with all of this. Courtney eventually gets out and we wave as Peter's Mazda pulls away.

'He'll let us know what the police say,' says Courtney. 'Come on, let's get inside.'

I follow her down an alleyway that leads around the back of the pharmacy and up some rickety steps to her flat. It's small, and smells of Glade plug-ins with an under-lay of damp. It's strange to think this is where Una lived too. It's like I'm walking in her shoes, living her life. It's a strange feeling and I shiver, wrapping the anorak further around my body.

'You can stay in Una's old room,' says Courtney, going to the little kitchen, which is tacked onto the end of a living room, and putting the kettle on. Everything is immacu-lately tidy: no strewn shoes on the floor or magazines thrown on the table. No dirty plates and cups in the sink. I lean back against the rickety units. It's worlds away from Elspeth's elegant townhouse. 'It's full of Kris's stuff but her bed is still there.'

'Are you sure Kris won't mind?'

'It's not up to him,' she says, folding her arms defiantly. 'And you can't go back to The Cuckoo's Nest. It's not safe.'

I sigh. I know she's right. Now, after finding Viola's bag and Jemima's passport in Kathryn's gallery, well, things have turned up a notch. The danger is real. Kathryn must be involved somehow, maybe even Elspeth. How far do their crimes go back? Did Kathryn hurt Viola? Did Elspeth? Despite her advancing years, she's a lot more sprightly and healthy than she tries to make out. There's something weird going on in that house. I might never know what it is but I'm relieved to be out of it. I can't deny that I'll miss the money, even the luxurious surroundings, but if I went back there I wouldn't be able to rest, wondering if I'd be their next victim.

'Why do you think they did it?' I ask Courtney, as she pours us each a mint tea.

Courtney shakes her head. I can see she's trying to suppress her emotions and she can't speak for a while, her lips pressed tightly together. She hands me a mug, which I take with thanks, then opens a kitchen drawer full of sweets, the kind I haven't had since I was a kid. She offers me one but I decline. Courtney takes out a handful of Black Jacks, which is so at odds with the sort of thing I thought she'd eat. We go to the sofa and Courtney sits with the sweets in her lap. She unwraps one and pops it into her mouth.

'I don't know what to think about all this,' she says, as she chews.

'I hope Peter will be okay.'

'Me too.'

We fall silent for a few moments. Then I say, 'I'm going to have to go back there to get my stuff.'

'I can come with you tomorrow. It's Sunday so I'm not working.'

I nod and sip my tea. 'I sort of feel bad for leaving them in the lurch.'

Courtney gasps. 'Willow! For fuck's sake! They might have killed Jemima and Una.'

'But . . .' I say, my mind spinning '. . . what if they didn't? What if something . . . someone else links them?'

'Like who?'

I rack my brains, trying to remember everyone I've come across since working for Elspeth. 'Daisy! She works for Kathryn at the gallery. She's a bit odd.'

'But what would her motive be?'

'I don't know. Maybe she's doing something dodgy at the gallery. Maybe Una and Jemima found out.'

Courtney shakes her head. 'Don't get me wrong, I love a mystery but this is too close to the bone now. People have died. My best friend has been murdered. This isn't a game. Maybe we should leave it to the police.'

'You're right.' I curl my fingers around my mug. Suddenly I remember something Daisy said to me the first time I met her. 'She told me Elspeth sacked her boyfriend. She sounded . . . I don't know . . . bitter about it.'

Courtney turns to me with a frown. 'Who?'

'Louis. No. Lewis. Lewis something.'

'Lewis?'

'Did Una mention him?'

Courtney leans over to place her cup on the little side table next to the sofa. A Black Jack slides onto the carpet but she doesn't notice. 'Actually, yes, she did. She said he was hot. But she hardly knew him. She'd only been there a day or so before he was sacked. Peter had told her that Jemima was in love with someone, and Una thought it might have been Lewis but it wasn't. Lewis said they'd dated for a bit but not seriously, and then they'd split up.'

'Can you remember what else Una said about him?'

Courtney pushes back her hair anxiously. 'Oh, God, let me think . . . No. Nothing else, really. I think she liked him but she hardly knew him. Anyway, Una found what she thought was Jemima's bag in the cellar of Elspeth's house. She told me Kathryn had come into the cellar while she was there and acted all weird. She believed that Kathryn had stowed the bag there, so when she went home Una took it and hid it in her room. Kathryn obviously found it and hid it at the gallery. I honestly don't think it has anything to do with Daisy and Lewis, even if they are dating.'

Before I can reply we hear the front door slam and male voices in the hallway. I notice Courtney's eyes flicker to the large wall clock in the kitchen. It's only eleven but feels much later. 'Looks like Kris has brought his mates home,' she says, but it's only Vince who follows him into the living room.

'You're back early,' says Kris, with a wide grin,

addressing Courtney. 'I thought you'd be out ages playing Miss Marple.'

Vince doesn't say anything but gazes at his feet, cheeks flushed.

Courtney ignores Kris and says to Vince, 'You remember Willow?'

'Of course, hi.' He looks up and smiles at me shyly. My heart beats faster. It's ridiculous – I can't have a crush on Una's ex-boyfriend! It's just too weird.

There's not enough room for them on the sofa so they turn the kitchen chairs around so that they're facing us. Vince is wearing a chunky black leather jacket and a T-shirt advertising a band I've never heard of. His jeans are tight. He looks around the shabby room, at the woodchip walls and the drab brown curtains, his gaze landing on a framed photo of Courtney and Una, their arms around each other and pouting for the camera. It hits me now how closely I resemble her. 'This is the first time I've been here since – since Una and I split up,' he says, his tone strained.

Nobody says anything, and I suddenly feel awkward, like an intruder when I realize they must often have made a foursome.

I watch him as he scratches the back of his neck, where his dirty-blond hair touches the collar of his jacket, and wonder what happened to the money Vince owed Una. Did her debts clear with her death? Does he feel guilty for making the last few months of her life stressful?

Kris gets up from his seat and bounds over to the fridge. I'm sure he's on something. 'Beer, anyone?'

Courtney and I decline, but Vince nods and takes a can from him.

'So, did you find out anything interesting from Peter the Plod?' asks Kris.

'He's not a cop, he's a firefighter . . .' I begin, but catch Courtney's eye. She's subtly shaking her head. Oh, I see. Kris is being facetious. It's totally inappropriate and I decide I don't like him.

'I don't want to talk about it,' says Courtney, primly.

Kris turns to Vince. 'Oooh, she doesn't want to talk about it!' He laughs. 'Did I tell you she thinks Una was murdered?'

I wince at his insensitivity.

'Yes – and I –' stutters Vince.

'The police believe it now too,' snaps Courtney, her large chestnut eyes flashing. 'So I'm not the lunatic you make me out to be. You know, Kris, some support might have been nice.'

He rolls his eyes theatrically. 'Support!' He chuckles but there's no warmth in it. 'I've been living here with you, haven't I? Helping with the rent when Una left you in the lurch to live in that Cuckoo house?'

Vince shakes his head. 'Mate, that's too far.'

He shrugs in a what-do-you-want-me-to-say? kind of way.

I've had enough. 'I don't know why you're not taking it seriously,' I pipe up. 'Someone was seen on the bridge with Jemima the night she died so it's doubtful it was suicide. And the police think Una wasn't alone either.'

'It's what I've been saying all along,' interjects Court-ney. 'Someone lured Una onto the bridge, pretending to be Peter.'

Vince pales. Then, 'Well, who knew Una was in touch with Peter?'

'Kathryn did. She was cross that Una was in touch with him and that she'd had the gall to question her about a necklace.' She fills me in on the locket Una found in her room with a photo of Jemima inside it.

'That solves the mystery, then, doesn't it?' says Kris, a smug look on his face. 'It looks like it's Kathryn.' He claps his hands. 'Anyone for more drinks?'

There's a shocked silence. Vince opens his mouth to say something, but Courtney stands, drawing herself up to her five foot seven inches, the sweets in her lap slipping to the floor. 'Get the fuck out of my flat,' she snarls, her voice low. 'We're finished.'

The look on his face is so comically surprised that my first instinct is to laugh.

'What? What did I say?'

'You're not exactly sensitive, mate,' says Vince, also standing up. A muscle throbs in his jaw and I can see he's upset. 'We cared – fuck it, we loved Una, even if you didn't give a shit about her.'

'Hold on a minute . . .'

'Get out,' repeats Courtney. 'I mean it.'

Kris reluctantly gets to his feet. 'Fine. I'll go and stay with Stan. Just until you've cooled off.' He heads into Una's old room.

'I'm sorry,' says Vince, in a low voice. 'He's a prick.'

'I don't know why you hang around with him.'

'He's an excellent drummer.'

Courtney laughs and he pulls her into his arms and kisses the top of her head. When he draws away, he says firmly, 'What you've both done is amazing. I hope that bitch Kathryn gets what she deserves.'

His eyes flash above Courtney's head and there's something about his expression, his suppressed anger, that makes me feel uneasy.

39

Kathryn

It's been three days since Willow left.

Kathryn was still at the house on Sunday afternoon when Willow called in to collect her stuff, accompanied by a tall pretty girl she'd met before. Courtney. Una's best friend. Kathryn had refused to speak to them but Elspeth had been her usual sycophantic self, begging Willow to stay. 'The police don't think Kathryn has any involvement in the deaths of Una and Jemima,' her mother had said, her voice reedy and desperate, 'and neither do I. Please, this is a strange situation for all of us, but you're in no danger.'

It had baffled Kathryn as to how her mother could have made such a grand statement on something she knows nothing about. How does she know Willow isn't in danger?

Willow had apologized and said she felt, under the circumstances, that she couldn't stay. She'd gone upstairs with her friend and packed all her stuff. Kathryn had hovered around on the landing outside to make sure Willow didn't decide to take anything that didn't belong to her.

Elspeth was practically crying as she hugged Willow goodbye. 'I'm so sorry,' she said again, pressing some money into the girl's hand. 'I didn't want things to turn out like this.'

If Willow thought it was a strange thing to say, she didn't comment on it. Neither did she mention the money. Instead she heaved her rucksack – so large it might have crushed her – onto her back, and got into the waiting taxi, Courtney close behind.

'What am I going to do now?' her mother had wailed, leaning back against the front door. 'I can hardly get *another* companion after what's happened.'

'You've got me,' Kathryn had said, reaching out a placatory hand.

But Elspeth had batted her away. 'Of course I haven't got you. How can I have you when you've a husband and two sons to look after?'

Kathryn hadn't known how to answer that. Because her mother was right.

After Willow had left, Kathryn rang Ed and told him she wasn't coming home for a few days. 'Just until I can work something out,' she'd said. He hadn't shouted at her, that wasn't Ed's way, but she could hear the disappointment in his voice. She'd let him down. And Harry. But most of all Jacob. She thought of her eldest son's big brown eyes, his flop of sandy hair. He needed her now more than ever.

And now, in the three days she's been staying with Elspeth, she grasps how futile it all is. Because it doesn't matter what she does for her mother, or how much she cares, she's just a poor substitute for the daughter Elspeth really wants. The daughter she's spent years pretending to forget.

*

It's not until Wednesday morning that Kathryn has plucked up enough courage to tell her mother she's going home.

Harry and Jacob had FaceTimed her last night, Harry's beaming face filling the screen, Jacob lurking behind him, pretending to look nonchalant while Harry nattered away about his day. She could see Ed in the background, with one of her gingham aprons tied around his waist. It looked like he was cooking something, although he didn't come to the phone. He had the radio on in the background and the scene before her was like everything she'd always dreamt of as a child. A loving family home. Ed actually cooking a meal.

She couldn't stop thinking about it last night as she lay alone in the room that had never been hers. When she eventually fell asleep, she dreamt that Ed told her he had fallen in love with someone else and was leaving her. She'd woken up in a cold sweat, her heart pounding.

Her head still feels woolly as she sits at the breakfast table. Elspeth is tearing into one of Aggie's freshly made croissants while holding court, as usual. She's telling Aggie how Kathryn had failed to pick out the right clothes for her this morning. 'That's the thing about Willow,' she says, her voice braying. 'She knew instinctively what I wanted to wear. She had style, that one. Not my style, granted, but she knew how to put things together. Unlike this one here.' She laughs. It sounds cruel and humourless.

All Kathryn can think about is Ed and the boys eating breakfast in her cosy kitchen without her. And it suddenly strikes her that she doesn't belong here, in this posh house with her cold mother. Perhaps she never has. She could have lost Jacob to drugs. Ed might decide he's had enough and leave her. And then where would she be? Stuck in this soulless house, which she coveted while she was growing up. It's brought nothing but unhappiness, with a mother who is always putting her down by telling her (and anybody else who will listen) that she's not good enough.

She can't stand it a moment longer. She gets up from the table, her chair scratching against the tiles in her haste. Elspeth looks up, confused. 'Where are you going?'

'Home, Mother. I'm going home. To my husband. To my kids.'

'But . . .' Elspeth drops her croissant onto the plate, sending flakes of pastry flying across the table '. . . who's going to look after me?' She glances at Aggie, who quickly turns away and busies herself with washing-up.

'You can look after yourself. You're more than able. It was never about having a carer anyway, was it?'

'What are you talking about? You know I need someone to look after me.'

'Then you'll have to pay for a live-in full-time nurse. You've got enough money. I'm sorry, Mother, but I can't do it anymore. It's not fair on Ed. Or the kids. I have to put them first for once.'

Elspeth draws herself up to her full height, a flush blooming up her neck and into her cheeks. 'I've done more than enough for those boys. They go to that school because I pay. I've given you a job in my gallery – which, by the way, you seem to be running into the ground. I paid the deposit so you could buy your first house.'

'Yes. You've never let me forget it.'

'How dare you? You ungrateful little brat.'

Kathryn swallows her tears. That's what this relation-ship has always been about. Shut up, put up and be grateful. And she has. For so many years. She takes a deep breath. 'I don't want to fight but you have to understand why I can't stay here indefinitely.'

'You offered once before. So what is it now? The girls have gone and you no longer want me either?'

'Don't be silly. Yes, I did offer to be your full-time carer and you told me – quite rightly – why it wouldn't work. But the companions haven't worked out either, have they?'

'Well,' she hisses, 'you made sure of that.'

Kathryn notices how Aggie's shoulders tense but she doesn't come to her rescue. Is that what they think? That it's all her fault?

'Do you think I killed those girls?' she asks incredulously.

Elspeth crosses her arms. 'I tried to give you a good home despite your bad beginning. But you're so jealous and possessive over me, Kathryn. First with Viola and then with my companions. Do you want me to die alone? Is that it?'

Words fail Kathryn. She can only stare at her mother in shock.

Elspeth sinks back in her seat. She seems small and vul-nerable and, despite Kathryn's righteous anger, she feels bad. 'Look, if you can't cope on your own why don't you come and stay with me, Ed and the boys? Just for a while.'

Elspeth's eyes widen in shock. 'And leave my beautiful house? I don't think so.'

Kathryn sighs. This fucking house. It's like a millstone around all of their necks. 'Then you'll have to make alternative arrangements. I need to go. I'm sorry.' She bends over to pick up her handbag from the floor, her heart in her mouth. 'I miss my boys. I want to see them before school.'

Elspeth stares at her as though the thought of missing her own children is alien to her.

The phone in the hallway rings, breaking the tension. 'Can you get that on your way out?' Elspeth asks casually, picking up her croissant and continuing to eat it as though their argument never took place. Aggie still has her back to them, pretending to be engrossed in the washing-up.

'Fine,' says Kathryn, inching her bag strap over her shoulder.

Elspeth doesn't speak and Kathryn walks up the stairs to the hallway, her heart thumping so hard she feels dizzy. She goes to the telephone on the little art-deco moon table and lifts the receiver. 'Hello?'

'Is this Elspeth McKenzie?' asks a gruff voice. Kathryn wonders if it's the police.

Kathryn checks her watch. If she doesn't hurry she'll miss seeing the boys before school. 'Can I ask what it's in regard to?'

'My name is Jim Sutton and it's in regard to her daughter Viola.'

Kathryn freezes. Before she's even thought about it she says, 'Mrs McKenzie speaking.'

'I've done numerous checks, as you know, hoping to find your daughter, like we agreed.'

'Yes,' she lies. She's had no clue her mother was looking for Viola and the betrayal is like a fist in the gut. Out of the corner of her eye she sees Elspeth walking towards her, a questioning look on her face. Kathryn turns her back on her mother, pressing the receiver against her ear. She can hardly hear over the thumping of her heart.

'I regret to inform you that she's . . .' He clears his throat and Kathryn realizes she's holding her breath. She knows what's coming. 'I'm afraid she's dead.'

40

Willow

Courtney sits on the sofa, holding her mobile as though Peter is still there, although they finished speaking a few minutes ago.

'Any news?' I ask.

She shakes her head. 'He doesn't know. The police aren't telling him anything. I don't even know if Kathryn has been arrested. What if they never catch Una and Jemima's killer?'

'Kathryn will slip up,' I say, with a confidence I don't feel. I'm still not totally convinced Kathryn is behind the other girls' deaths and I'm surprised to find I miss working there. I had a good thing going. And now I have no clue what I'll do next.

'I bloody hope so. I keep asking myself why,' says Courtney, falling back against the sofa, her long copper hair fanning across her shoulders.

'Jealousy. Money maybe. Who knows?'

Courtney throws her mobile onto the sofa and leaps to her feet. She begins pacing the tiny room. 'When I went to that house and saw your room – *Una's room* – I don't know . . . I can't stop thinking about it all. I can't bear that we may never know what really happened.'

We fall silent, each deep in thought. Then I get up too. I can't put it off any longer. I need to go. I pull on my floral bomber jacket from where I'd left it on the back of the kitchen chair. It's been a weird few days living with Courtney. I was here when Kris came back for his stuff on Monday. He was angry when he found that Courtney was serious about not taking him back, calling her cold-hearted one minute, then begging her to change her mind the next. I was proud to watch her standing firm. She's moving out too. She's going to live with her mum and brother for a while until she's got her head together, as she puts it. She says the flat has too many sad memories. I think she's doing the right thing.

I hope it doesn't take her and Peter too long to realize they're perfect for each other.

Courtney comes over to me and pulls me into a hug. 'Take care of yourself. Promise to keep in touch.'

'I promise.' I have no idea what I'm going to do with my life now that the job with Elspeth has fallen through. I'm back to square one. I haven't broken the news to Arlo yet. He'll be disappointed in me. He was so happy when I got the job. I know he's worried about me since Mum died and I sensed he was reassured that I was settled. I also think he liked me being out of his hair. I know it's not good for his reputation to be living with his little sister.

'Will you be okay?' she asks, her pretty face full of concern.

'Of course. I'm always okay.' I laugh, which hides my real fear. I have no idea if it's true. 'I'm going back to my brother's flat – he'll be chuffed, no doubt – and then, well, we'll see.'

She puts her hand on my arm and what she says next sends chills through me. 'I think you've had a lucky escape.'

It's still light when I leave Courtney's flat. My heart feels unexpectedly heavy. I've only known Courtney a few weeks but all of this has bonded us. I feel we could become proper friends. And I love Bristol. Maybe I'll come back. When I've decided what I'm going to do with my life.

I head to the bus stop through the unfamiliar streets. It's much quieter here than in Clifton but as I amble along the pavement I get the familiar feeling that someone is behind me. I quicken my pace, telling myself not to be paranoid. The footsteps are getting closer but I daren't turn around. It's probably someone making their way to the bus stop too, I tell myself. But apart from me and the person behind me, the street is quiet. I hear them speed up and I tense. I can see the bus stop ahead. To my dismay, nobody else is waiting and, even though it's not yet dark, the area has a ghost town feel to it. I slow down as I approach the bus stop and as I do so someone brushes past me, shoving me hard in the shoulder. I cry out in shock but they continue walking briskly, a hood pulled over their head. It looks like a bloke. I want to shout at his retreating back and call him a wanker, but I feel vulnerable, worried he might turn and attack me. I'm relieved when the bus to Temple Meads station pulls in.

The area might have been quiet, but the bus is heaving with commuters and the great unwashed so I have to stand for most of the journey. Temple Meads is even busier and I run to catch my train, just making it on time. I wander through the carriages until I find a seat next to a man in a smart suit with a laptop. His eyes slide towards me and I can almost see him wrinkle his nose when he takes in my hair and clothes. I might look a bit eccentric, I want to tell him, but I don't smell.

It's dark by the time we pull into the station at Weston-super-Mare. Even so I decide to walk the ten minutes to my brother's flat. Now I'm no longer in Bristol, the fear of being followed dissipates and I breathe in the fresh sea air, the backpack heavy on my shoulders.

The streets are still busy and the sun is setting in the distance, streaking the sky dusky pink and ochre. I can see why Arlo ended up here. It has a certain charm. Not unlike where we grew up, I suppose. Since Mum died two years ago we've both been in limbo, unsure of what to do with our lives. Not that we could ever accuse Mum of being a helicopter parent. Her philosophy was to make us as autonomous as possible and to do what made us happy. The problem is, Arlo and I are still figuring that out.

Arlo lives in a top-floor flat in a row of equally dingy buildings that have been battered by winds. Unfortunately there are no sea views from his street, just grey rooftops and overfed gulls that wake you up with their squawking too early in the morning. It's the antithesis of where Elspeth lives. There are no lights on in the window of Arlo's flat, which isn't unusual. He often sits in the dark. Sometimes he meditates with just a flickering candle and a spliff in his hand. Although this is usually after a hangover. He could be out with his weird hippie friends – after all, it is a Friday night.

I let myself in with the spare key. The one I took before I left for Bristol. He doesn't know I have it. I found it in the kitchen drawer among the elastic bands and rolled-up balls of string and pocketed it, just in case the job didn't work out. It was an unusually savvy move on my part because here I am, barely a month later.

The flat is pretty much as I left it. It's even smaller than Courtney's: one bedroom, a small living room, with a futon, and a tiny kitchenette overlooking the street. There are posters of Bob Marley tacked to the walls and a lingering smell of weed. I suddenly feel a stab of something akin to homesickness for the elegant townhouse in Clifton that always smelt of Jo Malone diffusers and beeswax. I *swanned* – there really is no other word for it – around that house like I was in a Jane Austen film, and I can't deny that I devoured every minute of living there despite its lack of homeliness. Yes, the job was dull, but the house and location more than made up for it. I doubt I'll ever get to live anywhere so glamorous again.

I dump my rucksack by the table, then rummage in the cupboards. There's little food – a tin of baked beans and a jar of pickles in the cupboard and a pint of milk three days out of date and some margarine in the fridge. Great. My stomach rumbles. I open the beans and eat them straight out of the tin with a fork, which would make Arlo gag. He can't eat beans unless they're heated up first. I think wistfully of Aggie's homemade meals. On Fridays she usually cooks a delicious fish dish.

It's freezing in here. I finish off the beans, then go to the airing cupboard in the tiny hallway and switch on the heating. The switch is near the back of the immersion tank so I have to lean right in to reach it, almost pulling my arm out of its socket as I do so. My hand brushes against something. It's a padded envelope that has been wedged down the side of the tank. I know I should leave it but I'm intrigued, so I grab it and pull it out. It's heavy and has been secured at the top with brown tape. Before I've even had a chance to think about what I'm doing, I rip the tape apart with my teeth. When I peer inside I can't help but gasp. There's money. Wedges of it. All in twenty-pound notes and tied with elastic bands. I flick through it. There must be a couple of grand here easily. Maybe five. Where the hell did Arlo get this kind of money?

Tucked behind the money is a phone. I take it from the bag. It looks old and the screen is cracked. It must be a burner phone. What kind of shit is Arlo involved in?

Why did I rip apart the tape? Now Arlo will know I've seen what's inside. It might not be what I think it is. I slip the phone into the bag and put it back where I found it. A noise on the stairwell makes me jump.

I hear the key in the lock and I slam the airing-cupboard door and rush into the kitchen to make a black coffee.

Arlo is whistling to himself as he walks in, more dishev-elled than ever. His hair is long and messy and there is a rip in the arm of his parka. He starts when he notices me. 'What are you doing here?' He doesn't sound pleased to see me. He has a duffle bag on him, which he chucks onto the sofa. My eyes flick towards it, and I wonder what's inside. More money? Drugs? Is my brother involved in something illegal?

We had an unconventional childhood, growing up in the commune, and normal rules didn't seem to apply to us. Arlo, some of the other kids and I were home-schooled. The rest of the time we were able to run wild through the many acres of fields, helping out on the farm at weekends. It was idyllic in lots of ways but Arlo in particular seemed to struggle in his late teens, especially with authority. As a result he never lasts long in a job. Not that I'm one to talk. But Arlo has always said he wants me to make something of myself, have a secure future after our childhood. He'd acknowledge he's a bit of a fuck-up. 'But you,' he'd say, his voice sad, 'have your head screwed on right.'

'I left the McKenzie house,' I say.

He rubs his hand across his chin. He doesn't look like he's shaved for days. 'What? Why?'

'Because something weird is going on there, that's why. I don't want to be their next victim.'

'For fuck's sake,' he mutters, under his breath, as he pushes past me to get to the fridge. When he sees it's practically empty he closes it again. 'You had a good thing going there. You're mental. I've told you before you can't rely on me. I've got nothing.' He was furious when I admitted I'd dropped out of uni and equally annoyed when I told him I was going to India for a few months. I feel like I've continuously disappointed him since Mum died.

'I know it was well paid, but –'

'And now you've fucked it up.'

I feel a rising sense of indignation. 'No, I didn't. Two, possibly three of my predecessors were murdered in that job.'

He sighs. His eyes are baggy and bloodshot. 'We've talked about this.'

I tell him about finding Jemima's passport hidden at Kathryn's gallery.

He shrugs, unconcerned. 'There could be many explanations.' He slumps onto the sofa. He looks exhausted. 'I've got a lot on my plate. I don't need this.'

I sit beside him. He smells of stale smoke. 'I'm sorry. I'll sort something out. But can I stay just for a bit?'

'You're twenty years old. I can't keep babysitting you.'

'You're not.'

'I've been working all hours, putting in nights down at the factory. And you can't even keep a job for five minutes.'

I hang my head in shame. Since Mum died I've just floundered. 'I've saved up money at Elspeth's. I can pay you rent.'

'The flat is too small.'

'Just for a few nights. I might go back to Bristol.'

He turns to look at me, his blue eyes intense. 'I thought you got on with that Elspeth.'

'I did. I think she liked me.'

His face brightens. 'Then she'll forgive you leaving. I think you should go back.'

'But –'

'You're being ridiculous. An old woman can't harm you. What do you expect her to do? Stab you in the night with her knitting needles?'

'Well, no, but –'

'And, okay, the daughter sounds a bit odd, but she doesn't live there. Just be aware, that's all. Don't let her lure you onto the bridge like you reckon she did with the others.'

'But Courtney thinks –'

'Who the fuck is Courtney?'

'She's Una's best friend. She was the one who told me I should be careful, that I should –'

He stands up, his face red and more animated than I've seen it since I arrived. 'I don't believe this. You've been listening to conspiracy theories. That's messed up.' His expression softens. 'This was a good job. You had a beautiful place to live and a great wage. The old woman sounds loaded. If you'd played your cards right you could have been left a fair wedge in her will.'

'What? Is this just about money to you?'

He sighs. 'It's always about money.'

'Is that why you have a bag of it in the airing cupboard?'

His face darkens. 'Have you been nosing about my flat?'

'No. I turned the heating on when I got here and found it.'

'I do a bit of cash-in-hand work. I've not had time to go to the bank.' The explanation slips off his lips smoothly, but I don't buy it. He's been acting shifty for months, when I think of it. Ever since I came back from travelling.

He lowers his voice. 'I'm just looking out for you. That's what Mum would want. You need that job. Do you want to do what I do, huh? Lugging washing-machines around all day at that factory? You had a cushy number.'

Maybe he's right. Maybe I let Courtney drag me into the drama of it all when really there was no basis for me to suspect I was in any danger. The only thing linking Kathryn with Jemima is that passport – and there could be any number of logical explanations as to why she had it. And she hid it because she knew it looked suspicious.

I lean back against the worn sofa. 'Okay. I'll ring Elspeth in the morning. Beg for my job back.'

He beams at me, his whole face brightening. 'That's great. You've made the right decision. I'm going to pop out and get us some beers to celebrate.'

41

The Cuckoo, 1988

Viola still hated Katy, that much was obvious. Since Mittens had gone missing Katy had given up trying to form some kind of friendship with her, and as the years passed she realized they would never be close, that Viola would never be the sister she so desperately wanted. Katy had been with the McKenzies for five years now and she finally felt more secure, less scared that they would send her back to the home. And even though Viola was still nasty and cold towards her it was as though she'd got bored of the pranks. Most of the time she treated Katy to a contemptuous silence.

That was until she met Danny O'Connor.

He was a traveller. She was never quite sure what to call them. All she knew was that he hung around with the group of people who parked their caravans on someone else's land until they were told to move on. Katy had seen him lurking around the newsagent's on the corner, usually with a mangy dog in tow. He looked out of place on the clean, wide streets of Clifton. But he was handsome – even Katy, at sixteen, could see that – with his long dark hair, olive skin and sparkly blue eyes. Although she daren't even contemplate having a boyfriend. Elspeth was dead against it and it had been drilled into Viola and herself that she wouldn't stand for them bringing boys home. That they had to have left school before they even thought about a serious relationship, and even then it had to be with the 'right kind of boy'. Katy knew that the 'right kind' meant someone who'd gone to a good school, and was from a 'nice family'. Not some traveller of no fixed abode.

One crisp Saturday in early March, as she walked past the newsagent on her way home from the shops, she saw him talking to a pretty blonde girl in a puffball skirt and over-the-knee socks. With a jolt, she realized it was Viola. And from the way Viola giggled and twirled her hair, she could see that her sister was smitten.

Katy couldn't help smiling to herself as she scurried past them and let herself into the house. Elspeth would never approve. Oh, no. Elspeth had plans for Viola that included university and law school, not relationships with out-of-work Travellers.

Katy hugged the secret to her chest as the days passed, relishing that she, for once, had something over Viola. She watched from the attic window as Viola sneaked off to meet him whenever she could. Elspeth was still grieving for Huw, and coming to terms with becoming a widow at the young age of forty-seven. Katy had been devastated by Huw's death. She had come to love her gentle, dependable father. The house seemed vast and empty without him. And even though Elspeth employed a new cook and housekeeper called Aggie, whose warm smile and kind eyes went some way to helping Katy feel more secure, she missed Huw fiercely. He'd been her protector, and fear plagued her that Viola's nastiness would turn up a notch now he was dead. Elspeth had changed since his death too, becoming more brittle and harder to please.

Luckily, Viola was distracted by Danny.

One warm May evening, Elspeth and Katy were in the kitchen – they'd stopped using the dining room since Huw died – Aggie dishing up fish and salad, when Elspeth said, her eyes narrowed, 'Kathryn, where's Viola?'

Katy had fidgeted in her chair. She knew exactly where Viola was. She could tell her mother now and get Viola into trouble or she could cover for her. That way Viola would owe her. 'I think she's still at the library. Studying. She's got her A levels coming up.'

'Yes,' said Elspeth, spreading a cloth napkin over her lap. 'I'm well aware of that, thank you, Kathryn.' She always refused to shorten her name. She looked down at the elegant Cartier watch on her wrist. 'It's past her curfew on a school night.'

Just then Viola bounded into the kitchen, her cheeks flushed, her hair escaping from her ponytail. She looked more beautiful than Katy had ever seen her. 'You're late,' snapped her mother, without glancing up from her food.

'I'm sorry, I –'

'I told Mother you were at the library,' chimed in Katy, her eyes meeting Viola's. 'I assumed that's where you still were after I left.'

Viola widened her big blue eyes in surprise. 'I – Yes, I was. Studying.'

Afterwards, as they were getting ready for bed, Viola cornered Katy in her attic room. 'Why did you lie for me?' she hissed. 'I don't need you doing me any favours.'

Katy shrugged, enjoying herself for once. 'Okay, fine. Then I'll tell her where you really were.'

'Where I really was? What do you know about it, you brown-nosed little shit?'

'You were with that Danny O'Connor. You've been sneaking off to meet him for months.'

Her face paled. 'What?'

'You heard,' said Katy, sounding braver than she felt. 'I've seen everything.'

The fight seemed to seep out of Viola and she sank to the floor, her head in her hands and groaned. 'Mother would kill me if she knew. She'd stop me seeing him.'

Katy joined her on the floor, her legs crossed. She tentatively reached out to touch Viola's shoulder, feeling she was about to pet a lion. But Viola didn't move, or bite her head off, like she'd expected. Instead she continued to sit there, her head in her hands. When she eventually looked up her eyes were red-rimmed. 'I love him,' she said, in a small voice. 'I can't bear to be apart from him. Will you help me?'

She locked eyes with Katy, desperation reflected in the deep blue irises that were so like Elspeth's. Katy hesitated, pretending to think about it, and the air around them seemed to still, as though the oxygen had been squeezed out of the room. 'Of course,' said Katy, eventually.

For the next few months, Katy helped cover for Viola whenever she could, and as a result her sister was nice to her. After Elspeth went to bed Viola would sneak up into Katy's attic room, sit on the edge of her bed and tell her all about her secret rendezvous with Danny. And even though Katy couldn't help but feel a little jealous that

Viola had found such a handsome, sexy boyfriend, she was honoured that she, geeky, shy Katy, who spent hours in her room with only her books for company, was the confidante of the popular, beautiful and vivacious Viola. She even began to let go of her years-long conviction that Viola had done something awful to Mittens.

Viola sat her A levels and Katy her GCSEs, then the school broke up for the holidays. For the first time, Katy actually looked forward to the summer ahead. She envisaged time spent with Viola and maybe even Danny. Perhaps she could suggest they set her up with one of Danny's crew. She daydreamed of walking over the Downs with her younger version of Danny, picnics in the sunshine, trips to the cinema as a gang. She'd have a social life for once, apart from just Mandy. Lots of friends. Maybe even a boyfriend of her own.

The summer holidays flew by, and just as she hoped, Viola accepted Katy into her group, allowing her to join them when they went shopping or to the park. Cass always eyed Katy with suspicion, as though she couldn't understand why she was suddenly allowed to hang out with them. But she didn't make any trouble and Katy basked in Viola's attention. One day, Viola took her to Tammy Girl and helped Katy pick out a pair of stone-washed jeans. Katy had never felt so fashionable.

Elspeth seemed delighted that her 'two best girls' were getting on so well and every time they went shopping she'd hand them some more cash. 'If I'd known being friends with you would make Mother so generous I'd have done it years ago,' laughed Viola, linking her arm through Katy's as they boarded the bus. Sometimes they sneaked off to the Downs to meet Danny. Viola would disappear under the bushes with him while Katy kept watch. On the way home one day, Katy asked, 'Do you think Danny has a friend you could set me up with?'

Viola flicked her long hair over her shoulder while she pouted in her little pocket mirror as she applied her new pearl-pink lipstick. 'Maybe,' she'd said noncommittally and Katy had spent the rest of the journey wondering what he'd look like.

One stifling hot Friday night in August, when Elspeth was due at some charity do, Viola asked Katy for another favour.

'I want to sneak Danny into the house. Will you help me?'

Katy faltered. This was different from the other times. This felt dangerous. If Elspeth caught them it wouldn't only be Viola who'd get into trouble. The fear of being sent back to the home reared its head again. The threat was always there, lying dormant. It was in the subtle ways Elspeth expected Katy to be constantly grateful and the perfect daughter. When Huw was alive, he'd always come to Katy's defence on the rare occasions Katy had done something Elspeth disapproved of, and the deep-seated fear of being sent away had lessened. But since Huw had died, Elspeth had taken to finding more and more ways for Katy to disappoint her. The most recent being her end-of-term report at Easter. 'Oh dear,' Elspeth had said, her voice cold as she sat across the desk from Katy in what had been Huw's study but was now hers. 'This report isn't as good as I expected. After everything we've done for you, all the money we've spent. Please don't make me regret choosing you, Kathryn.' Katy had apologized and promised to do better until Elspeth was mollified.

'Please,' begged Viola, looking up at her through her ridiculously long eyelashes. How could Katy say no? 'You need to be on the lookout. As soon as Mother comes back, let me know. Once she's in bed I'll sneak Danny out through the kitchen. Okay?'

Katy felt sick at the thought but she agreed.

They hovered in the kitchen as Elspeth faffed about with her hair and makeup upstairs. When she eventually came down in a taffeta ballgown, her tightly permed blonde hair falling to her shoulders, Katy could hardly speak she was so nervous.

'What's up with you two tonight?' Elspeth said, as she wafted over to them in a cloud of Chanel No. 5 so they could diligently kiss her rosy cheeks.

Viola giggled nervously. 'Nothing.' She snaked her arm through Katy's. 'We're going to paint each other's nails and order pizza.'

Elspeth flashed them an indulgent smile, told them she'd left some money on the side, and to 'be good'.

'It's so great to see my two best girls getting on so well at last,' she said, dabbing at the corner of her eyes. She was wearing blue mascara. 'It would have pleased your father.'

A lump formed in Katy's throat. Her mother trusted them and they were about to betray her. When Elspeth had left Katy turned to Viola. 'I don't know about this . . . I feel bad.'

Viola waved a hand dismissively. 'Don't start getting all Goody Two Shoes on me now.'

'But —'

She put a finger to her lips. 'Sssh. He's here!' She jumped up and down, then ran to the French windows, throwing them open. Danny emerged from behind the big oak tree in baggy jeans and a tight T-shirt. It was still light outside. How long had he been hiding there?

Viola grabbed Danny's hand and dragged him into the kitchen. 'Thanks for doing this,' he said, throwing Katy a charming smile that melted away all her doubts. 'We owe you big-time.'

'Come on.' Viola giggled, still holding Danny's hand. 'We don't have long, let's go.' And they disappeared out of the kitchen.

Katy wondered if they were going to have sex. Is that what all this was about? Somewhere comfortable to go instead of where they usually sneaked off to.

She watched them as they ran up the winding staircase, hand in hand, excitement bouncing off them. Then she wandered into the library to read, feeling alone.

She was slumped on the sofa, unable to concentrate on her book, when her stomach rumbled. She'd forgotten to order the pizza. Elspeth had left the money specially. If she came back and saw they hadn't bought pizza it would look suspicious. Katy jumped up and raced upstairs. She'd ask Viola what she wanted – she could share hers with Danny. They couldn't risk buying enough for three because that would also raise questions.

Katy hovered outside Viola's door, which was ever so slightly ajar. She should knock first, in case they were in the middle of doing it. She was about to rap her knuckles against the door when she heard her name mentioned.

'What – so you don't see Katy as your sister?' This was Danny's voice. Strong and sexy.

Her stomach turned over. Why were they talking about her?

Viola laughed. It sounded cruel. 'No, of course not. I can't stand the little bitch. She's made my life hell since she arrived. Such a lick-arse. Always trying to make me look bad to my parents. I hate her.'

Katy felt as if she was going to throw up. So nothing had changed? Viola really despised her that much? After everything? All those shopping trips and sunshine-filled afternoons in the park, the confidential chats and bus excursions, the makeup sessions and advice on clothes and boys: the closeness she had felt to Viola had seemed so real. She had begun to care about her, love her even. See her as the big sister she'd always wanted.

'Then why are you being nice to her?' And then Danny laughs. 'Oh, don't tell me. So she'll cover for you and you can see me?'

'Of course. She's so pathetic, she'll do anything I ask. She . . .'

But Katy couldn't bear to hear any more. She stumbled away from the door, angry, humiliated, tears stinging her eyes. How dare Viola use her like that, make her believe they really could have a close relationship? Fury flooded through her as she fled back downstairs. She couldn't let Viola get away with this. She flung open the front door. It was only nine o'clock and still light outside. She ran all the way to the Assembly Rooms where she knew Elspeth had gone for her charity ball. She begged the doorman to let her in, that it was an emergency, and she waited, pacing the hall while someone went to summon her mother.

'What is it? What's happened?' Elspeth cried, as she rushed up to her, the hem of her ballgown making swishing sounds as it trailed on the floor.

'Viola! It's Viola! She's got a man in her bedroom. She made me lie for her. He's a Traveller. I think he's taking advantage of her. You need to come quickly!'

Elspeth turned white, her mouth pinched. Without saying another word she gathered up the hem of her skirt and fled the building, Katy close behind.

Elspeth arrived home just in time to catch the two of them in the act. Katy had never seen her so angry. She threatened to disown Viola if she ever saw Danny again. 'And if I ever see you with my daughter again I'll call the police,' she raged at Danny. Katy hid in her room, waiting for the shouting and the recriminations to stop. What had she done? Viola would never forgive her.

Much later, Viola came to Katy, her eyes red and swollen from crying. 'How could you do that to me? You promised. Mother said you went to fetch her. How could you betray me like that? She's forbidden me to ever see him again.'

'How could *you*?' Katy screamed back. 'I heard what you said about me. You were just using me. All this time. I thought . . .' she started to cry '. . . I thought we were friends.'

Viola fell silent. When eventually she spoke, her voice was quiet but each word punctured with anger: 'Then you're thicker than you look. I hate you. I've always hated you. Interfere in my life again and I'll kill you.'

Katy, always a light sleeper, heard Viola sneak out of her room in the early hours of the morning and she knew. She knew Viola was running away to be with Danny. She lay on the bed, frozen with indecision. If Viola left, her life would be a lot easier, but it would break Elspeth's heart. She couldn't have that.

Throwing off her covers, she slid out of bed and crept down the stairs just in time to see Viola opening the front door.

'Don't go,' she pleaded.

Viola turned around, shock on her face. Her eyes were puffy and swollen. 'Don't . . .' Her voice cracked and she held up her hand.

'Please. I'm sorry for telling on you. But you'll break her heart.'

Viola shrugged. 'She's got you.'

'She loves you.'

She shook her head. 'I can't stay. I feel caged here.'

Katy moved slowly across the hall so as not to frighten Viola away. 'I know you hate me . . .'

'I don't hate you. Not really. It's . . .' She swallowed and looked at the floor. 'It's complicated. Mother and I have never got on, even before you came. It's being here.' She sighed. 'I don't know. When I'm with Danny I'm a better person. When I'm here I'm full of hate.'

Katy hung her head. This was all her fault. 'I'm sorry.'

'No,' said Viola, surprising Katy. 'I'm sorry. Really. For what I said to Danny. I don't know why I have to act like a bitch all the time.' And then she gave Katy a quick, firm hug. 'Promise not to tell on me this time.'

Katy nodded, blinking tears away. 'I promise.'

'And look after Mother. She's going to need you.'

'I will.'

Viola drew away and disappeared out of the front door, pulling it gently shut behind her.

Viola left a note for Elspeth saying that she was in love. That there was nothing anyone could do about it. And that she wanted never to see either of them again.

Elspeth took the news hard. She wiped away any sign of Viola, taking down photographs from the walls and stripping her bedroom with a white-hot fury. 'As far as I'm concerned, Viola is dead,' she said. In one way Katy was pleased to see the back of Viola and all the arguments that her presence had caused, but she could see how much Elspeth was hurting. She often wondered, in the years that followed, whether Viola had meant her parting words or if she had been pacifying her so that she could run away without Katy telling Elspeth.

Elspeth grew more brittle as time passed, as though she blamed Katy for sending her real daughter away. There were occasions when she refused to speak to her for days at a time, never giving a real reason. But Katy knew that the resentment was there, bubbling beneath the surface, every now and again rearing its head.

But it wasn't until later, when Katy grew up and became Kathryn, when she had her own children, that she began to doubt her mother's actions. How could she have wiped her only daughter so easily from her life?

Now here they are, thirty years later, and Viola is dead. Elspeth will never have that chance to say sorry.

Kathryn stares at Elspeth. When Jim called and said Viola was dead, she'd passed the receiver wordlessly to her mother. Now Elspeth's face is ashen, her mouth trembling.

'Here, come on, let's sit down,' says Kathryn, gently, taking the receiver from Elspeth's hand and leading her into the sitting room.

'She's dead,' she says again, her voice wobbling.

'I know,' she soothes. 'But . . . you must have expected it?'

'Of course I didn't,' she snaps. 'Why would I? She was only forty-seven.'

'I know . . . It's just that you never heard from her and I thought that must have been why.'

'It was only two years ago she died. All those years she could have been in touch.' She puts a hand to her heart, her face pallid. 'I suppose I hoped I'd see her again before I . . .' She trails off.

'Before you what?'

She draws herself up so she resembles the formidable woman Kathryn was in awe of as a child. 'I'm nearly eighty. I've been suffering from bad health.' She still has her hand on her heart. 'I know I won't make more than a year or two.'

'Nonsense!'

'I've got heart disease, Kathryn.'

Kathryn doesn't know what to say. She swallows. What does this mean? 'Are you saying . . . are you saying you're dying?'

'We're all dying.' Her eyes glisten. A heart attack had killed Viola, according to Jim.

'Oh, God.' Kathryn doesn't know what else to say. If only things could have turned out differently. If only Viola had been kind when Kathryn was adopted into their family. Kathryn had wanted a sister, a friend, not an enemy. Then none of this would have happened.

Kathryn reaches across and takes her mother's hand. It's small and frail in her own and she can feel all the bones and veins. If she could turn back time she would change it all. She'd be the bigger person because, in the end, she had succeeded in causing this pain.

Elspeth looks up at Kathryn with pale, watery eyes. 'There's something else that Jim told me.'

Kathryn braces herself.

'Viola had children. A daughter. A twenty-year-old daughter.'

This hits her harder than the news of Viola's death and the room spins. A daughter. And a much longed-for granddaughter for Elspeth. Probably beautiful and blonde and petite, like Viola herself.

But Elspeth hasn't finished. She is grabbing her hand and telling her there's more. Kathryn's stomach turns over because she thinks she knows what Elspeth is about to say and she clutches her mother's hand, like she's eleven years old again, not wanting to let go. Not wanting to lose her, to lose everything she's worked so hard for. She doesn't want to hear the words but they float towards her anyway in her mother's clipped tone.

'When Viola ran off with Danny, they lived in a commune in Norfolk somewhere. Eventually they separated and Viola met another man, Dominic Green, and they had a daughter. A daughter called Willow.'

I can see you through the window. You've left the lights on and the curtains open; a great view into your shabby little flat. You should be more careful. All those potential Peeping Toms. You needn't worry. It's only me here tonight. Watching you. Waiting. You wear your grief well. Less makeup, not so tarty. You're quite pretty beneath all that slap. Not like the others, though, with your copper hair. But that doesn't matter to me. You see, I have a taste for it now. The kill.

    And I've decided that you're next.

42

The flat feels empty, not homely, now that Willow has left, the walls bare of all the photos of Courtney and Una, just patches of lighter-coloured magnolia paint where the frames had been. Courtney surveys the place she once thought of as home. It was never much, but she and Una had made the best of it. Now it's just an empty shell, devoid of Una and her warmth, Willow and her chatter. Kris, thankfully, has taken his stuff and she's begun to pack her belongings into boxes. Her mum and dad will drive over tomorrow to take them to their house in Filton.

Yesterday she'd found one of Una's hairbands down the back of the sofa. She'd held it for ages, staring at the long blonde hairs interwoven around it.

Una's death has hit her harder than she'd ever imagined. She feels as if her old self – the Instagramming, selfie-taking girl, who was obsessed with hair and makeup and childish retro sweets, is now a thing of the past. The things she used to love now seem so . . . so *frivolous* in light of Una's murder. Because, despite the lack of evidence to back up her theory, she still believes Una was murdered.

She's on her knees on the scratchy brown carpet as she packs the last of the boxes when her mobile vibrates. She stands up wearily and goes to the kitchen table where it sits.

Kathryn's number flashes up on the screen. They'd swapped numbers after Courtney had collected Una's things after her death in case Kathryn found anything else, but she never had. What does she want? Why would Courtney want to speak to Kathryn after everything she's done? She ignores the phone and continues packing. She doesn't know what to do with Una's stuff. She thought about giving it to a charity shop – Una would have wanted that – but she can't bring herself to part with her clothes, not yet. Sometimes she gets out her maroon coat with the velvet collar that had been her eighteenth-birthday present from her mum, and inhales the scent that still lingers on the fabric.

The phone rings again, then stops, then rings. Courtney continues to ignore it. As far as she's concerned, Kathryn can go to Hell. If she wants to find out where Willow is, she can do it some other way.

It's dark now and, although it's April, the flat is cold. It's her last night here. She feels as though she should have had a get-together or something, but now that she's no longer with Kris she wonders if the rest of the band will want to remain friends. She's heard from Vince a few times, but nothing from the others.

A crash from outside breaks the silence and she jumps. What was that? She gets up and goes to the little window that overlooks the lane that runs alongside her flat. An old metal dustbin that belongs to the old man in the flat next door has been knocked onto its side. She presses her nose to the glass, her heart racing. Someone's there, crouching by the bin. A man dressed in dark clothing. She darts to the window that looks out onto the street. There's a white van parked outside. It's gone seven. Who does it belong to? She stands still, not knowing what to do. Is it a burglar? Why is he lurking around her building? She goes to the little side window again. The man's no longer there. But the white van is still parked outside.

Courtney grabs her phone from the kitchen table. There are six missed calls from Kathryn. She's about to dial her brother Theo's number – he lives nearby – when her phone rings again. 'Hello,' she says breathlessly, her heart still pounding.

'At last. I thought you'd never pick up,' says Kathryn. 'I really need to see you. I've found something out. About Viola. And Willow . . .'

Courtney can't grasp what she's saying. All she can think about is the man lurking outside her flat.

'Courtney? Are you listening?'

'I'm scared.'

'Look, how many times do I have to explain myself? I never hurt Una. Or Jemima or Matilde. Please. Whoever is doing this, it's not me. It's –'

'No. I mean there's someone outside my flat. A man –' She's interrupted by another bang. She strains her ears. She can hear footsteps on the concrete steps outside. 'Some-one's here,' she whispers, her heart pumping so loudly she can't concentrate.

'Don't answer the door. I'm coming over.' Kathryn sounds so authoritarian that Courtney finds herself agreeing. She reels off the address and hangs up. Then she runs to the front door and double-locks it. Kathryn should be here in fifteen minutes. She just won't open the door until then.

A shadow passes in front of the frosted glass of the front door. Oh, God. Someone's there. Someone's right outside her door. She stands in the little square hallway that smells of feet. She looks frantically around for an object to use as a weapon when her eyes fall on an umbrella that Una had bought from Bristol Zoo. She picks it up. It's huge with a metal spike poking out of the top. She'll stab them in the eye if they dare to break in, she thinks, wielding it in front of her.

Despite her bravado, she lets out an involuntary scream when a fist pounds the door.

Bang. Bang. Bang.

Shit. Her hands are trembling but she doesn't move. What will she do if they break the door down? Oh, God, she can't believe this is happening.

And then a familiar voice calls through the glass. 'Courtney?'

She stands up straight, umbrella still in her hand. 'Vince?'

'Are you okay in there? I heard a scream.'

'What are you doing here?'

'Open up.'

She hesitates. She's known Vince for years, even before Una started dating him. He wouldn't harm her, would he? He's gentle. Kind. Then why was he lurking outside by the bins in the dark? Does the white van belong to him? Jemima was seen getting out of a white van the night she died.

'Courtney? It's freezing out here. I need to speak to you. Please let me in.'

She's being ridiculous. This is Vince. Una's ex-boyfriend. He practically lived with them when he and Una were together.

'Hold on,' she says, dropping the umbrella to the floor and unbolting the door to let him inside.

43

Willow

Arlo's been gone for ages already, and although I switched on the heating when I arrived, the flat is still freezing. I perch on my brother's ripped leather sofa, which will be my bed tonight, waiting, the television on in the background. It's dark for seven thirty, the sky moonless and thick, like a fire blanket has been laid out over the town.

I rummage in my bag for my phone. I've not looked at it all day and I'm surprised to see ten missed calls all from the same number. *Kathryn.*

Shit. Is she phoning to berate me for leaving without notice? Or to beg me to return? I hesitate, remembering what Arlo said earlier about trying to get my job back. I call her and she picks up instantly. 'Willow?' She sounds breathless.

'Yes?'

'I've been trying to get hold of you for hours. Where are you?'

'I'm at my brother's.'

'You have a brother?' She sounds surprised. Have I never mentioned Arlo to her? I can't remember. After all, it's not like we sat having cosy chats. She's barely ever said two words to me.

'Yes. Arlo. He lives in Weston.'

'Weston in Bath?'

'No. Weston-super-Mare.'

'Oh.' A pause and a rustle. It sounds like she's walking, her breath coming in short, sharp gasps. 'I really need to talk to you. Can I come over?'

I frown. Bristol is at least forty minutes away. 'If you want, but –'

'It's urgent,' she interrupts.

'Is everything okay with Elspeth?'

'Yes. No. Look, I'll explain everything when I come over. Can you give me your address?'

I rattle it off. 'Great. See you later.' She ends the call. I stare at my phone for a few moments, still puzzled. What's the urgency? She didn't even ask me why I'd left. At least Arlo will be here. If Kathryn is dangerous she can't exactly hurt me with my six-foot-two-inch brother in tow.

But as the time ticks by, Arlo fails to return home. I ring his mobile but it goes straight to voicemail. He's probably run into some mates and they've persuaded him to go to the pub. It wouldn't be the first time. And why is it still so bloody cold in here?

I go to the airing cupboard again to check the immersion switch. The little red light is on so why aren't the radiators heating? Has Arlo been paying his bills? My eye catches the envelope. It's as I left it but I can't help reaching for it anyway. Something about Arlo's story doesn't add up. It's his life, I know, and I shouldn't be nosy but . . . I delve into the bag and grab the phone. Why has he got a second phone anyway?

I take it into the lounge and sit on the sofa, the phone

in my hand and the envelope on my lap. The phone has been switched off so I turn it on, half expecting it not to be charged, but the screen brightens and blood pounds in my ears as I stare at the phone's wallpaper. It's a photograph of Una and Courtney, their arms wrapped around each other, their smiles wide. They look young, maybe mid-teens. I've seen the same photograph on the wall in Courtney's flat. My hands begin to shake, my brain not quite understanding what I'm seeing. Is this Courtney's phone?

Or – and the thought makes me want to vomit – is it Una's?

There's a whooshing in my ears and my face is hot with panic. It has to be Una's phone. Una's missing phone. Why the fuck would Arlo have it?

A movement in the stairwell makes my heart beat faster and I shove the phone back into the envelope and run to the airing cupboard, dumping the bag behind the tank. I return to the sofa just in time before the front door opens and Arlo walks in, whistling to himself. He's got a plastic carrier bag in his hand, which he holds up to me, a rueful smile on his face. 'Got 'em. Sorry it took so long.'

'Did you run into some mates?' I ask, trying to keep my voice even, trying to quell the screaming in my head.

'Yep. Bumped into Gaz. We went for a quick one. Hope you don't mind.'

'Not at all.' I sound like a strangled cat and I cough to cover it up. Is this why Kathryn is travelling all the way here to see me? To tell me she suspects my brother? But she'd sounded surprised to hear I had a brother on the phone, so it can't be that. Arlo goes to the tiny kitchen.

He has his back to me but I can tell from the sound of a can opening that he's having one of his beers. He doesn't offer me one. I stare at the back of his dark head. I can't believe he'd hurt Una. He didn't even know her. And, as far as I'm aware, he doesn't hang out in Bristol. Maybe one of his dodgy mates asked him to keep the phone. Maybe that's what the money is, a pay-off to keep quiet. But I can't imagine any of his mates are secret psychos either. Most of them are too stoned and stupid to be capable of murder.

Arlo's always been a bit of an enigma. A free spirit. Five years older than me, he's always danced to his own tune. But still. He was a good kid growing up in the commune, a little intense at times perhaps, obsessive about certain things, certain people. Once he spent an entire summer trying to mend an engine in an old car, and wouldn't give up until it was working. He was often a bit of a loner. He was handsome, though, and girls always liked him. He cared about Mum. About me. He was the man of the family after Dad left. He wouldn't hurt a fly. I've never even seen him kill a spider. No, there has to be some logical explanation as to why he has Una's phone.

He slumps down next to me, can in hand. He's still wearing his parka and there is a smudge of dirt on his cheek. There is an energy radiating from him and his legs won't stop moving. Has he taken something? I've always known he liked to smoke pot but he always said he'd never touch any class As. Yet he's buzzing.

'Are you okay?' I ask.

He shrugs in answer and takes a swig of his beer.

'You're right about the job,' I say. 'I've been hasty.

I don't think Kathryn had anything to do with the deaths of those girls.'

He turns to me, his eyes too bright. 'Great idea.'

'Then you can have the flat back to yourself again.'

He punches me playfully in the arm. 'Hey, are you saying I'm trying to get rid of you?'

I force a laugh. 'No!'

It used to be so easy between Arlo and me when we were growing up, but now our banter is off. I feel as though I don't know the man sitting beside me. I don't know how to tell him Kathryn is on her way here. I don't know how to broach the subject of the phone. For the first time ever I feel a little . . . *scared* of Arlo.

I open my mouth to say something, anything, to dispel the awkwardness but I'm interrupted by a knock on the door.

There is a flicker of alarm in Arlo's eyes.

'That will be Kathryn,' I say, getting up.

'Kathryn?' He sits upright, panic on his face. 'As in Elspeth's daughter? She can't come here.'

I frown. 'Why not? You wanted me to get my job back, didn't you?'

He stands up too. He looks as though he's about to bolt. 'What's going on?' There is fear in his voice. It must be the drugs making him paranoid.

'It's Kathryn.' I laugh. 'You look like you're about to get arrested by the police.' I reach for the door but he throws his body in front of it to prevent me from opening it.

'Arlo? What the fuck?'

'I don't want visitors.'

'Get out of the way.' I try pushing him off me but he's so strong he won't budge. 'Don't be stupid!'

I don't understand. Why doesn't he want me to see Kathryn? We wrestle for a bit and then, reluctantly, he stands aside to allow me to open the door. He sighs almost resignedly.

I let Kathryn into the flat. She's alone. She doesn't smile or say anything but she follows me into the living room where Arlo is sitting with his head in his hands. When he senses us standing in the middle of the room he looks up, and I see shock register on Kathryn's face.

They just stare at each other for a few moments and Kathryn nods imperceptibly. 'Of course.' She shakes her head, as though she should always have known it. 'I thought there was something familiar about you. Hello, Lewis.'

44

Kathryn

As Kathryn surveys Lewis, everything falls into place. He stares back at her with Viola's defiant eyes. No wonder her mother fawned over Willow. She was the most like Viola because she's made up of her DNA.

'Why are you calling him Lewis?' asks Willow, her eyebrow raised.

'Because that's what he told me he was called. When he worked for us.'

'What?' Willow spins around to glare at her brother. 'You worked for Elspeth?'

'Earlier this year,' continues Kathryn. 'As our gardener. Until Elspeth sacked him for smoking pot.'

Lewis stares at her for a few seconds. 'When did you find out?' he says.

'Find out what?' interjects Willow, her cheeks flushed. 'Will someone tell me what the fuck is going on? Arlo, why did you tell them you were called Lewis?'

He shrugs. 'I didn't want them to know.'

'Know what?' cries Willow, throwing up her hands.

Kathryn turns to Willow. Does she really not know? 'That Viola – Elspeth's daughter – is your mother?'

Willow gawps at Kathryn, shock written all over her

face. It's clear to Kathryn that she had no clue. 'W-what? But that can't be. My mother was called Lily.'

'She changed it.'

'B-but . . .' Willow's mouth hangs open.

'And Arlo here pretended to be a gardener called Lewis so he could work for my mother.' She turns to him. 'I don't know what you were hoping to achieve.'

He folds his arms across his broad chest. He still has his coat on. 'I wanted to see the old bag. She's my grand-mother, after all.'

Willow sits heavily beside Arlo. 'But why didn't you tell me? Why didn't you tell Elspeth?'

'It was obvious as soon as I started working there that she didn't like men. She was smitten with the girls. The pretty little blonde girls. I thought it was because they reminded her of Mum, so I thought you'd be perfect for the job. It was supposed to be so easy. You'd work for her, she'd fall in love with you and then –'

'And then your money worries would be over. Isn't that right, Arlo?' says Kathryn.

Arlo stands up, his fists clenched at his sides. Kathryn's tall but he's over a head taller. 'It's rightfully mine. Right-fully Willow's. Not yours,' he spits. 'You're **adopted**. You're not flesh and blood.'

Kathryn doesn't say anything at first. She could be wrong. So wrong. But she has a feeling that she isn't. 'Is that why you got rid of Una?'

'What?' he splutters, looking at his sister with a per-plexed expression. 'You're crazy, lady. I hardly knew the girl. If you remember, we only overlapped by a few days before I got the sack. The most I did to her was steal her breakfast.' He hesitates, watching their faces. 'What? Don't judge me too harshly. I was starving and it was just there, in the kitchen under a tea-towel.'

Kathryn delivers her sucker punch. 'Then why did I see you kissing? Just a few days before she died.'

Willow groans, her head in her hands. When she looks up there are tears in her eyes. 'Why did you do it?' she says to her brother. He opens his mouth to object but Willow adds, 'I found Una's phone.'

Something changes in Arlo then. There's a coldness in his eyes and time seems to freeze. Suddenly he lunges at Kathryn, grabbing her by the throat and pinning her against the wall.

'No!' screams Willow. 'Please! Arlo!'

Kathryn can hardly breathe. His hands are so tight around her throat and, despite Willow's protests, he keeps squeezing her windpipe. She tries to kick and punch him but it's no good. She can feel herself getting weaker. 'You meddling bitch,' he hisses, spit flying from his mouth and landing on her face. 'Why couldn't you have left it alone?'

Willow leaps on him but she's so tiny he simply shrugs her off, like she's an irritating insect.

Kathryn's vision starts to recede, black crowding in at the edges of her eyes. This is it. This is how she's going to die. She thinks of Ed and the boys. All the regrets of the last year bearing down on her. Now she'll never have a chance to put things right.

Without warning, he releases her. She falls to the floor, like a ragdoll, clutching her throat, unable to believe he's let her go. And then she sees why. Arlo is flanked by two police officers, one of whom is reading him his rights. 'We are arresting you on suspicion of the murder of Una Richardson . . .' Courtney stands in the doorway, pale-faced, her mobile in her hand and Vince behind her. Willow is on the sofa, sobbing.

A plain-clothed detective she recognizes as DS Holds-worth is suddenly kneeling beside her. 'Are you okay?' she asks, reaching out a hand gently and helping Kathryn up off the floor.

Kathryn doesn't say anything. She just watches as Arlo is led out of the door, his hands cuffed behind his back. She can't take it all in. It feels unreal, like she's watching a police drama on TV.

Arlo doesn't look back. All she can hear is Willow's quiet weeping.

She clutches her throat. It feels sore.

'I don't understand,' says Willow.

Suddenly Kathryn feels sorry for her: the girl had no clue as to what was going on. Willow's head whips around and she spots Vince and Courtney in the doorway. 'Why are you two here? Please,' she says, as she looks from Kathryn to DS Holdsworth, 'can someone please tell me what the fuck is going on?'

45

Willow

The detective, who introduces herself as Christine Holdsworth, comes and sits beside me on the sofa. 'I'm going to have to go to the station and interview Arlo,' she says, her voice kind. 'But I'm going to send a colleague here to sit with you.'

'I don't need anyone to sit with me,' I cry. 'I'm not a child.'

'She can come and stay with me tonight,' pipes up Courtney. She's still hovering in the doorway with Vince.

Why do I feel like I'm the last to know what's going on?

'I'll need to take statements from you all in due course,' DS Holdsworth says. 'I'll be in touch.'

I nod, blinking back tears. Arlo a killer. I still don't know if I believe it. Although the way he lunged at Kathryn tonight was so out of character it's made me wonder if I know my brother at all. Christine Holdsworth stands up, dusting down her long dark coat as though the sofa contains germs – which, to be fair, it probably does. 'Did you turn on the phone?' she suddenly asks.

'The phone?'

'Una's phone?'

'Yes. I didn't know it was hers. I found it . . .' I get up and show her to the airing cupboard '. . . in here.'

She holds out her hand and, without speaking, I reach for the envelope and give it to her, knowing that this evidence will help put Arlo away.

I suddenly feel utterly and helplessly alone.

DS Holdsworth flashes me a sympathetic smile and, tucking the envelope under her arm, leaves the flat, closing the door behind her. When I return to the living room/kitchenette, Kathryn is sitting on the sofa with Vince and Courtney. They all glance up at me with glum expressions.

'How did you know?' I say to them, as I slump into the leather armchair by the window.

Kathryn speaks first. 'Mother hired a private detective to find Viola. He discovered that she died two years ago but also that she had a daughter called Willow and that she'd married a man called Dominic Green.'

I nod. 'That's my dad. But . . .' I frown, remembering what she'd said on the phone earlier '. . . you didn't know I had a brother?'

'Not at that point.'

'Kathryn rang me,' pipes up Courtney.

'I wanted to see what she knew about you,' adds Kathryn. 'Because I realized it couldn't be a coincidence that you'd decided to take a job at your grandmother's house.'

'But when I picked up the phone I was scared because I'd seen a man lurking outside my flat,' says Courtney.

'So I drove straight round there,' adds Kathryn.

'I'd gone to see Courtney too,' says Vince. It's the first thing he's said so far this evening and his male voice sounds abrasive in this small flat. It reminds me of Arlo. 'It was silly, but I knew she was leaving the flat and I wanted to . . . say goodbye to it. Goodbye to Una.'

'I think Vince interrupted the intruder because as he was walking towards my flat the man suddenly pushed past him, got into his van and sped away,' says Courtney.

'And when I turned into the road, I saw the van speeding towards me,' says Kathryn. 'I recognized it as Lewis's. I didn't think much of it. Until Courtney told me what had happened.'

I fidget in my seat. 'So Arlo was Lewis?'

'Yes.'

'Which means he's dating Daisy. Who works with you.'

Kathryn purses her lips. 'I guessed that. Someone's been fiddling the books in the gallery. But that's another story.'

I flop back against the headrest. My mind is aching. 'I just don't understand.'

'There's a lot I don't understand, either,' agrees Kathryn. 'But Lewis – sorry, Arlo – took a job with my mother because he wanted to get in with her. He must have known that she'd disinherited Viola. I don't know how. And thought it was a way in. But when he realized my mother was having none of it –'

I'm puzzled. 'Wait! Your mother knew who he was?'

Kathryn shakes her head. 'No. He never told her. He had a better plan. He wanted to install you in the job. It's obvious when you think about it. He knew my mother would take to you.' She looks embarrassed. 'Anyone can see my mother gets infatuated with pretty young blonde girls.'

'So – what? He murdered the others so that I could get the job?'

'I think he planned for you to get the job after Matilde.

That was when he started working with us. And when she died, my mother gave the job to Jemima pretty swiftly.'

'But when Jemima took the job last October I was travelling. I only got back after Christmas.'

'I think he killed Jemima hoping you'd get the job, but my mother employed Una before he had the chance to show you the advertisement. So he must have felt he had no choice but to kill Una as well,' explains Kathryn.

I swallow a lump in my throat. My brother has killed three people. Needlessly. And for what? Money?

'I just . . . I can't get my head around this.'

Courtney sits forward. 'I'm so sorry, Willow. When Kathryn was at mine, I had a phone call from Peter. The police had contacted him to say they had located a signal for Una's phone at an address in Weston-super-Mare. Because of what Kathryn had found out about you being Viola's daughter we thought . . . We came here thinking it might have been you.'

I stare at her, like she's grown an extra head. 'What do you mean? That you thought I might have killed those girls?'

'Only for a minute. When we pulled up outside the flat and saw the white van, we guessed it must be your brother.'

'I knew the police were on their way,' Kathryn adds. 'That's why I was brave enough to come inside.' She touches her throat. 'Although for a moment there I thought he'd kill me too.'

'I'm so sorry,' I say, tears forming again.

'I'm sorry, too,' says Kathryn. 'For being so awful to you. And to Jemima and Una. Even Matilde. If I'd only reported Jemima missing earlier the police might have – I don't know – found Arlo sooner. Una might not have died.'

'Why did you hide Jemima's passport?' asks Courtney, sharply.

Kathryn looks shame-faced. 'I'm not proud of what I did. Money. It does strange things to you. Ed and I, we were struggling. I was worried that my mother would become so infatuated with one of the Viola-lookalikes that she'd push me out into the cold. She's harsh like that. She cut off Viola for good because she didn't approve of her boyfriend. When Matilde joined, Mother changed her will. She was going to leave a huge lump sum to her. To a girl she'd known five minutes!' Her voice rises and, as though conscious of this, she lowers it again. 'Anyway, I argued with Jemima. I didn't trust her. Rightly or wrongly, I don't know. When she flounced off with her bag but without her passport I thought she might be back. But when she didn't appear, I was relieved. I hoped she'd just taken off, maybe moved in with that mystery man of hers – who, I think now, must have been Arlo – so I took it from her room and told my mother she'd resigned. I forgot all about the passport. And then when she died I was scared to throw it away, in case it was found and somehow traced back to me and looked suspicious. So I hid it. I panicked.'

'And the necklace?' I ask. 'Was it Jemima's?'

Kathryn shakes her head. 'No. It was my mother's. The photo inside was of Viola. I found it in the bin after Viola left. I fished it out and kept it. I'd forgotten all about it until Una found it.'

There's a beat of silence before Courtney says to me, 'Did you ever suspect that Arlo was capable of murder?'

I shake my head vehemently. 'Never. I'm not going to lie, he was always a little obsessed by wealth. He hated living in the commune, everyone having the same. He hated "being poor", as he put it. But I never . . .' my stomach turns '. . . I never thought he'd be capable of murder.'

How will I ever trust anyone again?

46

Three months later, Willow

We're in the middle of a heatwave. The city feels stagnant with it. The air is breezeless, cloying with traffic fumes and cut grass. I can't even walk to the end of the street without sweat running down my back.

But Clifton in July is a joy to behold, and I love it here. I love the little pavement cafés and the boutiques and the beautiful old buildings that shimmer in the sun. I love the view of the suspension bridge, even with the knowledge of what took place there, and the hot-air balloons in the cloudless cornflower-blue sky.

When I'm out and about I feel a bounce to my step for the first time since Arlo was arrested and subsequently charged with the murders of Matilde, Jemima and Una. He's denying it, of course. But the evidence mounting up against him is undeniable. His van was taken away and analysed. Fibres from Jemima were found in the back. Una's phone was in his flat, plus another phone, a spare with the message he sent on it pretending to be Peter. He also had a backpack containing Jemima's clothes. Plus there's the CCTV footage of a man fitting his description on the bridge at the same time as Jemima. He's also been charged with obtaining money fraudulently and the assault on Kathryn.

I visited him once in prison, not long after he was charged. He sat there in front of me with unwashed hair and a cut down his face from some fight. He never admitted anything to me, and as I sat opposite him, I could barely look at him without disgust. 'Why can't you plead guilty and save everyone the stress of a trial?' I hissed.

But he just smiled, refusing to say anything. Refusing to admit that he'd driven into Matilde with his van, or charmed his way into Jemima's affections only to kill her, or pretended to be Peter to lure Una onto the bridge. And why had he been hanging around Courtney's flat? Was he planning to murder her, too?

My brother might have thought he had his reasons but, when it came down to it, they were just excuses when, really, his instincts are animalistic: to *kill*. And with each kill his need grew more insatiable.

As I got up to leave he did say, 'I was only thinking of you. Why should we get nothing? She's family, for fuck's sake.'

The irony is he didn't have to kill for the money. If he'd only told Elspeth who he really was I'm sure she would have wanted a relationship with him. He'd grown up with tales from our own mother about what a wicked mean old woman Elspeth was, rich but controlling, with her little pet cuckoo who had kicked Viola out of the nest. My mum had vowed never to have anything to do with her mother again. I didn't know any of this. Mum never talked to me about her childhood. I didn't even know that she'd had rich parents. She told me they were dead. That was it. Arlo, being so much older, must have heard a different story. The real story. And maybe, back then, Elspeth had been a harder woman. How was he to know that she was softening in her ripe old age and that she'd wanted a reconciliation with her biological daughter? How was he to know that Elspeth had left it all too late?

Elspeth has taken me under her wing. I've moved in with her and she's showing me the ropes of the businesses. Since they found out that Arlo and his girlfriend Daisy were stealing from the art gallery, it's starting to have a healthy turnover again. Kathryn has hired a carer who comes in each day to help Elspeth, and between us we do the rest, although we agree that Elspeth is perfectly capable of doing things for herself and we shouldn't pander to her, despite her heart condition. This was hard for Kathryn at first – her constant fear of being 'cut off' still ever present. But she's learning that as much as she needs her mother the feeling is mutual. It's taken the pressure off her, and I like to think she no longer feels threatened by my presence.

Kathryn and I had a heart-to-heart when I first moved in. She admitted to me how badly my mother treated her, and how she'd betrayed her trust by telling Elspeth about her relationship with a boy called Danny. I feel ashamed of how my mother was. She sounded spoilt and selfish, with a nasty, sadistic side to her. Maybe that's where Arlo gets it from. But no. I'm not going to make excuses for him. As far as I'm aware, my mother wasn't a killer. She was a good mother to me. I like to think that running off and joining a commune, living a non-materialistic life, meant that she wanted to be a better person. And even though our childhood was unconventional, living as we had on a large farm with twenty other people, I was happy. Even when Dad took up with another member of the commune and left us all behind I didn't really miss him. He was never particularly paternal and I sometimes wondered if living on a commune was a way for him to bow out of his parental responsibilities, knowing there was always someone else to keep an eye on us, or to give advice or discipline. Mum, on the other hand, I miss terribly. But I'm glad she's not around to see what Arlo has become.

I enjoy working with Kathryn at the gallery, and I hope she knows she can trust me. I'm not interested in taking her place or my grandmother's money. I'm just happy to have a semblance of a family after my own has fallen apart so catastrophically.

Grandma, as Elspeth likes me to call her now, enjoys the tales of my childhood. She doesn't want to hear about Arlo. To her, it's like he doesn't exist – and we know she's good at that because she did the same when my mother left. But now she asks endless questions about Viola, as she still refers to her.

'Did she ever mention me?' she asked once, and I lied and said, yes, of course. And Elspeth – Grandma – would lean back in her chair with a serene smile at the thought that her daughter hadn't forgotten her after all.

On Sunday Courtney calls for me and we amble into the village for lunch.

Courtney and I have become good friends. I was worried at first that she'd blame me for Una's murder, that I was somehow accountable by proxy because it was my brother who killed her. But on the contrary we're bonded by it, and the same applies to her and Peter. They're dating, and she's moving to London to be nearer to him.

'When are you leaving?' I ask her, as we link arms and head to our favourite café.

'Next weekend. I've found a job in a salon in Covent Garden and a house-share in Streatham. Not far from Peter.' She blushes when she mentions his name. She's got it bad. 'You know, you could come too. We could find a place together.'

'I've thought about it. But I can't leave Elspeth – Grandma. It still feels weird to call her that. Not yet, anyway. Not when I've only just found her. I've moved around so much in the last few years, it'll be nice to put down roots for a while.'

'I understand. But you'll visit, won't you?'

'You bet.' We fall into a companionable silence before I ask, 'How're things going with Peter?'

'Really well.' She grins. 'I've never felt this way about anyone.' Then she looks sad.

'What is it?'

She shrugs. 'I don't know. I suppose I feel like I'm leaving Una behind. And I know it's a big ask, but will you visit her grave for me? She's buried in the same cemetery as her mum.'

Although I never knew Una, my eyes smart. 'Of course I will.'

'I think Vince goes sometimes.' She gives me a knowing look. I know she's trying to set us up but that would be too weird. I already feel like I'm living Una's life, inhabiting her space, getting close to her best friend. Going out with her ex would be one step too far.

By now we've reached the café. There's a party atmosphere in the village today. A busker strums a guitar on the corner, while groups of young people sit outside drinking iced lattes and chatting.

We find a table. Courtney goes off to get some menus and I sit, watching the world go by. Today I refuse to think about Arlo and the girls he killed or the trial date that's looming. I refuse to be quashed by the guilt of his crimes. Instead I give thanks to the universe for my life, for Courtney and my new family. And for the future, which Una and Jemima and Matilde never got the chance to have.

47

Kathryn

The sun beats down and Kathryn can feel her shoulders starting to burn as she meanders through the grounds of the National Trust's Tyntesfield, the boys running in front of her and Ed by her side. It warms her heart to see her sons so carefree, particularly Jacob. For once he's acting like a kid instead of a surly teenager, teasing his brother and not caring what he looks like as he races Harry and pushes him over. They roll around on the grass in a play fight.

'It's beautiful here,' says Ed, taking a deep breath. He grabs her hand and she smiles up at him. Her lovely, dependable, affable Ed. In some ways he reminds her of Huw. Maybe that was why she fell for him when they first met. Huw had made her feel safe, and Ed does too. They are now in a new stage of their marriage, almost like they're falling in love all over again. After she came back from Weston-super-Mare that evening, she sat Ed down and told him everything – well, nearly everything. About Arlo and Willow, and the part she had played in Viola's disappearance. She admitted how she's been feeling over-whelmed by her job and her role as the dutiful daughter. She told Ed that she needed him to step up and stop tak-ing her for granted. He'd been shocked to hear she felt that way, and the next day, after coming home late from work, she noticed he'd cleaned the kitchen and put the dishwasher on. Little things.

She also knows her new-found happiness is because she's finally let go of her insecurities. She no longer has to feel solely responsible for her mother now that Willow's on the scene. And she doesn't have to feel that her inheritance is threatened – even though, ironically, it is, more so now than it ever was with the other girls. After all, Elspeth has a new granddaughter to dote on so she'll be well cared for after Elspeth dies. But it no longer seems to matter to Kathryn in quite the same way. Maybe because she's finally grasped that there's more to life than money. There's family: Ed and the boys are hers. She was in danger of losing all of that because of her obsession with wealth, always second-guessing what her mother would do with the money. Plus the guilt of thinking she was running the art gallery into the ground, when the drop in profits was down to Arlo and Daisy. Elspeth is a law unto herself. She uses money to control the people around her but Kathryn refuses to play that game. From now on, Ed and the boys come first.

Things have taken an unexpected turn with Willow. Kathryn had always been so fearful that Viola would return and claim her share of the house, or the girls her mother became infatuated with would be left everything after Elspeth died. But with Willow she's found the opposite is true. She has an ally. Willow is clever, more savvy than she'd thought. She knows exactly what Elspeth is like, and the two of them have decided to stick together against Elspeth's ludicrous demands.

So far it seems to have worked. Willow is her niece but she is everything that Kathryn has always wanted in a sister.

For the first time in years, Kathryn can truly relax. Well, almost.

There's still one cloud she's living under. She'll never be able to tell anyone the truth about that, even Ed.

And that's about the night Matilde died.

It had been a rainy night in August and Ed was away on a stag do. It was in the midst of all the problems they'd been having with Jacob. The constant running away and the drug-taking. She'd let Jacob go to his friend Wilf's house, a boy she trusted from school, because they were supposed to be working on a project together. Except when he wasn't home by eleven – long past his curfew of ten – she began to worry. She rang Wilf's home, only to be told Jacob had left around nine. Two hours unaccounted for. She was desperate, knowing he must have gone down to the estate to meet up with those druggy mates of his. She didn't want to wake Harry so she'd slipped out of the house, grabbing her car keys from the dish on the side table in the hall. But when she opened the front door she was puzzled to see the driveway empty. Ed had taken his car to Manchester for the stag do, but where was her Golf? It was at least fifteen years old so she doubted anyone would want to steal it. And then the thought hit her. Had Jacob taken it? She tried ringing his mobile but it went straight to voicemail. And just as she was contemplating calling the police, he rang her. She couldn't understand what he was saying at first he was crying so much, she only caught bits of the conversation – 'I hit someone' ... 'They just walked out into the road' ... 'What am I going to do?'

And it suddenly dawned on her what he was saying, and she had a sick feeling in the pit of her stomach.

She told him to stay where he was. He'd driven to the Downs, where he'd stopped in the middle of nowhere. Then she called a taxi to drop her off just around the corner. When she eventually reached him, panting and soaked through by the rain, he was sobbing hysterically onto the steering wheel.

She got into the passenger seat. He reeked of alcohol. 'What the fuck have you done?' she snapped.

He told her, through sobs, that he'd taken her car for a spin. That one of his new 'mates' wanted a ride to score some drugs – she was amazed by how honest he was being about it – and he'd wanted to look 'hard' in front of this mate. So he'd stolen her car, thinking he could return it before she even noticed.

'You stupid, stupid boy,' she'd cried. 'You don't even know how to drive.'

'I'm sorry. I'm so sorry. It was raining. And I couldn't see, and I'd had a few drinks. Then suddenly there was something in the road and I hit it. I –'

'It was probably an animal,' she said, hoping she was right.

That made him cry even harder as though that was the worst prospect.

He had to get out of the car to be sick then, and she waited for him, unable to work out if she felt more fury or pity. What if he had knocked someone over and left them for dead? When he eventually stopped throwing up, she made him lie down in the back seat while she drove slowly home. The roads were quiet, no sign of any accident. Maybe he was confused. She put him to bed with a bucket on the floor and prayed that nobody had been hurt. Then she'd gone back outside and checked over her car. It was hardly damaged, just a little dent to the front bumper. Surely there would have been more damage if he'd knocked over a person.

But just a few hours later she received the phone call from her mother to say that Matilde had been found dead in the middle of the road outside their house and that the police suspected a hit-and-run. And she knew. She knew Jacob had killed her.

She had two choices. To ring the police and confess all. Or cover it up. If she turned in Jacob to the police it would ruin his life. He'd go to a young offenders' institute and, with his tendency towards drugs and crime, he might never recover. She had to protect her son.

So, Kathryn left the boys in their beds and drove the car to the compound they sometimes used to store paintings. When things died down she'd sell it. But until then, she'd keep it locked away. Out of sight. She'd invent some story for Ed about how it had broken down and she'd had to get rid of it.

Later that night she woke Jacob up and told him the truth. There was no way she'd be able to keep it from him.

'You have to sort yourself out,' she'd told him, sitting on the edge of his bed, like she used to do when he was little. 'You can't go on like this. Your reckless behaviour has cost a girl her life.'

'I don't think I can live with it,' he'd sobbed. 'What if there were witnesses? Or I was caught on CCTV?'

'If you turn yourself in, you'll go to prison. You can make amends, Jake. You can live a better life.'

And that was what he'd promised to do.

Every now and again he'd come to her, wide-eyed and panicking, worried that he'd be found out. And she lived in constant fear, too, that there would be a knock on the door from the police. But now that Arlo has been arrested and charged, they can rest easy. Arlo is wicked. He deliberately took the lives of those girls. Jacob made a mistake. It was an accident. He doesn't deserve the same punishment as Arlo. She feels no guilt for letting everyone assume Arlo killed Matilde too.

Now, as she watches Jacob messing around with his brother, she hopes he can live with it, that he's telling her the truth when he says he's not touched drugs since. She has no choice but to believe him.

Ed would have made her turn him in. She knows that. He's always said she panders to the boys. That's why she has to keep it from him too.

Her and Jacob's secret. It binds them.

She just prays it doesn't destroy them.

But she'd do anything for the people she loves. For her family.

Author's Note

Although the setting for *Just Like the Other Girls* is Sion Hill in Clifton, Bristol, which is a real (and very lovely) place, Elspeth McKenzie's house, The Cuckoo's Nest, is just a figment of my imagination and is not based on any house in the street.

The character of the social worker in the initial 1983 chapter was named after Fiona, who won an auction for Doctors Against Borders. Thank you so much, Fiona.

Acknowledgments

This book wouldn't have been possible without the wonderful team at Michael Joseph, particularly my brilliant editor Maxine Hitchcock, who is always so encouraging of my ideas, always calm, kind and clever. I love our meet-ups and talks about everything from writing to must-watch Netflix documentaries. This book is so much better than it would have been thanks to her hard work and insightful editing skills. A huge thank-you also to Rebecca Hilsdon, Emma Plater, Olivia Thomas, Sriya Varadharajan, Bea McIntyre, and everyone in Marketing, Sales and Art for all their hard work, dedication and creativity. I'm so grateful for everything you do, from the amazing covers to getting the book onto shelves. I'm so lucky to work with such a great team.

As always, a huge thank-you to Hazel Orme for her meticulous copy-edits, picking up on my continuity errors and grammar, as well as her enthusiasm for my stories.

So much love to my family: my mum, dad, step-parents, sister Sam and step-sister Sharon and brothers-in-law Mark and Jeff. To my amazing husband, Ty, for his continued patience and endless support and my lovely children, Claudia and Isaac, who might now just be getting old enough to read my books – not that they want to! To my in-laws, Lu, Steve, Tam, Rick, Teresa, and my cute little nieces. To my wonderful friends; particularly Alex (who kindly let me use her name in this book), Carinne,

ACKNOWLEDGMENTS

Elizabeth, Jacq, Nicky, Esther, Tanya, Magda, Verity, Jeanine, Claire, Carey and Liz. And a special thanks to Justine for all the word races. I don't know what I'd do without you all.

Thank you to the West Country writers crew, Tim and Gilly for all the meet-ups, chats and laughs. And to other writer friends, Liz, Jo, Fiona, Gilly, Fleur and Sarah for support, word races and WhatsApp messages.

A huge thank-you to all the amazing readers for buying, borrowing, talking about and recommending my books. I wouldn't be here without your support. To all the bloggers, who take time to read and review my books: you do such a great job. And to the supermarkets and bookshops and libraries. I'm so grateful.

And finally, to the person this book is dedicated to, my agent Juliet Mushens.

Juliet offered to represent me back in 2013 after I won a novel-writing competition run by *Marie Claire* magazine, where she was one of the judges. At the time there was no guarantee my book would even be published, but as soon as I met her I could see she is a force to be reckoned with. Since then she has worked tirelessly on making sure that that book, which became *The Sisters*, was a stepping stone to a writing career. She has been responsible for getting me fantastic publishing deals, both here and abroad. Not only is she a brilliant agent but she's a fabulous person: a fashion icon, funny, super-smart, supportive and loyal. And she loves cats! Thank you so much, Juliet. Six books! This wouldn't have been possible without you.

About the Author

Claire Douglas has worked as a journalist for fifteen years, writing features for women's magazines and national newspapers, but she has dreamed of being a novelist since the age of seven. She finally got her wish after winning Marie Claire's Debut Novel Award for her first novel, *The Sisters*, which was one of the bestselling debut novels of 2015. She lives in Bath, England, with her husband and two children.

DON'T MISS THESE OTHER NAIL-BITING THRILLERS!

THEN SHE VANISHES
A NOVEL

"*Then She Vanishes* lifts the stone on a cold case disappearance and asks chilling questions about friendship, loyalty, love, and obsession."
—Gilly Macmillan,
New York Times bestselling author

DO NOT DISTURB
A NOVEL

"Douglas is a true must-read thriller author. . . *Do Not Disturb* is yet another reminder of just how good she is at putting the reader on the edge of their seat and keeping them there until the final page."
—*PopSugar*

LAST SEEN ALIVE
A NOVEL

"Thrillingly tense and twisty, a great read."
—B. A. Paris,
bestselling author of *Behind Closed Doors*

LOCAL GIRL MISSING
A NOVEL

"*Local Girl Missing* has a supple, twisty shape and a sense of menace that never flags."
—*New York Times Book Review*

S-11-22
MEYER

O